DEVIL'S DREAM

SHADE OF DEVIL BOOK 1

SHAYNE SILVERS

ARGENTO PUBLISHING

COPYRIGHT

DEDICATION

To that person in front of me at the coffee shop who didn't pay for my drink...
this book is dedicated to someone else.

And to anyone who thinks I didn't deserve that drink, I once won a race
against a billion other competitors. It was do or die. If you're reading this, you
probably deserve a coffee, too.
And a laugh.
Enjoy my words. This book is for you, because you're a winner.
I'm not buying you a coffee, though.

-Shayne

EPIGRAPH

"There is no death. Only a change of worlds."

— Chief Seattle

CONTENTS

THE SHADE OF DEVIL SERIES—A WARNING

Many vampires were harmed in the making of this story. Like...a lot of them.

If you enjoyed the *Blade* or *Underworld* movies, you will love the *Shade of Devil* series.

The greatest trick the First Vampire ever pulled was convincing the world that he didn't exist.

Before the now-infamous Count Dracula ever tasted his first drop of blood, Sorin Ambrogio owned the night. Humanity fearfully called him the Devil.

Cursed by the gods, Sorin spent centuries bathing Europe in oceans of blood with his best friends, Lucian and Nero, the world's first Werewolf and Warlock—an unholy trinity if there ever was one. Until the three monsters grew weary of the carnage, choosing to leave it all behind and visit the brave New World across the ocean. As they befriended a Native American tribe, they quickly forgot that monsters can never escape their past.

But Dracula—Sorin's spawn—was willing to do anything to erase Sorin's name from the pages of history so that he could claim the title of the world's first vampire all for himself. Dracula hunts him down and slaughters the natives, fatally wounding Sorin in the attack. Except a Shaman manages to secretly cast Sorin into a healing slumber.

For five hundred years.

Until Sorin is awoken by a powerful Shaman in present-day New York City. In a world he doesn't understand, Sorin only wants one thing —to kill Dracula and anyone else who stands in his path. When the descendant of an infamous vampire hunter steps into his life, Sorin is torn between conflicting feelings in his heart—revenge or love. But to a woman like Victoria Helsing, it might just be considered a bloody good date.

The streets of New York City will flow with rivers of blood, and the fate of the world rests in the hands of the Devil, Sorin Ambrogio.

Because this town isn't big enough for the both of them.

Now, our story begins in a brave New World...

DON'T FORGET!

VIP readers get early access to all sorts of goodies, including signed books, private giveaways, and advance notice of future projects. AND A FREE NOVELLA! Click the image or join here: www.shaynesilvers.com/l/219800

FOLLOW AND LIKE:
Shayne's FACEBOOK PAGE:
www.shaynesilvers.com/l/38602

I try my best to respond to all messages, so don't hesitate to drop me a line. Not interacting with readers is the biggest travesty that most authors can make. Let me fix that.

1

I stared out at the forest, smiling absently at the sounds of laughter and conversation coming from around the crackling campfire behind me. I felt like the luckiest man in the world as I let the vibrancy of the American Indians' lifestyle—my new family—pour over me. None referred to themselves as Indians, of course—that was a term my fellow Europeans had given them.

My new family were part of the Mohawk tribe, but they were led by a peaceful man named Deganawida who had been adopted into the tribe. It had been rather difficult to get an accurate understanding of the various tribes and how they interacted with one another due to the different languages they spoke, but Deganawida knew enough English for me to parse out a vague concept of their cultural climate. Essentially, there were several other neighboring nations, and they often warred with each other for goods, territory, or over personal feuds, but Deganawida longed for lasting peace between them all.

Overall, the Americas—or the New World, as many called it—were wild, savage places compared to the other civilizations across the ocean, but there was also a crisp honesty to the air here. No one pretended to be anything other than what they were.

No one cared about my bloody history. Thinking about that past—even *obtusely—always caused my shoulders to inch higher, paranoid that my enemies were watching me from the darkened woods. I took a calming breath, familiar with the sensation now.*

It had been too long. I was safe. No one was coming for me. They probably didn't even know where I had gone.

The world's first vampire, Sorin Ambrogio, had simply disappeared.

Along with the world's first werewolf, Lucian, and the world's first warlock, Nero. The three unlikeliest of friends.

No one knew we had fled to the Americas to find a new life.

The air here in the Americas was brisk yet refreshing, perfect weather for hunting. Upon seeing our virginal new home for the first time—vast stretches of relatively unexplored forests and trails and mountains—Lucian had instantly displayed the exuberance of a youthful puppy, while Nero had complained about the lack of rowdy taverns. The resident animals had wandered these lands for thousands of years, sharing them only with the occasional hunting party.

They had never known the chilling howl of a werewolf like Lucian.

The incredible powers of a curious warlock like Nero.

Or the hunting scream of the world's first vampire—me.

My two friends were off hunting now, preferring the wild to the company of humans. Even Nero. It wasn't that they didn't appreciate our hosts but that they longed for the wild adventure possibly lurking over the next new hill.

We had each come here to escape our dark, bloody pasts. I had once been a simple, humble adventurer named Sorin Ambrogio—a man who found a treasure that wasn't mine to find.

I had visited the fabled Oracle of Delphi in Greece to learn my destiny. Her cryptic words had forever changed my simple, curious life:

The Curse.

The Moon.

The Blood will run.

Troubled by my grim prophecy, I had remained near the temple. As the fates would have it, I met a woman named Selene, who just happened to be the Oracle's sister. Over time, I grew to love Selene.

Thus began my descent into blood. I had found a treasure that would cost me my soul.

The merciless gods punished me for this crime, cursing me to become a vampire—to feast on the blood of men for eternity. I never saw Selene again.

In bitter retaliation for my unfair punishment, I had chosen to become the world's most notorious murderer, and to amass an army of men and women just like me.

I turned a man named Dracula to help me in my quest—to spit in the gods' eyes and laugh.

And then I made more...and more...and more. My appetite had been insatiable.

Over the centuries, my vampires—and my human victims—had given me a new name, one that I relished. They had called me the Devil, and I had let them.

In fact, I had loved them for it.

But as the centuries of conquest drew on, I found myself growing increasingly bored with my vocation, and concerned about what I had birthed in my army of vampires. I built a castle to help restrain them, but it wasn't enough. My vampires spread across Europe like a plague.

Soon, my apprehension became known, and chasms of division split between me and Dracula, between me and my vampires. They all wanted their Devil back, but I was beginning to think that I wanted the man, Sorin, back.

Following in the footsteps of my second-in-command, Dracula, my vampires evolved into a violent, ruthless, soulless group of killers who wanted nothing more than to spread across Europe in a red tide of blood, toppling the rulers of any country who stood in their way. For many, many years, I had enabled and encouraged such behavior, harboring great disdain for mankind and their precious freedoms from internal demons.

But once I began to object, my vampires had turned on me—encouraged by Dracula, who had gradually turned them against me.

Rather than attempting to kill every single one of my creations—and likely die against such overwhelming numbers—I had fled, no longer wanting anything to do with their quest for power. I handed Dracula my figurative crown, gave him my castle, and left it all behind.

To become an adventurer again. To find the man, Sorin Ambrogio—the man I had once been.

Lucian and Nero shared similar stories, and chose to accompany me on my grand new adventure to the Americas—a land of uncounted opportunities and new beginnings.

Where we had run into the American Indians—a people unlike any we'd known in Europe. They took us in, unafraid of our strange powers, believing us to be great protectors. Avenging spirits trapped in the bodies of men.

"*Regretting your decision not to go hunting with your friends?*" *a man asked from over my shoulder, snapping me out of my memories. His voice and the usual herbal smell of his pipe had a relaxing effect on my shoulders, and I let out a sigh. I'd sensed him lurking nearby for some time, now.*

"*There will always be another hunt, Shaman,*" *I replied, turning to face the tribe's Medicine Man, Deganawida. He narrowed his eyes at the term I'd flippantly used, even though he knew I only used it to antagonize him.*

A Medicine Man was not the same as a Shaman.

And neither of those were the same as a warlock, although I couldn't rightly explain the specific differences—all three used magic, bending the elements to their wills. Nero had been constantly on edge every time Deganawida began peppering him with questions on his powers.

Which amused Lucian and me to no end. This new life had encouraged me and my friends to open up, to act more like men than monsters. Rather than frequently sneaking off to hunt and explore, I'd chosen to focus my transformation from monster to man by jesting with tribe members. My prior life had not permitted me such a temperament.

Deganawida was a strong, imposing man with light brown skin and rich black hair that was braided down his back all the way to his waist. He looked to be in his late thirties, but his aura was that of a priest or a boxer—without the raw violence, judgment, and piety I was more accustomed to from those noble professions. The Medicine Man commanded respect, wielded wisdom like the sharpest of swords, and had a broad, angular face always on the verge of laughter.

Deganawida nodded, glancing past me at the woods. "The others fear to hunt with Lucian."

I furrowed my brows. "Lucian would never harm—"

The Medicine Man held up his pipe, leaving a trail of blue smoke in its wake as he cut me off. "He harms their pride, Sorin," he said, chuckling. "Every hunt increases their shame when they fall short of his collections."

I let out a sigh and nodded my agreement. "He does do that, I'm afraid," I admitted, not bothering to hide my grin. "I find myself missing him and Nero. I wish that they would find stronger ties to your tribe, but they are explorers, conquerors, and wanderers at heart."

"They will find their peace eventually, if that is what they seek." He paused thoughtfully, thumbing a stone on a leather cord tied around his neck as he glanced at me sidelong. "This is your tribe, too, Sorin. I would think that marrying my daughter, at least, made that clear."

I grunted, smiling as I noticed his daughter—my new wife—carrying a basket of vegetables to the fire. She smiled at my attention before continuing on. Although she was my wife, she was a stranger to me in many ways, our cultures so vastly different. Painful memories of Selene slipped into my thoughts, but I shoved them back down.

Love had cursed me before, so I was understandably hesitant.

"Bubbling Brook is a fine woman," I told Deganawida, "although there is much for me to still learn about her."

The old man nodded. "Her English will improve and you two will flourish."

I narrowed my eyes at him, hating how quickly he had begun to improve his own English. "Your swift grasp of my language is rather unsettling, you know. I should never have agreed to educate you."

Deganawida chuckled. "My previous tutor was much more...academic. I find your barbaric practice of the language more...useful."

I scoffed, smirking at him. "I do not speak like a politician or a man of God, you mean."

"You speak like a humble man, yes," he agreed, puffing contentedly on his pipe, "which I find more honest and genuine. There is a time for both, of course. Especially with our newest...neighbors building settlements all along the coast," he said tiredly. "I believe communication will be vital in the years to come. Words or weapons...words or weapons."

I nodded regretfully. "I'm glad to hear you are finally beginning to see what I warned you about years ago," I said gently.

I realized I was licking my lips absently, thirsty for the blood I had stored back in our teepee. I pushed down my hunger. I'd been working on controlling it, and I had wanted to see if Lucian and Nero would return before I chose to eat. It would give us something to do while we caught up. But it had been two days since I'd drunk any blood, and I was beginning to feel noticeably weaker.

I couldn't wait much longer. Still, I willed the hunger away, waiting for my friends' return.

I noticed Deganawida was holding a journal in the crook of an elbow, scribbling on the pages as he held his pipe clenched in his teeth. "What are you writing, old man?"

"Our story," he said happily. "The true story," he added meaningfully, glancing at my son, my wife, and then me. "How three monsters remembered that they were man, and that their hearts were stronger than their hate. Even if I had to browbeat one of them into believing it," he added wryly.

I grunted, eyeing the journal warily. "That is a dangerous story to put to paper, Deganawida. If the wrong people ever learned the truth about me, it could bring trouble upon your—" I cleared my throat at his arched brow. "Our people. Words are indeed weapons, and they will be held against your own throat as often as not..."

The Medicine Man waved a hand. "Our people are devoted to our stories, and one such as yours...it's compelling. A valuable lesson that the spirit is stronger than the shell," he said, first tapping his heart and then tapping his teeth to indicate my fangs—which only extended when I chose to use them. "Perhaps one day you will be written into our myths and legends as a great protector."

I scoffed. "Hardly. And I still counsel that this journal is a foolish risk. It only paints a target on your back—another reason for the settlers to hunt you down. Trust me, I know the minds of the men from across the ocean—and I'm not even speaking of my own cursed offspring." I winced as a nearby child giggled upon falling to his rear.

My son.

He was not the cursed offspring I had been referring to, of course. I had been speaking of the vampires I had left back home—my first children.

I found myself smiling as I watched my new wife laugh as she helped the tan-skinned young boy back to his feet, encouraging him to try again. The moonlight struck her black hair, glinting like polished obsidian.

I had taken to calling her Bubble. She hadn't liked that at first, demanding to know why I wanted to steal her name. It had taken some time to convince her that it was a term of endearment—because the tribe used their full names in all but the most intimate of situations.

I was stubborn and had eventually won out.

Even more impossible than finding the beginnings of what I hoped would one day become a deep love, we had conceived a son together—no doubt thanks to her powerful bloodline from her father, the tribe's Medicine Man. On that note, the boy was growing faster than naturally possible. It had only been a few months, and he was already on the cusp of walking. From conception to birth had also been concerningly fast—much to the anxiety of the midwives.

The world's First Vampire had conceived a son—something that had been deemed impossible.

"You know what I mean," I finally said, turning back to Deganawida. "My story is dangerous to tell. If the wrong people heard it..." I trailed off, knowing the futility of our endless debate.

"That describes men everywhere, Sorin." I shot him a dubious look and he waved a hand. "We have monsters here, too, Sorin. Skinwalkers are rare, but they can be unspeakably evil." I nodded somberly, having heard only a single story—in the privacy of a closed tent—about the dreaded skinwalkers. "I'm certain there are as many good settlers as there are evil settlers. Men struggling to find a new life..." he said, arching a pointed eyebrow at me.

"Doesn't seem that way," I said, thinking of the settlers constantly herding us further inland.

"I hold the same fears, Sorin. But this journal is just for our family—only to be spoken around our fires. Rest easy."

With a tired sigh, I let it go. He closed his journal and continued standing beside me. I studied the man sidelong. In him, I saw a greatness waiting to emerge. Whether that would be as a warrior drenched in blood or a statesman brokering peace between the white settlers and the numerous—sometimes ruthless—other tribes living in this brave new world.

I turned at a strange sound from Deganawida to find him staring in horror behind me towards the tree-line.

The hair on the back of my neck suddenly stood on end as my senses informed me that something was very, very wrong.

Then came the screams.

2

Everyone leapt to their feet, snatching up weapons as a small army descended upon our camp, having silently overrun our sentries. I pulled back my lips in a snarl, frantically searching for my wife and son as fire erupted across the tents and the longhouse. It hadn't rained in some time, so the land was dry and barren, the perfect tinder.

I dove behind a stump as arrows slammed into the dirt all around me, preventing me from diving deep into the mayhem. Screams filled the night, and time seemed to slow as my predatory senses took over. I hadn't feasted on much blood in recent days, so my powers were limited, but I had more than enough strength to slaughter our mortal, human attackers—unless I was feathered with arrows. I wore none of my old armor. I'd only just woken up, after all.

But my family was out there—two people who depended on me to keep them safe.

It was time for the Devil to go to work.

Smoke filled the clearing as the tents raged with flame, obscuring the vision of the archers, and I began to sprint with unnatural speed from cover to cover, searching out any of the invaders. Through the smoke, men in armor and leathers stalked the camp, laughing as they searched out victims for their blades.

My claws tore and rent flesh from bone, removed organs, severed limbs.

I didn't even have time to feed for fear that I was too hungry and might lose myself in the meal, providing a perfect target for the next attacker. Death now, dinner later.

But as I slaughtered and eviscerated invader after invader, I caught faint glimpses of superhuman speed, heard feral roars and screams that didn't belong to anything natural.

The invaders weren't all human. So, not an enemy tribe or conquering settlers. Something from my side of the world.

I screamed and roared, my fury redoubled to learn of the non-human threats, and my arms soon glistened with hot, crimson blood, but the invaders had targeted our warriors first, and it seemed I was the only one fighting back. The only man left to defend the women and children.

I listened in distant horror as my tribe was mowed down by both traditional weapons and blurs of monsters tearing my tribe limb from limb, faster than I could protect them.

I lashed out, snatching up a creature as it tore past me. I sank my fangs into his shoulder, risking a swift drink before ripping a chunk of his flesh from his body as easily as a razor-blade. The man gasped and shrieked as he went down, clutching at his wound and screaming with abandon.

But as I stared out through the smoke, I realized his allies had already fled, likely knowing full-well the sound of my hunting cry. Their attack had been surgical in its swiftness. No matter. I would feast and pursue every last one of them.

The parched earth gorged on the spilled blood and I had to force my baser instincts to ignore the savory hunger it ignited within me. The thirst for blood was overwhelming, even knowing it belonged to my family. Because everywhere I looked, the dead I had left in my wake were mingled with those of my tribe, making it impossible to see where one body ended and another began.

Impossible to discern enemy blood from the blood of my tribe.

Impossible to find clean blood not tied to my own family.

I screamed in rage, even my own ears popping at the sound. I needed blood to pursue the cowards—especially since they had their own monsters in their number.

I had scented both werewolves and vampires and...

My lips curled back. A merchant of magic. A warlock of some kind. That was why I hadn't sensed the attack until they were already upon us. Someone had blanketed the clearing with magic, dulling my senses. Dulling even Deganawida's senses, apparently.

But there were no warlocks or werewolves here in the Americas—other than Lucian and Nero. And I had heard of no new boats landing ashore.

Where were my wife and son? Where was Deganawida?

I prowled the camp, searching for survivors, enemies, anyone who could give me answers, stumbling at each scream and cry. Dead, glassy eyes stared up at me, piercing my soul, praying to their great protector to help them...

Me.

But there were so few actual survivors.

Finding all my enemies dead, I finally made my way back to the last man I had attacked. Surprisingly, he wasn't supernatural at all, but a human. I snatched up a fallen spear and slammed the butt into a puddle of soaked earth hard enough for it to sink a foot into the ground. Then I hoisted the man up with one claw and carefully impaled him on the blade.

It never ceased to amaze me how quickly a man could wake up when a spear entered his rear.

But I didn't have time to enjoy this justified torture. I let him scream and beg, so terrified and tortured that he dared not kick his feet for fear of increasing his current level of agony. I supported him enough not to let him die too quickly, literally holding his life in my claw, as I leaned in close to reveal my fangs. It took everything in my power not to drain him dry, but I needed information.

And he was soaked with blood from my own tribe; he had been lying atop a trio of young girls. Young girls who had earlier made me a wreath of white flowers, singing and laughing as they danced up to me.

"What was the meaning of this attack?" I demanded. "Who are you?"

The man's eyes were wild with horror and pain, his neck bleeding freely. I shook him and hissed, opening my jaws wide. His eyes finally locked onto mine and a look of smug pride briefly flickered across his face as he saw that his fate was sealed. "No one can escape their past," he rasped. "Dracula sends his regards, Devil."

Before I could press him on the answer, I felt a sudden bloom of pain in my chest. I dropped him instinctively, the tip of the spear tearing out through his throat as he let out a gurgling gasp. I stumbled back as fire raged through my body. I stared down to find a rough wooden stake in my chest, close enough to shave my heart but not pierce it or I would have already died. I blinked in disbelief, staggering. The human had been sent by Dracula, my old servant—the first man I had turned.

The man I had left everything to when I fled Europe.

But to a man who lived on a never-ending thirst for blood...even my last gift had not been enough. He had finally sent men for me, and that mistake had slaughtered my new family.

It was the move of a man desperate enough to bite the hand that fed him, in hopes that it would be enough to let the world think he was more important than he truly was. A man so terrified of letting the world discover that the only reason he held my throne was because I had cast down my crown, giving it to him without so much as a backward glance.

Dracula...that pestilent, pitiful plague of paranoid paucity.

I fell to my knees, staring at the dead man. But his lifeless gaze stared into the eyes of the Devil, and I wanted nothing more than to bring him back to life so that I might kill him again. Slowly. Over centuries. All the while, imagining him as Dracula—the spawn of my hubris.

The world began to spin and my claws sank into the bloody earth. I spat dark blood, grimacing at the strange taste in my mouth. His blood. It...was tainted with something.

And I had drunk from him.

What was it? What had he done? What had Dracula made him do to his own blood?

I knew that his claim must be true. No one I had met in the Americas knew of vampires—and they definitely hadn't heard of Dracula. Deganawida had said so, asking me to explain what was different about me since he had never run across a man such as myself. He had kept that secret—mostly—from the rest of the tribe. They knew I was a man with demons and that I had some sort of power, that I drank blood, but none of them had seemed to particularly care, being well familiar with magic since they had a powerful Medicine Man like Deganawida to guide them. If he thought me and my friends were safe, that had been enough for them.

So how had these invaders known? How had they found me?

"I need to find Bubble...My son," I mumbled, realizing I was now sitting in *a pool of bloody mud beside the trio of young girls. Their hands reached out to me, begging for my help, my vengeance.*

Some of those arms were no longer attached.

And as I stared down, struggling to fight down my own dizziness, I heard their laughter from earlier—superimposed over their lifeless bodies. I began retching, desperately trying to expel the poisoned blood from my body, but each attempt reminded me of the stake in my chest.

Deganawida shambled from around a smoldering tent, his eyes locking onto me. His face was covered in ash and mud and blood, and his fingers were blistered and burned—either from using his magic or from pulling survivors from the flames. But the look in his eyes told me there weren't many—if any —of the latter.

He stumbled closer, eyes riveted on my chest wound, and his lips tightened.

"Sorin," he whispered. "What do you need?" He crouched down to study the stake in my chest. It was obvious he wanted to help me in the only way he knew how—to heal—but with me being different, he didn't know what that entailed.

"Blood," I admitted with a pained groan. "And I see no enemy bodies to drink," I snarled, scanning my surroundings. My previous victim was dead, not far away, but his blood was poisoned. Likely, all of the invaders had poison in their blood—to practically guarantee my death. If I hadn't been the target, I would have been impressed at the tactic.

I'd taught my protégé too well.

I stared out at the moaning tribe, those still alive, knowing they were only moments from death—if they were lucky. All the blood. The only thing that could help heal me was all around me.

And I knew that I would forever damn my own soul if I tasted even a single drop of my own tribe. And with a wound like mine, a simple taste would not help. I needed buckets of blood. The kind of blood I had once celebrated with, enough to make me drunk with rapture.

The situation sickened me. "I need to find my family," I rasped, grasping at his sleeve desperately. It was shredded from claws, and I saw angry gouges in the meat of his shoulder. He didn't wince at my grip so I looked back up at the tough bastard. "Bubbling Brook. My son," I whispered desperately. "I need clean blood!"

His filthy face was streaked with trails of tears. "They burned the tent with your blood stores, and—" his voice choked off and his shoulders slumped. "My daughter and grandson...did not make it," he whispered, his voice cracking at the end. "I could not find them!"

My world jolted as if I had been struck upside the head, and a steady whining sound filled my ears. No...that couldn't be right. They had been so close to me when it all began. They had to be just around the corner. My vision swam and spun wildly as I waited for my wife and son to walk out from behind one of the burning tents, eager to show me that they had survived—that my unnamed son had learned to walk!

Seeing my son walk unaided might have been enough to cure me. Even if it cost me the last of my strength to avenge the tribe. Surely, it would. I just wanted to see that my son could walk. Was that too much to ask?

Had the Oracle of Delphi been right?

As if in answer, all I heard were more moans, wails, and cries of anguish. The hellish choir of the damned. The Devil's prayer.

Deganawida slapped me across the jaw, snapping me out of my night-mare. "Sorin! You are the only one who can avenge us. You must feed."

I shook my head adamantly, gagging at the thought. "Never. You cannot ask such a thing of me. Their blood has been poisoned. And yours would likely kill me!"

We'd tried that once—just a sample. It had been disastrous. I had sworn to never again drink the blood of a Medicine Man. I would likely end up killing the few who had survived in my wild, uncontrollable bloodlust.

Understanding dawned upon Deganawida's face and he shuddered, nodding sadly. "There is...perhaps one other way, Sorin. Someone must make them pay for what they did, and I must assist the wounded. Get them to safety..."

I locked eyes with him, momentarily forgetting the flame of pain within my chest. "Tell me."

He was silent for a moment, his eyes distant as he weighed options or perhaps considered whether his plan could even work with a man like me—a vampire. "I can put you into a sleep that would heal you. I think. It has worked on other patients—even a few with unique abilities," he added with a meaningful glance. "But not specifically one such as you. I could bind us together."

I nodded. "Do it. If it will heal me, I must try. I will return and track down every last Godforsaken soul who dared harm our family this night," I swore. "My family will be avenged. Our family will be avenged," I told him, my voice oozing with anticipation. "Do it. Now. I don't know how much longer I have without blood to sustain me."

"There is a chance it will not work," Deganawida admitted. "And it will also put me at great risk," he said, not in fear, but in responsibility. If any had survived, they would need Deganawida.

I grimaced. "Then nothing changes, for I will surely die without blood, and I don't think I have enough time—let alone the strength—to go hunting now. You need to heal those who you can. I will be our vengeance if I am able, but the survivors will need you. Do as you must, and I swear I will do the same. You must find Lucian and Nero. You will need them for protection until I return. And I will need their righteous fury when I return," I snarled. "Just don't wait too long to wake me."

My wife's father nodded as he placed his hands upon my forehead. I heard a wolf howl—too late if it was my friend Lucian—as my spirit was suddenly cast up into the heavens to drift among the stars, seeming to leave my shredded heart and my mortal coils far, far below...

A phoenix of vengeance rising up into the stars, waiting for the day, in a few weeks, when it would return to rain fire down upon every member of the invaders—and every blood relative of theirs I could find.

I would return and make Dracula choke on the blood he had spilled this day. Choke on the blood of his own people.

Because those people were rightfully mine.

I, Sorin Ambrogio, would remind the world who truly ruled the night—the vampire who didn't need a crown to reign.

The Devil would rise again...

Darkness consumed me for a time, and then the haunted memories started all over again...as it had repeated countless times before—an eternal pit of woe and shame that I could never escape.

A Devil's due—a Devil's Dream.

I STARED out at the forest, smiling absently at the sounds of laughter and conversation coming from around the crackling campfire behind me. I felt like the luckiest man in the world as I let the vibrancy of the American Indians' lifestyle—my new family—pour over me. None referred to themselves as Indians, of course—that was a term my fellow Europeans had given them.

3

G od damned me.

He—in his infinite, omnipotent wisdom—declared for all to hear...

Let there be pain...

In the exact center of this poor bastard's soul.

And that merciless smiting woke me from a dead sleep and thrust me into a body devoid of every sensation but blinding agony.

I tried to scream but my throat felt as dry as dust, only permitting me to emit a rasping, whistling hiss that brought on yet *more* pain. My skin burned and throbbed while my bones creaked and groaned with each full-body tremor. My claws sunk into a hard surface beneath me and I was distantly surprised they hadn't simply shattered upon contact.

My memory was an immolated ruin—each fragment of thought merely an elusive fleck of ash or ember that danced through my fog of despair as I struggled to catch one and hold onto it long enough to recall what had brought me to this bleak existence. How I had become this poor, wretched, shell of a man. I couldn't even remember my own *name*; it was all I could do to simply survive this profound horror.

After what seemed an eternity, the initial pain began to slowly ebb, but I quickly realized that it had only triggered a cascade of smaller, more numerous tortures—like ripples caused by a boulder thrown into a pond.

I couldn't find the strength to even attempt to open my crusted eyes, and my abdomen was a solid knot of gnawing hunger so overwhelming that I felt like I was being pulled down into the earth by a lead weight. My fingers tingled and burned so fiercely that I wondered if the skin had been peeled away while I slept. Since they were twitching involuntarily, at least I knew that the muscles and tendons were still attached.

I held onto that sliver of joy, that beacon of hope.

I stubbornly gritted my teeth, but even that slight movement made the skin over my face stretch tight enough to almost tear. I willed myself to relax as I tried to process *why* I was in so much pain, where I was, how I had gotten here, and...*who* I even was? A singular thought finally struck me like an echo of the faintest of whispers, giving me something to latch onto.

Hunger.

I let out a crackling gasp of relief at finally grasping an independent answer of some kind, but I was unable to draw enough moisture onto my tongue to properly swallow. Understanding that I was hungry had seemed to alleviate a fraction of my pain. The answer to at least one question distracted me long enough to allow me to think. And despite my hunger, I felt something tantalizingly delicious slowly coursing down my throat, desperately attempting to alleviate my starvation.

Even though my memory was still enshrouded in fog, I was entirely certain that it was incredibly dangerous for me to feel this hungry. This...*thirsty.* Dangerous for both myself and anyone nearby. I tried to remember why it was so dangerous but the reason eluded me. Instead, an answer to a different question emerged from my mind like a specter from the mist—and I felt myself begin to smile as a modicum of strength slowly took root deep within me.

"Sorin..." I croaked. My voice echoed, letting me know that I was in an enclosed space of some kind. "My name is Sorin Ambrogio. And I need..." I trailed off uncertainly, unable to finish my own thought.

"Blood," a man's deep voice answered from only a few paces away. "You need more blood."

I hissed instinctively, snapping my eyes open for the first time since waking. I had completely forgotten to check my surroundings, too consumed with my own pain to bother with my other senses. I had been asleep so long that even the air seemed to burn my eyes like smoke, forcing me to blink rapidly. No, the air *was* filled with pungent, aromatic smoke, but not like the smoke from the fires in my—

I shuddered involuntarily, blocking out the thought for some unknown reason.

Beneath the pungent smoke, the air was musty and damp. Through it all, I smelled the delicious, coppery scent of hot, powerful blood.

I had been resting atop a raised stone plinth—almost like a table—in a depthless, shadowy cavern. I appreciated the darkness because any light would have likely blinded me in my current state. I couldn't see the man who had spoken, but the area was filled with silhouettes of what appeared to be tables, crates, and other shapes that could easily conceal him. I focused on my hearing and almost instantly noticed a seductively familiar, *beating* sound.

A noise as delightful as a child's first belly-laugh...

A beautiful woman's sigh as she locked eyes with you for the first time.

The gentle crackling of a fireplace on a brisk, snowy night.

Thump-thump.

Thump-thump.

Thump-thump.

The sound became *everything* and my vision slowly began to sharpen, the room brightening into shades of gray. My pain didn't disappear, but it was swiftly muted as I tracked the sound.

I inhaled deeply, my eyes riveting on a far wall as my nostrils flared, pinpointing the source of the savory perfume and the seductive beating sound. I didn't recall sitting up, but I realized that I was suddenly leaning forward and that the room was continuing to brighten into paler shades of gray, burning away the last of the remaining shadows—despite the fact that there was no actual light. And it grew clearer as I focused on the seductive sound.

Until I finally spotted a man leaning against the far wall. *Thump-thump. Thump-thump. Thump-thump...* I licked my lips ravenously, setting my hands on the cool stone table as I prepared to set my feet on the ground.

Food...

The man calmly lifted his hand and a sharp *clicking* sound suddenly echoed from the walls. The room abruptly flooded with light so bright and unexpected that it felt like my eyes had exploded. Worse, what seemed like a trio of radiant stars was not more than a span from my face—so close that I could feel the direct heat from their flare. I recoiled with a snarl, momentarily forgetting all about food as I shielded my eyes with a hand and prepared to defend myself. I leaned away from the bright lights, wondering why I couldn't smell smoke from the flickering flames. I squinted, watching the man's feet for any indication of movement.

Half a minute went by as my vision slowly began to adjust, and the man didn't even shift his weight—almost as if he was granting me time enough to grow accustomed to the sudden light. Which...didn't make any sense. Hadn't it been an attack? I hesitantly lowered my hand from my face, reassessing the situation and my surroundings.

I stared in wonder as I realized that the orbs were not made of flame, but rather what seemed to be pure light affixed to polished metal stands. Looking directly at them hurt, so I studied them sidelong, making sure to also keep the man in my peripheral vision. He had to be a sorcerer of some kind. Who else could wield pure light without fire?

"Easy, Sorin," the man murmured in a calming baritone. "I can't see as well as you in the dark, but it looked like you were about to do something unnecessarily stupid. Let me turn them down a little."

He didn't wait for my reply, but the room slowly dimmed after another clicking sound.

I tried to get a better look at the stranger—wondering where he had come from, where he had taken me, and who he was. One thing was obvious—he knew magic. "Where did you learn this sorcery?" I rasped, gesturing at the orbs of light.

"Um. Hobby Lobby."

"I've never heard of him," I hissed, coughing as a result of my parched throat.

"I'm not even remotely surprised by that," he said dryly. He extended his other hand and I gasped to see an impossibility—a transparent bag as clear as new glass. And it was *flexible*, swinging back and forth like a bulging coin purse or a clear water-skin. My momentary wonder at the magical material evaporated as I recognized the crimson liquid *inside* the bag.

Blood.

He lobbed it at me underhanded without a word of warning. I hissed as I desperately—and with exceeding caution—caught it from the air lest it fall and break open. I gasped as the clear bag of blood settled into my palms and, before I consciously realized it, I tore off the corner with my fangs, pressed it to my lips, and squeezed the bag in one explosive, violent gesture. The ruby fluid gushed into my mouth and over my face, dousing my almost forgotten pain as swiftly as a bucket of water thrown on hot coals.

I felt my eyes roll back into my skull and my body shuddered as I lost my balance and fell from the stone table. I landed on my back but I was too overwhelmed to care as I stretched out my arms and legs. I groaned in rapture, licking at my lips like a wild animal. The ruby nectar was a living serpent of molten oil as it slithered down into my stomach, nurturing and healing me almost instantly. It was the most wonderful sensation I could imagine—almost enough to make me weep.

Like a desert rain, my parched tongue and throat absorbed the blood so quickly and completely that I couldn't even savor the heady flavor. This wasn't a joyful feast; this was survival, a necessity. My body guzzled it, instantly using the liquid to repair the damage, pain, and the cloud of fog that had enshrouded me.

I realized that I was laughing. The sound echoed into the vast stone space like rolling thunder.

Because I had remembered something else.

The world's First Vampire was *back*.

And he was still *very* hungry.

4

The blood slaked my thirst and washed away the last of my pains like sheets of cool rain on sunbaked boulders. It wasn't enough blood—there would never be enough—but it was enough to repair my most concerning ailments and sustain me until I could hunt down some more.

I finally opened my eyes again, licking the blood from my lips and chin. Sudden claws spouted from my fingers and I ripped the clear bag entirely open, lapping up a few last drops of blood like a hound at the table.

I heard that delicious *thump-thump* sound again—a heartbeat—and locked onto the source, propping myself up. The man was studying me thoughtfully, keeping me at what he presumed to be a safe distance.

I really would be much more content if I guzzled down all of his sweet, sweet blood. The only balm capable of quelling my fiery emotions.

After all, I had always been taught not to play with my food. I ignored the strange lights between us. I would study them after this meat-sack was out of my hair. The obvious sorcery of the lights made me uneasy, and feeling uneasy in front of my prey was stoking my anger to even greater heights.

I locked eyes with the man and was surprised to find him smiling at my initial reaction to the blood rather than fleeing in terror at the sudden hunger in my eyes. Which made me hesitate.

More chunks of my memory were slowly trickling in, but I still had trouble connecting the pieces together into a full picture. So, I decided to assess my guest to buy myself some time.

He was a tall, middle-aged man with sun-kissed skin and he wore his thick, ebony hair in a wavy mess that managed to look at least somewhat presentable. His face was like a chiseled boulder with high, dominant cheekbones and a harsh, angular jaw—almost guaranteeing he was of an American Indian bloodline. He had very light stubble and his eyes were like dark, melted chocolate. In those bold, brown eyes, I sensed a calm serenity as powerful and dangerous as any man I had ever met. He was broader of the shoulder than me and wore pants of a thick blue fabric with a white, stained undershirt of sorts.

I found myself wondering if his clothing would fit me after I killed him.

To a man of my years, he would always be a boy—an adolescent, at best. Rather than running in terror at my bloody, hungry grin, his amused smile slowly faded and he shook his head in warning at the look in my eyes. "It is generally considered unwise to drink the blood of a Medicine Man," he warned.

I belted out a mocking laugh. "You expect me to believe you are a Medicine Man? Your balls haven't even dropped, boy. Have you ever even gone on a hunt? Killed a man? Made love to a woman?"

He glared at me, his eyes narrowing. "You will soon learn that the requirements for becoming a man have changed in...recent times. And my name is Nosh. Not *boy*."

I grunted, rolling my eyes at his pathetic excuse.

I couldn't necessarily confirm or deny whether he was truly a Medicine Man, but his blood did smell potent. And he had that magic light on those metal stands...

He obviously had some type of magic at his command. I appraised him pointedly. "Medicine Man," I repeated doubtfully, deciding I needed to find what this man was truly made of—to provoke him, even though I presumed he was telling me the truth. Having magic was one thing, but knowing how to effectively use it was quite another.

True Medicine Men were *extremely* dangerous, and I knew only the vaguest of details about the limits and capabilities of their power. I vaguely recalled living with the American Indians for a few years, as strange as that sounded. But I felt like I knew quite a bit about Medicine Men, so it had to be true.

Nosh smiled faintly. "I prefer the term Shaman. Although not as accurate, it incites more fear these days. And fear is a weapon in and of itself. When a mere word can give an enemy pause, it is wise to wield it."

I grunted my agreement, memories still slowly trickling in, but they were a confusing jumble like they were out of order or context. But I was absolutely certain of a few things.

To square off against a Shaman, I would need to drink a figurative ocean of blood—which would likely leave me dazed and lazy after such starvation as I had obviously suffered. Blood would help me recover, but as much as I would need to fully heal would also put me at risk. I had never been as hungry as I was now. Despite the bag of blood reviving me, I still felt weak. I must have been asleep for a long time. The real question was *why*?

Drinking this Shaman's blood might help me recover faster but a more persistent whisper in my mind warned me that drinking a Shaman's blood was the worst thing I could possibly do. I couldn't recall why, but I was confident that my instincts had never steered me wrong before.

Nosh held up a hand to reveal a wooden stake in his fist. He waited for me to react but I managed to keep my face blank. A real Shaman wouldn't need a stake to battle a vampire. It was like introducing a wooden practice sword to a duel. His fist shook ever so slightly but I sensed no fear from him. It was almost as if he was testing me, wondering how feral I was—that he believed that if I attacked him for such a slight we would both lose something much more important than our pride. A Medicine Man—or Shaman, as he preferred—was a unique type of man. They looked at the simplest of situations in very complicated ways, inferring deeper meanings from the most common of occurrences.

Typically, vampires were very wild and erratic types—reacting on impulse more often than not. Their hunger and dominance rose above all else.

I decided I was very interested in letting this situation play out before I contemplated eating him. Because I wanted the rest of my memories to clarify before I did anything rash.

Also, this man's actions were...intriguing.

In me, he apparently saw a potential for something that he considered important enough that it warranted risking his own mortal life. The look in his hard eyes practically shouted that if he had to stake me to save his own life, he would do it, but I could tell that he felt he would be starting some cataclysmic chain of events that would doom us all—meaning he would lose either way. The only hope he saw was in our conversation continuing—for us two entirely different men to overcome our baser natures and stereotypes.

I needed to know why he felt such a thing. I was no hero.

I was entirely sure that I was quite the *opposite* of a hero, in fact.

"I'm still thirsty, and your fear is not helping," I lied.

"One Medicine Man a day is beyond impressive, Sorin. Two would surely kill a vampire. Even the world's First vampire."

I blinked twice, staring at him. What was he talking about?

I realized that he was not looking at me but beside me. I glanced over to see that we were not alone. Three dead bodies lay on the ground beside a bowl of smoking incense—the source of the thick herbal scent in the cavern.

Two roasted men were propped up against a stack of crates, their faces blackened and melted to reveal fangs where their teeth should have been.

Vampires.

They were smoking, their bodies still warm with both blood and fire. I was surprised I hadn't smelled them before now, but the herbal scent in the air had masked it.

A wizened old man was sprawled out beside the stone plinth I had been resting upon. Blood trailed down the side of my temporary bed, and I realized it was emitting a smoking vapor—magic. Tendrils of that magical vapor fused with the smoke from the incense, growing thicker and more pungent.

The old man's wrist was a mangled ruin, and something about him looked...vaguely familiar, although I was certain that I did not know him. Recalling Nosh's comment, my body froze.

One Medicine Man a day is quite enough...

This old man had fed his blood to me—that was why his wrist was shredded. He had given his life to wake me from my slumber. And he had been a Medicine Man. How had that not killed me? Their potent blood was enough to possibly overwhelm me, even poison me. I'd learned that the hard way with—

I grunted as a dizzying cascade of memories slammed into me. After a few seconds, I blinked rapidly, trying to process it all. I *had* lived with the American Indians, even befriending their Medicine Man, Deganawida! That was where I had acquired my knowledge of their people.

Deganawida had adopted me into his tribe soon after I first came to the Americas. I remembered him once offering me some of his blood during a meal, fascinated to meet a vampire—since there hadn't been any vampires in the Americas. I had hesitantly agreed, and had instantly regretted it. I remembered only a bolt of lightning followed by sudden unconsciousness.

A cold chill raced up my spine as my eyes latched onto his chest. I eagerly scooted closer, snatching at a familiar necklace around the old man's neck. My hands shook as I stared at it—a simple stone from a creek-bed.

Deganawida had worn such a necklace. He had found the stone the day his daughter was born, while impatiently waiting outside the tribe's longhouse for her to enter the world. It was how he had chosen her name, Bubbling Brook, and he'd worn it as a memento ever since.

A larger flood of memories abruptly hammered into me, seeming to physically hit me like punches to the gut. I rocked back and forth, gritting my teeth as I began to remember. To remember why I was here.

It all came back to me in a deluge of body blows, and all I could do was sit there and take it like a man.

As the mental beating continued, it took every fiber of my being not to explode in a murderous rage, because the ramifications of my returning memories were forming a bleak, terrifying picture.

I stared down at the necklace, quivering. This man wasn't just familiar. I knew exactly who he was. This was Deganawida—only decades older. Many decades older.

And he'd finally chosen to wake me from my slumber, to fulfill his promise to me. To give his life to do so.

Except...judging by his apparent age, he was decades overdue.

I was too late to avenge my family.

5

I recoiled in disgust, dropping the necklace like it was a burning coal as I spat and gagged, wanting nothing more than to vomit his blood out of my body, no matter that it had been willingly given to bring me back to life. I must have been on the verge of death for his blood not to kill me outright. I remembered his last words to me. Something about bonding us together. Was this what he had meant?

"No!" I rasped, shaking my head in denial as I stared at the Shaman's kind, hopeful, lifeless eyes. He...had died smiling.

"Do you remember?" Nosh asked in a gentle, meaningful tone, his voice limned with what sounded like hope.

I snapped my gaze his way, hissing instinctively—both at momentarily forgetting that he was present and with unbridled rage at Deganawida's contradicting betrayal and sacrifice.

"What have you done?" I rasped, not wanting to accept the fact that Deganawida had obviously chosen his fate of his own volition, evidenced by the dying smile on his face. "How could you let Deganawida do such a thing? And why is he so old?" I snarled, my panic rising at an alarming rate. "It was only supposed to be days or weeks! Not *decades*!"

Nosh's jaw dropped. "Degan...awida?" he whispered, making it sound like two different words. His face was as pale as a sheet. "*The* Deganawida?" he asked as if speaking of a legend given flesh.

I stared at him, my hands still shaking. As much as I suddenly wanted to rip the man's spine from his body, he was the only survivor of the obvious battle that had taken place around me. And...the look of raw agony on his face was convincing—enough to grant him a few more precious moments of life, anyway.

That didn't mean that I felt any sliver of patience. "You will tell me everything you know, boy. I might not dare to drink two Medicine Men in one day, but that doesn't mean I wouldn't take particularly cruel delight in skinning you alive and handing you over to the settlers on the coast."

The man didn't even look at me, too busy staring at the dead old man to even register my threat. "He told me his name was Richard Degan..." he whispered, sounding hurt and...deeply furious, for some reason. "I assumed he was named *after* Deganawida," he breathed, shaking his head and licking his lips subconsciously. His eyes looked a little wild around the edges, as if he was watching his world collapse around him.

"Why do you act so surprised? He brought you here, to see me. How could you not know who he really was?" I demanded, growing suspicious. Deganawida would have never told anyone about me unless he trusted them implicitly.

The man blinked, finally turning to face me. "Deganawida died *hundreds* of years ago," he murmured incredulously. "You haven't been asleep for *decades*, Sorin. You've been asleep for *centuries*. Five hundred years."

I attempted to mask my reaction, but I must have failed miserably, because I sensed a noticeable spike in his pulse as he watched me. Five hundred years. That couldn't be right. That shouldn't even be possible.

A wave of panic roared through me and I realized that I was panting. That meant...

The entire reason I had been put to sleep—the cause of my unceasing nightmares, reliving that night over and over again.

Had all been for *nothing*.

Nosh abruptly glanced at the smoke, which had suddenly stilled in an entirely abnormal manner. He cursed. "Shit! I almost forgot about the fucking ritual!" Without explanation, he turned to one of the far walls and flung up a hand as if warding something away. He snatched up a dreamcatcher I hadn't noticed sitting in his lap, and then he began to hum and chant a powerful song as he wafted the dreamcatcher back and forth, fanning the smoke—like I had seen Deganawida do many times when calling upon the rain or any other number of rituals as the tribe's Medicine Man.

The smoke didn't eddy or move. At all. Even when the dreamcatcher physically touched it, and the hair on the back of my arms shot straight up as goosebumps pebbled my flesh.

A swarm of icy blue lights bloomed to life from the eerily still blanket of smoke, and I felt his magic suddenly swamp the air—just like Deganawida's magic. He truly was a Medicine Man.

A...*Shaman*, I thought to myself with a sad frown, recalling how I had always teased Deganawida with the incorrect term. Yet Nosh had seemed to prefer it.

The blue lights flitted through the air like crazed butterflies, revealing a painted mural on the wall. I gasped as the paint began to glow in the hypnotic dance of the blue lights. And Nosh kept on chanting, rocking back and forth now.

I stared at the dozens of images covering the surface of the wall from floor to ceiling, and I felt my stomach drop. It told a story...one I was well familiar with.

The story of a white, skulking, cloaked figure—me—huddled over a corpse, feeding. Of another man drawn in bronze paint—Deganawida —seated beside him, smoking a pipe.

An image of me standing before a tribe—my skin again colored with white chalk rather than the bronze faces of everyone else.

And dozens of other images.

Two white-skinned men—a werewolf and a man holding a flame in his palm—standing beside me as I married a beautiful bronze woman, Bubbling Brook.

My son struggling to walk. The chaotic battle of that fateful night when everything had changed. Me lying with a stake in my heart and Deganawida praying over me.

Then a cavern, laying me to rest on a raised dais.

White invaders attacking villages of bronze families.

Bronze warriors attacking villages of white families.

Deganawida addressing hundreds of bronze-painted stick-figures. An image of a tree and five arrows bundled together.

And many more that I didn't understand but...images that obviously depicted a changing world—some horrifying and some revered.

The chanting suddenly stopped, and I turned to see Nosh panting, covered in a sheen of sweat. He set the dreamcatcher down and slowly looked up at me. "If this works," he growled, "shit's about to get very weird. If you have any questions for him, this is your chance. I know I've got a few questions for the lying bastard, all of a sudden."

The steady gaze in his red-rimmed eyes told me he was speaking the truth—that, and the calm but thunderous beating of his heart. He felt just as betrayed as me. But what the hell was he—

A sudden rattling noise made me stop short, and I looked up to see that the cavern was filled with dreamcatchers. I hadn't noticed them before. They were vibrating and swinging wildly, and the blanket of smoke was suddenly cresting and falling like waves in a turbulent ocean. Deganawida's blood was practically spraying more vapor up into the air. I gasped as I spotted his old pipe tucked into a pocket on his shirt. Because it was also emitting thick vapor of its own.

My eyes widened in disbelief.

"I think it's working..." Nosh warned. "The crazy bastard wins again."

Before I could demand an explanation, an apparition of Deganawida—the younger version I had known long ago—suddenly coalesced before me, formed from the incense and magical vapor cloying the air. I grunted incredulously as he stared down at me.

"It worked!" he crowed, clearly pleased to see me alive. Without missing a beat, his cheer evaporated as if I had only imagined it. "Sorin Ambrogio..." he whispered. "I owe you the greatest of apologies. Your punishment has been my life's greatest regret."

I nodded stiffly, pretending that this was all entirely normal. "Keep your apologies, Shaman, but I demand an explanation for your betrayal of my trust."

He nodded sadly. "The spell I used on you did not work the way I had intended. It did indeed bond us, but I learned that the only way to bring you back was for me to die. And the tribe needed me to protect them. And then other tribes needed me. And then..." he waved a hand vaguely, "there always seemed to be one more reason for delay. Until I noticed that my magic had begun to fade. Maybe as a consequence of my betrayal to you, my powers evaporated."

Nosh grunted. "I could sense the power in you, and I always wondered why I never saw you use it, even while you taught me..." he said, as if trying to make sense of Deganawida's claim. Then his features hardened. "And you never told me you were *the* Deganawida."

Deganawida nodded. "That was the cruelest aspect. I still *felt* all my power—like nothing had changed—but I couldn't *access* it. And my identity was my own secret to keep, Nosh. Knowing would have changed nothing."

"Then why didn't you just open a vein and give me your blood?" I demanded testily. "That was all I needed, right?"

Deganawida shook his head, and I saw Nosh stiffen in sudden understanding. "You needed a Medicine Man to perform the ritual *and* my blood to wake you up," Deganawida explained.

Nosh growled angrily. "You used me. And you didn't tell me that I was helping you commit suicide tonight, although I should have anticipated it when you forced me to learn the summoning ritual with the incense and dreamcatchers. I figured that part out pretty quickly. You know, after I saw the vampire drink you dry."

Deganawida shot him a stern look. "I used you to do what Medicine Men do, Nosh. Chastise me for lying, but not for asking you to perform the magic that you asked me to teach you in the first place, boy."

Nosh stiffened at the reprimand, but he still didn't look pleased about only just now learning Deganawida's true identity or any of his other secrets.

"Although I kept much from Nosh," Deganawida explained, turning to face me, "I did tell him *why* I woke you, which is what actually matters right now. You two strangers will need each other in the coming days."

I glared at him. "I'm not sure I'm too inclined to do anything to help you, let alone babysit the angry man-child over there."

Nosh growled warningly, but Deganawida cut him off with a stern look. "His anger is justified, Nosh. As is yours. But I am the one who has earned that anger, so direct it at me so that I may carry it with me as I depart this mortal plane."

His statement cut the tension like a knife, and we both lowered our heads. Deganawida was about to go to the afterlife. We were witnessing a man delaying his own death to give us a warning, and we were bickering like children. I nodded. "Speak your piece, Deganawida. I make no promises to comply, but I will at least listen."

Because no matter what justifications he gave me, his actions had forced me to live for centuries in my own personal hell—forced to relive that fateful night on repeat for centuries—a prisoner in my own mind. An experience worse than any hell the Devil could give me.

The more I thought about my slumber, the more I began to realize that some small part of me must have been entirely aware that the memory had been playing on repeat. Encore after encore, keeping track of the number of repetitions. Because my current rage was more at his betrayal than any immediate emotional reaction for my dead family.

Like my subconscious mind had already processed and accepted that crime long ago, while I slept. If it hadn't, I would have been in a blind rage over them right about now. But...my anger was deep and sterile, like a long-held grudge that had been forgotten but never forgiven.

Which made me feel incredibly uneasy—almost guilty.

Deganawida nodded somberly. "Your kin and other supernatural associates of your past have come to New York, and I fear it is my fault," he admitted, gesturing at the two charcoal vampires on the ground.

I leaned forward, narrowing my eyes suspiciously. I didn't want to interrupt him, though, fearing how much time he had left before this ritual was over and he was called to the afterlife.

"It will be some time before you are back to full strength, Sorin. I know how hungry you must be. How weak you must feel right now. You once warned me about the dangers of you drinking too much blood too quickly."

I nodded, having already considered that problem. My body was so depleted that I would need a hundred humans to even *begin* to feel like normal, and drinking that much blood at once would turn me into a mindless, feral beast with no sense of friend or foe—no rational mind whatsoever. The only way back was gradually.

"In the coming days, you will need every power at your disposal, which is one of the other reasons I brought Nosh into my confidences. I needed his power to wake you, but you will also need his power to battle this new threat. He is a competent Shaman and knows the ways of the world—which has drastically changed over the last few hundred years. But Nosh can catch you up on all of that. My time is limited."

I nodded. "I'm going to need more blood. Now. Are you absolutely *certain* I need the meat sack over there?" I asked, pointing at Nosh.

Deganawida nodded firmly. "More than you know, Sorin. More than you could believe. He is one of the last few remaining descendants of our tribe, after all."

I stiffened, glancing sharply at Nosh. A descendant of our tribe? I couldn't place any physical similarities between him and the tribe members I had known, but it had been five hundred years, so that wasn't surprising. What was surprising was that we had any descendants at all after Dracula's savage attack.

"Give him the blood bags. All of them," Deganawida said, pointing at an orange and white chest against the wall. Nosh nodded and bent over to lift the hinged, white lid. It wasn't metal, but it was a slightly reflective, firm material that I had never seen before. He reached inside to grab a heavy satchel before tossing it my way. I caught it, flipping open the top to see it was bulging with more of the transparent packets of blood. I didn't even bother marveling at their substance. There would be time for that later. I tore into one and began to guzzle it down as Deganawida continued talking.

6

The blood hit my lips like oil on a dry wagon axle, my body drinking it down deep. I tried not to shudder as I felt my emaciated muscles growing denser and stronger, my flesh no longer on the verge of tearing like dried paper, my aching joints and bones suddenly relieved of strain and pressure, no longer creaking and groaning with each movement.

"Nosh might be the last true Medicine Man in the world, believe it or not," Deganawida mused, eyeing Nosh with fatherly pride. "Over the years, the pool of potential Medicine Men has grown smaller and smaller. Those who might have had the potential to learn did not have the desire, preferring to abandon our Native American culture in favor of modern society. Nosh had no interest in that world, thankfully. But his parents have always been historians at heart."

Nosh nodded with a faint smile. "They should have been museum curators."

Deganawida smiled warmly, nodding his agreement. "In a way, they were."

Nosh cocked his head at a sudden thought. "They would have lost their mind had they known you were the real Deganawida. You were their hero," he said, smiling sadly. "Mine, too."

Deganawida sighed tiredly. "I told no one. If I had, they would have locked me away in an asylum." Nosh nodded his agreement, letting out a frustrated sigh. "Immortality is a curse, as I'm sure Sorin knows well."

"Everyone wants immortality until they get a true taste of it—and realize it's simply the opportunity to watch generations of cruelty rather than just one. And that it makes you more paranoid about death than any mortal."

Deganawida nodded. "The allure fades rapidly, but the desperation only increases. It truly is a curse—a double-edged sword."

I studied the two men, trying to process this new world so I could decide my place in it. Hundreds of years had passed, and now they expected me to help. Like a good soldier.

I'd never been very obedient. I reached for another bag of blood, discarding the empty packet on the ground. "What became of Lucian and Nero?" I asked. "Surely they could have come to your aid."

Deganawida winced. "When they returned and heard of the attack, I showed them your body. They waited three days to verify you were not going to wake up, and then they went straight after the culprits. They swore to avenge you and your family by any means necessary."

I grunted, sucking down the bag of blood with more violence than necessary.

"I never spoke to them again—they wouldn't even accept an audience with me decades later—"

"Because you lied to them," I growled.

Deganawida nodded, not bothering to deny it. "I do not know what happened to Nero, but I know that Lucian created a new pack of werewolves almost immediately—building an army to keep himself safe. They were beholden to none but their werewolf king, claiming the Americas for themselves. No vampire dared set foot here in the years since—upon threat of eradication. Until recently."

I shook my head grimly, recalling the particulars of the attack. A small part of me remembered the taste of magic in the air, the howl of a werewolf before Deganawida's spell had put me to sleep.

Had...my own friends been a part of the attack? No one else had known we were there. And I'd had many contacts at the nearby ports and coastal towns. None had spoken of any ship landing ashore in the days or weeks leading up to the attack, and none had been expected for months.

As much as I hated to consider it...there was a possibility my friends had betrayed me.

I punched my fist into my palm. "I gave Dracula everything I owned. I don't understand why he would bother hunting me down years later. It doesn't make any sense," I muttered, speaking more to myself than anyone in the room.

Deganawida shifted uncomfortably and my eyes latched onto him. "I believe he wanted even the memory of you erased. In the numerous myths and stories about vampires, your name is never mentioned. The world believes Dracula is the father of vampires—the First—not you."

I snarled furiously, but Deganawida pressed on before I could speak.

"But I think there is more to it. Bubbling Brook and your son...I never found their bodies after the attack," he all but whispered. "I spent decades searching, speaking with other tribes, following strange rumors. But I never found them."

The cavern grew silent as I stared at him, opening my mouth wordlessly. "You think...Dracula took them?" I final whispered. "Why would he do that?" I asked, my throat raw.

Deganawida frowned. "I think he *tried*," he said carefully, "but I doubt he was successful. I think he learned about you conceiving a child and wanted that for himself. The fact that I never heard about baby vampires leads me to believe that they managed to escape his clutches. You told me that Dracula hated you—especially when you gave him your castle and figurative crown. Hated that he had to live in your shadow."

"He will *die* in my shadow, too, Deganawida. This I swear." As furious as I was at the moment, I knew I needed to calm down. I could entertain my rage later. Right now, I needed answers. But my mouth began to work of its own accord. "I will kill Dracula for myself, not for you. Never for *you*. I want you to know that—to carry that burden with you to whichever cursed afterlife you inhabit, if any. Do you know that the entire time I was asleep, I relived that fateful night on repeat? But that I still cannot recall if I told my wife that I loved her? Or whether or not I embraced my son with a loving hug? Even such simple memories as those were washed away in your cursed slumber. I watched that attack *millions* of times, Deganawida. Because of you."

Nosh murmured uneasily, sounding disgusted. "That...is unbelievably sickening," he whispered. "Enough to make a man go crazy."

I slowly turned to look at him, flashing him the coolest glare I could manage. "Then you should be thankful that I am not merely a man, boy. I am a monster. The Devil, as I was once known."

Nosh studied me thoughtfully—not looking afraid, but thoughtful. I dismissed him, turning back to Deganawida. "What does any of that have to do with you waking me up now?

Deganawida pursed his lips, weighing his answer. "The tribe is not what it once was, Sorin. The world has changed, and not for the better, despite my efforts. We may as well have all died that night."

Nosh grunted. "Oh, I think you achieved quite a bit," Nosh grunted. "Uniting the tribes was no small feat."

Deganawida waved a hand dismissively. "I recently hosted an interview to tell the world the story of our people, our way of life, our culture. A documentary. Of course, I couldn't let on that I had been around since the beginning. At any rate, the reporter was particularly callous and unsympathetic. I grew defensive and mistakenly showed him my journal from hundreds of years ago—the journal which you reprimanded me for, Sorin. The one that tells of your story. That a monster became a man, and that all things are possible if one attempts to fix their heart."

I stared incredulously. "I doubt many would believe this reporter, judging by what you've told me...I'm also guessing that Dracula was not best pleased with your revelation."

Deganawida nodded. "That's just it. The reporter suddenly grew very interested when I mentioned your name. He asked questions about your story and the attack. He was particularly focused on the story that a vampire had conceived a child."

I grew very still, considering the numerous consequences. How furious Dracula would be for that information to be made public.

"Days later, there was a theft at my home, and my journal was stolen. It is going up for sale tonight at a private, illegal auction—

claimed as a recovered item from an archaeological dig. It is rumored that Dracula wants this journal—the only proof that he is not the First Vampire—silenced."

I grinned mirthlessly. "Something like that? Yes. He would burn the world to destroy it." I considered his words. "How would you know about an illegal auction?" I asked. The Deganawida I had known would never associate with that kind of immoral activity. But he had obviously changed from the man I once knew.

Nosh cleared his throat. "My parents associate with...several nefarious individuals." I blinked at him, waiting. He sighed. "Gambling halls and casinos. Legislation has provided legal benefits to Native Americans opening casinos. My parents were involved in the beginning and set up a dynasty of sorts, although they are mostly retired now." He looked guilty as he spoke, but I wasn't entirely sure why. It wasn't a sin to own a casino. I wondered what type of world I was about to encounter when we left the cave.

Deganawida continued. "I fear Dracula wants more than your existence erased, Sorin. I think he wants knowledge on your ability to conceive a child—something no vampire has ever done before or since." I realized my lips were pulled back and that my fangs were bared. "I fear that the reason for the attack so long ago might have been twofold. To kill you and kidnap your family so he could reenact the miracle of vampire childbirth. I believe he must have failed on both accounts, but now my journal—which tells the full story—is going up for sale."

Nosh cleared his throat. "Our people are in danger," he explained. "If Dracula gets his hands on that text, he will likely target our bloodline, or you specifically, thinking one of the two holds the key to the procreation of monsters. Creating a brood of baby vampires. Because with everyone thinking you are long dead, that is the only lead. Vampires have already begun abducting our tribe." He pointed down at the dead vampires on the ground. "Which means Dracula already knows about the journal."

Deganawida nodded. "The werewolves will have nothing to do with us, as we are small and not worth their alliance—and they have enough going on with trying to take down the vampires and witches. And with most of the world not even knowing that the supernatural exists, we have no one to protect us. We need you, Sorin. As cruel as it sounds to have denied your vengeance for so long, I now beg your help in correcting my many, many mistakes. And, to finally offer you vengeance. Perhaps if I would have honored my promise to you, we would never have come to this."

I realized that the smoke was beginning to fade somewhat, reminding me that we were on borrowed time and that Deganawida would not last much longer.

"Why would I care about any of this?" I rasped, clenching my fists. "My family is long dead, no matter what Dracula did that night. If I decide to kill him, it won't be for you or your stupid journal."

Deganawida lowered his eyes, nodding in understanding. "My journal contains many dangerous spells, but I doubt you would care about those. It also documents my search for your family. Particularly, your son."

I stiffened incredulously. "*WHAT?!*"

"In my search, I found legends and folktales of a mysterious, cunning little boy who allegedly lived in the forests, leaving behind feathers on the animals he killed. Animals drained of blood, often-times. I was never able to prove or disprove the story, but the coincidence was concerning. He could be dead for all I know, but with your immortal bloodline, I find that doubtful. And if the story is true, I imagine that Dracula would be very interested in finding him."

I was unable to move as I considered his story. Was it possible?

"My parents have tickets to the auction," Nosh said. "No matter what you feel, I believe it's in all our best interests to reclaim the damning evidence before Dracula does, if for no other reason than to infuriate him," he said, eyeing me. "We can meet my parents tonight to get the tickets and go to this auction. They have the money to at least get us inside—but I doubt it can stand against Dracula's accounts. Although my parents are wealthy, they are not immortal. In the end, compound interest wins. So, we might need to get our hands dirty..." He smirked at me. "If you're interested in that kind of thing."

I shot him a hungry smirk. "Perhaps."

"I would like a moment with Nosh, Sorin," Deganawida said,

sounding tired and sad. "You aren't the only person I've wronged in this room." He smiled at me, looking regretful. "I would ask that you be a better man than me, but perhaps being the Devil is better than being a man," he murmured tiredly. "I'm truly sorry for betraying your trust, and I'm glad I was able to see you again, old friend."

I climbed to my feet, wincing as my threadbare clothes ripped, falling in tatters of disintegrating fabric. "I do this for our tribe, Deganawida. I do this for the man you once were. The man who taught me that joy was within my grasp. I will do this to right a wrong that I am responsible for. I will not do this for *you*."

Then I dipped my chin and prepared to leave the room, spotting crude stairs and smelling fresh air. Well, fresher air.

"You'll find a change of clothes in the satchel under the blood. I had to guess on the sizes," Nosh said softly. "If they don't fit, we will find you something else at my parents' place."

I didn't acknowledge his comment as I left, hoisting the pack over my shoulder and leaving the empty blood bags behind me.

7

I climbed up the stairs to find a ladder made of metal bolted to the wall, leading upwards. At the top was a wooden trapdoor that opened into a large cavernous tunnel that looked to have been designed for hundreds of people but had been adapted into living quarters of some kind. Several of the metal stands with lights illuminated several racks of shelves laden with all manner of strange ritualistic items, boxes of what looked like food, and clear containers that looked to be made of a stiffer form of the material that held blood but filled with what appeared to be water.

I finished off the remaining packets of blood in the satchel as I studied the make-shift room, noticing a private corner behind the shelves with a cot, a table, and a comfortable looking chair.

Had Deganawida lived here?

Once finished with my blood bags, I emptied the satchel to find the clothing and boots like Nosh had told me. I easily tore off the raggedy clothes I was currently wearing and tugged on a pair of pants from the satchel, but the strange boots and undershirt didn't fit properly. I fingered the blue fabric of the pants, wondering exactly what it was made of. It reminded me of canvas, although it wasn't as rough.

A tag on the interior said *Levi*, and I wondered if that had been the name of the tailor. Regardless, it felt nice to wear clothing that wasn't falling apart.

I stared at everything beyond the transformed living area, wondering where we were. I presumed it to be part of an extravagantly rich castle hall—a large, arched, tunnel-like hallway of some kind. I shook my head in wonder.

Behind me, the platform dropped off in a perfectly straight line with yellow paint marking the ledge. Below the ledge was a graveled, muddy area with two metal bars set into the earth that ran parallel with each other as they stretched off into the depths of the dark tunnel like twin veins of precious metal. Enough polished metal to buy a *country*.

Beyond the depression was another platform like mine, similarly abandoned but not illuminated and changed into living quarters. I turned to my right and saw that the platforms ended as the tunnel narrowed on the strange tracks, but this tunnel was blocked off by a gigantic metal wagon. I could only see the front of it from my position, showing me a glass window that enclosed the front. There were no lights inside, but I could see that the wagon was massive, stretching beyond the curve of the narrowing tunnel.

"Incredible," I whispered to myself, marveling at the underground tunnel and wondering why such a thing had ever been left buried away. I turned back to my platform, shaking my head. Against the far wall, a wide set of stairs led upwards, but there were no lights to tell me where they went.

I studied the entirety of the extravagant hall. *My new home*, I decided, wondering what other marvels this strange palace held for me. Some instinctive part of me knew that we were underground—which was ideal since I wasn't a fan of sunlight.

I heard a sound behind me and turned to find the trap door open, and Nosh struggling awkwardly as he tried to maneuver the orange and white chest ahead of him without falling down the ladder. He noticed me watching and grunted, craning his neck to hold the door open with his head. "Little help, please," he grumbled.

I stared him in the eyes as I slowly lifted the blood bag to my mouth and began loudly slurping up the last drops of blood. "I'm recovering."

He growled unhappily, contorting his body in what looked like a painful position before he finally managed to shove the chest ahead of him, sliding it across the ground.

I lowered the empty blood bag as I studied the trap door, wondering how many people had walked on this platform when the area was in use, none of them aware that my tomb was directly below them. I was surprised that I hadn't been discovered years prior when they had first built this place. Likely, Deganawida had brought me here after the tracks were constructed, hiding me in plain sight.

"There's more blood in the cooler if you've finished the others," he said in a grumpy baritone, kicking the chest with a boot. Seeing him standing upright, I realized that he was larger than I had given him credit for. Judging by the wary look he was giving me, he must have underestimated my size as well. I wasn't as big as most men, but I had often been broader of the shoulder, and a hand-span taller than average.

"Cooler," I repeated, staring down at the orange crate. The chest was made of no material I had ever seen—not wood, metal, or horn— unless mankind had discovered a creature with vibrant orange bones.

Nosh flipped back the hinged lid and reached inside of the chest, never dropping his eyes from mine. Then he tossed me two more of the flexible clear bags—both pregnant with blood. I caught them and stared down at the sorcerous material, inspecting them curiously.

Who would make water-skins specifically designed for blood?

"What hellish material is this?" I finally asked, tilting the bag upside down and watching the crimson liquid inside slosh back and forth.

Nosh coughed strangely. "It's called plastic." I squinted up at him suspiciously, sensing amusement at my expense. Nosh smiled good-naturedly, the motion making the skin at the edge of his eyes crinkle. He was either incredibly naive or overly confident. Time would tell. Despite my instinctive doubt, something about his calm posture screamed that he was dangerous, perhaps even more-so when considering his age. What kind of boy could impress Deganawida enough to earn the title of Shaman unless he had extraordinary power? "I didn't consider that catching you up to speed would be this difficult, but I should have," he admitted, his tone letting me know he wasn't mocking me.

I nodded, waiting. "Enlighten me."

"We've come a long way since you went to sleep," Nosh said, closing the lid of the chest and sitting on top of it. "Those are made of plastic," he said, pointing at the clear bags in my hand. "You'll see it everywhere. It's..." he trailed off, searching for an analogy or explanation that would make sense to me.

I scowled. "I am not uneducated, boy, just unfamiliar. You're saying that this is not magic?"

Nosh shook his head. "It's a man-made substance we use for many things. It can be soft and transparent like that," he said, pointing, "or it can be hardened and sturdy like this," he said, patting the chest on which he sat. I stared from one to the other in disbelief. They were *both* plastic? How was that not magic? They were entirely different—one object was clear and flexible and the other was solid enough to support his bodyweight!

Then I thought about trees, and how they could be used to make paper, or how plants could be used to make clothing.

He waved a hand tiredly, urging me to drink the blood rather than discussing the history of plastic. I used my teeth to tear off the corners of the plastic and guzzled both bags in a marginally more civilized manner this time, careful not to spill any of it. The effects were almost immediate, a pleasant buzzing sensation coursing through my body. I had recovered enough so that I could actually grimace at the stale taste of the blood. It was nothing like drinking from a fresh human, but it was all I had available to me.

My litany of pains and aches had mostly dissipated, but I could tell that the blood I was consuming was going deep into my body, healing and repairing me in ways that I wasn't even aware of. Which meant that none of the blood was necessarily making me stronger or more powerful in a combative sense. I wasn't even sure which of my typical powers I had access to now, if any.

Nosh watched me finish the blood, grunted, and crouched down beside his plastic chest. He rummaged inside for a moment and pulled out three more bags. He wore a frown as he turned back to me. He approached close enough for me to murder him and handed me three bags. "That's the last of my supply. Will that sustain you until we get to my parents' home?"

As much as I instinctively wanted to get a taste of real, fresh-from-the-source, blood, I didn't slaughter him. I might have been the world's first vampire—but I was a gentleman, foremost.

"Am I to understand that you are offering your parents up to me as a meal?" I asked, smirking suggestively.

Nosh didn't laugh, and I saw a flash of deadly heat in those youthful eyes. "Drink these and we can be on our way. You still look a little peaked, obviously suffering from the delusion that you think you are funny."

I grinned. "Don't worry. It's probably just the company."

Nosh smirked at my gibe, flashing brilliantly white teeth. "Right. Well, the auction is in a few hours, so we need to get moving. You will need a suit." He eyed me up and down. "Are you going to get any bigger after that blood or is this your usual size?"

"If only the vampire had a mirror..." I said tiredly.

Nosh blinked at me, and then burst out laughing. "That myth is true? You cannot see your own reflection?"

I shrugged. "There really is no need for me to care about my appearance when my very pheromones attract whoever I want to attract," I said. "And I already know that I am ridiculously handsome."

Nosh coughed, shaking his head in objection. "You look like a vagrant in desperate need of a haircut and a line of coke. At least the blood allowed some of your hair to grow back. I thought I was going to have to buy you a wig or some clippers."

I scowled at him. "Jealousy is an ugly trait, Nosh."

He chuckled as he reached into his pocket and pulled out a black rectangular slate that was the size of his palm. He held it up to me in a threatening manner with an evil grin on his face.

A bright flash momentarily blinded me. I hissed, dancing back and tripping over a crate as I fell to my backside.

8

Nosh burst out laughing, holding the device out for me to see. I snapped out my claws and crouched, squinting against the anticipated attack light. Then I paused to see...a glowing painting on the slate.

It...was *me!*

The breath left my lungs and I snatched it from his hand, staring down at it in awe. The glowing painting was set beneath a sheet of glass on one side of the slate, but the other side looked to be metallic. "What in the world is this?" I whispered, staring at the painting. I truly did look sickly and pale, and my cheeks were gaunt and hollow. My hair was matted and long, but it wasn't tangled up in knots, at least.

Nosh placed his finger and thumb on the glass surface and spread them apart. I almost fell back again to see the painting zoom in like he had whipped out a magnifying glass. I could see individual follicles of hair on my cheeks!

"It's a picture," Nosh explained, grinning at my innocence. "This is a phone. It's made of metal, plastic, and glass. I can use it to call people over long distances. Or find answers to questions. Or directions to go places. Or to order food."

I blinked, dumbfounded. "A demon familiar..." I breathed. I

snatched it back from his hand and held it to my mouth. "Bring me blood, demon. Your master is thirsty." I pulled the phone away and stared at it, wondering where the food would appear.

Nosh was cackling with laughter. "This is going to be fucking amazing," he wheezed. "Truly."

"The familiar is disappointing me," I growled. "Where is my blood, Shaman?"

He sighed. "It's not that simple, and I don't know any places that deliver blood. Toss on a coat, at least. People might get the wrong impression if we walk out of the basement with you half naked." He reached into his pocket and handed me a pair of dark glasses. "Put these sunglasses on so no one thinks you're a junkie."

Realizing that I was about to enter a world completely unlike anything I had been equipped for, I followed his advice, putting on the glasses. I was impressed to find that they darkened the room without impeding my vision. They had been around in my time, to a degree, but glasses had not been even remotely comfortable in my day.

I plucked them off my head, inspecting them as Nosh grabbed a coat from a nearby table. "Plastic," I told him proudly, tapping the sunglasses.

"Yep. You're going to see a lot of it when we get above ground. Pretty much everything is plastic, now that I think about it. Even our cars." He scratched at his jaw as I put the sunglasses back on and then I slipped into the long leather coat he was holding out for me.

I spun in a circle, letting the knee-length coat flare out as I grinned. "This reminds me of my old clothing, in a way."

Nosh let out a sigh. "A stereotypical vampire. Leather coat, no shoes or shirt, and sunglasses."

I held the phone out to him. "Light-paint me, Shaman. I wish to see how dashing I look."

He arched an eyebrow. "A picture?" he asked, looking confused.

I nodded. "Yes."

He sighed, lifted the phone, and then pushed a button on the glass. I hurried over to stare at myself, marveling at the instant results. "I look amazing. I am keeping this demon familiar."

Nosh sighed. "Phone," he said, correcting me as he slipped it into his pocket and out of my reach. "I'll buy you a phone of your own."

I gasped. "There are more of these?"

He nodded, looking amused. "You're going to want to keep the sunglasses on, so no one notices you gawking at everything."

I frowned. "If it is night, why would I need sunglasses?" I asked.

He pointed at the lights on the metal stands. "The entire place is illuminated with lights. There is no such thing as darkness these days. Not unless you go looking for it, and especially not in New York City," he said, tugging the coat's hood over my messy hair.

I felt anxiety creeping into my shoulders, wondering what other marvels I was about to see. As exciting as it was, it was also terrifying. To go from being the most dangerous man in the world to feeling like a naive toddler was...humbling.

Also, the last few years of my awake life had been spent living in the forests away from civilization, so seeing a village was going to be shocking. I would have to find a tavern willing to rent out rooms by the day, so that I could avoid sunlight. Unless Nosh intended to take me back here to the underground castle.

Nosh patted me on the shoulder. "Sorin, I'm not sure Deganawida truly considered the difficulties we are about to face together."

I narrowed my eyes. "What other monsters are there for me to slay?" I growled.

Nosh shook his head. "That's just it. I'm not worried about the monsters. I'm worried about civilization. The little things. Like that phone. Everyone has one. Everything you see is going to look like magic, so I need you to hide your shock and keep a running list of questions that we can discuss later when we are out of public view. If people see how amazed you are by the things that they accept as normal, we're going to draw attention, and that could lead our enemies directly to us. So...try to hide your surprise."

I nodded. "Nothing can shock me, Shaman. I've seen magic so dazzling that it would be enough to make your testicles explode."

He coughed, his eyes widening. "Right. Well, um, don't let your testicles explode, I guess."

"Understood."

"And you're about to see more people than you've probably ever seen in your entire life, all living here in New York City—very close to where you originally lived with Deganawida, in case you were wondering. You cannot eat the people. Everyone has a phone and will get it on video—think of that as a moving picture," he explained, noticing the frown on my face. "Then we will have the police and monsters to deal with. So, play it cool and don't freak out. Maybe listen in on the conversations around you to get a feel for how we talk these days. You speak formally, but not ridiculously so, which is good. I guess I can always say you're a rich trust-fund kid from one of those old pretentious families."

I nodded firmly, trying to hide my anxiety. "That would be the truth, technically." He smiled, nodding. I ticked my fingers off as I repeated his advice. "Lot of people. Lot of lights. No killing. No freaking out. I'm rich and pretentious. I know how to handle that last one," I said dryly. "Also, my general aura and scent will enthrall anyone who gets too nosy. I won't even have to kill them. I can simply make them look the other way—as if they never even saw me."

Nosh blinked at me. "Really?"

I shrugged. "In the past, yes. Although I'm still recovering, so I do not know which powers I still have access to. Everything I'm consuming is going to repairing the last several hundred years of malnutrition rather than fueling any sort of reserves for my abilities."

Nosh nodded thoughtfully. "Then pretend you don't have those powers. This is a stealth operation. Just follow my lead and do as I do. Don't make eye contact with people, don't be friendly, and don't answer any questions if someone starts talking to you."

I slowly peeled off my glasses. "I am not as incompetent as you seem to think, Nosh. I know how to play a part. Do not treat me like an ignorant child."

Nosh shook his head. "I wasn't. That's just how New Yorkers act." Then he was walking away, motioning for me to follow him up the wide stairs I had seen earlier. "You'll see." He pulled out his phone and hit a button. A bright light suddenly shone from the front, illuminating his path like a torch.

I followed him, drinking down another bag of blood as naturally as if I had been doing it my entire unnaturally-long life. "Plastic," I muttered, tossing the strange material on the ground and moving onto the next.

His light didn't illuminate much beyond our path, so I didn't have anything to do but think. A few minutes into our walk, I began to laugh, the sound echoing off the walls.

"What is it?" Nosh asked curiously.

"This is the second time I've set out to explore a brave New World—but this time I didn't have to leave to do it. This one came to me."

Nosh glanced back at me from over his shoulder, smiling. "Just don't let your testicles explode."

I laughed harder, shaking my head. "Sage advice, Shaman. Sage advice."

9

I followed the Shaman from our shadowy palace, my mind racing with questions, demands, and potential plans that would hopefully result in torrents of blood raining down upon me. A cleansing waterfall of absolution.

If I couldn't have my vengeance, I would have my notoriety. I would remind the world just how terrifying a vampire without a heart could be.

"What about the vampires who followed you here? Does that mean the tomb is no longer safe?" I asked, feeling territorial.

Nosh paused, glancing back at me. "That depends. Is the threshold myth true? That vampires can't enter a home unless they are invited in?"

I nodded, suddenly grinning as I understood his line of reasoning. I held out my arms, focusing on the blood coursing through my veins. Then I bit my own wrist and sprinkled my blood around me in a circle. "This entire building is my home," I said authoritatively, drawing on the power of my blood.

I felt a sudden thrum of power and Nosh jolted, his eyes widening. "Jesus!"

I grunted smugly, nodding. "What is my home called?"

"Grand Central Terminal," he said, his face paling.

I nodded. "I approve. I have lived here for centuries, so I barely had to use any power to activate the threshold," I murmured, impressing even myself.

Nosh stared at me for a few moments. "Well, I had a fancy ward ready, but I guess that works, too. Except now the vampires won't be able to use the subway here, which is bound to draw attention."

I shrugged. "I was here first. Not my problem."

He scratched at his head, muttering under his breath. "Nothing we can do about it now. But you could have just protected the downstairs area, not the whole goddamned building."

He continued walking, leaving me no choice but to follow along or get lost.

After a few more minutes of winding hallways and squeaking doors, we entered an illuminated area with lights affixed to the walls, much like the ones below on the metal stands. I glanced back at the door as it closed. *Do not enter*, was written in capital letters, covering the door.

"They abandoned that section a long time ago," Nosh explained, noticing my attention. "Now we're technically in the operational area, but Deganawida told me he'd never seen anyone here before. It's why he chose it for your tomb. Let's be careful just in case."

With that, he pressed onward, clicking off the light on his phone.

"What was so important that it required a private conversation?" I asked, watching his shoulders for a reaction.

Nosh sighed, not turning to look back at me. "He warned me about my parents."

"The gamblers? Why? Do they work for Dracula?" I asked, narrowing my eyes.

Nosh glanced back at me, shaking his head adamantly. "No. He was just warning me that we were about to enter a very deadly game and that it would put my parents in danger. Anyone involved will be in danger."

I allowed myself to relax, nodding along.

"He apologized for not telling me the truth—about who he really was."

"You truly did not know?" I asked, finding it doubtful.

Nosh growled angrily. "Why would I? Deganawida lived hundreds of years ago. It would have been ridiculous to think such a thing. I knew he was an old, powerful Medicine Man, so I reached out to him to teach me how to use my magic—how to honor the old ways."

"What is so different about the new ways?" I asked.

Nosh shrugged. "It's louder and everything is connected. It's hard to find anywhere to sit and think in peace. Everyone is in a rush, overly dramatic, shallow, narcissistic, and ignorant—with no interest for opening their minds to informative debates." He let out a calming breath, realizing he'd raised his voice by the end. "It's not all bad, I guess. In fact, it's pretty incredible—especially when compared to what you lived through. But...I just wanted a quieter, more meaningful life."

"The quest for meaning is a painful, bloody path, boy," I agreed, considering his words. "Things change. I lived through periods of both stagnation and rapid growth. Things I once thought impossible became the new reality dozens of times. Children hide and throw tantrums, but men face change and adapt. Survival of the fittest. Which are you? A child or a man?"

Nosh grunted. "A man, of course. I adapted by leaving my old life behind and pursuing what truly mattered to me. A life of meaning and introspection. In fact, I heard of another man doing that once."

I scowled at his back. That was exactly what I had done when I came across the ocean. When I had joined Deganawida's tribe.

"Would you mind filling me in on the blanks of your story?" Nosh asked curiously. "I've heard it from Dr. Degan—" he cut off abruptly, grunting. "*Deganawida*," he corrected himself, "but upon hearing of his flexibility with the truth, I prefer to hear it from you."

I studied his back, thinking. I was impressed to hear the sincerity in his voice—that he wanted the facts rather than taking Deganawida at his word. And, since I had been thinking about it in the back of my mind anyway, I decided it could only help our partnership. It would also help me pinpoint any discrepancies that Nosh might point out.

Rather than telling him how I had first become a vampire, I started with my journey to the New World with Lucian and Nero. How we had agreed to leave our pasts behind us and begin new lives. Better lives.

How I had first met Deganawida, married his daughter, Bubbling Brook, and ultimately conceived a son—an impossibility for vampires. And, of course, the night of the attack.

Nosh had slowed to walk beside me so he could glance over at me now and then, listening intently. He finally let out a breath once I finished, shaking his head as we reached another door. "That is much more detailed than any version I've heard, but the bones of the story are the same," he said reassuringly.

I nodded stiffly. "That is good to hear—"

A great rumbling sound suddenly shook the walls and I froze, my claws extending as I crouched defensively.

"It's just one of the trains," Nosh explained, smirking at me. "It's how most people travel around town."

I relaxed, glancing up at the ceiling nervously. "It sounded like an army of bears beating at the walls," I said uneasily.

Nosh grunted. "Welcome to civilization." He pointed at the door. "This is it. The great outdoors," he said theatrically. I rolled my eyes, squaring my shoulders as I faced the door.

"I'm ready."

"Vampires could be anywhere," Nosh reminded me. "Those two downstairs tracked us all across town and we didn't even notice. Keep your eyes out and let me know if you see any, but don't let on that you noticed them. I'll guide us somewhere that we can dispatch them without witnesses. Without anyone recording it on their phones," he reminded me.

"Can we just go already?" I snapped. "You said we are on a timetable and that I need a suit. One thing I don't need is a babysitter."

He sighed, nodding. Then he opened the door and held out his hand, gesturing for me to go first. I kept my hands free as I approached the New World for the second time in my life.

I felt the cool rush of fresh, moist, nighttime air on my cheeks as I strode out into a deserted alley. I instantly scrunched my nose and let out a horrendous sneeze. "Gah! That is foul!" I cursed, rubbing at my nose and trying not to inhale too deeply. My eyes were even watering!

Nosh chuckled. "Welcome to New York City, also known as the Big Apple. That's the refreshing aroma of civilization—trash, cars, and too many people living on top of one another. Wonderful, isn't it?" He was grinning at me. "It tastes better than it smells," he teased.

I gagged, realizing that I could actually taste the stench, thanks to the moist, thick air. I blinked the tears out of my eyes and gasped as I really noticed my surroundings for the first time. We stood in a modern forest made of towering structures that were taller than anything I had ever imagined mankind creating without magic. The buildings—dozens of them all around me—reached up to the very clouds, making me suddenly dizzy.

The only structure I had seen that compared to their size was my own castle overseas. The one I had abandoned to Dracula so long ago. Except that had been built with the aid of dark magic and hadn't been limited by the basic laws of reality that the rest of the world had to adhere to.

Standing before Castle Ambrogio, the very air reeked of magic.

I sensed none of that magic here. This had all been built by mankind.

"Centuries," Nosh murmured, holding out his hand to encompass the structures. I heard distant, frequent honking sounds, but Nosh didn't seem concerned by it. Was it some form of modern music spilling out from a tavern? If so, I understood Nosh's preference of escaping it for some peace and quiet. The horns sounded like an audible expression of impotent rage at shattered dreams.

I frowned as I realized that the foul stench seemed to be growing stronger with each breath, and I found myself staring down into the darkness of the alley. I narrowed my eyes as it suddenly hit me. The stench was familiar.

Beneath the putrid smell of decay and rot of damp trash and over-population, I smelled wet fur.

Nosh noticed my attention and immediately cursed. "Werewolves. Degan never mentioned this was their territory. How the hell did they find us so fast?"

I slowly shook my head. "Doesn't matter," I said, staring into the darkness. I couldn't see them, but their scent was undeniable. Even to Nosh, apparently. I cocked my head, focusing my senses through the hubbub of horns. I reached out and immediately felt two thunderous heartbeats. They were hiding behind a large metal wagon that was overflowing with garbage, huddled close together. I pointed. "Two of them. There."

Nosh nodded. "Behind the trash dumpster," he growled, "trying to hide their scent. We should get out of here. They're not attacking, so maybe they are giving us the option to leave."

I smiled, not looking over at him. "It is far too late for that, Shaman. Watch out for the other two coming up behind us," I told him.

"What?" he hissed, spinning. "I don't see anything. Can you sense them?"

I shook my head. "Not yet, but they always move in groups of four or more, and their typical tactic is to flank and catch their prey on two sides. They will be close. I'll scratch my head if I sense them."

Nosh grumbled unhappily. "I'm not scared of a fight, but if we're in their territory," he said, pointing at a blue marking on the wall of my Grand Central Terminal, "then fighting these wolves will only bring the rest of their pack down on us. We have to move at least three blocks to reach neutral territory." He cupped his hands around his mouth, speaking loudly and amicably. "Our mistake! We didn't realize where we were! We'll be leaving now!"

I studied the blue marking curiously. It was a crude crescent moon drawn in blue paint. Definitely a territory marker. I frowned at it thoughtfully. Then I scowled at a sudden realization. "It seems we have a misunderstanding," I murmured under my breath.

Nosh gripped my arm. "No, Sorin. Not a misunder—"

I shook free of his grip with a snarl. Then I cleared my throat and held out my arms, taking two powerful strides towards the werewolves. "Territorial challenge!" I shouted out to them.

Nosh cursed.

A wolf howled in the distance.

Then another.

I smiled and bent down low enough to touch the wet stone. I used a claw to score a line in the ground, straightened, and then clasped my hands behind my back, staring towards the dumpster with an expectant grin.

Two huge men stepped out from the shadows, glaring at me as they advanced in long strides. They were bearded and built like black-smiths, proving they didn't need their werewolf forms to deliver a lethal beating. The moonlight glinted off their eyes, and I welcomed the familiar gleam of the Grim Reaper's scythe.

It reminded you that you were still alive.

I glanced back at Nosh. "This is how a child became a man in my day, Nosh. A man would never let another man claim his territory. Ever. And Grand Central Terminal is mine, remember?"

He muttered something that sounded unhappy, which made me happy. "I hope you enjoyed New York," he muttered. "We can kill a lot of them, but reinforcements are inbound."

I snarled with an expectant grin, rolling my neck to the left and right, and extending my claws with a thought. "Maybe they will be amicable to negotiation. They could even be friendly. Allies."

I actually felt excited at the thought of gaining allies so soon upon waking. If vampires and werewolves were sworn enemies like Deganawida had claimed, then I could explain the situation to them. Werewolves were exceedingly intelligent and well-spoken, only resorting to anger at personal offenses.

Reasonable creatures.

Except I really did need to address the illegality of their territorial claim, which would certainly put a strain on any potential alliance.

Nosh scoffed incredulously. "Werewolves are not friendly. Ever. You fucking lunatic. Whatever you think you know from your past existence you need to forget it. Or talk to me about it ahead of time. If you think werewolves are anything but blood-crazed, psychopathic thugs, you're delusional."

I frowned. "Well. One Shaman and a vampire should have no problem taking down a few werewolves," I said confidently.

"You're fucking insane, Sorin. You're going to get us killed long before we make it to Dracula."

I knew I wasn't back to full strength, but long before I'd become a vampire, I'd learned to hold my own in a street brawl. Of course, that had been against humans—when I was a child.

Not werewolves.

This little scrap would give me the chance to confirm just how powerful I was. And how useful Nosh was. How much I could rely upon him. Testing a man in battle was the most honest way to judge a man's character.

And after my long slumber...

I needed to work out some stiff muscles.

10

The two werewolves stopped on the other side of my line, studying me up and down with strange looks on their faces. I smiled, dipping my chin but not breaking eye contact. "My name is Sorin. It is a pleasure to make your acquaintance, however unfortunate the circumstances."

The taller man glanced at my bare feet and lack of shirt again. "Stevie," he said, drawing out the word as if he suddenly had doubts about our confrontation. He was bald-headed with startlingly blue eyes, and his thick, iron-gray beard stretched down to his chest. His arms were easily as thick as my thighs

The shorter man had wild, greasy brown hair and his beard was patchy and unkempt. He sneered cockily, showing off a crooked row of teeth. "Ralph," he said, puffing out his chest and then pounding his fist against it in an aggressive manner. "And who the hell is that?" he demanded, pointing over my shoulder.

"That would be my associate, Nosh," I said, choosing to focus my attention on Stevie rather than the hot-tempered fool. "He's pleased to make your acquaintance as well."

Ralph glared at me, rising up on his toes. "And is he unable to speak for himself?"

I shook my head, still staring at Stevie. "No. But when he speaks, things die," I said conversationally. Stevie's eyes widened as he grunted in surprise, eyeing Nosh with more concern than a moment ago. I sensed Nosh's pulse double and had to bite back a smile. "Also, he has no qualms with you," I added.

The pair focused on me, and Ralph clenched his fists with a toothy, maniacal grin. "Oh yeah?"

I frowned at him for a moment, wondering if he was drunk. Stevie elbowed him sharply before shooting him a stern glare. He'd obviously caught on that Ralph was quickly becoming a liability.

"And you do have a problem with us, I take it," Stevie said neutrally, looking amused.

I frowned, glancing down at the line I had drawn as if to make sure it was still there. "Of course. That is what the line is for—your safety while I present my legal challenge. I'm sure we can discuss this in a civilized manner. Like gentlemen."

Ralph took an aggressive step forward, but Stevie grabbed his sleeve, stopping him short. The constant eye contact was truly agitating them—especially Ralph—so I kept at it.

"I wasn't aware that this was a courtroom," Stevie mused, caressing his beard pensively. He was obviously in charge, and the more rational of the two. Where Ralph hoped to intimidate me, I was fairly certain Stevie had picked up on the serious danger I represented.

"Wherever two or more men meet may become a field of judgment —a courtroom or a field of death. I suggest we consider this a courtroom."

Stevie grunted. "I like that. But I think I already have a verdict."

I sighed disappointedly. "I'm afraid that is not how it works."

"Just let me kill him," Ralph snarled.

Stevie glanced over at him with a resigned weariness in his eyes. "You do see the line, don't you?"

"I don't give a fuck about his line, boss!"

I saw the exasperated look in Stevie's eyes as he finally had enough. "As you wish, but I'm staying here," he said tiredly. And he was staring into my eyes as he said it. I got the message.

Ralph lunged forward to tackle me. I remained motionless until the moment he crossed my line. Then I took a single step to the side, unclasping my hands from behind my back.

In one swift motion, I severed both of his wrists with a downward strike of my claws. He stumbled forward as his hands flew and blood spurted into the air, gasping as the pain finally registered in his brain. I swung my hand upward like I was intending to uppercut his jaw, but I left my claws outstretched rather than making a fist.

My claws tore through his throat and out the back of his neck, decapitating him instantly. His body struck the ground in an undignified heap, and his head rolled into a puddle, his eyes blinking once.

His hot blood had sprayed over my face and I shuddered, forcing myself not to lick my lips in front of Stevie. I managed to control my lust and remained motionless as I locked eyes with the boss. "I warned him about the line," I said dryly, pointing at the line I had gouged into the ground. "I told you that I wanted to have a civil discussion. And you're welcome."

Nosh's pulse had grown calm, all of a sudden, which was an interesting development. Only the bravest of warriors grew calmer in the heat of actual combat, letting me know that he would be perfectly dependable as a partner. The best kind of ally I could hope for, actually.

In my raised hand—like I had caught a falling apple—I held the dead werewolf's throat and part of his severed spine. It steamed in the cool, evening air. Blood dripped down my claws and wrist as Stevie stared from it to my face. Although he knew he had enabled Ralph's last ignorant act, he still looked surprised that it had happened so incredibly fast and with practically no effort on my part.

In fact, Nosh hadn't even *attempted* to help me. I glanced over to see that he actually looked incredibly bored, with his arms folded across his chest.

I turned back to Stevie, dropping the gore and shaking my wrist clean as best as I could. "Now, can we get back to our polite conversation?"

He blinked at me, and I could see his mind racing—but not with fear. He was calculating odds and probably his inbound wolves we had heard, wondering how best to handle this situation. "This just became complicated," he finally said. "My wolves are going to see Ralph dead and me speaking to the enemy."

I sighed. "I'm sure we can explain it to them. And by *we*, I mean *you*. Since you're the boss and I was merely trying to have a cordial conversation with a future ally."

"That's a strange word for a vampire to use with a werewolf, but I'm listening. Talk fast. The smell of blood travels quickly, vampire," he said, and I could tell he was struggling to hold himself together—to not shift. "You mentioned a territorial dispute."

I nodded and pointed at the Grand Central Terminal behind me. "This is my home. I've lived here ever since it was built, but I don't get out very often."

He glanced at the colossal building, scratching at his beard. "You live here?"

I nodded. "And I would like to keep it that way. I actually prefer having you control the territory around my home. I would even be willing to help you defend it, if necessary. But this building," I said, pointing again, "is mine. Does that sound fair?"

Stevie had a truly bewildered look on his face. "Let me get this straight. You, a vampire, want to live in the middle of werewolf territory, and you're willing to help me defend it?"

I nodded. "Precisely."

"That's insane. Vampires aren't allowed *anywhere* in the United States by order of the werewolf council. The Crescent would kill me."

"It seems the vampires are doing whatever the hell they want, right here in the United States, as a matter of fact," Nosh said calmly. "Despite the noble laws of the Crescent."

Stevie shot him a stern glare.

Before he could respond, I cleared my throat. "I might be a vampire, Stevie, but I can guarantee that I am no friend to other vampires. In fact, I wager that I hate vampires more than all your werewolves combined. All the werewolves in the Crescent, even."

He grunted, staring at me in disbelief. "No way."

I shrugged. "Head through that door and track my scent. You'll find two dead vampires who tried to kill me in my sleep," I said, shrugging. "In fact, I came out here to see if they had any friends lurking about. I didn't know I was in werewolf territory until I met you."

"It's true," Nosh said, shrugging.

Stevie studied the two of us, shaking his head. "This is insane. I can't make that kind of decision without consulting the Crescent. And besides, their laws don't even allow you to live in the country, let alone here."

I considered his words. "What if I spoke directly to the Crescent and told them my story? That I want to side with the werewolves and hunt vampires."

He stared at me with a stunned look on his face. "You would be willing to personally talk to the Crescent?" he asked incredulously. "A pack of werewolves who hate all vampires?"

I shrugged. "If they are willing to hear me out, sure. We share the same enemy, after all."

He scratched at his ear as if he hadn't heard me correctly. As he did so, his eyes settled on Ralph's dead body and he cringed. "Well, that's not going to help matters. Not at all." He let out a long sigh. "Although I consider it a favor, to be honest—"

He cut off abruptly, his gaze jerking over my shoulder as he let out a vicious snarl.

I spun in time to see a large, fully-shifted werewolf skid across the ground before slamming into the wall. Judging by the trail of blood and the lack of movement, the werewolf was already dead.

11

Werewolves came in all shapes and sizes when they shifted, but their overall structure was always the same. They stood upright like a man, but they could drop down to all fours and run as fast as a horse if necessary—which meant that they walked rather strangely when standing vertically, like they were creeping up on you. Their heads were entirely indistinguishable from a real wolf, but the rest of their bodies were primarily human—just much more muscular and hairier than before shifting.

It was a relief to see that some things hadn't changed from my time. Since I hadn't seen Stevie or Ralph shift, I hadn't been sure until now.

Two extremely tall, pale men entered the alley. One of them was dragging a second fully-shifted, brown werewolf by the scruff of his neck. He bent down and calmly snapped its neck. Then the two men began swaggering our way, and I instantly knew they were vampires. I had been so distracted by my talk with Stevie that I hadn't even sensed their approach until their grand entrance. Or my powers hadn't been strong enough to sense them, which was concerning.

"Well, well, well," the skinnier vampire said, looking like he had absolutely no meat on his bones. "What do we have here, Gabriel?" he asked his partner, staring directly at me.

Gabriel had messy blonde hair and looked scrappier. He narrowed his eyes, also staring at me—as if Stevie and Nosh didn't even exist. "Looks like a traitor, Alex, although I don't recognize him. Must be from out of town." He cocked his head. "He smells old," he added in a warning tone.

Alex—apparently—sniffed disdainfully. "I don't care where he's from or how old he is. He should know better than to consort with—"

"I did not give you permission to talk," I interrupted in a cold tone. "Wait your turn." Then I calmly turned back to Stevie, who was panting furiously—torn between his rage at the dead wolves and disbelief that I was picking a fight with the vampires. I nodded reassuringly. "I told you they don't like me. On a positive note, it looks like we might have found Ralph's killers," I suggested with a faint grin. "If you're willing to set up that meeting for me."

He gave me the barest of nods. "Deal."

"Who the *hell* do you think you are?" Alex demanded in a sputtering shout. "Do you have any idea who I am?" he roared.

I calmly glanced over my shoulder and met his eyes. "You're dead, of course."

Before I could follow up on my threat, Nosh clapped his hands together and bellowed out a chilling, animalistic roar—a sound no human should have been able to make. It was as if a great beast had just spoken through him.

And then a damned grizzly bear of opaque, icy fog suddenly appeared in front of him between one moment and the next. Nosh began to chant loudly, clapping his hands and dancing with a savage grin on his face. His eyes seemed to glow with the same light as the bear's form.

I'd never seen Deganawida do anything like this. Not even close.

The vampires forgot all about me as they stared slack-jawed at the spirit bear towering over them—easily twice their height. Then they each pulled out short metal sticks and pointed them at the bear. I frowned, thinking the weapons looked vaguely familiar for some reason.

A sudden cacophony of thunderous booms exploded from the handheld weapons and I snarled, crouching down with a hiss. Guns!

I'd never shot one before but the sound was unmistakable. They'd obviously improved them over the years, because both of them let off half a dozen shots each in the span of a few seconds—no reloading necessary.

Nosh continued singing as he began to run towards the vampires in a zig-zagging motion. The bear lunged forward with a feral roar and tore one of the vampires in half.

He didn't even have time to scream. His partner grunted incredulously, pointing his gun at the apparition, his eyes wide with horror as more explosions rocked from the surprisingly small weapon.

Luckily, it had no effect on Nosh's spirit bear. The beast swallowed the vampire's hand and gun, biting the entire arm off at the shoulder. Then it gored into his stomach, eating him alive.

Nosh waited a few moments before halting his singing. He said a single word, and the bear slowly evaporated, leaving behind the partially-eaten vampire.

I glanced over my shoulder to see Stevie staring with his mouth hanging open.

I cleared my throat. "Want to be friends, Stevie?"

He nodded.

Instantly.

"Excellent."

Nosh walked over, a dark grin on his cheeks. "I would greatly appreciate it if you could wait until tomorrow to mention this to the Crescent. We have an appointment this evening that I'm afraid we cannot miss."

I kept my face blank, realizing what he was getting at. Werewolves might attend the auction.

Stevie nodded woodenly. "Sure. I think I'll go grab a coffee or something while I try to think of a story." He glanced at the two dead werewolves and I saw his eyes darken. He slowly turned to look at me and then Nosh. "Thank you. It doesn't do them any good, but you convinced me."

Nosh dipped his chin. "Vampires suck," he said, smirking at me. Stevie chuckled, shaking his head. "Now we just have to convince the Crescent," he sighed.

I nodded, turning to Stevie. "I expect you to keep knowledge of my hideout to yourself. I would hate to hear that you betrayed my trust. A friend would never do such a thing. We are friends, aren't we, Stevie?"

"Having a rogue spirit bear running around can be dangerous," Nosh added conversationally. "The neighboring vampires might even decide to relocate, not wanting to live in a neighborhood with a spirit bear lurking about. You'd have to expand your territory to protect everyone from the bear. Think you could do that?" Nosh asked, grinning widely.

Stevie chuckled, shaking his head. "I think I'm actually beginning to like you two. And I never met a vampire I didn't hate, so that's saying something."

I nodded. "To new friendships," I said, extending my hand—which was still covered in Ralph's gore.

Nosh clucked his tongue. "Poor taste, Sorin. Poor taste."

Stevie grunted, gripping my hand in his much larger palm. "Ralph was an asshole who caused more problems than anything else. You tried your best to establish a peaceful conversation. The way I see it, he sealed his own fate."

I smiled. "I'm glad you feel that way."

"What's your number, Stevie?" Nosh asked, pulling out his phone. "I'll call you tomorrow so we can set up a meeting with the Crescent—as long as our vampire hunting schedule permits it."

I glanced up at the cloudy sky, listening absently as Stevie told Nosh his contact information.

With all the commotion and gunfire, I was surprised no one had come by to check on us.

"I'll talk to you tomorrow," Stevie said after giving Nosh the information. He waved at us one last time before jogging towards the alley's exit—the same one the vampires had entered from. It began to rain and I sighed irritably.

Nosh walked over, looking pleased. "You're covered in blood. Rain is good. Might clean you up enough to let us catch a cab. Come on," he said, motioning for me to follow him towards the opposite end of the alley from the one Stevie had taken.

"That worked out well," I said.

Nosh grunted. "That just proves how little you know."

12

I walked through the rainy streets of New York City, struggling to process the onslaught to my senses. Nosh had quickly over-whelmed me with explanations for the modern marvels all around me, but I knew it would take time to truly comprehend it all. For now, all I could do was accept his litany of terms, phrases, and inventions that were seemingly taken for granted by the humans all around us.

The smells of roasting meat, fresh bread, trash, flowers, and humanity danced through the air like unseen tendrils vying for my attention. More languages than I'd ever heard buzzed in my ears, and the unbelievable number of people walking up and down the street—all ignoring each other or speaking into their phones—produced a staccato of heartbeats that threatened to make my eyes bulge.

I don't know what I would have done without Nosh's sunglasses because the city seemed to be made of light—coming from lampposts, shop fronts, massive *screens* as large as some of the smaller buildings, and red and green lights hanging from some type of small metal rope, over the streets.

It was so much to take in that I could almost ignore the light rain plastering my hood to my head, soaking me to the bone. I glanced down to avoid stepping into the oily puddles of water with my bare feet, even though I was too wet for it to really matter at this point.

Thousands of people walked past me, all averting their eyes from one another—a city of strangers packed together like rats on a sinking ship. Many had frowned at my ensemble, but most didn't even seem to notice. It took every fiber of my being to keep my hands shoved into my pockets and my fangs to myself. Free food surrounded me, and the way everyone ignored each other...

This city was *begging* for vampires to invade. I doubted anyone would even notice if a tenth of them suddenly went missing, because none of them cared about each other, let alone knew each other.

Nosh had kept up a steady stream of conversation, explaining the magic of his era. He told me about electricity powering the city, illuminating the streets and providing guidance for the hundreds of metal coaches—cars—zipping back and forth down the streets, faster than any horse I'd ever ridden, all powered by a liquid called gasoline.

The cars honked and swerved around each other with abandon, barely dodging pedestrians who were too busy trying to take light-paintings of themselves with their phones.

And the roads and sidewalks were all made of smooth stone rather than cobblestones or packed dirt. We'd walked by a shop selling televisions, and Nosh had pointed at the moving images, explaining how phones could also be used to record video, not just pictures. He'd even recorded me walking down the street to accompany his fumbling explanation.

I could do little more than stare and soak it all in, especially when we came to an area with screens attached to the very buildings, all playing videos of some kind or another. Nosh had spent five minutes trying to reassure me that the explosions and the flying man with a red cape on one screen wasn't real but rather an upcoming movie. Like a book brought to life.

To me, it was magic, and no one else seemed to care, taking it all for granted.

"Watch where you're walking!" a man shouted. I flinched in surprise to realize that he was talking to me—the first person to have done so on our long walk. He and several others dressed in identical dark blue uniforms stood beside a black and white car with flashing red and blue lights attached to the top. They wore silver badges on their chests and each had a compact metal gun affixed to their belt—where a sword would have hung in my day.

The men were staring at my bare feet with suspicious frowns before realizing that I also wore no shirt beneath my coat. I was grateful the rain had washed away all of the blood, because it was obvious that these men were constabulary of some sort.

"Sorry, officers," Nosh chimed in hurriedly. "My friend has had too much to drink and I'm trying to get him back home. Which way is the Aristocrat?" he asked, smiling brightly. "Poor guy doesn't have things like this in Kansas, and he has no head for his liquor."

The lead officer frowned dubiously. "They don't have shoes or shirts in Kansas either? Fucking moron is going to get sick."

"Easy, Tommy," one of the other officers teased, "or I'll start blabbing about how you lost your clothes in Atlantic City."

Tommy grunted, his face flushing red, and I had to keep my mouth closed for fear that seeing the rush of blood would make my fangs snap down, because I was feeling incredibly hungry again.

"I lost more than *that* after I bought Jenny a drink!" another hooted. "Best night of my life!" His fellow officers roared with laughter as he puffed out his chest, grinning.

The other officers began pestering him to tell the story, already turning away from us. Tommy looked relieved as the attention shifted away from him. He pointed back over his shoulder with a grunt. "Two blocks that way. Keep an eye on your pal. Lot of pickpockets in town robbing tourists blind. And get him some goddamned shoes!"

"Of course. Thanks, officer." Nosh quickly ushered me away as if fearing I might ask a question or make a scene. But I had no intention of drawing any attention to myself. "Come on, Sorin," Nosh said under his breath. "We're almost there and we need to hurry if we want to make it to the auction on time. I'll show you more of the city later."

"Lead the way," I said, honestly relieved. Because I was beginning to feel rather overwhelmed by everything. I kept my eyes downcast, focusing on my feet so as not to get distracted by the city around me.

A few minutes later, Nosh guided us towards a large building with a grand staircase and several men in black suits waiting by a huge glass door. *Aristocrat* was etched into the glass, outlined in gold paint.

Apparently, many people lived in the building. His parents lived in one of the penthouse suites at the top. I glanced up and cringed, realizing I couldn't actually see the top of the building. I feigned casual nonchalance, doing my best not to consider how many steps it would take for us to climb that high. An older man in a suit rushed towards us with an umbrella clutched in his fist, and I instantly squared my shoulders, fearing an assault due to the panicked look on his face.

"Mr. Griffin! You're soaked to the bone, sir!" He handed Nosh the umbrella, looking scandalized at how close I stood to his charge. Nosh motioned for me to stay close and I watched the servant's face contort in confusion, realizing that I wasn't a threat but an acquaintance. He suddenly looked alarmed, torn between staring at my bare feet and finding me an umbrella.

Nosh waved a hand, smiling familiarly. "Too little, too late, Redford. I'm just stopping by to introduce my parents to an old friend. They are expecting me."

Redford frowned. "My apologies, Mr. Griffin. They left an hour ago. I believe they were attending a dinner party with some friends."

Nosh hid his concern well, showing only a faint, thoughtful frown, but I picked up on the slight spike in his pulse. "Some friends, you say," he mused thoughtfully for Redford's benefit. "Ah, yes! They invited me, but I completely lost track of time after running into my good friend, Sorin," he said, gesturing in my direction. "We've had an eventful evening, as you can see," he murmured in a low tone, winking conspiratorially.

Redford dipped his chin politely, offering no comment, but I could see the wheels turning behind his eyes. "As you say, sir."

"I'll run upstairs and get him a change of clothes so we can meet them. What was the name of the restaurant again?" Nosh asked, sounding distracted.

This was obviously a common occurrence, or Redford was well-versed in not pressing for details. "They did not say, Mr. Griffin. You could check with the front desk."

Nosh waved a hand. "I'll just call them while my friend gets changed. Could you have a car pulled around?"

"Of course, Mr. Griffin. How soon?"

Nosh glanced at me with a thoughtful look. Then he glanced down at his phone, reading the time—which had been another shock for me to process, that his phone was also a clock. "Twenty minutes should suffice."

Redford nodded. "I'll have everything ready and waiting for you in fifteen minutes. Please take your time. You know how your mother gets if you don't dress appropriately," he suggested in a politely respectful tone.

Nosh sighed, shaking his hand. I saw the exchange of money, but Redford accepted it and pocketed the cash so smoothly that I knew he had been doing this job for decades. "Her definition of *appropriate* is a tuxedo for every occasion," Nosh murmured with a rakish grin. "We'll be down shortly. Come along, Sorin."

I nodded woodenly, flashed Redford a warm smile, and did my best to look inconspicuous as I followed Nosh—Mr. Griffin—into a palatial lobby.

I kept my eyes downcast so as not to gawk at the chandeliers. Gold and crystal adorned everything, and the room was decorated with white leather furniture. My wet feet slapped loudly against the white marble floors, echoing through the vast space. A row of attendants waited behind a chest-high counter, but Nosh went straight for a row of gleaming metal double-doors against the back wall. Another man in a suit stood guard outside the doors and pressed a button on the wall, opening them for Nosh.

"Thank you, Justin," Nosh said absently, stepping inside and motioning for me to join him.

"Good evening, Mr. Griffin. You just missed your parents and their friends," Justin said. "Your mother didn't look pleased. Is that why you're in such a rush?" he said, smiling politely.

Nosh grimaced. "Yes. I imagine she's not very happy with me. Do you recall what their friends looked like?" he asked seeming nonchalant, but I could tell he was concerned.

Justin shrugged. "I've never seen them before, sir. White men with dark hair, and a young, beautiful woman in a red dress. She looked disappointed. Perhaps you were expected sooner? She was beautiful enough that I imagine she was intended for the city's most eligible bachelor," he said, smirking faintly.

Nosh grunted. "I wish my mother would just stop parading them all in front of me. Love is not a buffet line," he muttered as if by rote, seemingly a conversation he'd had a dozen times before.

"Of course, sir," Justin agreed, stepping a few paces away from the door as he smiled at me.

I ignored all the perfectly concealed looks of astonishment at my attire and stepped into what appeared to be a metal room. The walls were mirrors, and the double-doors closed behind us, trapping us inside. I let out a shaky breath. "What is troubling you, *Mr. Griffin*?" I asked anxiously. "I thought we were meeting your parents?"

Nosh frowned uneasily, pressing a card up against the wall near the door. It beeped and flashed green, and then Nosh folded his arms, waiting. "They never mentioned going to a restaurant, and it's highly uncommon for them to not tell Redford where they are going—especially knowing that I was coming over tonight. And I don't recognize the people they were with. Their business dealings are typically with other Native Americans or the Chinese."

I studied him thoughtfully, wondering if they had been taken. The metal room suddenly shifted, feeling like the floor had dropped out from under me. I gasped, clutching at the walls, realizing the entire room was racing upwards at an alarming pace. "This is a lift?" I asked, still gripping the railing nervously.

Nosh turned to look at me, wincing guiltily. "Yes. Sorry. I forgot to explain that in my distraction. Lifts—or elevators, as we call them—were designed so we didn't have to walk up so many stairs. New York was built *up* rather than *out*. It was apparently necessary to see how many rich people they could fit on one island," he said dryly.

I nodded, watching as glowing numbers above the door rapidly counted upwards. "Your parents are...royalty?" I asked, not certain what word to use, and fearing to look at what number the elevator would stop on.

Nosh grunted. "There is no royalty in America. Well, no *official* royalty. But they are exceedingly wealthy and have lived here a long time. They run one of the biggest casinos in New Jersey. Atlantic City, like the policeman mentioned."

"Why do you look concerned about your parents' friends?" I asked carefully.

He pursed his lips. "Because I'm concerned that my parents were taken. Abducted."

I snarled angrily, hating to hear that my assumptions were correct. "The vampires?" I asked.

Nosh shrugged. "Perhaps. Or it could be totally innocent. My parents knew I was coming over. If their plans changed, they would have called me," he said, pulling his phone out of his pocket. He showed it to me, pointing out at a green square on the screen. "This one is for phone calls. It would have a red symbol on it—a notification—if they'd tried calling me." There was no red symbol on it. He pointed at another green square. "This one would have a similar notification on it if they'd tried sending me a message," he explained, tapping the symbol.

The screen changed to reveal a list of names.

He tapped one that said *mom*, and the screen changed again to reveal several short messages back and forth.

"Those are from earlier today," Nosh explained, shutting the phone off and slipping it back into his pocket. "Nothing about going to dinner."

"Perhaps they went to the auction," I said, knowing that my commentary was worthless in a world that I hardly understood.

Nosh met my eyes as the elevator stopped. I glanced up to see *100* above the doors, and I shivered. The doors opened to reveal a lavish foyer with a single round table in the center. A crystal vase full of red roses decorated it. Nosh froze, staring at them with narrowed eyes.

"What is it?" I asked, stepping out of the elevator for fear that it would go back down with me still inside it.

A card was nestled among the flowers, and I watched Nosh storm over, snatching it away to read it with a grim frown. "My mother hates roses," he abruptly snarled, swatting the vase of flowers down to the ground. It shattered, splashing water and glass everywhere. "They were taken," he snarled.

Two slips of paper also rested on the table. Nosh met my eyes, and I could practically taste his rage. "They're taunting me," he said, pointing at them.

I leaned down, reading them. They were invitations to the auction. Two typed names had been crossed off at the top—*Mr. & Mrs. Griffin*—and replaced with two handwritten names, along with a crimson drop and the impression of red lipstick where a woman had kissed the crimson drop so that it hung between the imprint.

His parents' blood. The lipstick was definitely a cruel taunt.

Nosh Griffin. Degan Smith.

I frowned. "They did not invite me." I mused. "That might be good news. They don't know I have awakened."

Nosh was glaring at the invitations. "True. Dr. Smith—or Dr. Degan, as I always called him—was a close friend of my parents." His eyes grew animated, coming up with plans. "We should get ready. I'll turn the shower on and find something for you to wear."

Not knowing what a shower was, but growing increasingly comfortable with just following along when he mentioned strange phrases, I nodded, walking behind him through the penthouse. Scanning the furniture, art, and bric-a-brac decorating the tables and shelves, one thing I knew for certain; Nosh's parents were beyond wealthy. They were richer than any royalty I had ever met. Was that a factor in all of this? If so, how much of one? "I hope your bath tub fills up quickly," I said, feeling the pressing of time on my shoulders.

Nosh just laughed.

13

I stared at my reflection in the floor-to-ceiling window that overlooked New York City from one hundred floors up. I'd grown brave enough to walk up to it and place my hand on the glass as I stared down an impossible distance at all the cars far, far below. I felt like I was flying—like Zeus staring down at mankind from Mount Olympus.

Thinking of the Greek pantheon, my mood rapidly soured and I let out a growl.

The glass of wine shattered in my palm and I cursed, stepping back on reflex. Luckily, I had finished the drink already and the glass hadn't cut my palm. I bent down, sweeping the glass into a neat pile on the marble floor and then carefully brushed off my hands. I walked over to the kitchen and washed my hands in the sink, not wanting to later discover a sliver of glass stuck to my finger the next time I rubbed at my eye. I dried off my hands, grabbed a fresh glass, and filled it with wine, appreciating the vintage. It was comical to think that the vintage was hundreds of years younger than me, considering that wine took time to mature and ripen.

I had made the decision that I was going to install a shower in my home at Grand Central Terminal. Rather than the bathtub I had anticipated, Nosh had ushered me into a glass-walled room with hot water spraying from metal spouts on the walls. Like a private waterfall. I'd even had six different scents to choose from when it came to picking my soap!

I'd showered quickly, not wanting to waste any time with Nosh's parents in danger. The hardest part about hurrying was not letting myself pay too much attention to all of the other amenities in the bathroom. Nosh had shown me a device that blew hot air out of one end, designed specifically to dry long hair. After mastering the device and brushing out my hair, I'd quickly made my way out of the bathroom before I could find something else to fascinate me.

Studying myself in the glass again, I noticed that I still looked worn down, but the blood I'd consumed had filled out my cheeks, the skin below my eyes no longer as sunken and dark. My Greek heritage was now beginning to overpower the sickly gray pallor to my skin, and my blue eyes shone brightly. My hair had filled out, no longer matted and patchy—thankfully. I'd brushed it back into a tail, using one of his mother's hair ties—a band of some strange, stretchable fabric, and I wore a simple but well-fitted, navy suit coat and trousers. I was larger than Nosh, but close enough in size for his clothes to fit me. I was unable to button up the white dress shirt all the way, so I had chosen not to wear a tie. Nosh's father had black dress shoes that matched my outfit and fit me well enough, completing my ensemble.

I sighed, shaking my head as I recalled the closet—how many suits, clothes, and shoes that had been available—enough to fill a tailor's shop.

If this family wasn't royal, I couldn't imagine seeing how actual royalty fared.

Thinking of money, I wondered how Dracula now lived—how much money he'd accumulated in his unnaturally long life—the life I had given him. The money and castle I had given him. Five hundred years of accumulating interest, not even considering new investments he may have made over time.

It would make Nosh's family look like paupers. Money also bought influence. How would I manage to stand up against a man of such means? Not even considering his physical and magical powers—of which I knew I was his better—his money was a very real weapon. Money bought guards, and mountains of money bought mountains of guards, which would make it impossible for me to get near him.

I needed to find a way to make him come to me. To cripple his business interests. Even though I was stronger one-on-one—or at least I had been—how could I get close to him? He would have an army of powerful vampires shielding him. Vampires who had lived hundreds of years—as long as I had lived before I had been put to sleep. Hell, many of them would technically be older than me, if I considered their time spent actually wandering the earth. They would have more experience than me in the real world. It was humbling to consider that a fledgling vampire—turned on the day I had been put to rest—would technically have lived longer than I had.

I shook off the thought, feeling the shoulders of my coat stretch at the motion. The cut of the suit was much different than anything I had been familiar with, but at least it fit well. Tight but not uncomfortable, silhouetting me in a flattering *V* shape from shoulder to waist. I wondered if it was easier to wash blood from clothes these days.

I would certainly be putting that to the test.

I turned back to the penthouse, taking a few steps from the glass wall for peace of mind. I studied the rich furnishings, listening as Nosh finished getting dressed in one of their other bathrooms, because the penthouse had four of them.

Rich vases lined the mantle above a white stone fireplace, and I froze upon seeing the painting hanging above. I stared incredulously at a tribal chief who looked eerily similar to Deganawida in his prime. He looked older than the man I had known—the painting created sometime after I had known him.

I strode closer, barely allowing myself to breathe. Text below the image drew my attention. *Iroquois Confederacy.* Deganawida knelt before a giant tree. He held five arrows clutched in a fist, bundled together with a single cord, and a dozen other American Indians—or Native Americans, as Nosh had called them—were seated around him. I smiled sadly, sensing the significance of the event, even though I didn't know what it entailed. For that many chieftains to gather together without killing one another was...astonishing.

"Some kind of peace agreement," I mused out loud, studying the arrows bound together. One for each nation, perhaps. Which implied that he had accomplished something worthwhile with his extended life. That neglecting to allow me to avenge my family had at least allowed him to broker peace between other tribes.

I'd never personally come across any other tribes in my time with Deganawida, but I'd heard about many—some friendly, most not. At least not to each other. And definitely not to the white settlers from across the sea.

Hanging on the wall on either side of the painting were ornate, matching tomahawks. The haft was carved from a strange black wood, and the blades gleamed of polished steel—too polished, as a matter of fact. Despite their beauty, I knew they were functional rather than decorative, because they looked old, featuring gouges and dents on the haft from where they had deflected enemy weapons in battle. I walked closer, frowning at the blades. The edge of the blades shone brighter than the rest of the steel, and I noticed faint etchings in the metal. A feather decorated the side of each.

Nosh cleared his throat behind me, and I turned to look at him. He stared up at the painting and weapons. "Passed down from generation to generation. My parents said it belonged to Deganawida. Too bad none of us knew Deganawida was eating dinner with us every week or we could have verified it," he said bitterly. "Dr. Degan would often stare up at them for long periods of time, but I always took it as reverence for our ancestors. Apparently, he was reminiscing."

I nodded thoughtfully, glancing at them. "They have magic of some kind."

Nosh turned to study me, looking surprised at my awareness—but not at my claim. "How did you know?"

I shrugged. "I think they were made with silver, but I don't understand how they were ever used as weapons if that were the case. Silver is too soft of a metal for a weapon of war."

Nosh nodded, glancing up at them. "I always wondered about that as well. You're right, though. I thought that maybe the hafts had belonged to some great chieftain and that they had been remade into these ceremonial pieces," he said, waiting for my thoughts.

I shook my head. "They have tasted blood. I can sense it. As if they are sentient in some way." I paused, curling my lips. "Vampire blood."

Nosh blinked, striding closer. "You're sure you aren't sensing blood on the haft?"

I shook my head and pointed at the pommels of the tomahawks. A silver point had been hammered into the base, concealed by a leather cord with two black feathers dangling from the base. "A stake," I explained. "But the blades have tasted blood as well. So long ago that I'm surprised I can even sense it. Almost like it was never cleaned after the battle."

Nosh studied me thoughtfully. "Silver is deadly to werewolves."

I nodded. "And vampires. At least me, anyway," I muttered, thinking back on the Greek gods.

Nosh frowned. "Really?" I nodded tersely. "We will come back and inspect them more thoroughly after the auction. If we take weapons with us, the guards will confiscate them. Best to leave them here."

"This penthouse is not safe," I reminded him. "They took your parents with minimal fuss. What if those weapons are important? What if that is what they wanted from your parents?" I asked, itching to get my hands on them.

Nosh thought about it and finally nodded. He climbed up atop a chair and lifted them from their holders on the wall. Then he turned to assess the room. I was too busy staring at the weapons, though. The moment he'd grabbed them, I'd felt a thrum of power from them, almost like a purr of anticipation. Nosh spun them absently, glancing about for a place to hide them.

"If they come back before us, they might notice the empty spots on the wall," I said, pointing.

Nosh grunted, pointing one of the tomahawks at a bookshelf with a wooden case on display. "Grab that." I walked over and opened it to find two basic tomahawks with stone blades inside—the kind given to children for training. I grabbed them and the box, walking back over to Nosh. I handed him the box since it was large enough to hold the ornate weapons. "Put those inside to hide them." He nodded, tucking the ornate tomahawks within and clasping it shut. I spun the cruder weapons in my wrists like Nosh had done. I hadn't used them often, but

Deganawida had taught me enough to be formidable. They still felt familiar in my palms. I switched places with Nosh atop the chair to hang them on either side of the painting. Finished, I nodded satisfactorily.

"Let's go," Nosh said, clutching the box under one arm. "Redford will watch them for us. No one would think to ask him for them, and I trust him with my life." He noticed my doubtful frown and rolled his eyes. "In the event my trust is misplaced, he can be easily bought. I'll tell him that I will double the price of anyone asking about them, so he doesn't betray us."

I nodded grimly. "And I'll remind him how dangerous greed can be."

Nosh glanced at me with a tight frown. "He is a friend."

I shook my head firmly. "There are no friends when it comes to those who abducted your parents or anyone choosing to profit from deceit. Unless you prefer to reward them for their hard work."

Nosh clenched his jaws and shook his head. "No. I don't think I would prefer that. If we leave now, we will still be early. As long as traffic isn't ridiculous."

I nodded eagerly, wondering if Dracula would attend this auction. Or perhaps some other old friends from back home. I could imagine the surprised looks on their faces when they came face-to-face with a malevolent ghost.

We walked into the elevator and began to descend. I glanced over at Nosh. "We will need gold."

Her frowned over at me. "No one uses gold anymore. I brought our checkbook."

I frowned thoughtfully, wondering if that would be acceptable. "In my day, these sorts of transactions were always done with gold—so as not to have to bother with exchanging different currencies."

Nosh frowned. "I've never gone to a black-market auction, but in typical auctions, a checkbook has always sufficed," he said, not sounding entirely confident. "Is this a rule of vampire auctions, or just an outdated element of your time period?"

I shrugged, letting out a sigh. "In my long, lucrative life, I had never pissed in an ivory toilet until today, Nosh. How the hell would I know what currency is used in an auction, let alone a vampire auction?" I admitted.

Nosh burst out laughing. "We call it ivory, but it's actually just porcelain."

"Well, it was infinitely better than a chamber pot, and my old one was solid gold," I said, folding my arms.

As the elevator descended, I caught Nosh glancing at the invitations in his hand, his mood growing darker by the moment. "We have to get that journal, Sorin," he finally growled.

I frowned over at him. "And your parents, of course," I said carefully, watching his reaction.

He shot me a grim, bitter look, staring into my eyes without blinking. "I know you don't know me very well, Sorin, but I'm an incredibly rational person when I need to be. Rational enough to admit that I believe my parents are already dead." I nodded ever so slowly, waiting for him to continue. "They were taken from their own home, and the abductors didn't bother trying to hide their faces. They left these invitations for me and Deganawida as a challenge. They want the journal and are willing to kill to get it. I believe they are already dead—hence the roses."

I had already considered as much, but I was surprised to hear Nosh so calmly admit it. I definitely hadn't anticipated his cool headedness. I asked him one question in response. "What do you propose we do about that?"

He shot me a cruel, chilling look, tapping the chest with his fingers. "I propose to end each of their lives by burying a hatchet in their foreheads. *After* we get the journal back."

The rest of the elevator ride was silent. Nosh grew colder and calmer as the elevator descended—just like I'd seen him do when I killed Ralph, the werewolf—his instincts taking over.

The elevator opened and I followed Nosh into the lobby, surprised to see no employees walking around. We caught Redford on the street just as he was about to climb into the back of a yellow car with a driver up front.

"Mr. Griffin," he said, straightening. "Your car should be waiting for you near the valet station," he said. "Is everything alright?"

Nosh nodded. "I have a favor to ask you, but I need your utmost discretion, Redford."

He nodded firmly, closing the car door so as not to be overheard. "You have it, Mr. Griffin. No question."

Nosh handed him the chest with the tomahawks, and I paid very close attention to Redford's pulse, searching for any hint of his involvement or knowledge of the abduction—any sign that he might be untrustworthy. But Redford seemed about as honest and loyal of a man as I had ever met. In fact, he was *exactly* the kind of man I would have personally hired to manage my day-to-day affairs.

He accepted the chest with a protective nod, tucking it under his jacket and out of sight. "I will guard it with my life and tell no one. I swear."

Nosh locked eyes with him. "This might be the most important thing I have ever asked you to do, Redford. Don't give that chest to anyone but me." I cleared my throat pointedly and Nosh nodded. "Or Sorin. No one else ever needs to know about it. Ever. Not even my parents."

Redford licked his lips at Nosh's tone. Then he gave us a final nod. "You have my word, Mr. Griffin. You or Sorin only."

Nosh gripped his shoulder and squeezed. "Thank you, Redford. I will see you soon."

Redford climbed into his car, and we made our way over to the valet station in silence.

Despite Nosh's poor attitude, I had an absolutely lovely time during my first experience in a car.

As we made our way to the auction, I pushed every button within my reach, opening and closing the window dozens of times, and I annoyed the driver to no end as I fiddled with the radio stations, gasping every time I turned the dial and heard a new song on the radio. When we finally pulled up to the auction, Nosh had practically leapt out of the car, and the driver had wasted no time abandoning us the moment we climbed out.

As if the Devil himself was on his heels.

I stared up at the large mansion and the guards out front. They looked decidedly menacing, even though they were dressed much like the men working at the Aristocrat.

Nosh was already walking up the steps, leaving me behind. "Here we go," I muttered, hoping his mood improved soon.

But I knew it wouldn't. Because I was pretty sure he was absolutely right about his parents.

Vengeance and tomahawks buried between the eyes had always been a mood enhancer for me, so I vowed to show him how cathartic a little violence and torture could be to a wounded heart.

14

One of the guards held a wand in his hand, waving it up and down my body. Nosh waited beside an open door on the other side of the guards, deeper inside the mansion since he'd gone through first to reassure me that they were merely checking for hidden weapons. The guard nodded, handing me my jacket back. "Enjoy your evening, sir," he said politely.

"Thank you." As I was slipping back into my suit coat, I heard a commotion behind me and turned to see a guest snarling at the guard.

"I don't need weapons, fool. I've always preferred to eat with my hands!" he snapped, openly brandishing his furry claws. The guard grunted—not looking even remotely concerned or impressed—and a trio of beefy looking men with guns on their hips firmly escorted the werewolf from the building.

I arched an eyebrow at the guard, and he shrugged. "Manners matter, sir." He gestured further into the mansion. "If you need refreshment, the bar has a diverse drink menu," he said, smirking suggestively.

I nodded, not knowing what he meant but appreciating his courtesy. "I'll have a look."

He turned to the next guest in line—a woman bedecked in so many furs that I first mistook her for a pregnant werewolf.

I made my way over to Nosh, shaking my head. No one seemed to be hiding their powers.

Nosh nodded, studying me thoughtfully. "A drink to take the edge off? I know I've been poor company."

"As long as the drinks are still warm," I murmured, glancing about the old mansion.

"Freshly squeezed, from what I hear."

He was walking away before I could ask him what he meant.

I followed him into a large living area that had been modified to serve as the auction floor, featuring rows of chairs facing the front of the room. Thankfully, the mansion had a wide, open entryway leading into an adjoining room. I saw a well-stocked bar against the far wall and tall tables evenly spaced throughout, allowing the guests to have some privacy or mingle, depending on their preference.

My shoulders immediately tensed as I observed a pair of vampires. They noticed my attention and smiled at me before continuing their conversation. I nodded back, eager to get away from their immediate view. I let out a small sigh, glad to realize that muting my vampire aura was working appropriately. They hadn't seemed to notice what I was— or maybe they just hadn't cared.

With my blood reserves so depleted, I had been grateful to see that it didn't take much power to mask my aura—but it did take a lot of concentration.

I hadn't been sure what to expect tonight, but I found myself surprised to count more than forty guests, and that *none* of them were bothering to conceal their true natures. They huddled in small groups of two or three, forming pointless alliances for safety. Pointless, because I knew any of them would betray those heartfelt alliances the moment the claws came out. The nefarious twinkles of betrayal in their eyes were identical to those from my time. It was oddly reassuring to see that some things never changed.

Deceit was a dependable, old friend.

Nosh guided me towards the adjoining room and over to the bar. "Relax, Sorin. You look like I feel. We can't both look like assholes hungry for a fight," he said with a whisper of a smile.

I grunted. "It's always served me well in the past. Especially in these circles." But I did let out a sigh, forcing my shoulders to relax. Beside the bar, a dozen naked men and women sat in leather chairs, staring docilely out at nothing. Nosh hesitated and I sighed in understanding. I walked up to the barkeep, scanned the selection, and pointed at a beautiful, red-haired woman with freckles on her delicate shoulders. "Just a glass, thank you."

The bartender nodded, picked up a bulbous wineglass, and walked over to her. He withdrew a scalpel from his apron and sliced her palm in a practiced, precise cut. She didn't even flinch. Judging by her dilated eyes, I doubted that she even felt it. She squeezed her blood into the glass, filling it halfway before the bartender murmured to her and she unclenched her fist. She then wrapped some gauze over her wound without a word. He walked back over to me with a polite smile, his thick, curled mustache bobbing up and down as he extended the glass. "Sir," he said, not meeting my eyes.

I took the glass and inhaled through my nose, appreciating the faint spiciness. Nosh's face was as hard as granite as he asked for a scotch on the rocks. Three fingers.

Once we both had our drinks, we leaned back against the bar, surveying the room and making sure we were private.

"Are you sure you don't want to be a vampire?" I teased gently. "Your scotch is aged twelve years, and I'm betting my wine is aged thirty."

He grunted, shaking his head distastefully.

Since he obviously didn't want to talk, I surveyed the room and brought the glass to my lips. I took my first drink and shuddered as the blood hit my tongue in a wave of creamy spiciness. The blood coursed down my throat like a flame to oil and my fingers tingled faintly, savoring the food. Along with it, I sensed my strength blooming faintly and smiled to myself. Not all of it was going to repairing me, which was a great sign.

Although I wanted to chug it down and then take all twelve of the naked humans into a private room for a full meal, I lowered the glass from my lips. Control was essential. I wasn't out of the woods yet. I realized Nosh was watching me discreetly, making sure I was alright.

I nodded faintly. "I'm fine."

Nosh grunted, discreetly pointing out a pair of women just walking into the main room. They paused beside a pillar, speaking softly to one another. Each wore white scarves with a red, ornate crucifix emblazoned across the front. "I dare you to go shake their hands. Don't underestimate the Sisters of Mercy. Monsters know them as Nuns of the Gun," he murmured, chuckling.

I eyed the women thoughtfully and then shrugged. Before Nosh could comment, I strode up to them and introduced myself. "Good evening. My friend over there was just commenting on how exquisite you two look. I've heard tales about the Sisters of Mercy, but I have never had the pleasure of meeting one before tonight. Thank you for holding the line," I said, smiling. One had fiery red hair and was taller than any woman I had ever seen. Her green eyes were like fire, and she assessed me up and down with a coquettish smirk.

Her associate had dark, inky hair that was tied up into a tight bun on the back of her head. "Is that so?" she said, sounding amused.

I nodded, stepping to the side and holding out my hand to indicate Nosh. His cheeks darkened with embarrassment—no small feat on his complexion, and he waved back lamely. "He's terribly shy, I'm afraid."

They studied him with mixed looks of surprise. "Is he a Shaman?"

I smiled. "I think the proper term is Medicine Man, but yes."

The fiery haired woman studied me curiously. "And you work with him?" she asked doubtfully, unable to place my specific flavor of power —because I was still concealing my aura, preventing anyone from instantly recognizing that I was a vampire. Which was why I'd taken Nosh up on his dare. If I could coerce these Sisters of Mercy into a conversation without them calling me out for being a vampire, then the others in the room should take it as evidence that I was not a vampire and wouldn't bother me.

Or they would become doubly curious about what I might be since I wasn't a vampire.

Then again, it wasn't a crime to be a vampire here, so I'd seen minimal risk in my little game. And the look on Nosh's face made it all worth it. Also, contrary to what Nosh had assumed, I didn't have adverse reactions to any religion, let alone Christianity. My vampire spawn did, but I never had.

I had always assumed that my immunity was a result of me growing up on the streets as an orphan, never learning about gods or religion until I was well into adolescence. And by that age, I'd been too street-wise to believe that any gods were looking out for me. The only time I had considered seeking the help of the gods—years later when I consulted the Oracle of Delphi—they had ultimately cursed me, turning me into a vampire.

So...I'd never been even remotely religious.

My vampire spawn, on the other hand, had been raised fearing and respecting the Christian faith. Some kernel of belief must have resided deep within them that allowed the power of Christ to compel thee.

"Would you mind if I borrowed one of your scarves to show to him?" I asked, smiling politely.

They shared a long look with each other and finally nodded. The red-headed woman untied her scarf and handed it to me with an expectant smile. I accepted the scarf without bursting into flame, and I could practically feel Nosh's eyes bug out of his head in shock. For that matter, the Sisters of Mercy looked equally stunned, their smiles fracturing in an instant.

"How..." they gasped in unison, staring from the scarf to my drink.

Damn. I'd been holding my glass of blood, so they'd instantly known I was a vampire. All that energy spent trying to conceal my aura and I may as well have been carrying around a sign that declared what I was.

15

I smiled reassuringly, hoping to appease their alarm. "The priests skipped my village long before I became what I am."

They stared at me, still looking shaken to the core. "That's... not possible," the dark-haired woman said. "Even Dracula is affected by religious artifacts."

I nodded. "I know. Evolution, perhaps," I said in a soft, calming tone. I stared at the drink in my hand, gathering my thoughts and debating how much I wanted to reveal since I was in a building full of both his likely allies and foes. And almost everyone had enhanced senses of hearing. "Dracula has brought more harm to this world than I ever thought possible," I said, speaking in a low tone. "I despise the man more than anyone in this room."

They stared from me to each other, licking their lips. The red-haired woman regained her composure first. "You have given us much to think about."

I smiled, dipping my chin. "Would it be too much trouble to ask if you could further embarrass my friend? I find great pleasure in his torment," I said, grinning mischievously.

She smiled, her eyes twinkling. "I've never met a Shaman before."

I extended my wrist, palm down, dangling the scarf from my fingertips. She hesitated only a moment before resting her callused hand atop my forearm and walking with me towards Nosh, who looked to be on the verge of choking on his own tongue. "Might I ask your name?" I asked gently. "Mine is Sorin, but that is a dangerous name to know in this den of vipers," I warned.

She nodded, storing the information away for later analysis. "My name is Isabella."

"Charmed." We strode up to Nosh and I smiled. "Sister Isabella, this is my good friend, Nosh Griffin."

Nosh bowed politely, attempting to hide his anxiety. "It is a pleasure," he said, his gaze discreetly flicking to the scarf in my fingers. I gently withdrew my forearm and handed her back her scarf. "Thank you for entertaining me. I believe I will walk the room to get a better sense of what we might be up against." I frowned at my choice of words. "I mean, to mingle with our host and his or her guests."

Isabella nodded with a light smile, her eyes latching onto Nosh like a bird of prey. She leaned closer to me and spoke under her breath. "Be careful, Sorin. I've seen representatives from every supernatural faction here. Witches, wizards, shifters, and vampires. Even the Nuns with Guns are in attendance," she said with a wry grin, referring to herself.

I nodded warily. "Den of vipers indeed. Be careful with Nosh. He's a gentle soul."

Nosh narrowed his eyes at me, grumbling under his breath, but Isabella's dazzling smile soon made him forget all about me. More people had entered the building, but there were no more than fifty attendees altogether. I scanned the room, debating whether I should go strike up a conversation with any of the nefarious guests. I finished my drink and set the glass on the tray of a passing waiter.

I strolled up to the bar, seeing a half-dozen people ordering drinks, and I decided it was the most natural way to meet strangers at an event such as this. Rather than ordering another fresh blood and inadvertently announcing my vampire nature, I ordered a red wine that I'd overheard another guest praising.

I swirled the wine in my glass and then took a deep sniff, smiling contentedly.

"You're a tall glass of water," a woman said from behind me.

I smiled reflexively and turned to stare into the pale blue eyes of a woman so stunning that she momentarily left me speechless. I hadn't seen her wandering the room, and she definitely hadn't been at the bar moments ago. It took me a second to clear my head and formulate a response, which only seemed to increase her amusement as I watched her grin stretch wider. "I'm not sure I've ever heard that phrase," I finally admitted with a warm smile.

Her long brown hair was pulled back into a complicated weaving of individual braids—some thick and some thin—held in place by two silver sticks that formed an X on the back of her head. Her skin was pale and fair, and I noticed a faint, thin scar across her right cheek, making me instantly envision a hairline crack on an elegant marble statue I had once seen. Rather than diminish its beauty, the fracture had only served to highlight it.

She was tall and lithe, but she had wide shoulders, indicating attention to physical fitness that was typically only found in warriors. She faced me openly with her shoulders squared, staring at my face without shame or fear, her pale blue eyes seeming to glow, and I felt a sharp resonance between us. It wasn't magical in the literal sense but in the most *meaningful* sense—two individuals sensing an undefined kinship in each other.

Like two pieces of stone fitting together so precisely that there was no space between.

"My name is Victoria," she said, flashing her teeth in a wide grin.

I started, realizing I'd been staring at her without speaking. "Thank you," I breathed.

She cocked her head curiously. "For what?"

"For showing me what it meant to feel truly speechless," I admitted.

Her cheeks bloomed with faint spots of color and her eyes widened in surprise. "Oh. It's the dress, isn't it," she said, glancing down. "I never wear them."

I blinked. "To be entirely honest, I didn't know you were wearing one until just now," I chuckled. She smiled even wider, revealing dimples big enough to stick my finger in.

"Oh. Thank you, I think," she said, sounding slightly flustered.

I remembered that I hadn't introduced myself. "My name is Sorin,"

I said, confident that no one would know it. "I'm not usually this distracted," I admitted, lowering my eyes. "I hope I didn't offend."

She lifted my chin with two warm fingers, making my stomach drop. "You didn't offend me, Sorin. I don't think I've been complimented quite like that before. It was...nice," she said, blinking long eyelashes. "Sorin is an interesting name. Greek?"

I shrugged. "Bit of Greek, bit of Italian. Who knows how much of each. I'm a mongrel, in all honesty."

She laughed lightly, sipping a white wine she held in one hand. "Aren't we all. You could do a blood test if you were really curious, but then you would have to find a company that would hide your...unique anomalies. And then hope they didn't sell your information to some marketing firm."

She'd said *unique anomalies*, making me wonder if she'd sensed my aura and had already surmised that I was a vampire. I tried sensing hers, but I picked up no obvious signs of what she was, other than human. But what human would be brave enough to come into this place, knowing we were monsters?

Having no idea what she was talking about regarding a blood test, but fully understanding her references to privacy, I nodded. "Too many answers can get a humble man into trouble."

"Nothing wrong with a little trouble now and then, is there?" she asked playfully.

I was hyper aware of the blood that suddenly pumped to her lips as she said it, and I sensed that her pulse had ticked up ever so slightly when she met my eyes. I was very careful in my response. "Well, there is trouble, and there is trouble," I said, enunciating the difference. "And I often get them confused, so I try to avoid them altogether."

She nodded, eyeing me sidelong. "I know you're trying to hide what you are, but I can't fathom why. Everyone is a monster, or monster hunter, here," she said, shooting the women from the church a significant look. Isabella and her friend were both talking to Nosh now, having moved to a table as the bar's business increased.

I smiled. "I'm not familiar with the players in this game, and I've learned to hold my cards close to the chest when playing at a new table."

"And you still didn't answer," she added.

"That is because we're playing cards at the same table," I said, smiling. I was actually enjoying this conversation. "If you want to show your cards first, I can show you mine."

She shrugged, eyeing me thoughtfully. "You truly don't recognize me?" she finally asked.

I noticed that Nosh was staring at me with a bewildered expression from over her shoulder. He discreetly shook his head—a clear warning. I wasn't entirely sure what he was trying to warn me about though. I noticed all this with a mere flick of my eyes, using my peripheral vision so as not to alert her. "I'm a new settler to New York, if I'm being honest," I said carefully. I scanned the room with a faint frown. "I wasn't sure I liked it until a few moments ago," I said, settling on her.

"So clever," she smiled, sipping at her drink. "Vampires vying for power, you mean? It happens everywhere. It's like no one here has even heard of Dracula's true tyranny."

I locked onto her more directly—enough so that she hesitated from taking another sip. "If I'm being entirely honest, I detest Dracula and pretty much everything I hear about him. Admittedly, I have precious few facts."

She nodded. "I'm glad to hear you dislike him as well, but I wouldn't make that too public if I were you. Especially not if he waltzes through that door," she said, licking her lips at the prospect.

I glanced over my shoulder, licking my lips for entirely different reasons. "Is he to attend?" I asked, doing my best to conceal my interest and rage.

She made a frustrated sound and I turned back. "I doubt it. He hardly ever leaves his precious castle. I've never seen him anyway. He hides where no one can reach him, sending his minions out like a plague to infect and invade in the subtlest of ways. It's the only reason he has lived this long."

I shook my head, sneering. "Coward."

She smiled delightedly. "Agreed. I think I like you, Sorin. I'll admit, I had you pegged as a vampire—"

Nosh sidled up to the bar, coincidentally bumping into me. "We should probably find our seats," he said. Then he glanced at Victoria with an embarrassed look. "My apologies, my lady. Is this rogue bothering you? He uses fancy suits like that to ensnare a woman's sensibilities."

Victoria was staring directly into my eyes, unblinking. "I hadn't noticed the suit," she murmured. And then she flashed me a discreet wink.

I grinned, catching her reference to my earlier statement about not noticing her dress.

Victoria turned her attention to Nosh. "Rogue, is he? Well, I've always been attracted to the bad boys. And it really is a nice suit," she said, finally eyeing me up and down.

I smiled in spite of Nosh's obvious concern. Attracted...was she? I knew how women could use flirtatious guises in order to trip men up, but something about her felt pure and honest. I knew she was dangerous, but she was also reckless—in what seemed a calculated way. She'd spoken against Dracula, even after assuming I was a vampire and would therefore be under his control.

Little did she know that I was actually the man who had created the monster, and that I was beholden to no one. Was her disgust against vampires in general or Dracula specifically? I would have to ask Nosh once we found some privacy.

16

Victoria leaned past Nosh, sliding a card my way. It was a simple white card with a vertical wooden stake and a horizontal sword, forming a crucifix. "Victoria Helsing," I read out loud, not recalling the name from any of my conversations with Nosh.

She watched me with an expectant smile on her face, but it soon transformed into a look of curious intrigue, as if I had passed some test. "I wrote my cell phone number on the back. I would love to speak with you again. Perhaps over dinner."

I smiled, nodding along as I silently wondered what had caused her reaction. "I do not have a card or a phone," I said.

Nosh rolled his eyes. "Stolen at the airport, so he says. I'm sure it's just a ploy to attract the interest of women who should know better," he said with a teasing smile aimed at Victoria. "My name is Nosh Griffin."

"Oh, I know exactly who you are," she said, smirking. "How is business?"

He smiled politely. "Like selling water in the desert, but I try to distance myself from my parents' empire. It is an honor to meet such a renowned vampire hunter, Miss Helsing. It also concerns me to see you here," he said. I did my best to conceal my surprise. Vampire hunter? "I hope you don't paint me with the same brush as some of the guests. I'm here in a personal capacity—to right a wrong."

"Me too," she admitted with a tired sigh. "You have no idea how many times I've considered changing my last name."

Before I could ask a question that I was obviously supposed to already know the answer to, Nosh smiled. "You are preaching to the choir, Victoria. A Native American is the heir to a casino. We are all unfairly painted with the brush of our ancestors—and only the most notorious of them."

Victoria thought about that and finally nodded. "Fair point."

The lights dimmed twice in rapid succession, and the hum of conversation quieted as a gentleman in a tuxedo stepped up to the pedestal in the main room. At some point during my conversation with Victoria, they had brought out the items going up for auction. "Good evening, ladies and gentlemen," the man said in a nasally, high-pitched whine. "Thank you for attending this private auction. Know that ten-percent of tonight's proceeds will be donated to the Blood Center of the Empire State."

"Of course it will," Victoria murmured under her breath. "Like a sales tax."

Nosh grunted, nodding absently. "They don't even try to hide it, do they?" He leaned back, whispering something that only I could hear. "Vampires own the blood bank where I got your snacks."

I narrowed my eyes and nodded. Victoria hadn't overheard him, thankfully.

"If you could please find your seats, we will begin in two minutes," the man at the podium said, clapping his hands twice. The lights flickered two more times and people began to make their way over.

Victoria climbed to her feet and turned to face me. "Don't forget to give me a call, mystery man. I haven't dined with a rogue in quite some time," she said suggestively.

I bowed, clutching her card to my chest. "I will hold this close to my heart," I told her solemnly.

She grinned brightly. "And he manages to bring it back full circle while still being charming," she said. Then she gave me an awkward curtsy, trying to mimic the sincerity of my bow. I was beginning to realize that bowing and curtsying was no longer a common act—but the women I had met sure seemed to appreciate it, regardless. Why abandon such a simple act of courtesy if it was so well-received?

Yet another failing of modern times to add to Nosh's list.

Victoria turned to walk away and I sensed the stiff tension in Nosh's shoulders as he gestured for me to follow him. I studied Victoria in her blue dress for longer than was entirely appropriate, but I couldn't make myself look away. It wasn't hunger and it wasn't lust.

It was...

I wasn't entirely sure what it was, to be honest. But thoughts of my past lovers were vying for power in my mind, demanding my attention. Because it was undeniable that a part of me obviously fancied Victoria Helsing, even though I was currently on a quest to avenge my wife, Bubble.

Thinking of Bubble and the slumber I'd been put into by Deganawida, I remembered the strange sensation from when I had awoken below Grand Central Terminal. That having relived that night so many times had somehow served to numb me to it—like an adult reminiscing on an old childhood memory. It would always be there and bring a smile to your face or a tear to your eye, but you knew the world was full of bigger and better things that better aligned with the current version of yourself. Not that one was better than the other, overall, but that they now occupied different rooms in your heart.

Reliving that night over and over, hundreds of thousands of times—at least—had subconsciously turned my love for Bubble into an old forgotten memory. Even if she had survived the attack, she was long dead now. Time mattered, and I was beginning to consciously realize—long before I'd met Victoria this evening—that some part of me had died alongside Bubble that fateful night long ago, dousing a spark that hadn't truly had the time to grow into a proper fire. My relationship with Bubble had been budding and full of potential, except conceiving a son—and having him develop and then grow so rapidly—had forced us to advance our relationship faster than was natural.

Like cutting buds off a flower before they had the chance to bloom.

And I would never see her again.

All I could do was avenge her. But my motivations for doing so were more out of honor than from a freshly stabbed heart. The emotions now fueling my vengeance were tied to Dracula—for his crime in destroying my family when I had given him everything he'd ever wanted.

His ingratitude.

My brief interaction with Victoria had been entirely different from what I experienced with Bubble.

Rather than a spark for a potential fire...

It had felt more like an instant conflagration. More so than I'd even felt for Selene back in Delphi, and *that* brief romance had literally ruined my life. Eternally. The Greek gods did not appreciate poaching from their figurative herd, and they had no empathy for the hearts of men.

My shoulders itched instinctively, wondering which god was about to come down and punish me for my heart's desires this time.

Despite what romantic sensations I was feeling now, I realized that I had every right to open my heart again. That it was already open, as a matter of fact. And that unnecessary guilt was...unnecessary.

As long as I was willing to suffer some *other* god's wrath, of course, since they seemed to take particular delight in watching me squirm for the sake of love. That seemed to be my real curse—to live eternally with half a heart.

I watched Victoria take her seat and realized I was smiling absently. On a strictly platonic level, something about her seemed to calm me. Perhaps it was her utter lack of fear for vampires. Perhaps it was her dominance—becoming a vampire hunter. Victoria was brave, bold, and cunning. When she'd said she hated Dracula, it had come from the same place where my own hatred for Dracula resided. Genuine, soul-deep dedication.

Dracula had wronged Victoria Helsing. I decided that I would find out how, and that I would help her shoulder that hatred. If she let me.

Nosh sat down in a chair far from the other guests. As I joined him, I noticed others were also choosing seats far away from their fellows, only congregating in the same small groups in which they had spent the evening thus far. Nosh eyed the Sisters of Mercy—particularly Isabella, who was smiling at his blatant attention—like a wolf on the prowl. Victoria sat by herself near the front, not far from the Sisters of Mercy, sitting up straight and discreetly watching the other guests like a falcon.

I had been so focused on the guests, that I hadn't taken the time to inspect the items available for auction. There were only a handful of items, but they looked exquisite and old. I saw a painting, a small pottery collection, a few rusted weapons, golden jewelry, and a single leather-bound book. I discreetly studied it from my seat, wanting to shake my head in disbelief. From here, I noticed a familiar marking on the spine that I had seen on Deganawida's journal so long ago.

Nosh was staring at the book, confirming my suspicion. I scanned the room and noticed that many people were studying the journal, more with curiosity than interest. Or so it seemed. "Do we have enough money to compete?" I asked Nosh in a muted whisper.

He pursed his lips. "I don't think anyone does, to be honest, but I was never planning on buying it. I wanted to see the other players." He leaned closer, pretending to brush something off my shoulder as he whispered, "We are going to steal it. I refuse to pay for something that was stolen from our tribe." Then he straightened, flicking away the imagined debris from my shoulder with a satisfied grunt.

I swept our surroundings to make sure no one had overheard since several people were still walking past us as they chose their seats. "Generally, theft works best when no one sees your face," I murmured in a stern reprimand.

Nosh shook his head. "I needed to know who we were up against, and to take note of who bids on it."

"Why? We're stealing it, remember?"

"To learn whether or not we have any potential allies," he murmured, smiling discreetly.

I agreed with his sentiment, but I also knew how bloody this auction was about to become.

17

Bidding began on the paintings, first. The Sisters of Mercy seemed particularly interested in them, but when I heard the bidding amount repeated by the nasally voice at the podium, my mind momentarily fragmented, shattering into pieces like a broken vase. "The hell?" I spluttered to Nosh, careful to keep my voice down.

Nosh frowned at me, and then finally seemed to understand. "Inflation. Things cost more these days."

I grunted. Isabella purchased one of the paintings for two hundred thousand dollars. Her associate bought the other one for half-again as much money and I shook my head incredulously. Now I knew why Nosh wanted to steal the journal. And then I thought about how much gold it would have been and I was abruptly convinced that Nosh's checkbook was more efficient.

I leaned back in my seat, doing my best not to look like a fish out of water. Nosh didn't look concerned, but he hadn't intended on paying for anything. I began to wonder just how wealthy his parents were for him to seem so indifferent. Either that or he was too busy ogling Isabella to listen to the ridiculous sums being shouted back and forth across the room.

I also wondered just how wealthy Dracula might be after a few hundred years of compounding interest. Exactly how much had he increased my coffers?

I sensed Nosh stiffening and glanced up to see the journal carefully set on display for all to see. "This is the journal of Deganawida, the man who founded the Iroquois Confederacy that first united five Native American nations together. The journal was recently discovered—or at least unveiled—by Dr. Degan Smith, a Medicine Man and retired professor of Native American studies at NYU. With Dr. Smith being named after the vital historical figure—and obviously an astute scholar of Native American history—his claim on the journal's authenticity carries significant weight. This finding is currently unknown to the public." He paused, not bothering to clarify that it had been stolen since everyone could read between the lines. "The bidding will open up at one hundred thousand dollars."

I didn't spot any familiar faces from my day and age, but I hadn't really expected to. The friendly pair of vampires I had seen upon entering the auction were back at the bar, not participating in the bidding at all. I did take note of a trio of vampires—I could sense their auras—discussing the journal in a silent but intense exchange. They looked to be in their mid-thirties, which meant absolutely nothing in the grand scheme of things. I sensed Victoria eyeing them with an open scowl, but the group pointedly ignored her as one of them raised a paddle, interrupting the other bidders who had been raising each other in ten thousand increments. "Five hundred," he said in a voice like warm honey.

I grunted. The agitated sounds from the rest of the bidders mirrored my sentiments.

The Sisters of Mercy perked up, likely wondering why this old journal was so expensive. So, they hadn't arrived to bid on it. The two began conversing softly, lowering their heads together as they likely debated whether to jump in and attempt to bid on the item the vampires so desperately wanted.

Nosh raised his paddle, catching me off-guard. "Six," he said, his face utterly relaxed.

The auctioneer nodded. "Six! Do I have a six fifty?"

I maintained my composure as all the heads suddenly swiveled our way. The vampires simultaneously locked onto us, scowling furiously. Their faces grew grim and suspicious, which meant they had no idea who we were. I smiled, waving back at them.

"Six fifty!" the auctioneer shouted, pointing at me. Nosh shot me a dark look and I very carefully lowered my hand.

Victoria had been watching the exchange, her eyebrows furrowing. "Seven fifty," she said, lifting her paddle and glancing at me curiously.

"One million!" Isabella said, drawing every eye to the Sisters of Mercy.

I felt like I was sweating all of a sudden. Good lord. What did they think was inside the book? Only the vampires knew the truth. I wasn't even entirely sure what was inside. I glanced back at the bar to check on the two friendly vampires, wondering if they had been involved in abducting Nosh's parents, but they seemed to be having more fun drinking blood than anything else.

I turned back to the other group of vampires, wondering if they had been involved in the abduction. They huddled together, gesturing angrily at each other.

"One million!" the auctioneer repeated. "Would anyone like to bid higher than one million? Going once, for one million dollars." The crowd began to murmur excitedly, but no one lifted a paddle. "Going twice!" the auctioneer crowed.

The same vampire finally lifted his paddle. "Six million."

The crowd went silent for about two seconds, and then the hum of discussion doubled. No one lifted a paddle, and Victoria and the Sisters of Mercy looked utterly pale as they stared at the vampires.

"Seven," Nosh said calmly, not batting an eyelash.

The crowd exploded into chatter, loud enough that the auctioneer was forced to bang a gavel on the podium to calm everyone back down.

I realized I was gripping my seat, just as stunned as everyone else. I now knew how wealthy Nosh was. Or at least how wealthy his parents were.

A woman calmly walked into the room as the gavel struck the podium, as if it had summoned her. She was swirling a wine glass, but it was definitely blood rather than wine.

She wore a red dress that showed entirely too much pale cleavage to be decent, and the fabric hugged her body like a second skin. It was slit at the hip so that each step showed off an alarming swathe of pale thigh. Her hair was as dark as night and her skin was as white as milk.

The three vampires bowed to her in an obedient manner and then backed away a step without raising their eyes. She ignored them, turning to glance over at Nosh with an amused smile. "Do your parents know you are here, Mr. Griffin? I would imagine they would be quite alarmed at your flagrant disregard for their hard-earned money."

Nosh stared back at her. "I am a signer on the accounts and have attended numerous auctions in their stead." He glanced at the podium with a grimace. "Even auctions of allegedly ill repute."

She laughed lightly, and I felt the hackles on my neck rising. This was the woman behind the abduction. A beautiful woman in a red dress.

"I just finished dinner with them, and they made no mention of you attending the auction this evening. It is concerning, to be honest. I would hate for irreparable harm to come between a boy and his parents."

"With all due *disrespect*," Nosh drawled, enunciating the last word, "I don't believe any of these distinguished guests should have to suffer through hearing family advice from you and your harem of impotent boys. Unless they're actually your back-up dancers—in which case I'd have to ask for a demonstration." He leaned forward, focusing on the vampire he'd been bidding against. "Dance for me, boy."

The vampire's fangs snapped out and he clenched his fists furiously.

Nosh sighed sadly, shaking his head as he addressed the rest of the guests in a solemn tone. "Premature e-fangulation is real, folks."

Victoria burst out laughing, and I was suddenly certain that we were no longer leaving the auction without a fight.

The vampire woman's features tightened in barely restrained rage. Instead of replying, she turned to the auctioneer, narrowing her eyes. "What trifling sum are we up to?" The auctioneer opened his mouth, but she waved a hand impatiently, cutting him off. "Never mind. Whatever it is, I'll double it."

The Sisters of Mercy gaped, lowering their paddles. No one had even noticed them raising it, but it was apparent that they'd reached their limit.

Victoria glared openly at the woman, reaching back to adjust her chopsticks even though they were not out of place.

The woman in red ignored everyone but Nosh, turning to face him. "We can play this game all night, but you know you cannot beat me. And I would like to remind everyone that the rules of the house state that other bidders cannot bid more than they are actually willing to spend. Otherwise we are devaluing our funds and enacting a charade of Monopoly money. Which would bring dishonor and harm upon our families." She took a healthy sip of her blood and then smiled deeply. "I always prefer to bring my own hooch to events like this. You never know what bottom-shelf libations the bar is serving." She licked her lips, the implication plain to Nosh.

She was heavily hinting that she was drinking his parents' blood.

Nosh's lips thinned and he nodded stiffly. "So be it. I'm man enough to admit when I'm defeated."

"Good boy," she purred. "What was the amount?" she asked absently, turning to the auctioneer. "I'll set up the wire transfer so we can end this farce."

"Fourteen million," he said, dabbing at his brow with a handkerchief. "Going once..."

No one spoke.

"Twice..." he said, looking as if he was praying that no one would challenge the woman.

They didn't. Nosh shifted in his seat, staring at the journal longingly.

"Sold for fourteen million!" the auctioneer crowed, hammering his gavel onto the podium to announce that the bidding was finally concluded. He let out a deep breath as four beefy men armed with long, metal weapons of some kind approached the journal with a small wooden chest. The auctioneer picked it up with his white-gloved hands and carefully set it within.

The guards left the stage, heading down a hallway I hadn't noticed —one that was closed-off from the guests.

The woman laughed lightly, shooting us one last look. "It was a pleasure, I'm sure. Oh, and my condolences on your loss, Mr. Griffin," she said with a fraudulent frown. "I hope they find the savage who so brutally murdered your parents. It's always those closest to us who stab us in the back," she said, her eyes flicking my way.

I frowned, suddenly alarmed. Condolences...

Had she already killed his parents? And why had she looked at me?

She had already turned on a heel and was leaving the way she had come in, her trio of vampires staring at us with smug smirks. They even licked their lips as if they were going to openly attack us before obediently turning to follow their mistress. Nosh stiffly climbed to his feet, his hands shaking. I gripped his shoulder to steady him as I turned him in the direction of the exit. His shoulders were quivering ever so faintly, and I feared that whatever he was about to do should not be done in front of the other guests.

"Let's go, Nosh," I hissed into his ear, guiding him towards the exit. He was staring down at his phone, typing furiously.

18

As we reached the bar area, Nosh began speaking into his phone in low, furious tones. I kept my eyes on the crowd, assuming he was trying to find some truth to the woman's claim. If I'd had my way, I would have simply chased her down and ripped off an appendage or two until she remembered that what she truly desired to do was give me the answers I sought.

Except I was certain that the rules of the auction prohibited such acts between guests—like a truce. Attacking her in front of everyone could very well start a war with every faction in town.

But if she had killed Nosh's parents...

I would find her the moment her foot stepped off the property and introduce her to the worst night of her life. I kept my eyes on the guests, taking note of who was watching us. Many of them were anxiously staring at their phones with sickened looks on their faces. Strangely, several of them glanced our way, their faces pale and furious as they studied me.

The Sisters of Mercy looked grim and confused, ducking their heads close together in a private, fervent conversation. Victoria's face looked so cold and emotionless that I almost took a step back. What in the world was going on here? Other members of the auction were bidding on one of the jewelry collections. Some distant part of me wondered what kind of price it would fetch, trying to get a grasp on how much inflation had changed in my slumber.

It was a strange feeling to stand in a room full of monsters and monster hunters and not know what to do or how best to respond to the woman's parting comments. To not be immediately recognized and feared by every person in attendance.

No one would have ever spoken to me like that in my day. Ever. Even before I had become a vampire, I had lived on the streets, having to fight every single day to stay alive. To stay on top. To use fear as a preventative measure. To destroy my enemies so utterly and horrifically that future threats were few and far between.

Reputation had been one of my greatest weapons.

Yet...I no longer had a reputation. No one even knew my name. I was starting over from the beginning in a world that had new rules.

Recalling Nosh's flippant wit, I felt a small flush of pride. Maybe I was overthinking it. Maybe the rules hadn't changed. Maybe the scenery had just changed.

I studied the guests with a thoughtful look. Many of them seemed to have forgotten the taste of true fear. Like monarchs with more advanced weapons than their enemies, they had grown complacent, forgetting what it was like to get their hands dirty. They were no longer hungry.

In that regard, I had an advantage.

Because the Devil was *always* hungry. Maybe that was what Nosh truly needed from me—a force of nature from the old days. One of the monsters of legend who hadn't bothered reading the present-day rule books. A monster who lived by his own rules.

These people had forgotten what it felt like to starve. They had forgotten how to be savage. They hadn't forgotten cruelty or violence, but their passions were hollow and lazy.

They didn't have the drive, the feral hunger I had used to dominate my world so long ago.

My instincts were a strength, a unique perspective. My endless appetite would be a virtue.

I felt my shoulders suddenly grow lighter as I made my decision. In that moment, I decided to proceed as I would have long ago, and to let Nosh nudge me in the right direction if he thought I was wandering off course in a manner that would cause us more problems.

Because I was beginning to realize just how much this strange new world had inhibited me. The advancements, the technology, the politics. I'd been so concerned with stepping out of bounds that I'd been tying my own hands behind my back.

The best military generals in history were not necessarily the best swordsmen or archers or cavalry or infantry. They were the best *coordinators*. Oftentimes, the general knew next to nothing about the particulars of a master archer or how to specifically turn a horse into a flanking maneuver. But he knew what each unit was fully capable of and how best to apply their skills.

When to apply their skills.

He didn't need to know how to hold a bow when it was cold and raining, how to shoe a horse, or how to use a sword against a man with a shield.

He needed to know how to use other men who already had those strengths.

So, Nosh would be my commander of the modern age while I would be the general of this war against Dracula. Otherwise, I was just a vampire on retainer. What he truly needed was the Devil.

Nosh slowly turned to stare at me, his face ashen and murderous. He gestured for me to join him, and that it was time for us to leave. Immediately. As I approached, I ignored the looks from Victoria and the Sisters of Mercy, but they weren't the only eyes seeming to focus on me. Had my identity finally been unmasked? I doubted it, since Nosh was the only one who truly knew.

According to him, no one knew there had even been a vampire before Dracula, so it was highly unlikely that anyone would let slip the true story. It would only reduce Dracula's credibility.

Once the auction had commenced, they had closed the doors leading back to the entrance. Nosh opened them, storming forward rather than waiting for me. I slipped through, hot on his heels, only to bump into him after two steps.

The double doors closed behind us with barely a click. The woman in the red dress and her cohorts were fanned out before us, blocking the entrance. The security guards from earlier watched us with menacing looks. No. Not us.

Me.

The woman studied me up and down, smirking as she drank her glass of blood. "And who do we have here?" she asked, studying me curiously. "You seem familiar to me. Have we met?"

I shook my head calmly, wondering what game she was playing. "Much to my disappointment, we have not."

"Disappointment?" she asked, sounding flattered.

I nodded. "If we had, I would have already had the pleasure of watching your slick body writhe beneath mine, squirming and crying out to god...as I allowed you to bleed out." I paused, licking my lips. "On the other hand, I now have something to look forward to, so there is a silver lining to my disappointment."

She stiffened, her smug smile evaporating in an instant. "Like you did to his parents?" she finally asked, glancing back over her shoulder at the guards. "It seems he has condemned himself with his own words. The article on the *New York Times* website was tragically correct."

The guards nodded grimly.

I turned to Nosh, frowning. "What is she talking about?" Out of all the animosity currently aimed my way, Nosh was the only one who wasn't looking at me like I was a wild beast. He had reserved all his ire for the woman before us.

He answered me in a crisp, clipped tone, never breaking eye contact with the woman. "It seems my parents were found murdered in their penthouse, and that a journalist somehow acquired a security feed image of the murderer entering the lobby of the Aristocrat just prior to the crime." He glanced at me briefly. "You are now the prime suspect." His rasping tone was the only sign that emotions were raging through him, because his face was as expressive as a stone.

The woman nodded with faux sadness. "So much blood," she said primly, lifting her nose. "It was truly...inspiring." For the span of a single moment, her eyes twinkled delightedly.

I stared at Nosh, ignoring her. "I haven't left your side. I haven't even *met* your parents."

Nosh nodded stiffly. "I know. But to everyone else in the city, the evidence makes it look like you just murdered a very high-profile couple. Biggest story of the decade."

"What evidence?" I demanded. "Walking into the lobby? That really narrows down the suspects," I sneered.

The woman smiled. "As long as the police don't find evidence of you inside the apartment, I'm sure you'll be fine. Maybe everyone will forget."

I felt my hands balling into fists, remembering that I had showered there. I'd left clothes behind—the same clothes I had been wearing when I'd first walked into the hotel—the very clothes from the security feed—whatever that was. But she'd said *image*, so I was assuming some kind of light-painting, although I hadn't posed for anyone to take my likeness.

"We left the apartment together and your parents were not there. Security can verify that, right?" I asked Nosh.

He shrugged, staring at the woman unblinkingly. "I didn't see any employees when we got off the elevator," he said woodenly. I stared at him for a moment. He...was right.

"It was a set up," I whispered, suddenly thinking about Redford. Had he deceived us?

"It doesn't matter," Nosh said. "She would have doctored up some other evidence if necessary. All that matters is the appearance."

She laughed excitedly. "Alas, their dinner reservation was canceled and they returned to their rooms just prior to this man's arrival. Strangely, security footage doesn't show you two together. Just him entering the elevator a few minutes after your parents."

Nosh nodded. "As soon as I saw that they'd been taken, I knew I would never see them again. I know how your kind operates. But slowly ripping the fangs from your mouth will be almost as good as a final goodbye," he said, his voice rough and dry. His hands were beginning to throb with white light. The guards and other vampires definitely noticed that, even though the woman seemed entirely unconcerned.

The woman smirked at his obvious magic. "A Shaman," she purred. "That should make this slightly more entertaining. It's a pity that this man murdered you after killing your parents. I can almost see the headlines now."

I narrowed my eyes. "You own the papers," I snarled. "You're rigging the story."

She shrugged. "It is one of the best ways to control what the sheeple think. My Master taught me well. No direct weapon is needed to conquer a country. Own the media, own the police, and own the judges. I could murder you in the middle of the street and skip away without concern. I would have a few loose ends to tie up, but nothing that couldn't be handled within an hour. I am Mina Harker, after all."

Knowing she had an exceedingly high opinion of herself, I kept my face blank. "Who?"

She clenched her jaw, and her glass of wine shook in her hand. "Mina. Harker."

Nosh had tensed very minutely upon hearing her name, but his pulse hadn't changed in the slightest. Also, Mina had been glaring at me so hadn't noticed his recognition. Picking up on my tactic, he turned to glance at me. "Never heard of her. Just another whore in Dracula's stable, I guess. They all ride the same." Then he very calmly turned back to Mina. "They all die the same."

I blatantly eyed her up and down as if I was eyeing a horse for purchase, enjoying the fury in her eyes. "Putting an expensive saddle on a mule doesn't make it a horse." I told Nosh, pointing at Mina's dress. "But for a penny a ride, I'm willing to see if I'm wrong."

Her face turned as red as her dress—which was quite difficult for a vampire. Her fellow vampires looked torn between disbelief and fear of her reaction, but she was too furious to take notice of them.

"Insolent fools!" she snarled. Then she took a calming breath, unclenching her fist as she shot Nosh a venomous sneer. "It's unfortunate that you will not survive the next few minutes. I would have loved to see your face when you learned that your parents changed their will to require that only a blood relative could inherit their company."

Nosh grew unnaturally still, and Mina sniffed triumphantly.

"I don't know what that has to do with anything, but I'm still waiting for my ride," I said, sensing that Nosh's pulse had somehow slowed even further as he sunk into an even deeper, colder calm. That was either very good or very bad.

Mina turned to me with a frown. "He was adopted, you fool. Not only has he lost his parents, he's lost his parents' company."

I studied her, frowning at a new thought. "You already have the journal. Why all this effort to destroy Nosh? Or me, for that matter."

She waved a hand dismissively. "We didn't want the Griffins to use their wealth to draw attention to the doctor's claims about a stolen journal. We intended to frame Dr. Smith for their murder to discredit him. You were just a happy coincidence. A scapegoat. You looked so sinister walking into the Aristocrat that I couldn't help myself."

That made sense. And it also told me that they had no idea Dr. Smith was dead, or that he was really Deganawida. I wasn't sure how important it was, but she also hadn't mentioned the tomahawks we had hidden. Which meant Redford might not be involved.

19

Mina cocked her head as she studied me. "What are you trying to hide from me?" she asked, frowning. Too late, I realized I hadn't been focusing as much on my concealment spell, and that Mina had noticed a slight change in my aura. I felt a brief surge in her power and then she suddenly froze, blinking at me in surprise. "Wait. You're a *vampire*?" she blurted, somehow managing to pierce the veil I had been holding around myself—which meant she was more powerful than I had given her credit for. "How do you not serve Dracula—"

In a single heartbeat, I moved.

I used all my dwindling power—which was alarmingly depleted after concealing my aura all night—and time seemed to slow. I saw tomahawks of light slowly crackling to life in Nosh's fists, but I was too focused on Mina Harker. I closed the distance between us and gripped her by the throat, sinking my claws into the soft skin beneath her jaw. Almost immediately, her skin hardened beneath my grip, preventing me from sinking my claws any deeper. It felt like I held plaster rather than flesh—still breakable, but not without effort. Which meant she was surprisingly strong. Time sped back up and I was suddenly in a battle of wills.

I managed to maintain my grip and fight her off, but that only seemed to alarm her more. That I had somehow slipped close enough to grab her by the throat, and that her hardening skin hadn't intimidated me or made me back off.

"Perhaps I wasn't clear," I snarled, extending my fangs. "You were never going to leave this building alive. You should have been long gone if you had any hope of living to see tomorrow, Mina Harker."

Her eyes bulged as she stared at me. I felt waves of power battering against my own will, and she slammed her glass of wine down onto my face, slicing into my cheek. I gritted my teeth as I stared deep into her eyes, drawing every pathetic drop of power at my disposal to withstand her physical and mental power. She was easily as strong as any vampire I had ever met. Stronger than Dracula had been when I handed him the keys to my kingdom. She had to be hundreds of years old.

I somehow managed to fight off her attempts to physically outmuscle me, and she gagged and choked as I lifted her a foot off the ground. Remembering the others in the room, I flung out my free hand, sending the guards slamming into the wall. Their heads struck the wall with sickening thuds before they crumpled to the ground, dazed but not dead.

Stars exploded across my vision, warning me that I was running dangerously close to my limits. I held on tight, knowing she was strong enough to kill everyone in the building if I let her go.

Her cadre of vampires stared at me, fearing to do anything that might hasten Mina's fate. Nosh lunged forward with a leonine roar, his blazing tomahawks a blur that left trails of light in their wake. Then they both sunk into the chest of the lead vampire and he simply exploded into crimson dust, his body instantly vaporized by whatever Nosh's blades were made of.

The other vampires lunged for him simultaneously, intending to grapple him, or at least take away his tomahawks of light. Nosh ducked, slicing off an offending wrist as he crouched. He let the momentum of his strike carry the tomahawk down and behind him, and I gasped as the tomahawk shifted into a long-handled axe as it continued its rotation high over his head.

He brought it down like he was chopping wood, and the axe of pure light split the vampire in half, starting at the point right between the eyes and tearing through past the crotch before it slammed into the marble floor with an explosive crack. It had torn through the vampire with the sound of paper being ripped.

There wasn't even a drop of blood or gore—the body immediately blackened and smoldered as the two halves began to topple. By the time they hit the floor, they were twin puffs of fine crimson dust.

"Timber," Nosh snarled, jerking the axe from the marble floor with one hand. His eyes glowed with a bluish-white fire that matched his axe, and I watched as it abruptly shifted back into a tomahawk to match the one still gripped in his other hand. He deftly spun them across his palms, grinning wolfishly at Mina.

The forgotten third vampire kicked him in the back, sending him crashing forward onto his chest. He rolled clear just as the vampire shambled after him, flinging a tomahawk behind his back without looking. The hatchet struck the vampire in the chest, pinning him to the wall. He hissed wordlessly, struggling to remove the hatchet before he disintegrated.

Nosh's second tomahawk struck him in the throat, decapitating him. Crimson dust collapsed to the ground and the tomahawks crackled and throbbed, still buried in the wall. They seemed to drink up the vampire's remains, devouring his energy.

Mina made a strangled sound as I locked eyes with her. I stared into her eyes and attempted to enthrall her, but she was too powerful for me in my current state. I was able to keep her neutralized, but not for much longer. Her eyes had widened at my attempt to enthrall her, alarmed that I had even tried. Only the oldest, most powerful of vampires would have dared to try such a thing against her.

Because when an underling attempted to enthrall a superior, he would typically drop to the ground in blinding pain, screaming as his own blood boiled in his veins.

And that hadn't happened to me when I tried to enthrall Mina, which instantly told her that I was either her equal or higher up in the food chain, which was understandably terrifying.

She also knew that I did not answer to Dracula, which should have been impossible. Despite her standing and age, she hadn't heard of Sorin Ambrogio either.

"Nosh?" I called out, gritting my teeth. I didn't want to admit my weakness to Mina, but I could see the sudden realization in her eyes. We were at a stalemate. I knew I was on the verge of collapsing. My only chance was to kill her. I knew I could manage that, but it wouldn't provide us any answers.

Nosh got the hint and stumbled over, cradling his arm as if injured. "Where is the journal, Mina?" he growled.

She shook her head stubbornly. "The Necromancer will destroy you for this," she hissed.

"The journal," Nosh repeated, holding his empty hand up by her head. The crackling tomahawk zipped through the air to strike his fist, slicing off her ear in the process.

She shrieked in pain. "I don't have it! I sent it off to the Necromancer!" she snarled, still struggling to match her will against mine, and I barely managed to beat her aura back.

"I'm losing my grip," I growled at Nosh. "We need to end this." I picked up sounds from beyond the closed doors. "Someone is coming."

Nosh held the tomahawk up to her face, slowly dragging the blade down her cheek. He smiled as her skin blackened and burned from the magical blade. "I really wish we could draw this out, Mina Harker. I loved reading your story in Bram Stoker's novel, but I don't have time for a book club discussion. Where is the Necromancer?"

She hissed and panted as the blade continued to slice from her cheek to her jaw. The smoldering wound continued to radiate outwards like an infection. "The Museum of Natural History!" she rasped, unable to take the pain any longer.

Nosh grunted. "No further questions," he muttered, turning back to the door.

Using the last of my strength, I shook her. "Where is Dracula?" I snarled.

She shook her head stubbornly, and I sensed her gathering her strength for one last attempt to overpower me. I knew I wouldn't be able to withstand it—especially not with someone approaching the doors, who might rise up to her defense.

"Keep that door closed, Nosh!" I rasped, licking my lips. "I need a drink before we leave."

Nosh lifted his hands and I saw chains made of the same light as his tomahawks suddenly whipped towards the door, wrapping around the handle three times. "Won't hold them for long."

Mina's eyes had widened with horror at my mention of drinking her. Quick as a snake, I lunged forward and bit into her neck. My teeth shattered through her hardened skin with a sound like breaking glass. I drank deeply, hugging her close to me. Her claws scratched desperately at my shoulders, but they rapidly weakened as I guzzled her blood.

It wasn't common to drink another vampire, but I felt as though I was about to fall over from exhaustion if I didn't get at least some type of blood into my system. If she had recently fed, it would give me enough energy to escape the auction without Nosh having to carry me.

Mina Harker was *old*. Surprisingly so.

Old enough for her many years of life to balance out the bitter taste of drinking my own kind. In fact, her blood gave me a slightly heady feeling, like I was floating. Not wanting to drink too much of her—which could be dangerous—I dropped her body to the ground, panting desperately. I steadied myself, waiting for the possible side effect of drinking a fellow vampire.

A moment later, the room abruptly tilted, and I fell to my knees as one of her memories hammered into my mind with flashes of light.

Her approaching a familiar, foreboding castle beneath the glow of a full moon. A lone candle flickered in the window of my old master suite at Castle Ambrogio as Dracula watched her approach. Her carriage jostled as it slipped into a puddle. A horse screamed as the wheel cracked, tilting the carriage over as it crashed to the ground. Rain poured into the carriage as Mina struggled to climb out. I heard a deep, evil, sadistic laugh echo out from that window.

A laugh I knew all too well.

Dracula.

I grabbed my head, trying to shake off the dizzying effect as I heard the doors rattling violently. Someone was trying to break them down.

Nosh had bent down and was reaching into Mina's mouth, tugging forcefully with a tool of some kind. He grunted as he pulled out an extremely long fang. He made short work of the other before shoving the prizes into his pocket.

"Get up, Sorin!" he growled, jostling my shoulder. I nodded woodenly as I obeyed. He stood and rushed over to the coat rack behind the groaning guards. He finally grabbed my long black coat from earlier before running back and shoving me towards the exit.

Fists began pounding on the door to the auction. "Open this door right now!" a familiar voice shouted. "I smell blood!"

Victoria.

Nosh flung a hand behind us and a brilliant flash of light erupted between us as the door to the auction blew open. I squinted against the flare in time to see Victoria Helsing and the two Sisters of Mercy recoiling in surprise, blinded by Nosh's light.

I backpedaled after Nosh—who was already outside—as I struggled to master my dizziness. The three women spotted me, but they didn't pursue.

I could tell from the looks on their faces that they had definitely heard about me killing Nosh's parents. And now they watched me flee the auction, leaving behind a dead woman in a red dress. They had no love for Mina Harker, a vampire, but that didn't mean they approved of the mess I was leaving behind. The friendly vampire from the auction had just killed a very old vampire. Did that make me a worse vampire or a potential ally?

Nosh yanked me into the night and kicked the front door closed behind me. He flung a blast of power at the door and I watched another rope of glowing chains whip around the handles, except much thicker than he'd used on the first door.

He flung my coat over my shoulders, yanked down the hood, and tugged me after him as he began to run from the mansion. "Now that you're a wanted murderer, we can't risk anyone seeing you out and about. The murder is already trending on Twitter, and I have no doubt your face will be plastered all over the news."

Having no idea what the hell Twitter was, I understood the rest of his statement. The picture of me in the hotel would be up where everyone could see—maybe on their phones?

We fled the auction, using the cover of darkness to hide from any cars or pedestrians. I tugged the hood down further as a car drove by, and I fought to keep my balance. Mina's blood flowed through my body, nourishing me but also disorienting me. Vampire blood could do that —much like alcohol made other people drunk.

Even though no one knew my name, I was now the city's most wanted criminal.

A new legend had been born.

The original legend of the world's first vampire was forgotten in the pages of an unwritten history.

20

I t took us over an hour to get back to my new subterranean
hideout beneath Grand Central Terminal. We'd jogged for a
while, avoiding the rare pedestrian or vehicle, not wanting to risk
my face being spotted. We also couldn't risk calling our earlier ride
from the Aristocrat, because we weren't sure who had been in on Mina's
scheme—whether knowingly or not. For all we knew, she had left
vampire underlings at the Aristocrat to make sure the employees kept
their story straight, threatening the lives of their families if they
aided us.

Nosh had tried calling Redford, but he hadn't answered.

For the same reason of wanting to keep me out of sight, Nosh also
hadn't wanted to risk calling one of the carriages for hire—yellow cars
driving up and down the street to pick up passengers who preferred to
avoid the misty, chilly streets in the middle of the night.

We also knew we would soon cross into werewolf territory—and
vampire territory, for that matter—so we couldn't continue on foot.
Ultimately, Nosh had consented to taking me to a magical place called
the subway. Coincidentally, it led straight to my hideout.

I marveled at the mass of humanity crowding to get into the subway
station, but kept my head downcast beneath my hood as Nosh bought

us tickets and ushered me through the crowds and down a few flights of stairs until we reached a platform that was eerily similar to the one outside my tomb. After following several brightly lit signs, he finally found the one that would take us to Grand Central Terminal, and we settled into a metal tube that had the aromatic stench of piss firmly soaked into the very walls—enough to make my eyes water. Not needing to breathe, I simply stopped, remembering to keep my head down.

Nosh did the same, but the grim look on his face told me he wasn't happy about our particular ride. "I haven't ridden the train in years. Now I remember why."

I stared out the window as we rocketed down the rails. It was stiff and jerky, rattling my teeth until I got used to the locomotion. We were underground, but dazzling murals painted the cavernous tunnel—some were words, others were full canvases, but all in bizarre, artistic portrayals—the likes I had never seen before. It was both primitive and astonishing.

"We should probably talk about—"

"Not here," Nosh growled, cutting me off. "Keep your head down until we get...home," he finally said, grimacing at the word.

"Castle. I prefer to call it my underground castle."

Nosh glanced at me sidelong. "It's not a castle, and it's not really yours."

"I've been there longer than anyone else. I lived there before any of this was ever dreamt of," I said, gesturing at our surroundings.

Nosh grunted, smiling faintly. "Fair point. But you need to stop talking about it. You already told the werewolf. The fact that it's secret is the only thing keeping us out of jail right now."

"Keeping *me* out of jail, you mean," I growled.

Nosh leaned closer, barely whispering. "If they saw you on camera, they had to have seen me. If I was Mina, I would have a contingency plan that also makes me an accomplice to their murder. For example, the moment I point a finger at her or her cronies, the missing video of you and me suddenly appears in the news. Then it becomes a new headline. *Heir to the Griffin fortune murders parents with mentally unstable accomplice.*"

I narrowed my eyes at his description of me, but his point was valid. "I had already considered that but had hoped that your generation had moved beyond such levels of depravity."

Nosh grunted. "I'm pretty sure we dug down a few new levels since you last walked the earth. What you consider depravity is probably considered virtuous by our standards."

I sighed. "Our only source of information is now...unable to tell us what she had planned. Who this Necromancer is, and why they're doing what they're doing. How did they have all of this set up if they didn't know about me? And if they didn't know about me, why target you?" I asked, choosing my words carefully. "I don't believe that it was just to protect the journal."

Nosh thought about it, his eyes growing distant. I watched him for any signs of emotion, but he was eerily cold. I began to wonder what kind of man I was working with. His parents had just been murdered, and he had barely reacted. Sure, he'd been angry, but no angrier than if they had been innocent strangers.

His parents were now dead, and he had yet to have a breakdown. He was either incredibly familiar with loss—as if he'd been a soldier in his past—or something very strange was going on. The longer he bit down his emotions, the worse the outburst would be. I knew that for a fact, having spent centuries as a murderer.

It was strangely ironic that after all the thousands of men I had killed, I was being held accountable for one I did not commit, against two victims I had never met.

Either someone had known I was back—which made no sense, since Mina had seemed aloof to my identity; she hadn't even realized I was a vampire—or Nosh had been specifically targeted for reasons yet unknown. With Nosh's cool sense of detachment, I was leaning towards that possibility more and more.

And to hear he had been adopted really stirred up my suspicions. He hadn't looked surprised to hear it, but he had looked surprised that Mina had known it, which meant it hadn't been public knowledge.

HE PLACED his elbows on his knees, leaning forward so our conversation couldn't be overheard. "It wasn't a secret that I worked with Degan Smith, but it also wasn't anything newsworthy. Up until the journal came into play, anyway. I hadn't even known his real name until a few hours ago, so I'm just as surprised as you."

"It doesn't seem like anyone knew who he truly was," I said, choosing my words very carefully. "I would have expected the woman in the red dress to admit such knowledge had she known of it. If for no other reason than to brag about it before we showed her our hand."

Nosh nodded. "I was present during the interview with the journalist. His questions were so derisive that Degan lost his temper and said more than he should have. I honestly think it was just bad luck that all of this happened. The journalist did his job, pushed some buttons, and a story popped out where no one had expected anything of importance. With Mina hinting that they own the news media, I wouldn't be surprised if the journalist reached out to tell his boss about his unlikely discovery, not knowing he worked for vampires. Or he *did* know who he worked for and got a nice payment for it," he muttered angrily. "Either way, here we are."

I nudged him gently with my elbow. "I'm sorry about your parents."

Nosh grunted. "Thanks."

The train came to a stop and the doors whisked open with a grinding sound. Several people got off, but just as many got on before the doors closed again and the train resumed its travels.

A trio of men with matching red hats and colorful clothing were dancing to a small metal device that was playing some kind of loud poetry with a steady thumping noise. They wore a ridiculous amount of jewelry around their necks but seemed to have no fear of thieves. The rest of the subway was a mix of all manner of people. Some in suits. Others in coats and scuffed shoes. All of them minded their own business, and a few of them were even reading newspapers or magazines. Most were staring down at their phones with worried looks on their faces.

I wondered how many were looking at pictures of me as I checked my hood and lowered my face from view.

21

I leaned closer to Nosh, speaking softly. "Why did you take her fangs?"

"They are powerful ingredients to a Shaman," he muttered dryly. That was well beyond my purview, since I had been the only vampire Deganawida had ever known back in my time. Nosh patted his pocket proudly. "Stubborn little shits, too. Like they were fighting me."

I nodded. "They *were* fighting you. It's not easy to acquire such things. They root down to the jawbone, unlike typical teeth."

He arched an eyebrow at me. "Well, that makes a lot more sense. I felt like I was breaking them off."

I shuddered, imagining such a sensation.

"What's our next play?" I asked, thinking of Stevie, the werewolf. "We are obviously going to need some allies. What we did back there will have consequences. The women from the auction saw me at the end. All three of them," I said, hoping he got my point. "The nuns and the hunter."

He sighed, scratching at his jaw. "The question is whether or not that makes us enemies or allies in their eyes. They had no love for the woman in the red dress, but that probably only makes us the lesser of two evils, not allies. And I doubt anyone wants what looks like a vampire civil war in their city—when they don't want any vampires here at all."

I nodded along, thinking. "They would be smart to wait it out, let us fight each other, and then attack the victor while he's weakened."

Nosh glanced at me with a surprised look. He slowly nodded. "That was a very quick deduction."

I shrugged. "It's what I would do. Which means we need to keep our guard up. We need to find a way to strike hard and fast before Mina's boss gets any more momentum. Have you ever heard of this Necromancer?"

Nosh thought about it for a moment and finally shook his head. "Never. No one talks about him. I've never heard anyone say his name, and I've never heard the term Necromancer to describe him. Whoever he is, he doesn't flaunt his position. He's incredibly secretive and stays under the radar. All vampires do, as a matter of fact. They didn't enter the city in a wave of murders. They were just suddenly here, owning dozens of lucrative companies, law and accounting firms, and other businesses. It was more like a hostile corporate takeover than anything. My parents were intrigued by the sudden flood of money and business ownership from overseas investors. That's how it was sold to the papers, anyway. Which makes more sense now that I know they own the news media."

I nodded. It was an old tactic of mine. Acquire the keys of industry in a city and pretty soon your enemy was working for you. It made the later war easier to manage. Of course, I had never attempted a takeover of anything on the scope of New York City. There hadn't been places this populated in my days.

"We have another problem, Sorin." I glanced over at him, not liking his grim tone. "My access to funds suddenly dried up. With the murder, my joint accounts will likely be frozen or at least severely restricted. Then the news about me being adopted will come into play, barring me from inheriting their company. And if I don't involve myself, fighting against the change in their will, it's going to look incredibly suspicious."

I grunted. "Which was their point. Mire you up in legalities and frame me for their murder so that we can't be seen together. Whoever this Necromancer was, he was exceedingly clever.

Nosh sighed tiredly, running a hand through his hair. "It's going to be sunrise in a few hours, and I'm sure you could use some rest and nourishment. Unfortunately for me, my day is only just beginning. I need to go check on Redford and get that chest back," he said, licking his lips anxiously.

I knew what he was thinking. That Redford might have been in on the frame-job from the beginning. Having assessed the man for deceit, I highly doubted it, but some of the employees had betrayed us, so there was only one way to find out.

"Then I have to make an appearance at the penthouse and learn exactly what happened," Nosh continued. "But before I do, I'm going to run to a store and pick up some clothes for you, because I don't know how long my talks with the police and attorneys will last. I'll get you a burner phone so that I can call you without being tracked."

I glanced over sharply. "Tracked?" I was inwardly pretty damned excited about getting a phone, wondering how many light-paintings I could take, but if they could track the phones...

He nodded, tapping his phone. "They can track these, and with the murder, I can almost guarantee they'll be taking a close look at my personal life. I can use cash to buy some temporary burner phones that aren't tied to my name, though. That way we can communicate without anyone listening in or potentially following me when I meet up with you—finding your hideout and catching me associating with my parents' alleged killer."

I narrowed my eyes. It really was the perfect setup. I glanced down to see my fingers shaking again. "I'm going to need some food," I said. "Soon."

Nosh pursed his lips, thinking. "Not sure how that's going to work. I'm all out of the bags, and if you get caught...eating, it's only going to reinforce their allegation that you're a murderer."

I grunted. "I know how to hunt without being seen," I growled.

Nosh glanced at me with a doubtful frown. "You know how to hunt without *people* seeing you, but there are cameras all over town." He leaned closer, lowering his head so that it was aimed at the floor, as if hiding his face. "Discreetly look at the ceiling. In the corner over there," he said, gently indicating the direction with his chin.

I glanced up to see a black orb tucked into the corner where the walls met the ceiling. It shone, reflecting the lights of the subway train. I averted my eyes, frowning. "Plastic. Looks like an eye."

Nosh nodded. "Technically, I guess it *is* an eye. It's a camera. Like the one that saw you in the Aristocrat, but not as high quality. They're on almost every street corner, too. And everyone has a phone with a camera." He grew silent, frowning at a new thought. "And those phones can also be tracked, so be careful when you're out hunting. If anyone gets a picture or video of you on their phone, you have to destroy it. And don't accidentally bring one of their phones back to your castle or the police could use it to find you and your tomb."

I nodded at the barrage of instructions.

A garbled voice spoke from a metal box up in the ceiling, and Nosh cocked his head, listening. I couldn't understand a single word. I didn't even know if it had been male or female. "The train doesn't speak very clearly," I commented, eyeing the metal box.

Nosh chuckled. "That was the conductor. The train doesn't talk," he said, grinning. "This is your stop. I'll meet you back down there in an hour. Be discreet and remember the cameras," he warned.

I nodded, scanning the trio of men, who also seemed to be exiting the train here. I'd been keeping an eye on them and listening in on their conversation, because they'd been bragging about some pickpocketing they'd done earlier tonight. They'd even compared their collections of wallets, not bothering to hide it from any of the other passengers—who were pointedly ignoring them as if afraid of attracting their attention.

I glanced at Nosh's wrist and spotted an expensive looking gold bracelet. "Give me that," I told him.

Nosh frowned. "Why? This is really expensive. And it was a gift."

"I need it to go fishing," I growled.

He frowned, glancing at me and then the trio of men. His lips thinned, but he nodded. "Remember the cameras," he murmured, unclasping the bracelet and slipping it to me.

The train came to a stop and I climbed to my feet, stumbling woozily. I dropped the bracelet and then muttered under my breath, doing my best to slur my speech like I was drunk. "That expensive and can't make a proper clasp," I complained. The trio of men locked onto the bracelet like eagles seeing a rabbit. I awkwardly snatched it up, almost falling over in the process. I shoved it into my pocket on the third attempt, right as the doors screeched open. I shuffled out the door, weaving from side-to-side as I melded into the flow of humanity at Grand Central Terminal.

I smiled as my act drew the anticipated response. The trio of thieves murmured excitedly from behind me, sensing the easy score.

To be fair, I had to agree.

It had been an easy score.

Now I just needed to find a spot to enjoy my meal in peace and quiet, unobserved.

22

Nosh returned to find me seated on the cooler, leaning back against a pile of wooden crates with my hands clasped over my belly. I wore a dozen gold chains with large, bejeweled medallions around my neck, several gold bracelets, and a bright red hat with a flat brim on the front—all acquisitions from my conquests. "Welcome to Castle Ambrogio, humble Shaman!" I bellowed in a grand tone. "New York City is now a safer place." I licked my lips and pointed at a nearby table where an impressive array of wallets, silver jewelry—that I was unable to wear—and cash was on display. I'd included his bracelet to round out the collection's aesthetic. The thieves from the train had earned every right to brag.

Nosh blinked incredulously. "You're making my eyes hurt, Mr. T."

I preened smugly, ignoring his reference. "Dazzling, is it not?"

It hadn't been enough blood—not by a long shot—but it had restored me back to the same persistent hunger I had felt after feasting on Nosh's blood bags.

I was beginning to feel concerned about how much blood I might need to get back to my usual self, but I didn't voice my fear. Once I returned to normal, I would likely only need a single meal every few days. "Criminals have a new reaper to fear. The Devil absolved the three thieves of their sins."

Nosh winced at me, shielding his eyes dramatically. "I hope you were careful—"

"And four men who were attempting to molest a woman in an alley."

His eyes widened. "I see—"

"And a man selling bags of white flour for a truly exorbitant price," I added, pointing at a backpack full of cash and dozens of transparent plastic bags of the white powder. "Although I technically had to kill four of his guards when they jumped out of a nearby car and chased me into a warren of filthy alleys. They had guns. I put them all in the bag, drank every last drop of their blood, and then hid the bodies. You were saying something about a money problem? We could sell our own flour," I suggested. "It seems rather lucrative."

He clenched his jaw, squaring his shoulders. "Sorin. If you kill too many people here, others are going to notice. Even if it's not caught on camera."

"This place is infested with crime. As stunningly beautiful as it appears on the outside, it has a vile underbelly that is absolutely teeming with maggots of decay. I've always hated crime, so I decided to kill two birds with one stone." I eyed the backpack. "Well, to kill a dozen rats with two fangs, technically," I amended with an amused chuckle.

Nosh sighed tiredly. "Fine. Just be careful and try to spread out your feedings. Your victims have friends and family, and if too many people start disappearing near one specific alley, the police will start looking around."

I snapped my fingers. "Ah! I almost forgot. I thought you might want to speak to the police about your parents, and I found one accepting a significant bribe from the man selling the bags of flour. That's actually how I got involved in that whole meal." I pointed towards the corner of the room. A man groaned groggily, hog-tied and blindfolded behind a stack of crates.

Nosh lost his temper, dropping the bags in his hands. "What the hell?" he demanded. "You can't kidnap a policeman! Are you *trying* to get caught?"

I frowned. "A *corrupt* policeman," I corrected. "I turned off all of his electronic items and enthralled him. I needed the practice, to gauge how low I truly am on blood. It was rather difficult, to be honest. Quite concerning. I will drink him once you finish your questions."

Nosh's eyes were bugging out of his skull. "No, Sorin! You need to enthrall his ass right out of here."

"He was extorting the flour man, accepting a bribe to look the other way. I did this city a service. We already suspect that Mina has her hands in the authorities. What if he knows something that may help us? Going back to your parents' apartment will not permit you to ask the real questions. This, on the other hand..." I said, shrugging.

Nosh began pacing back and forth, muttering under his breath. "Can he hear us?"

I glanced over at the groaning man and drew deep on my power. I focused on his mental faculties, checking to verify that he was still firmly under my control. It had been alarming to see how depleted I was from my blood withdrawal—enthralling humans was the first thing I used to teach my new vampires. But I'd had to use a vast majority of my strength to coerce him to follow me down here without losing my control. Even now, just checking on him felt like lifting a great weight. I let out a weary sigh after a few moments. "He's an idiot. He's conscious, but believes he is dreaming. We can speak freely. When you're ready, I can wake him."

Nosh muttered angrily, but I could sense his heartbeat. As openly upset as he was, his pulse was slow, steady, and calm. Like a block of ice. I appraised him thoughtfully, wondering again about this stranger who I had accepted as a friend and ally. A man who was so blatantly a target of the vampires.

He finally turned to look at me, sighing dejectedly. "I brought you new clothes, hygiene products, and a burner phone so we can call each other."

I leaned forward eagerly, clapping my hands. My bracelets jangled loudly. "Does it make light-paintings?" I asked excitedly. "And what can it burn?"

He smirked, nodding. "Pictures," he corrected me. "It does, but burner phones are not as fancy as my phone. They call them burners because you can dispose of them—burn them—if you think someone is tracking you through it. The important thing is that they are harder to track, so we can talk privately. I'm sure my phone records are going to be reviewed soon, so I can't risk using it. In fact, I turned it off four blocks from here so that no one could use it to track me here."

I nodded, holding out my hand. "Show me how to make light-paintings."

He sighed, digging into the bag and pulling out a box. He opened it, tossed the packaging to the side, and turned the phone on. "Full charge, so we should be good. Don't take too many light-paintings or you'll drain the battery. I doubt there are any outlets down here to recharge it, so we'll have to buy you a new one when it dies."

I frowned. "Dies?"

He turned the phone to show me the back, tapping it. "There is a power source inside that needs to be regularly recharged with electricity. Much like you need blood. If it runs out of power, it dies."

I stared at it wonderingly. "My light-painter is an electric vampire," I breathed.

He sighed. "Sure, Sorin. Sure." Nosh tossed it to me, and I caught it. Like he'd said, it was nowhere near as fancy as his phone had been. I flipped it open and stared at the tiny screen, frowning in displeasure. "Did they not have any nicer ones?" I touched the screen with my finger, and nothing happened. "And it's broken."

He rolled his eyes. "It doesn't have a touch screen."

I glared at him. "Why. Not."

He rolled his eyes. "Not even a day into the twenty-first century and you're already an entitled brat," he muttered.

I grunted. "Next time get me the better phone so I can touch my light-paintings. Use my treasures if it is out of your budget," I said, pointing at my pile of valuables.

He closed his eyes and took a deep breath as if restraining himself. Then he made his way over to the policeman, squatting down before him. He snapped his fingers and a cool blue ball of light appeared in his palm, illuminating the blindfolded policeman. "Can he hear me?"

he asked me, not bothering to look over his shoulder.

I had already found the button to take pictures with my new phone, so I wasn't paying much attention. "Yes. But you must start every sentence with *My Lord*, or he will snap out of his enthrallment," I said, smirking over at him. He wasn't looking, so he didn't catch my sarcasm. It was a joke I had often used on new vampires when teaching them how to thrall their victims.

"Strange requirement, but whatever," he muttered. I aimed my camera at him, pressing a button that said *record*. I gasped silently as the phone began taking a moving light-painting of Nosh. A *video*, as he had called it—but I preferred using my terminology since I knew it annoyed him.

He cleared his throat. "My Lord, what do the police know about the Griffin murder earlier tonight?"

The policeman flinched at the sudden request. "I'm just a patrol officer, not a homicide detective. I only know what I heard on the scanner. Perp with no shoes or shirt followed them to their penthouse. Exsanguinated them. Blood everywhere. Horrible. I think we're looking for the victims' son. He was at the penthouse earlier, from what I heard."

"My Lord, who alerted the police?"

"Anonymous tip, I think," he murmured dazedly. "Why do you keep calling me Lord?"

Nosh glanced back at me, frowning thoughtfully. I gave him a thumbs up, still recording. He shook his head at my phone, rolling his eyes. "My Lord, were you taking a bribe from a drug dealer tonight?"

He stiffened. "Never. That's illegal—"

"Johnathan," I warned, drawing out his name in a stern tone.

His shoulders slumped guiltily. "Fine. But only a small take here and there, and only the low-level scum. I risk my life every goddamned day, and no matter how many dealers we bust on patrol, a dozen more pop up to replace them. I got bills to pay," he growled aggressively. "I'm a good cop and this town is going to shit. Damn wolf gang popping up all over the place, doing our job better than we can."

Nosh glanced back at me, arching an eyebrow. I nodded satisfactorily. "Told you." Although the wolf gang comment was news to me. Was he referring to the werewolves? Were they acting as a type of silent police? I suddenly wanted to talk to Stevie again.

"My Lord, do you remember how you got here?" Nosh asked, turning back to him.

The policeman hesitated, struggling through the fog I had placed over his memory. "Nice woman said she needed help. A strong policeman to catch a bad man. But it's too dark for me to see right now. I must have forgotten my flashlight," he said, obviously too dazed to realize he wore a blindfold.

Nosh grunted and I grinned. "Pretty clever," I said, preening.

"My Lord, you can rest quietly," he told Johnathan, grimacing distastefully. He climbed to his feet and I ended my recording. "You should get some rest while I go to the penthouse," he told me tiredly, obviously not eager to do so.

I shuddered. "I do not need rest. I've had quite enough of it recently. I'll find some way to entertain myself."

Nosh eyed me warily.

23

I couldn't even think about resting without feeling uneasy—like I would wake again to find a hundred years had passed. I was also being truthful. Despite the blood not bringing me back to full power, it was definitely enough to rejuvenate me and prevent me from sleeping. And I'd learned that I could go for days without rest. Sunlight was obviously a deterrent, but not as detrimental as it was for other vampires. I would get severe sunburns if I stood in direct sunlight, but I wouldn't burst into flame or anything. Younger vampires were not so fortunate.

I could go out in sunlight, but not for any prolonged period of time —unless I had protection and shade. Like an umbrella. But walking around with an umbrella and my skin covered might attract unwanted attention. If any vampires happened to see me out in sunlight, they would instantly know I was beyond ancient. Or they might doubt I was a vampire—especially since I could hide my powers from my offspring. Unless they were powerful enough to break through that protection.

Since I wasn't at full strength, I wasn't sure how strong one needed to be to break my defenses. It was a big risk, and I chose not to share the details with Nosh. He had enough on his mind without worrying about me.

"Just lay low, Sorin. I mean it," Nosh said. "I'll call when I finish with the police. I'll arrange a meeting with Stevie the werewolf for sundown. We can see about meeting with this Crescent."

I shrugged. "It's not like we're drowning in options. Unless we want to go visit this Museum of Natural History," I said, recalling Mina's claim.

Nosh shook his head. "We have no idea how many vampires reside there. They have catacombs beneath the building that reportedly cover city blocks."

I frowned thoughtfully. "Underground tunnels? Like this?" I asked.

Nosh shrugged. "New York has a vast underground world. I have no idea exactly how vast, but rumors make it sound like it covers a significant portion of the island of Manhattan. Where we stand right now," he elaborated, noticing the confused look on my face. I nodded but found myself idly wondering how far I was from where I had lived with Deganawida. We hadn't been on an island.

I turned to Nosh. "Werewolves might have answers about these tunnels. Or know a way inside this museum."

Nosh nodded. "That is my hope. If Mina worked for this Necromancer, he must be in charge of the city. Like I already told you, the vampires are quiet about their control. They don't brag, they just consistently spread their roots throughout the city. Which means innocent men and women will work for them and not even know it," he said, eyeing the policeman. "We can't kill them for ignorance."

I grunted. "The world would be a desolate place if ignorance was a crime punishable by death."

He glanced down at his burner phone. "I should be going. Can I trust that you've murdered enough people for one evening? Can't you just kill the Necromancer with your mind from here? He is your offspring, after all."

I shook my head. "I doubt he was bitten by me, and even if he is mine, I haven't had anywhere near enough blood to attempt such a thing. I could barely handle Mina Harker."

Nosh arched a stunned eyebrow. "Jesus. How many victims do you need on a regular basis?" he demanded fearfully.

I shrugged. "After Deganawida's slumber, I have no idea. It's never happened before. Remember that I spent hundreds of years without so much as a drop of blood. There is a lot to repair. A lot to wake back up. Like rebuilding atrophied muscles."

Nosh grumbled unhappily but nodded. "Makes sense. I brought you some newspapers and a map so you can familiarize yourself a little, although I'm sure much of it will only give you more questions."

I pointed at the backpack I had acquired. "One of the flour dealer's men had some textbooks in his bag." I'd always enjoyed reading. It had been my only method of escapism in my time, and I had learned to read quite rapidly. In several languages.

I had no idea if those languages were still in use, however.

Nosh nodded. "That's great. Skim through and I can answer any questions you may have when I get back." He glanced over at Johnathan. "It is not wise to kill a policeman. His absence could bring a world of pain down upon our shoulders. The police are a close brotherhood. If he doesn't survive, you will have a hundred of them surrounding this area, canvasing the neighborhood in search of him."

I nodded. "You may take him with you." I turned to the policeman. "Johnathan."

"Yes?" he asked groggily.

"My acquaintance will escort you from the hotel. Thank you for helping keep us safe, but I would prefer we remain anonymous. You will forget everything that happened from the time we met until...ten minutes from now," I said, arching a questioning eyebrow at Nosh. He nodded.

Nosh looked decidedly uneasy to become an accomplice but leaving him down here with me was a good way for him to end up dead, no matter the consequences. I was hungry enough to drink a village.

"Just escort him back to the exit and tell him to keep walking. Once the ten-minute threshold is reached, he will snap out of it."

Nosh nodded. "You didn't say My Lord."

I grinned wolfishly. "It was never a necessity."

Nosh narrowed his eyes at me, clenching his fists. "Let's go, Johnathan." I waved at the pair, even though Johnathan couldn't see me. Nosh ignored my friendly gesture.

Soon, I sat in relative silence. I absently took some pictures, wondering if I should try to rest or go read one of the books inside the backpack.

Instead, I changed into the clothes Nosh had bought—blue trousers that were both durable and comfortable—called *jeans*, based on the paper tag attached to them—a black sweatshirt with a hood, and some black, heavy boots.

They weren't a close match to the coat, but I decided that it sufficed as an appropriate outfit—judging from the dozen pictures I'd taken with my new phone. My leather jacket was slick and shiny and would do well to repel rain if we had any more of it. A downside was that it drew the eye by catching reflections of distant light, which wasn't suitable to stealth. I would just have to be exceedingly careful. On a positive note, it was thick and resilient—like some of the armor I had worn in my days, when I wasn't wearing one of the dozen metallic armors that I owned, of course. *Had owned*, I thought to myself with a faint, territorial growl.

I found a pallet of plastic water jugs lined against the wall, along with a collection of shelves holding all manner of electronic devices, batteries, medicines, and packaged food. Like some kind of storage room. Had Deganawida spent considerable time here?

I inspected the private area with the cot and nodded satisfactorily. The area had a small bookshelf, and an armchair pressed into the corner opposite the cot. A stack of books and an electric lamp rested on top of a rickety table, apparently a chosen reading nook.

I closed my eyes and inhaled deeply, picking up traces of Deganawida's repeated presence. He had spent a very long time down here, right outside my tomb. I frowned thoughtfully, uncertain how to feel about this revelation. Was it as my jailer or as a sorrowful friend?

I shook my head and went back to the main area.

I emptied the rest of the bag Nosh had brought me to find a hairbrush and a trio of plastic bottles labeled *shampoo, body wash*, and *conditioner*. I frowned, wondering what to do with each. The body wash was self-explanatory, and a quick study of the other two told me that the shampoo was for washing the hair while the conditioner was some kind of moisturizer for hair. I glanced about the room, not seeing any tub for bathing. I opened the various soaps, curious what *Call of the Wild* smelled like. I gasped in awe, shaking my head as the aromas assaulted my nostrils, making my eyes roll back in my head. How had they acquired such a fragrance?

"Old Spice," I mused, recognizing the company logo as a ship. "They must have a secret trade route with some mysterious warlocks living beyond civilization," I murmured out loud. As much as the world had changed without me, I felt that I was handling the numerous changes remarkably well—getting a firmer grasp on how the world currently worked.

I set the items on the shelf of medicines and nodded. I found myself eyeing the bookshelf Deganawida had left here but shook my head firmly. I felt too restless to sit down and read. I wanted to explore these underground tunnels. The policeman had told me a lot about them before Nosh arrived—not that he would recall any of our conversations, even to Nosh.

They were abandoned subway tunnels, or at least they connected to them somewhere nearby. Johnathan often had to clear homeless men and women out of the upper reaches. But he had agreed that New York City's underground world was thriving with disgruntled men and women.

The forgotten and downtrodden.

The Devil had neighbors to meet.

I pocketed my phone, scooped up the backpack, and decided to take a walk. I'd always preferred active learning to a book—no matter how intriguing and fascinating the story was. And although I didn't have baked goods to share, I had flour that was worth a fortune.

And money and jewelry to buy information.

If there was one thing I had learned how to do from an early age, it was how to hustle and hawk my wares. I had learned those skills long before the fateful night I had become the world's first vampire.

But thoughts of that night always made me morose, so I took a calming breath and shook my head, straightening my red hat. "Time to go make some friends," I said out loud.

24

I had spent several hours exploring the underground, meeting new friends and removing some of the more troubling residents. The lack of light was no deterrent to me since my eyes naturally adjusted to the numerous shades of shadow.

It was my natural habitat.

The herds of prey were surprisingly plentiful in my new realm. And I learned quite a bit about the present state of affairs. Ironically, many of those I met were well acquainted with monsters like vampires and werewolves and something called aliens. I had been intrigued at first, until I'd learned they'd been referring to beings from the night sky who had somehow traveled down here in metal ships to sexually assault humans.

I very quickly dismissed these wild claims, hoping they were false.

As malnourished as I was, drinking too much blood too fast was dangerous. It would make me blood drunk. So, I toed the line, drinking as much as I thought I could manage without incapacitating myself, and I was careful to only choose victims who were enemies of the friends I had made—of which I'd made plenty. Many of the less useful individuals had become incredibly pliable to my requests once I began handing out jewelry and the baggies in my backpack.

I'd learned that the flour was in fact something called cocaine—a drug that made people remarkably excited and energetic. I'd watched them snort the fine powder, of all things. I hadn't dared to take part in case it affected vampires differently than humans. Seeing how twitchy and neurotic many of my neighbors were, I feared myself entering such a state.

It closely resembled me when I'd once become blood drunk.

And it had taken a dozen of my strongest vampires to restrain me for long enough to return to my senses. Dracula had been one of them. Back when he had been a staunch supporter and, dare I say, friend. But that had been long before I decided to leave Europe. Before my motivations had changed.

They, led by Dracula, had continued to desire more blood. Power. Domination. I thought back on those old days, sighing sadly.

As powerful as I had been, I had been no match for literally hundreds of vampires, and I knew that a coup was being arranged behind my back. My only alternative to self-banishment would have been to start a civil war, which would have sent Europe back into the dark ages.

So, I'd chosen to explore the world, teaming up with my old friends Lucian and Nero—who had experienced similar power struggles in their own communities. Ultimately, we had chosen to adventure across the ocean upon hearing recent news from Spain about a New World. It had cost us a significant amount of money to fund the exploration, but money had never been a problem.

I'd made an arrangement with the King of Spain behind closed doors for passage, privacy, and food aplenty. I may or may not have enthralled him.

Nevertheless, he'd been beyond agreeable to my terms—a ship, a crew, and his silence about our secret voyage in exchange for my gold and the fact that I would relieve him of all of his prisoners to take with me on my travels. I hadn't elaborated why I wanted his criminals —for food, naturally—only promising him that they would never trouble him or his country again. He'd found us a drunken beast of a man who had spent thirty years braving the oceans, and we'd embarked on a long, tumultuous journey that had been both exciting and incredible for about one week. Then we'd grown restless and irritable.

Somehow, we'd made it—with the bare minimum of sailors, thanks to my appetite. Then we'd given the captain the boat and told him to forget we ever existed.

I sighed at the memory, recalling the adventures we'd experienced before running into Deganawida and his tribe.

I paced back and forth in my hideout, having spent an hour flipping through one of the textbooks I had acquired—*History of the United States of America*—as I sat in Deganawida's old chair. I'd been pleased to learn that my journey had never been documented.

But the rest of what I'd read had been both insightful and troubling. Much of what I had personally lived through had been grossly misinterpreted. And that was before I came to learn what had ultimately happened to the Native Americans who I had grown to call family.

Wars had raged across the beautiful land I had come to call home. More and more settlers came from overseas, pushing the natives back through war and conquest, and ultimately staking claim to the lands they had stolen. After many years, battles, and threats back and forth between a few countries overseas, an independent country had ultimately formed—The United States of America.

Of course, there had been no mention of me, werewolves, vampires, or warlocks, but I had seen suspicious events dotting the pages. The Great Fires of New York, the Salem Witch Trials, and a place called Roanoke that practically screamed of magic.

Deganawida had earned his place in written history, having formed the Iroquois Confederacy—like the painting I had seen in Nosh's parents' home at the Aristocrat. Reading about that, I'd gone back down to my tomb to study the murals on the walls. They told both a similar and vastly different story.

I'd read about the rapid advancement of technology, the Industrial Revolution—which had to have been sparked by warlocks—and the invention of factories, electricity, and the combustible engine. I soon felt that I was beginning to get a healthy understanding of the world.

Until I read up on the World Wars. Then I began to wonder if the world could have used a few more vampires to keep the humans in line. Or if maybe vampires weren't as terrible as everyone seemed to think.

I'd soon resorted to skimming the book, wanting to get only the highlights. Truthfully, I'd also read between the lines, searching for any clues about my own ordeal, Deganawida, Dracula, or my wife and son.

I hadn't expected to find anything, so I wasn't disappointed. But Deganawida's comments about their uncertain demise was beyond unsettling. As was Dracula's current obsession with my bloodline— finding a way to procreate.

I genuinely had no idea why he would care about such a thing. He'd always been the type of man who believed that the ends justified the means and had never been afraid of spilling blood to get what he wanted. So, if he wanted more vampires, all he had to do was turn more humans.

"Unless...he is looking to make heirs bound to him, heirs who couldn't betray him like he betrayed me," I mused. Finally, I shook my head. "But that would only matter if he was looking to pass off the crown—at which point he wouldn't care."

I was missing something. I glanced around the room, searching for a distraction to occupy my time. I spotted an umbrella hanging on the edge of the shelf and an idea began to form in my mind. It had been four hours since Nosh had left, which meant I likely had another six hours or so until dusk. I knew I stood no chance of falling asleep, so I stared at my phone, debating internally.

Because I still remembered the phone number that the werewolf, Stevie, had given Nosh.

Memory had been a valuable asset in my rise to power. Having grown up never able to afford pen and paper, I'd been forced to hone my memory to the sharpness of a razor, never knowing when I might need to recall a particular detail.

And I'd once heard a traveling priest say, *idle hands are the Devil's workshop.*

He'd told it to me and a dozen other young boys who lived on the streets while we were waiting for a baker to turn his back so we could steal some food.

The priest hadn't elaborated on it, and I'd never even heard of

Christianity at that point. It was only many years later that we crossed paths again—by pure happenstance—when I caught him molesting a woman in his own church.

I had reminded him of his message to a young group of boys, wanting to make sure it was the last thing he heard before I killed him. He had tasted particularly bitter and spoiled, much like his hypocrisy.

Too bad for him that all those years earlier, neither of us had known that the future Devil of Italy had been seated in his assembly, and that the Devil would one day return to hold him accountable to his own lessons.

I'd been known as the Devil of many countries, over the years. "The Devil of New York," I mused out loud, considering some of the...negotiations I'd made on my travels through the underground earlier. I smiled, nodding. "I like the sound of that."

I picked up the phone and called the werewolf.

"Who is this and how did you get this number?" a suspicious growl demanded by way of introduction.

"It's the bloodsucking kin-killer," I replied. "I have questions."

"We're not hiding you from the law. You stirred up a hornet's nest at the Aristocrat," he snapped.

"Believe me when I tell you that I recall and relish in almost every kill I've performed, Stevie. But I never met those people, let alone killed them. And the man you saw me with in the alley?" I asked, letting the silence stretch for a few seconds. "That was their son."

I could practically taste his curiosity as he told me where to meet. "But don't you need to wait until sunset?"

I grinned. "Only the kids have to worry about sunlight, Stevie. But some shade would be preferable. Tans don't work with my wardrobe."

He burst out laughing. "I'll bet. One hour. You know how to get there?"

"I've got a map and a phone. I'll figure it out."

"This better not be a trap, Sorin. That won't go well for you."

"I'm here to eviscerate Dracula. If our goals coincide, all the better. If not, you'll read about my success in the news. I'll admit, I don't mind making some new friends along the way. I've been making plenty, as a matter of fact," I said, thinking back on my neighbors underground.

"Friends..." Stevie mused. "That's a dangerous word." I grunted my agreement. "Protocol requires me to have security in place. Is that going to be a problem?"

"Not unless they do something to annoy me or get in my way."

"You're pretty goddamned honest, you know that? Blunt might be too fine a word to describe you."

"Truths work best—and are deadliest—when no one believes them. The blade that cuts both ways shows no mercy for ignorance."

He grunted. "Right. I have no idea what that means, but we'll see you in an hour."

25

I stood in the shade beneath a massive tree in a place called Central Park. Colossal buildings formed a wall around the wooded landscape, boxing it in on all sides, but the park was large enough to almost feel like I had stepped out of the city and back into a world more resembling the one I had left.

As long as you ignored the unceasing honking from the hundreds of cars filling the streets around the perimeter. Or the hundreds of people walking around.

I saw elegant structures nestled deeper into the wooded park, but I didn't have time to go see them up close. Sprawling walkways criss-crossed the wooded hills, and men and women in brightly colored, tight-fitting clothes jogged down the paths everywhere I looked— although I saw no one pursuing them, which was odd. Why run if you weren't being chased?

It was all highly suspicious.

It was an overcast day, so my umbrella had gone largely unre-marked. I knew for a fact that clouds were not always protection from sunlight, so I had chosen to walk the entire way here with it raised, protecting me from any potential breaks in the cloud cover. One thing I hadn't factored in was the natural shade cast down from the buildings —skyscrapers, as I had heard them called.

Meaning I merely had to choose the shaded side of the street in order to walk freely during the day. The umbrella was almost pointless —as long as it wasn't high noon with the sun directly overhead.

As requested, I hadn't ventured deeply into the park, remaining close to the street where Stevie had told me to meet him. I glanced down at my phone, checking the time. I had never truly needed to judge time by a number, having spent most of my time in my castle or living with the Native Americans—who gauged the time of the day by the angle of the sun.

A large black vehicle pulled up on the street and Stevie climbed out, motioning me over. I nodded, studying the large car—which was unlike any of the cars I had seen so far. It could fit three rows of people as opposed to two, and it was much taller. Judging by the number of heart-beats I sensed inside—and the overwhelming smell of werewolf—they had filled the car to the max, leaving only one seat open.

For me.

I walked up to Stevie with a polite smile. He wore jeans and boots like me, but had a checkered collar shirt that was rolled up at the sleeves. He glanced down at my feet and smiled. "You found shoes!" he said, clapping his hands.

"And a shirt," I said, lifting my arms to show it off.

He laughed, his blue eyes twinkling. He studied my umbrella, his humor slowly replaced with concern. "If it's that simple, why don't more of your people use those?" he asked.

I shrugged. "I'm special. Umbrellas aren't enough protection for most of my kind. And it's not just the sun's light that harms us. Most of my kind grow deliriously tired the moment the sun *rises*—even if they're underground."

He studied me pensively. "But not you," he said flatly.

"I've been around for a while."

He grunted. Then his eyes locked onto the crucifix on my neck. "You're kidding. None of you can do that. I'm pretty sure even…your nemesis can't do that," he said, not wanting to say Dracula's name in such a public place.

When I had given away all my jewelry, the simple crucifix necklace had slipped under my shirt. I hadn't even realized it until I got back to my hideout. Knowing how uncomfortable it made people feel to see a vampire unharmed by a religious artifact, I'd chosen to keep wearing it.

I smiled mischievously at Stevie's concern. "That is correct. *Dracula* can't," I said, speaking his name clearly. It was daytime after all. Any potential spies lurking in the park would have drawn attention to themselves by spontaneously bursting into flame.

He studied me warily, as if reconsidering how wise it was to get involved with me. "I'm beginning to think I was very lucky last night," he finally said.

I nodded. "You used your logic rather than your emotions. That is a rare and admirable trait, and it will take you very far in life. I'll cut straight to the point since I can tell that you are concerned. I called you for assistance. If you are unable or unwilling to assist, why did you agree to meet me? With or without you, I'm going after my target. But my chances of success improve with allies." I paused. "As long as they rely on rational logic rather than passionate feelings."

After a considerable pause, he finally nodded. Then he lifted a hand to reveal a black, canvas bag. "I need you to put this hood on so you can't see where we're going. I'm also going to need to take your phone and check you for bugs."

I frowned. "How dare you accuse me of having bugs? I bathed last night. In a shower. It was delightful."

His smile faltered. "Um. Bugs, like electronic recording devices or trackers. Like they have in phones. I'm not talking about insects."

I blinked. "Oh. Of course. This is a new burner I picked up," I said, proud to use the modern term Nosh had told me as I flashed him my phone. "The only call I made was to you earlier. I had just taken it out of the box."

He took it and pressed a few buttons before clicking it shut. "I'll hold onto it just in case." I shrugged. Then he took out a metal wand— much like the ones the guards at the auction had used. He began waving it up and down my legs and arms, then up my neck and back. It made a faint whining sound as he moved it over the surface of my body, but that was about it.

Finally, he held out the black hood, permitting me the honor of blindfolding myself. I met his eyes, not blinking and not accepting. "I hope this isn't an elaborate plan to betray me, Stevie. That won't go well for anyone." I took a measured step forward and extended my hand for him to shake mine in agreement. "I'm a man of my word, Stevie. I mean you no ill will and will give you ample warning if that ever changes." Stevie slowly nodded, but he didn't look entirely convinced. "And you will do the same, correct? None of those big scary wolves in the back intend to club me the moment I step into your car?"

He shook his head, clenching his jaws. "If we meant you harm, we would have simply invaded your hideout. Think about this from my perspective, Sorin," he said with a frustrated sigh. "Here's what the werewolves know. You—a vampire—show up out of nowhere and kill a werewolf—Ralph—with minimal effort over a territorial dispute."

"Ralph was unspeakably rude and ill-mannered," I added.

Stevie nodded. "True. Then you defend another werewolf—me— from two fellow vampires." I nodded, fully aware of his concerns. "Then you demand a meeting with the Crescent and tell me you want to kill Dracula. Then you agree to meet with me outside in *daylight* while wearing a *crucifix*. Any of that sound a little strange to you?"

"I understand," I sighed, nodding.

"Good. Because my fellow wolves think it's *very* strange. That you might just be trying to discover the location of the Crescent so that you can lead your fellows right to our front door. That kind of information is well worth sacrificing a few underling vampires in an alley last night to buy my trust."

I took another step forward, extending my hand more forcefully as I glared at him. "I am a man of my word, Stevie. I meant everything I said to you. Tell me that you are a man of yours, and that you aren't intending a trap for *me*. Otherwise, we can call this quits right now. I have only one purpose, and my energy is fully devoted to that purpose. I want nothing more than to eradicate every vampire in town. Except for myself, obviously," I admitted.

"You want to take over New York City for yourself?" he asked, frowning.

"I just want to right a wrong," I said, avoiding his actual question.

Because I didn't have an answer to it. Did I want to take over New York City? I might not have a choice in the matter. I might need to take over in order to withstand Dracula's armies.

He finally nodded and shook my hand. His palm was hot and calloused, dwarfing mine. "No wolf will harm you unless you attack them first. Or provoke them. They are nervous about you, so I would avoid provoking anyone."

"No teasing," I agreed. "And no teaming up with my sworn enemy to put you and your fellow wolves in danger."

He nodded. "Then we have a deal."

We stood that way for about a minute, listening to a rather obnoxious bird chirping at us from a nearby tree. Neither of us spoke.

"You still want me to put the hood on," I finally said.

He nodded. "It would be better for everyone."

I sighed. "This better be good, Stevie. I'm not a fan of submission." I tugged the hood over my head and was suddenly unable to see a thing —which was a strange sensation for a vampire. I was accustomed to being able to see in the dark.

"Then you're coming to the right place. Werewolves only submit to our alpha or those above us," he said, chuckling as he guided me by the elbow towards the open door.

"I'm well aware of how your kind operates," I mused. "I used to be good friends with a werewolf," I said.

"Oh? What happened to him?"

I thought about it, unsure how to answer. "Our past caught up with us, tore us apart, and ruined our lives. I think. I never found out what happened to him."

"Maybe I know him," Stevie murmured from behind me as I climbed into the seat. I scooted across the leather until I bumped up against a large body. The werewolf sniffed at me curiously, but I ignored him as Stevie continued. "What was his name? We might need to verify your story." I could sense the powerful thuds of werewolf hearts from my fellow passengers, although I couldn't see anyone.

I shrugged as Stevie climbed in behind me and closed the door, boxing me in. "Lucian."

The car grew alarmingly silent as I felt every heartbeat ratchet up alarmingly fast. I began to grow uneasy, fearing they were all about to shift and simultaneously attack me.

They recognized the name, obviously. But the silence didn't necessarily make that a good thing. "Impossible," Stevie finally said. "He died hundreds of years ago."

I nodded. "Yes. He was the first werewolf in the United States. I brought him here."

Again, the tension in the vehicle was a physical presence, and I had to fight not to tear off my hood, wanting to keep an eye on everyone. That would, of course, be taken as an act of hostility.

"Drive," Stevie muttered, sounding distracted.

The rest of the car ride was silent, which I took for a good sign.

26

I sat on a stool in the middle of a vacant warehouse that smelled vaguely of sawdust. The werewolves had taken the hood from my face once inside the safety of the building, and I counted over two-dozen werewolves within eyesight. Thankfully, most of them were lounging on couches or chairs a good distance away, leaving me to sit with only Stevie and two others. But every werewolf in the room was watching and listening, no matter how far away they sat. Benefits of enhanced senses. And they all watched me like a fox in the chicken coop.

Not necessarily in an aggressive manner, but they definitely were not friendly looks.

I had spent the last hour telling them my story and answering Stevie's follow-up questions.

Two of his lieutenants listened in. A short, ridiculously muscular black man named Benjamin wore a perpetual grin and his hair was meticulously groomed into a flat surface on top that looked thick enough for me to set a cup on. His eyes were so light of a brown that they almost looked orange, seeming to glow against his deep brown skin.

A tall, curvaceous woman named Natalie wore tight jeans and a thin, long-sleeved shirt that hung loosely enough to show off one shoulder and her collarbone—which was incredibly distracting to a vampire. She had bright green eyes and short, blonde hair that was cut in a solid line at ear-level to form sharp points down her jaw.

I told them everything I'd learned since I'd awoken underground— that the vampires were led by a man known as the Necromancer, and that he lived in the Museum of Natural History. That this Necromancer had sent Mina Harker to an auction to acquire Deganawida's magical journal and that she'd managed to send it off to him before I killed her. That Mina had framed me for murdering Nosh's parents and that Nosh was currently with the police trying to get some answers.

I'd played aloof to what the journal contained because it was none of their business and because I wasn't entirely sure why the vampires wanted it so badly. I surmised that telling the werewolves that the journal possibly contained an explanation about my ability to procreate and make baby vampires would get me instantly torn to pieces, so I had left out that detail.

Understandably, the tension and suspicion in the air was thick enough to poke with a stick. Because Stevie had already commanded seven wolves to step away to call their contacts in order to verify some of my claims, not wanting to take my word for it. I didn't blame them.

It sounded downright ridiculous, even to me. And every answer I gave only seemed to bring up more questions, invariably leading back to me.

My story before waking up beneath Grand Central Terminal.

But I didn't have time to get into my life story. I needed to get to the Necromancer before he sent the journal off to Dracula.

The werewolves had seemed particularly impressed—and doubtful —that I had killed Mina Harker. Until my story, they had thought she ran the city. When I had mentioned that Nosh took her fangs and could corroborate my claim, one of the wolves had stepped out to try getting a hold of him on my burner phone.

He hadn't answered, which was mildly concerning because it had been almost an hour ago and he hadn't called back.

Stevie was leaning over a table covered in a map of the city. I saw a dozen red circles drawn on the map, marking locations. He pointed at one with a thick finger, thumping the table three times. "We had the museum marked as one of their hideouts, but we weren't sure how significant it was." He leaned back, scratching at his beard. "The place is a fortress. You think you can just walk in there with your vampire membership card and kill him?"

I frowned. "Well, I don't have a membership card, and there might be a few additional steps, but yes. I need to get to this Necromancer, get the journal back, and find out what he knows about Dracula. How I can get to him."

Stevie watched me like I was some strange creature he'd never seen before. "Dracula isn't in America. Everyone knows that."

"I'm sure you're right, but I need to be certain before I waste six months on a boat and then another few months trekking across the country to invade his fortress."

Stevie frowned. "Why wouldn't you just fly there?"

I grunted. "I'm not back to full strength, and no one can fly that far. Have you not met any vampires before?" I asked, frowning.

Benjamin cleared his throat. "Bro's never heard of a plane before, boss."

I glanced from one to the other, shrugging. "What's a plane?"

Stevie blinked and then nodded. "Right. I forgot. Because you're hundreds of years old."

Natalie leaned forward. "It's like a ship but it flies in the sky. You could get overseas in twelve hours or less, depending on where you're going and if it is a direct flight."

I stared at her. "That's incredible..." I murmured, shaking my head. That changed everything.

"Although you might wait in line for six months at JFK," Benjamin chuckled.

Natalie nodded her agreement, smirking at the confused look on my face. "He's exaggerating."

Stevie clapped his hands, drawing our attention. "You need to help us understand, Sorin. You say you knew Lucian, personally." I nodded. "That you can stand against Dracula because you *made* him—even though no one has ever heard of you. It all just sounds too good to be true."

I leaned back in my chair, empathizing with his dilemma. "I know you have questions, and that you need answers to trust me." They nodded eagerly, leaning forward. Even the wolves back on the couches grew quiet, listening in. "But I need you to focus. We're on limited time before the Necromancer sends that journal to Dracula and out of the city for good. I'll give you a quick summary of my story, but none of us has time to read my autobiography. We've already been here for an hour and we're no closer to getting the Necromancer. If we can get the journal back and kill the Necromancer, I'll host a party and tell you everything. If you can't agree to that, then I'll have to find another way to take him down. On my own."

Stevie nodded. "Go ahead. But I can't make any promises without hearing your story. I have to think of the pack, first. Because the moment we attack the vampires, everything changes. They will hunt us down without mercy."

I let out a deep breath, nodding. "My name is Sorin Ambrogio, and I'm the world's first vampire. Dracula was the first man I ever turned, and he worked for me for hundreds of years. Our numbers grew, and I soon faced a dilemma when it became apparent that their appetite for power and bloodshed exceeded even my own. Before that turned ugly, I passed my crown to Dracula and traveled to the Americas with Lucian —who had experienced a similar coup building in his own ranks—and another friend named Nero, a Warlock. We were each the first of our kind and wanted a new life here. We had a few years of peace before Dracula found me and destroyed the Native American tribe who had essentially adopted me. Deganawida's tribe. I was poisoned and injured, and Deganawida put me into a deep sleep of some kind so that I could heal and return a few weeks later to avenge our tribe. Except he never woke me up. Until yesterday when he gave his life to do so."

I had carefully chosen not to mention my family—my wife and son. That was personal and had no bearing on the matter at hand. It would only serve to muddy an already complicated story.

He let out a long sigh, shaking his head at the summary of what I'd already told them in bits and pieces. "That's insane. And completely unverifiable."

I shrugged. "I'm struggling to believe it myself. I thought I would wake up a few weeks later to go kill Dracula myself. I didn't expect any of this," I muttered, gesturing vaguely at the city beyond the walls of the warehouse. "But one thing you *can* verify is that I killed Mina Harker. Nosh has her fangs. You can't deny that I'm stronger than the vampire you thought was running the city. Why don't we just start there?" He nodded his head thoughtfully. "And remember, I intend to go after the Necromancer and Dracula one way or another. You can either help or stand aside. I don't require your belief, but your alliance couldn't hurt."

Stevie sat back down, grumbling unhappily. "I told them you were a crazy son of a bitch and that your goals aligned with ours, but I have no idea how I'm supposed to sell the rest of your story with the Crescent." He met my eyes, studying me.

"You can start by admitting that you run the Crescent," I suggested with a shrug.

Every werewolf in the warehouse stiffened.

"Oh, come on," I said, smirking. "It wasn't that difficult to figure out."

He watched me in silence, considering. Finally, he let out a breath, and his werewolves followed suit—an answer in and of itself. "The werewolves are indeed fractured, but perhaps not as much as I led you to believe. It is beneficial to let it be known that we are not unified. That way the vampires don't attack us in force, assuming we might just take each other out. It is a delicate alliance, but I was voted to head the Crescent. We have five Paws—gangs of werewolves—in New York City. One for each borough. I largely let each Paw govern themselves, but we can unite when necessary."

"Would me killing the Necromancer convince them to unite?" I asked dryly. "Or do I need to bake them a cake?"

Benjamin burst into a violent cough, turning away to conceal his obvious laughter. He cleared his throat and turned back to us, his orange eyes glistening. "I like cake," he finally said, smiling.

Stevie shot him a warning look before turning back to me. "Perhaps. Perhaps not. Many will just see you as a vampire. That this whole attack is so you can take control. None of it proves that you are a friend of the wolves. Vampires are cunning and deceitful. We've learned never to trust them."

I nodded. "That's why I'm here. To pay homage to my old friend, Lucian, and hope that a vampire can once again be friends with a werewolf. I called you, remember. And I didn't even know what a phone was before yesterday! That's progress."

Natalie flashed me a grin, nodding.

Stevie nodded absently. "What we need is a way to hurt them. To destabilize them. But we don't have the financial capability to harm them, and any attempt would only turn them all against us in one coordinated attack. It's a numbers game."

I nodded, having already thought about it. "We need to besiege them. From what I've learned, they aren't killing enough people to justify the number of vampires allegedly in the city. That many vampires would need a constant supply of blood. It would be impossible to ignore that many bodies. And guess who owns the Blood Center of the Empire State?" I asked, remembering Nosh's comment from the auction.

Stevie nodded. "We already knew they owned the blood banks. They hold blood drives, claiming to deliver the blood overseas to those in need."

I grunted. "*Those in need* would be vampires, and I very much doubt they are delivering it to anyone other than the local vampires. If we weaken their blood supply, we weaken all of them. My hope is that it would draw the Necromancer out. The vampires would have to retaliate to maintain their credibility, and to avoid a bloodbath in the streets in a few days when they all begin to grow maddeningly hungry. We could pick them off as they hunt."

Stevie frowned. "They have multiple locations. I'm not sure that attacking one would do much more than annoy them, and if they get a whiff of werewolf, they will descend upon us like a tidal wave. We would all die. No question." Several of the werewolves growled angrily, but Stevie rounded on them with a snarl. "Hate it all you want, but it's a fact. Their numbers are vastly superior to our own."

They calmed, still furious and territorial, but obviously knowing that he was right.

I glanced at the map thoughtfully. Finally, I cleared my throat and spoke softly. "I took over Europe all by myself, infiltrating the highest echelons of power—kings and queens—to do my bidding. Tell me where the biggest blood bank is, and I will eradicate it. You can keep your paws clean. For now."

He stared at me incredulously. "We're talking dozens of vampires and armed human security at each site."

I smiled. "I can be very sneaky."

He thought about it, calculating the odds in his head. "You and your Shaman could do some serious damage, but you would still probably die."

I shook my head. "Just me. I'm suspected of murdering Nosh's parents. He is now under constant scrutiny and obviously can't be seen in my presence without the police arresting him."

"The vampires will instantly blame the werewolves for the attack," Stevie growled. "We would have to go into hiding while we waited out their reaction."

I nodded with a smile. "Guess who has an underground home that is connected to miles of tunnels reaching all over the city? You are all welcome to move in. All I ask is that you leave the current residents alone. I've...befriended many of them."

He arched an eyebrow at my last comment. "Befriended..."

I grinned, nodding. "I might have begun sowing my seed for a new family."

Benjamin coughed again and Natalie blushed.

Stevie ignored them, folding his arms. "You've been awake for less than a day, and you're already building an army?" he asked.

I shrugged. "I will need allies. It would make sense for me to cast my net wide. I wasn't sure how this conversation would go. I hadn't expected any direct assistance, but I *had* hoped for a truce before you met any of my new friends and grew concerned."

He climbed to his feet. "Stay here."

I nodded. "Do you have something for me to drink?"

Natalie nodded. "We have a dozen blood bags on hand in our medical storage, but they're for emergencies."

"Natalie," I said confidently, "by tomorrow, you'll have an entirely full inventory. In exchange for my taking down their blood center, I would hope that you could offer some of my friends a truck to transport their inventory to my underground tunnels. I would have no problem with you stocking up your own supply in the process. Neighbors share with neighbors, after all." She shared a long look with Stevie, having a silent discussion. "Whatever we don't steal, I will have to destroy so they can't get their hands on it," I added.

Stevie finally nodded. "Do it. Then join us for a quick chat, Natalie," he said, motioning for the rest of the werewolves to join him deeper into the warehouse and out of my hearing.

27

Natalie brought six blood bags at first, rationing me. Rather than picking a fight, I accepted the gift. I drank all six of the blood bags while Stevie spoke with his wolves in an adjacent room. Several wolves stayed in the room with me, guarding me, even though we all knew they didn't have the power to prevent me from doing whatever I wanted.

I finished off the last bag and let out a sigh. I could feel the blood coursing through my veins, but it wasn't nearly as refreshing as fresh blood. Like stale bread when you were traveling, it did the job, but it wasn't remotely enjoyable.

All that mattered was that I could feel my strength slowly returning. Not fast enough for my liking, but the only way to do it rapidly was to get blood drunk and hope I came off my high before I murdered hundreds—because I wouldn't know friend from enemy in that state. All that would matter was blood. A feral, savage version of my inner monster.

Thankfully, that internal demon hadn't reared its head since I'd awoken from my slumber.

I didn't dare risk letting that side of me out, so these slow, gradual meals were all I could hazard. I wondered if that would be enough for me to take down this Necromancer, let alone Dracula. Judging by how close my strength had been to Mina Harker's, I wasn't feeling too optimistic.

Stevie finally walked back into the room, his wolves behind him. He approached and stopped about five paces away, staring at me. "You're asking me to make a decision that could put my entire pack at risk, and I have no way to verify your story, or anything else you've told me. The only thing I can do is trust your actions."

I nodded. "Understood."

"If it was just me, I would be willing to take that chance. But my wolves need more. I could give them a command to follow my orders, and they would obey. But it would put tension in the pack—tension that could very well end poorly for everyone. On top of that, I would be commanding them to move underground. To go into hiding. Wolves don't like hiding or submitting in any form or fashion."

"You phrase that as if I am demanding it, when all I did was offer your pack refuge."

Stevie gave me a tired shrug. "It could be seen both ways. As I've told you, we've been betrayed in the past. And although your goals indirectly benefit us, you haven't done anything specifically for the wolves—to show them you value them."

I clenched my jaw. "I'm not here to parcel out gifts to children," I growled. "I refuse to *buy* your trust, because that is what you're really asking me to do, no matter how you phrase it."

He narrowed his eyes. "Be careful, Sorin. Be very careful with your words."

I took a calming breath, closing my eyes for a moment. Then I opened them and walked up to the table with the map. I glanced down at it, memorizing the intersection of a circled location with a star drawn beside it. I tapped it, looking over at Stevie again. "I'm hitting this blood bank tonight, Stevie, with or without you. However you choose to proceed is up to you. Just know that there are consequences to cowardice as well as bravery. If you choose to stand on the sidelines now, then my trust in you will diminish. Perhaps when you need help, I will choose to stand on the sidelines. To wait for you to give me a gift," I sneered.

"Are you threatening me?" he asked in a very cold tone.

"Not in the slightest. But I refuse to enable your delusion. Standing by my side will have consequences. Hanging me out to dry will have consequences. Attempting to believe otherwise will have consequences. All these decisions could put your pack in danger. There will be a new master vampire of New York City soon. I believe wolves and vampires can work together, but there is no room for cowards in the days to come. We're approaching the dawn of a new world. Don't get stuck watching the sunset."

Many of the wolves' anger had shifted to concern upon hearing my words.

I dusted off my hands and stood. "Be ready with those trucks. Or don't. I'm not asking you to fight. I hope you consider the fact that I just killed one of the top vampires in the city and that I'm about to kill another. Dracula will have a strong opinion about that. Then remember that I came to you for an alliance. I know I will never forget this meeting. Whether it will be a fond or bitter memory...that decision is up to you."

Then I was walking past him without a backwards glance.

I paused as I neared the door. Benjamin was guarding it, studying me thoughtfully. I turned back to Stevie. "Thank you for the blood. I'll repay you as I promised, no matter what you decide."

He nodded stiffly. "Get out of his way, Ben," Stevie growled in a cold tone.

Benjamin stepped to the side, lowering his eyes. There was no animosity in his posture. Perhaps there was concern, but that wasn't my problem.

I opened the door and came face-to-face with a familiar woman. I smiled in surprise, but also confusion. Then she dove at me, driving a wooden stake towards my chest as her lips curled back into a snarl.

The werewolves all shouted out in alarm, accompanying her scream.

28

I rolled back, managing to deflect the stake by letting it slice into my forearm. I hissed and my claws snapped out as I regained my feet, facing Victoria Helsing who was crouching warily.

"Stand down!" Stevie roared, and Benjamin leapt between us, his own arms furry and clawed since he had partially shifted. Stevie rounded on Victoria, storming over to us. "Sorin has Guestright! How *dare* you attack a guest!"

Victoria instantly straightened, sheathing her stake and holding her palms out towards me. She looked surprised to see me. That made two of us. "I'm sorry," she said, sounding genuine. "I...didn't see that it was *you*. It's fucking dark in here and I smelled vampire! Do you guys have any idea how many people are looking for this man?" she said loudly, craning her neck to address Stevie. "I sensed vampire in a place where no vampire would ever be stupid enough to go. I thought you might have been attacked." She glanced back at me. "Hey, Sorin."

I released my claws with a grunt. "Good Evening, Miss Helsing," I said, noticing how dark it had become outside. I eyed her drastically different clothes with distant, inappropriate interest. She wore tight leather pants and a jacket. She looked positively stunning. The way the leather accentuated her curves was almost enough to be considered a weapon in its own right.

Even when compared to the veritable armory of blades, stakes, and guns hanging from her belt and shoulder straps.

"I liked you better in a suit. You look like a biker," she said, smirking at my outfit.

I frowned. "I don't know what that means."

She cocked her head, her lips quivering in amusement. Then she noticed that I was utterly serious. "Um..."

Stevie sighed loudly. "Both of you get your asses over here. I think I have an idea. A compromise."

"There will be no compromise, Stevie," I growled. "I believe I made myself perfectly clear. Either write your name on the pages of history or watch your world burn and pass you by."

Victoria arched an eyebrow. "Well. That's ominous. What did I miss?" she asked cautiously.

Benjamin leaned closer, speaking loud enough for us all to hear. "Sorin is the world's first vampire. Dracula was his bitch until Sorin took a vacation to America and let Dracula take over his empire."

Victoria's eyes widened and her jaw dropped.

Natalie picked up the story next. "Dracula hunted Sorin down, poisoned him, and a Shaman put Sorin to sleep to save him from death. Supposed to wake up a few weeks later to kill Dracula, but someone hit the snooze button and five hundred years went by."

"Th-that's ridiculous—"

And then Stevie piped in, displaying the tight-knit nature of were-wolves working together as a pack. "The same Shaman who first put Sorin to sleep sacrificed his life to wake Sorin up yesterday, because his journal was stolen and they needed his help to get it back."

Victoria stared at me, trying to process it all. "They left you asleep for hundreds of years and only woke you up when they needed you again?" she asked softly. "That's fucked up."

I nodded stiffly. "There are a few more details that I'd rather not share until I get a better understanding of them myself. But yes. I tried to get the journal back. Mina Harker got in my way, so I killed her, but not before she passed on the journal to her boss, the Necromancer. I came to ask Stevie if he wanted in on my revenge plot, but it seems werewolves today are not the same as those I used to know. So, I was just leaving—"

"You were just getting your ass back over here, mothersucker," Stevie growled, cutting me off.

Feeling his steadily increasing pulse, I bit back a smile. Benjamin shot me a discreet thumbs up. I sensed a brief flicker of hope inside Stevie. Why had Victoria Helsing's arrival changed anything? I sighed and extended my elbow to Victoria. "My Lady? Unless you intend to poke me with your stake again..."

"So smooth," Benjamin murmured. Natalie elbowed him sharply, but she flashed me an approving smile as she did it.

Victoria blushed, shaking her head. "No. Sorry. Just a reflex. Thank you for not counterattacking me. I could tell you held back on purpose," she said, slipping her hand into the crook of my elbow.

I nodded. "The sudden spike in your heart rate told me it was an instinctive reaction. I waited to see what you would do when your rational mind kicked back in. But you stabbed me fair and square, vampire hunter," I said honestly, not wanting to injure her pride. "You're very fast."

I sensed her studying me sidelong. "You did all that while rolling away and bouncing to your feet like a freaking ninja?" she asked, sounding impressed. I nodded, internally dismissing the question about whatever a ninja was, as I led her back towards Stevie. He was staring down at the table with the map, and his excitement was growing, even though his outward demeanor remained calm. I had to keep my mind focused as I walked beside Victoria, squashing down the sudden desire to kiss her neck. I shuddered at the thought, wondering where it had come from. It wasn't lust but something much different. It was her scent waking up something inside me, something I couldn't quite explain.

Because the desire had been to *kiss*, not *bite*.

But it wasn't just that. I felt a strange...resonance from her. A stronger sensation than what I had sensed at the auction, but of the same vein.

I removed my arm from her hand more awkwardly than I intended and approached Stevie, keeping my composure reserved—as much for the matter at hand as well as to conceal my suddenly turbulent emotions.

"Tell the mothersucker what he's still doing here," I said, using the term he'd tossed out.

He smiled, turning to address his wolves. "Take a look at him. Feel him," he said, emphasizing the word. "Notice anything different from a few minutes ago?"

The wolves drew closer, sniffing and studying me as if they could see through me. One by one, the looks on their faces began to change. Several of them sneezed, backing away to study me from a distance.

I frowned. "Nothing has changed from ten minutes ago."

"Wrong," Stevie interrupted. "Exactly *one thing* changed." And his eyes shot to Victoria Helsing. Everyone turned to look at her, and it was her turn to grow instantly uncomfortable.

I cocked my head, trying to keep my face calm. Were they sensing whatever I had sensed about her? That sense of kinship? But Victoria wasn't a vampire. To me, it wasn't any sort of blood bond that I had felt, but more as if she had awoken something deep within me. Something that I had honestly only felt once, very, very long ago...

When I had gotten my first glimpse at the gods. Before they cursed me to live in the shadows and suck blood as an immortal monster.

But what did that have to do with Victoria? I didn't know anyone from my day with her last name, and it definitely wasn't a Greek or Italian name.

"I don't understand," she said. "I haven't done anything other than try to kill Sorin by accident." She winced guiltily, mouthing *sorry* again.

I smiled, waving off her concern. "I'm used to it."

"You're right and you're wrong," Stevie said, folding his beefy arms as he studied the two of us. "I can't explain it because I don't understand it, but something happened the moment you opened that door. Enough for me to propose a compromise, if Victoria is willing, of course."

I frowned thoughtfully, wondering where this was heading. "Why are none of you concerned about a vampire hunter showing up at your door? Are you already working together?" I asked. "It's obvious that you are all well acquainted."

"Vickie is aces," Benjamin explained. "Honorary pack member. She's done a lot of good for us. I called her to ask about the auction, but I didn't mention you at all on the phone. The fact that you two instantly knew each other—and that she apologized for trying to kill you—actually speaks to her high moral character. She tries to kill everyone, and *never* apologizes," he said, grinning brightly.

Victoria narrowed her eyes. "Sorin killed Mina Harker. I saw it. Is that what this is about? Good fucking riddance." She glanced at me thoughtfully. "But I didn't know you were a vampire."

I nodded. "Because of how you are looking at me right now," I said, shrugging. "I'm not like the ones you know. I want to kill Dracula and his ilk."

She studied me thoughtfully before giving me a faint nod. "I can get behind that. But I have questions."

"He doesn't like questions," Benjamin murmured. "After he kills the Necromancer, he said he would throw a question and answer party, though."

She arched an eyebrow and I nodded. "No time for chit-chat."

Stevie cleared his throat. "Victoria has a real hard-on for Dracula. He killed her father. She's an immortal huntress, blessed by Artemis, as legend has it—"

My legs gave out and I dropped to my rear as the room suddenly tilted violently. Victoria was kneeling before me with a concerned look on her face as she patted my cheeks. "Sorin? Are you okay?" I nodded numbly, trying to shake off the sudden anxiety creeping through my veins. Artemis. Victoria had been blessed by Artemis.

"Just hungry," I lied. "I'm still regaining my strength."

"Get the rest of the blood!" Stevie bellowed, and I heard someone rushing to obey. Victoria helped me climb back to my feet even though I didn't need it. She studied me intently, a faint sense of doubt hidden in her eyes. "You don't need to lie, Sorin," she breathed—so softly that I barely heard it, even with my enhanced senses. "Whatever just happened, you can trust me. I saw what you did to Mina Harker, and that speaks louder than any words. I'm here if you need to talk to anyone. About *Artemis*," she added in an even softer tone. She smirked at my faint twitch, my reaction proving her point. Then she stepped back and guided me to a nearby chair. Everyone had been so preoccupied with Stevie's bellowing for a chair and more blood that they had missed her whispers.

Was that what I had felt from her? Mutual ties to Artemis, the Greek Goddess of the Hunt? But Artemis had *cursed* me, not given me a *gift*. Whatever it was, I wasn't about to entertain it in a room full of werewolves.

"Thank you," I said, sitting down. "It comes and goes. Not having eaten anything for five hundred years takes a toll."

Victoria shook her head, still trying to process my story.

Natalie approached with an armful of blood bags and dumped them on the table beside me. Then she knelt between my knees and held up a bag, placing her hand on my thigh as she watched me with her sharp green eyes, checking to make sure I was alright.

Her sleeves had bunched up, and my eyes instinctively latched onto the thin flesh at the top of her forearm, opposite her elbow. The thick vein beckoned, and my fangs popped out.

*Yes...*my inner demon cooed. *Fresh off the teat...*

I blinked, momentarily shaken. To hear that inner voice in my mind again was alarming. I hadn't heard it since waking up from my slumber. It also meant that I was hungrier than I'd thought.

I stiffly took the bag from Natalie's hand, averting my eyes from her arm and using all my mental strength to turn my back on my inner demon. For him to be rearing his head was a bad sign. He only came out when I was markedly hungry. And if I entertained him, I ran the risk of not being able to turn him off. Had he remained dormant due to my extreme blood withdrawal?

I say *him* like he was a separate being inhabiting my body and mind, but that wasn't the case. He was my conscience. The instinctive part of myself that wanted only to *take*. When I had first become a vampire, wanting nothing more than to make the world pay for my new affliction, I had been a close companion to that new part of myself. I hadn't known any better. Mountains of bodies and armies of angry villagers with pitchforks and torches had ultimately shown me the error of my ways, and I had fled Greece.

I had tried to flee that part of myself, as a matter of fact. It had only been when I found a cave out in the wilderness, as far from mankind as I could possibly find, that I had managed to come to terms with it. The inner demon, as I had taken to calling him, wasn't trying to harm me— he just had conflicting opinions about what I needed.

Much like Victoria had instinctively attacked me when sensing a vampire in the doorway. Her own instincts—or inner demon—had commanded her to end the threat to save her werewolf friends. When her rational mind kicked back in, she realized that I wasn't the threat she'd feared.

It had taken me more than a year to find a healthy balance—to know how much blood I needed to control my urges, maintain my strength, and survive without becoming a mindless killer.

And that was when I had first met Lucian and Dracula.

A traveling hunter named Dracula had encountered Lucian in a tavern, telling him a tale about a crazed monster terrorizing a village, and that he was hunting the beast down. Lucian, having nothing better to do, and knowing that the human hunter would need all the help he could get against such a beast, had agreed to accompany him.

Dracula hadn't known Lucian was a werewolf.

The two strangers soon found me and chose to observe their prey from a safe distance. I'd sensed Lucian's powerful heartbeat out in the mountains and had assumed it was some neighboring beast assessing the new occupant of the cave. Dracula, being a mere human, hadn't been powerful enough for me to sense. Since the werewolf's heartbeat remained a safe distance away, I let him be, not knowing what he was, but content to maintain my solitude.

His urgency to kill me had quickly faded upon seeing me feast only on animal blood—and only enough to survive. Nothing like the bloodsucking monster everyone had feared. When he had watched me feast on and then bury the corpse of an elk, he had been so baffled that he finally chose to approach my cave with Dracula, demanding to know what I was doing here and why the villagers wanted to hunt me down.

"Because I was a monster," I had admitted. "I wasn't in control of myself, *and it took a mountain of mistakes to realize it. So, I came out here where I couldn't hurt anyone."*

"Why do you avoid sunlight?" Lucian had asked.

"It burns. I was cursed by the gods."

Lucian had pursed his lips, nodding empathetically. "I too suffer a curse," he'd admitted. And before either of us could blink, he had simply...changed. One moment he was a large, imposing man, and the next he was a giant black wolf of the likes I had never seen before. His shredded clothes scattered around us, falling into the fire and making it pop and hiss.

Dracula had shouted, tripping over himself as he danced back a step, his hand settling on the hilt of his sword as he realized he faced two beasts rather than one. I had stared at the wolf, awed by its lethal beauty. That the man Lucian could learn to control such a monster living inside of him was remarkable. It gave me cause for hope. Then Lucian had simply changed back into a man, as naked as the day was long.

"Do you intend to live up here forever? All alone? Just you and your monster?" he had asked.

"I do not know. I've come to terms with my curse and no longer fear losing control," I had admitted, staring into his eyes.

"Are you willing to try to be a man?" Lucian had replied, staring deeply into my eyes. "To take control of your demon rather than letting it control your life? I will be there to hold you accountable."

"I will also stay by your side, Sorin Ambrogio," Dracula had agreed. "I will be your conscience. I see good in you."

I had stared into the flames of my campfire, considering the question with all the seriousness it required. "Yes. I think I would like to be a man."

And that decision had ultimately doomed the world.

Neither of us had realized that the real monster in our midst had been the only human at the fire that night—Dracula.

The memory faded, having taken only a moment in real time. I peeled my eyes away from Natalie, who was still kneeling before me. I drew strength from my old friend's confidence in me. It was one of the hardest things I'd had to do since waking from my slumber.

Natalie suddenly gripped my chin, turning me back to her. She let out a nervous breath and stared into my eyes, her jaw-length blonde hair framing her face like wings. "Do you swear you mean us no ill will?

That you truly want to end Dracula and his scourge?" she whispered softly, licking her lips.

"I do," I breathed, trying to ignore the heat from her fingertips.

"I can tell you want to drink from me," she whispered. "Will it harm me?"

"It will not," I rasped. "But it is not necessary—"

Stevie growled aggressively. "Absolutely not—"

"It is *my* blood, alpha," she snapped aggressively, silencing him with her vehemence. "I obey you unquestioningly, but this man might be our best chance at defeating them once and for all. I'm willing to do what I can to help." Stevie growled unhappily but relented. She turned back to me, smiling gently. "I take it that fresh blood is better?" she asked.

I nodded, eyeing one of the bags, considering how much it held. "Those taste stale. Six of them is like drinking one bag's worth from a living person. And nowhere *near* as powerful as freely given blood."

"How much would you need?"

"I can stop myself long before you suffer any harm. You might feel weak and euphoric for a few hours, but nothing that will prevent you from going about your regular day. One bag's worth would do wonders. Especially if I consume those after," I said, eyeing the bags on the table.

She nodded. "Then you have my permission, Sorin." She tucked her hair behind her ear and arched her neck as she turned her back to me. "This is how it's done in the stories, right?"

I shuddered, my mouth immediately salivating with the venom that would first replace her pain with euphoria and then heal the wound once I finished. I nodded stiffly, even though she couldn't see me. I stared down at her delicate neck, my stomach fluttering with anticipation. "Thank you," I whispered, barely able to form the sentence. The warehouse was deadly silent as I leaned down.

I placed my hands on her shoulders and she visibly relaxed. "I hope you enjoy the taste of the twenty-first century, Sorin," she said, sounding amused.

Her jovial demeanor made me smile. "It will be the sweetest thing I've ever tasted," I told her. And it was partly true. Freely given blood was significantly sweeter than stolen blood. Murdering or enthralling a victim to comply wasn't even remotely the same as freely given blood. Some form of magical bond between predator and prey—a sense of trust in the most intimate of acts. "You won't feel a thing, Natalie," I purred, drawing closer to the soft, berry-scented skin of her neck.

Before anyone could interfere, I sank my fangs into her neck. Electricity rocked through us as I lapped up her blood, inhaling the heady aroma of her powerful werewolf essence and the sweet, spicy smell of cinnamon in her hair. My eyes rolled back in my head, and I heard her moan in pleasure. My mouth tingled, and time slowed as we bonded together in a way I hadn't experienced in a very long time. Not since Bubble had permitted me to do the same—once, when we had conceived our son—and it had been a long time before I first met Bubble. I'd left my harem of willing blood slaves behind in Europe.

But they had been mortal, nothing like a willing, trusting werewolf.

Power rocked through me, and I began to drink deeper, squeezing her shoulders possessively, protecting this sweet, sweet prize.

"Ohmygod..." Natalie moaned, pressing every inch of her body into mine as she panted in delirious ecstasy. Her hips began to rock faster and faster and her hands suddenly gripped both of my ankles, squeezing desperately. "*Please don't stop, don't stop, don't stop...*" she begged, whimpering as her grip on my ankles tightened enough to give me pleasurable pain, urging me on. "*YES!*" she screamed loud enough for everyone to jump back a step.

And her body suddenly stiffened, every muscle clenching for the span of a single moment as she climaxed with a full-body orgasm. She gasped several times, clutching tightly to my ankles as if it was the only thing anchoring her to reality as her body continued to flinch with echoing tremors of pleasure. Her back was pressed so tightly to my inner thighs that we may as well have been the same person. I waited a few moments before I released her from my bite and licked at the wound, sealing it. She continued to shudder as I held her close, her body rippling with smaller, yet no less sensational, orgasms. I'd completely forgotten about that aspect. It could often happen with mortals, too, but it *always* happened with werewolves. Something about our magic bonding together.

I leaned down and kissed the back of her head. "The sweetest thing

I've ever tasted, Natalie," I whispered. And I meant it. It had been even sweeter than Bubble, my wife. I wasn't sure if that was because my body was so malnourished or if it was something specific about Natalie.

She trembled, whimpering since she was still unable to speak. I realized that I suddenly had an embarrassment of my own to conceal. I kept her pressed against me, leaning down to breathe a whisper directly into her ear, soft enough so no one else could hear. "Would you mind staying there for a few minutes? I'm not decent," I breathed, feeling my cheeks redden.

"Sorin," she purred dreamily, scooting even closer to me and caressing my calves with her hands in a subconscious, post-coitus gesture. "You can do whatever the living fuck you want to me," she laughed huskily. "Sweet motherfucking god. I haven't felt anything like that in my entire life. You just became my new best friend with benefits." She laid her cheek on my thigh, hugging my leg possessively.

"*Friends* don't know the way you *taste*," I murmured.

Her hand clenched my leg tighter and she trembled in pleasure. "And there's lucky number seven," she purred. "It's so nice to meet you."

I chuckled, brushing the hair back from her ear.

I finally lifted my gaze to see Victoria staring at me in disbelief. Several of the werewolves were eyeing each other meaningfully, fishing to see if anyone else wanted to go find some privacy for a little coitus of their own.

Stevie was struggling to light a cigar, staring at us with wide eyes. It took him a few tries because his hand was shaking.

Benjamin cleared his throat. I glanced over at him, arching an eyebrow. "Um. Do you need any more blood?" he asked, shifting uneasily from foot-to-foot. "No homo or anything."

Natalie shot him a menacing growl, squeezing my calf possessively.

Victoria burst out laughing, but I thought I caught a brief flicker of jealousy in her eyes. Interesting...

"What is homo?" I asked curiously.

They laughed harder.

29

Stevie cleared his throat and banged a fist against the table, drawing every eye. "Let's get back to business, unless you two need us to leave for a few hours," he said dryly, glaring at Natalie. "Unless you are now under his thrall."

I shook my head firmly. "She is her own woman. I did *not* enthrall her."

Natalie shook her head slowly, lowering her eyes. "Oh, don't worry, Stevie. This is me being independently dependent. I'm sure I can talk to Sorin at a later time," she said with a smile.

Stevie rolled his eyes before taking a puff of his cigar and stabbing a thick finger down onto the table again. "You would like our help for your raid."

"I would like your trust," I clarified, "while I risk my life for a mutually beneficial operation."

"Oh, he's *good*," Benjamin murmured, leaning closer to Victoria.

She elbowed him sharply, eliciting a grunt before she strolled up to the table to study the map. I watched as her face grew pale. "You're kidding me."

I waited until she lifted her gaze to stare at me before shaking my head. "Best way to weaken them. Cut off their blood supply and watch them starve or grow desperate."

I had to struggle to focus against the buzzing sensations coursing through my body as Natalie's blood empowered me—making me feel stronger than I had since waking from my slumber.

"Growing desperate would mean a hundred or more vampires getting hungry at exactly the same time. In New York City," Victoria said, frowning.

I nodded. "Unfortunately. Which is why I asked the werewolves to step up and be ready to catch them in the act and eliminate them. The vampires will break up into smaller factions, making them vulnerable, while they selfishly hunt for their own food. In war, there are risks. The consequences for doing nothing are to let them run amok and eventually do it anyway."

She pursed her lips, nodding slowly. She knew we were both right. "Unfortunately, I think he's right. How many wolves could you call to help?" she asked Stevie.

He shook his head. "That remains to be seen. If he's successful, I will call all of them. From outside the city if I must. If he fails…"

Victoria narrowed her eyes at him. "Come back with your shield or on it," she said. I blinked, surprised to hear a reference I knew—the Spartan Goodbye, a phrase often told to their soldiers before battle. Be successful or die trying.

I leaned forward, noticing that I was decent again. "This was my idea, Victoria. Stevie deserves no judgment on the matter. I want to hear about his so-called compromise. Because if it is useless, I have work to do."

"You and your fledgling vampires," Stevie murmured, not sounding best pleased. Victoria shot me a sharp glance and the alpha nodded. "Sorin has begun turning the residents of New York's underground community into vampires."

"I can assure you that I wouldn't risk turning anyone with questionable morality or addictions. And I can easily enthrall any of them since I personally turned them. In that event, they wouldn't be able to do anything I didn't deem acceptable, and I'm an excellent judge of right and wrong. Besides, I only offered the opportunity to those who turned down my cocaine or jewelry."

Every single head turned to gawk at me, but Benjamin spoke up first. "Cocaine?! You're a drug dealer?" he asked, stunned.

I frowned. "I was charitable and gave it away for free, so I don't believe you could call me a dealer of any sort. And I didn't know what it was, at first. I just saw that it was valuable."

"How in the *hell* did you get cocaine on your first day in NYC?"

I shrugged. "I acquired a backpack of cash and cocaine packets when I was out getting food this morning."

"Jesus. How much cocaine are we talking about? Do we need to be worried about the cops?" Benjamin asked, glancing back at the door nervously.

"There were at least thirty little bags," I said, trying to think back. "The policeman told me how valuable it was, so I used it to meet my neighbors."

"The *policeman*?" Stevie sputtered.

Benjamin stared at me in awe. "You're my new favorite person."

Stevie shot him a furious glare and Benjamin wilted. "Who the hell left you unsupervised and why?" the alpha demanded. Then he held up a hand and closed his eyes. "That's it. You need a chaperone. My plan is no longer a request but a *requirement*. And for the record, you are a *terrible* judge of right and wrong," he added in a humorless tone.

I frowned, feeling my shoulders tense at his tone. "I don't do well with orders or judgments, Stevie. I do, however, work quite well with mutual respect and constructive debates."

He leaned forward, biting the cigar between his teeth. "You just told us how you were an excellent judge of character, and then proceeded to tell us that you were handing out cocaine in the underground. That you killed a drug dealer and a cop. I fail to see why this needs to be explained as a *constructive debate*."

"I didn't kill the policeman," I muttered. "I just enthralled him. He doesn't even remember meeting me," I said, folding my arms.

Stevie puffed furiously at his cigar, shrouding him in a fog of smoke. "Because brainwashing a policeman is so much better."

"He lived," I said stubbornly.

Victoria slapped her palms on the table. "Pipe the fuck down and get on with it. What is your proposal, Stevie?" she demanded, enunciating the word.

He turned towards her with a dark grin. "That you team up with the Wolf of Wall Street on his adventure tonight. Be my eyes and ears, and make sure he's not a pawn for the vampires running this city. Convince the pack that he's on our side rather than his own side."

She blinked, looking like she was momentarily at a loss for words. "You think he will betray you?" she finally asked, her voice utterly calm. "The man who just killed Mina Harker?"

Stevie sighed, waving a hand. "That came out wrong. What I meant to say was that I have to think about the pack, first. If he was trying to set us up, it would literally mean the end for us because the vampires will immediately retaliate, assuming the raid was done by us."

Her anger cooled, her face growing somber. "Well, that is a fair point."

"I offered to move them into the underground with my fledgling vampires. They will be pretty worthless for a few more days as they get the hang of their new diet." Sensing the sudden tension in Stevie's shoulders, I held up a hand, forestalling him. "Don't worry. They are incapable of killing anyone. They are all heavily enthralled at the moment, but they will need blood in a few days. Like the bags of it that I'm about to steal. All I need from you are vehicles to transport it back underground."

Victoria nodded absently, processing my words, but I could tell her mind was on more immediate concerns. "If you're asking whether I'm willing to go vampire hunting, the answer is yes, but we'll have to be careful about it. I'm betting they'll have at least two dozen vampires on site." She shot me a quick look, gauging my concern. I shrugged with an easy smile.

She arched an eyebrow at my confidence. Then she folded her arms. "You're really the father of vampires, above Dracula, and you can't think of any other way to get him out in the open?"

I shook my head. "He was always a sneaky little shit, but he followed my rules—even when he didn't have to—but I think the power got to him as the decades stretched on. He began to subtly indoctrinate my vampires without my knowledge. He became my voice. To be fair, I was growing tired of the game, and he must have sensed it. It became obvious that there was a coup forming and that I could either get out of the way or wait to be executed. No matter how strong I was, I was vastly outnumbered. So, I came here to the Americas with Lucian and a warlock named Nero. Gave Dracula my crown and left with a satchel of gold and treasure buried all over Europe in case I needed to return."

Victoria frowned. "How were they able to rise against you if you were their Master?"

I grimaced. "I believe Dracula was feeding them his blood. If it doesn't outright kill them, it can slowly degrade a bond between a Master and said vampire. That's the only explanation I can think of. It's not like there was a handbook on vampirism." I glanced at the room. "No offense, but the werewolves are also a far cry from those I knew in my past. History changes us all."

Stevie bristled, but didn't comment. He knew I was right.

Victoria finally sighed. "Fine. But why now? What is so important about this journal? You show up, the journal goes up for auction, and now we're on the brink of war. What the hell is this thing?"

I shrugged. "I really wish I knew. The only thing I can say is that it chronicles my time in the Americas with Deganawida and his tribe, and that Deganawida wrote down powerful Shamanic spells. I'm not sure if the vampires are after those spells or information about me. My guess is a bit of both."

Which was true, but I was still leery about mentioning the fact that I had conceived a child and that Dracula might want to duplicate the process.

Not for the first time, I wondered exactly what the hell else Deganawida had written down in that cursed journal. The journal I had told him not to write in the first place.

"And Nosh Griffin can't be seen with you for obvious reasons," Victoria said, scratching at her jaw. "Is that why he isn't here right now? Because his magic was impressive at the auction."

I frowned, turning to Stevie. "He was supposed to call you to set up a meeting for us tonight. I grew restless so called you early. You haven't heard from him?" I asked, glancing towards the door. "He said he would return to my hideout after sunset. He would have called me the moment he saw I wasn't there. But you have my phone."

Stevie snapped his fingers. "Get his phone, Benjamin." Then he reached into his pocket and checked his own phone. "Nothing," he said, frowning warily.

Benjamin trotted back and handed me my phone. I opened it up to see an alert that said I had a missed text, whatever that was. I pressed a button to try and find the section that showed my calls, and a short message popped up on the screen.

I've been arrested. Stay hidden. Vamps own the cops. Phones no longer secure.

Nosh had sent it ten minutes ago. I stared at the screen in silence, reading it several times. Then I snapped it in half, tossing the pieces in a nearby trashcan. "The cops have the Shaman, and he thinks they're in league with the vampires," I growled, clenching my fists. The one person who had stood by me when I first woke up. The only tie I had left to Deganawida. The only person who could verify that I hadn't killed his parents. I locked eyes with Victoria. "I think I'm ready to go vampire hunting."

She nodded calmly, but I could sense the rage deep inside of her. She was funneling it into action. Into a plan. "Right." She turned to Stevie. "I've always found that the best way to prove loyalty was to collect some enemy heads. How many vampire heads will it take to prove his claims to your pack?" she asked without flinching. "Beyond a shadow of a doubt."

Stevie considered her question, a faint smile on his bearded face. "A dozen. That will prove they weren't murders of opportunity but that he went out of his way to hunt them down. No one will be able to dismiss that level of resolve. But let me state for the record that if it was up to me, the werewolves would already march by your side. This is simply a show of faith to remove all doubt, because we have all been deceived by vampires. Convincing them that not only are you the first vampire ever —which will be a hard sell—but that you want to overthrow your fellows...I don't want to leave any room for doubt. A dozen heads for our partnership. Hell, I'll put them on display in our new home," he muttered darkly. "Because you're not just asking us to pick a fight. You're asking us to start a world war on American soil. Every vampire answers to Dracula, so this could very likely affect werewolves in Europe, too. And I don't speak for them. A dozen heads will give them something to think about—both in backing up your wild claims and showing them that you are committed."

I shrugged unconcernedly, knowing that I was going to eradicate every vampire in the building anyway. "I already took down four at the auction. Do those count?"

"No," Stevie said firmly. "It needs to be twelve at one go. Also, you killed Ralph."

Benjamin cheered. "Finally! That guy was a prick." At least a dozen wolves nodded their agreement without any hesitation. "And Sorin just gave Natalie about four toe-curling orgasms," Benjamin piped up defensively. "That's gotta count for something."

"Oh, it should *definitely* count," Natalie purred. "And I had *seven* toe-curling orgasms, thank you very much," she reminded us proudly.

"I like you, Benjamin," I said, laughing suddenly. His comment had been just what the situation needed. A little levity. I turned back to Stevie, letting my laughter fade to address his statement. "I did ask him to stand down. I asked for a discussion and he attacked. You *let* him attack."

Stevie's face grew grim as the other wolves turned to look at him, frowning thoughtfully. So, he hadn't shared the specifics. But he also hadn't tried turning his wolves against me for killing Ralph. He was being very careful for some reason. Nothing like Lucian would have been.

"I stand by your actions, Sorin, but perception is all that matters. Especially to wolves overseas. They will only be reading facts, having to make a decision without meeting you in person."

I grunted, knowing all too well the prerogatives of kings. They had rules to follow. Steps in a carefully choreographed dance that must be acted out without stumbling. "So be it."

"And you have to do this without being seen. No witnesses or you will start an outright war. I want this Necromancer and his cronies to have no idea that they were even hit until well after the fact. And if he has the police in his pocket, you can't risk drawing their attention." I nodded, having already intended as much. Victoria was watching me curiously, not seeming remotely concerned. Stevie put out his cigar and let out a thick plume of smoke. His eyes glittered through the cloud. "If you really are the world's first vampire, show us how good you are."

"I'm going to get the Shaman back when I finish this errand. Whether it starts a war or not."

Stevie studied me for about five seconds before he gave me a firm, approving nod. "Bring me the twelve heads and maybe I'll help you."

I nodded. "We hit the blood bank. Tonight."

"What if this Necromancer is there?"

"I hope he is," I growled. "Because I'm collecting his head after I save Nosh."

"Are you recovered enough to face him?" Victoria asked. "If you waste all your energy collecting heads, the Necromancer could show up and take you down when you're exhausted.

I thought about it and shrugged. "Only one way to find out, but I can't risk drinking more blood right now. Drinking too much too quickly can send me into a bloodlust. I won't know friend from foe— just my hunger. So, regaining my full powers will take time. All I can do is hope that—even weakened—I am more than a match for my descendants. I'll be sure to take a few sips while we work," I added, grimacing. "Even though vampire blood tastes foul to me, it still counts as a form of nourishment."

She nodded warily. "There could be a lot of vampires there, not counting any mortals unknowingly working for them. Finding twelve should be easy. It's the getting back out that concerns me."

"Getting out will be easy," I said firmly. "Because we're not letting any of them survive."

She stared at me, blinking slowly. "And if there are thirty vampires?"

"Then I will collect thirty heads," I growled. "Betrayal has a price."

She finally nodded, as if her entire line of questioning had been asked for the sole purpose of making sure that I was a competent partner and that I wouldn't drag her down. "I'm going to need some more weapons," she said.

"We move in silence. No guns."

Stevie clapped his hands. "I'll keep an eye on the Museum of Natural History. Not sure if I'll notice anything since they're probably in the lower levels, but if I do, I'll have someone waiting within range of the blood bank to radio you two."

I frowned, cocking my head. "Radio?"

Benjamin walked over with a box and handed me a small rubber device. "Put it in your ear. You can talk to each other." He helped put it in my ear and showed me how to tap it to talk.

"Hey, handsome," Victoria's voice slithered directly into my ear canal in a breathy whisper.

I jumped straight to my feet—startling Natalie—and rounded on Victoria. She burst out laughing, lowering her hand from her ear. Then she turned to Benjamin. "You upgraded. These are definitely military issue."

"Fell off a truck," he said, smirking suspiciously.

"It's a phone without a phone," I said, shaking my head.

Benjamin shook his head. "No. Whichever earbuds are on this channel can communicate together, but it's not like you can make a call outside of that. Which is why Stevie will have someone close by on your channel. He sees something strange at the Museum, he will call them on their phone. They'll immediately tell you on the earbud."

I nodded, getting the main gist of it. "If I had something like this back in my day, I would have truly taken over the world." I mused. "This is incredible."

Benjamin nodded soberly. "Good chances that the vampires and guards will have them as well, but on a different secure channel. If you take your time killing them, or kill one too noisily, they could all be instantly alerted of your presence."

Victoria nodded. "I'll pick up one of their earbuds so I can hear what they're talking about. That way we know if they start getting suspicious about why some of their cohorts aren't answering their comms." Seeing the frown on my face, she tapped her earbud. "Radios, comms. Same thing."

I nodded, feigning confidence. "Got it."

"No planning and no preparation. This is going to be fun," she said, smiling.

"I've often favored instincts above plans. Once I get close, I'll be able to sense how many enemies are nearby so I can guide us."

Victoria frowned. "They won't be able to sense you?"

I shook my head. "I know how to conceal myself, much like I did at the auction. Even Mina didn't recognize me until it was too late, and I'm doubting these vampires are stronger than her."

She glanced down at my chest with a surprised look on her face. Then she sighed, shaking her head. I looked to see that my crucifix necklace had fallen free. I smiled, shrugging.

"Wear it. We could use the backup," she said, her face hardening much like I had seen soldiers do before a war.

I smiled. "This is something I remember how to do very well."

30

We crouched in a darkened alley across the street from the rear of the blood bank. A steady drizzle blanketed the street, and the cloudy sky rumbled ominously, threatening thunder and lightning. Luckily, there were limited lampposts in the immediate area, which would make our approach easier. The building was a large, three-story, brick warehouse that looked antiquated compared to its sleeker neighboring buildings. The third-floor featured windows along its entire perimeter, and we faced a large gate that opened to a loading dock—as Victoria had called it—that was butted up against the rear of the building. A tall brick wall surrounded the courtyard.

Several figures patrolled the courtyard, loading up a truck that was backed up against the building. I would have pegged it more as a prison than a blood bank. I counted four armed guards on the roof, all carrying long guns—rifles—that Victoria warned me were accurate at extremely long distances. They surveyed the property from their lofty perches, but I was hoping that the rain and darkened streets would mask our initial approach.

Victoria had some sort of scope in her hand and was scanning the building from left to right. I frowned, wondering what she was looking for since we had a clear view of the loading bay.

She held it out to me, and I pressed it up to my eyes. I gasped, almost dropping them as my field of vision drastically changed. The majority of the landscape became darker, colder colors of blues and purples, but flares of warm reds and oranges indicated the armed guards on the roof and those in the courtyard.

There were many more than I had seen with my eyes.

"The infrared binoculars are picking up on their body heat," Victoria murmured. "The walls are too thick to get a reading inside the building, but can you see the warmer colors in the loading bay?" she asked, pointing at the rear of the building.

I nodded, amazed at the rainbow of colors. "It's like a visual depiction of me picking up on their heartbeats—except this works from farther away."

She nodded, accepting the binoculars back. We studied the building in silence, gauging the length of each guard's rotation. I studied the streets, noticing only a single person on the sidewalk. He was huddled up under a blanket, hiding from the rain. A wheeled cart covered in blankets and dozens of plastic bags stood beside him.

"Homeless," Victoria murmured, noticing my attention.

I grunted noncommittally.

"What really happened earlier? When Stevie mentioned Artemis," she asked.

I continued studying the building, wondering how much I should tell her. Finally, I let out a sigh. "She's the one who cursed me with vampirism. Well, one of them. It was a joint effort, really."

Her eyes widened incredulously. After a few moments of utter silence, she spoke. "You're being serious..." she said, trailing off.

I nodded. "Let's get through this and I'll tell you all about it. Stevie's comment caught me off guard—to hear that she granted your ancestor a blessing when she granted me a curse. That she literally granted you immortality so that you could hunt down my kind—when I only exist *because* of her curse. Using your bloodline to correct a mistake she made."

Victoria considered my words in silence. "I understand a little of what you're going through," she said. "Dracula killed my father, Van Helsing. He was trying to save Mina Harker from his clutches back when she was still human, but he failed. I was just a little girl, but I saw it all happen. My father didn't hide anything from me, so I always knew I would one day become a vampire hunter. That moment sealed the deal, though."

I studied her in silence. Then I placed my hand atop hers. "I didn't know."

She nodded, wiping at her nose. "Sorry. It's just...I never thought there was anyone above Dracula. I just thought all vampires were the enemy. To find out that he wasn't actually the first vampire, and that you want to kill him even more than I do. It's...a lot to process."

I nodded, squeezing her hand. "When did this happen?"

"1890. About one hundred and thirty years ago. Almost." I arched an eyebrow, caught off guard. She batted her eyelashes playfully. "I told you I understood what you're going through. I'm older than I look."

I leaned back, shaking my head. "I had no idea. So, you've lived through all these changes?" I said. "Electricity, cars..."

She nodded. "Yes. But that was over decades. You're not even a day old."

I chuckled. "I'm just a babe," I agreed.

"Are our shared ties to Artemis why I can feel something between us? Some sort of bond?"

I looked over at her sharply. "You can?" I asked, surprised to hear she'd felt anything similar. I'd thought it was just me, but it made sense. Our powers came from the same source.

She nodded, looking slightly embarrassed. "I thought it was more... personal," she said, struggling for the proper word. Then, she continued on in a rush. "Because I felt a little jealous when you drank from Natalie. Well, not just a little. A lot."

I glanced over at her to find her blushing, lowering her eyes. I smiled. "I'll admit that I had similar hopes," I said, wanting to be honest after her confession. Because a very warm sensation suddenly ran through my body at her words. Nothing magical, but something deeply personal.

Water dripped from her chin as she smiled, staring down at the ground. "Oh. Good. Because I felt it back when you were masking your powers, too. It changed when I saw you after you killed Mina, though. They felt like different sensations to me."

I gently lifted my hand and touched her cheek. "Perhaps it is both..."

We broke apart, crouching low as a van suddenly pulled up to the gates. "New delivery," Victoria murmured. "We'll have to wait until they settle down. It looks like that van on the right is leaving soon."

I sighed. She was right. It would be too risky to attempt our incursion right now.

"Looks like we have time for a story," she said, smiling hopefully.

I closed my eyes, leaning back against the alley wall. "It's not a pleasant story," I said.

"It's better than thinking that Dracula was the first vampire."

I nodded. "Perhaps." I took a deep breath. It would feel nice to tell it to someone, and Victoria did have a unique perspective. She was also immortal and had been blessed by the gods—at least indirectly. Trying to tell Nosh my story wouldn't have been nearly as interesting. I turned to her and sighed at the hopeful look on her face. "I will tell you some of it," I finally said.

She nodded eagerly, pressing up beside me against the wall. "Ready."

"I grew up as an orphan on the streets. It was a difficult, unforgiving life. As a young man, I heard about the Oracle of Delphi, how the Sun God, Apollo, spoke prophecies through her. I traveled far to see if this Oracle could tell me my fate. But when she finally addressed me, she only had three things to say: *the curse, the moon, the blood will run.*"

I shifted in my seat, feeling uneasy about telling the story but forcing myself to continue.

"I struggled with my prophecy, obviously distraught. On my way back to the Oracle the next morning, I ran into a beautiful maiden of the temple named Selene, who just so happened to be the Oracle's sister. Long story short, we fell in love, and planned to leave Delphi at sunrise to start a new life together." I clenched my teeth for a moment, taking a calming breath. "Apollo punished me for trying to take his maiden away. He cursed me so that sunlight would burn my skin, preventing me from meeting Selene the following morning."

Victoria blanched, shaking her head. "That's terrible."

I shook my head. "It gets worse," I promised her. "I went to a nearby cave that led to Hades, God of the Underworld, begging for his help. He gave me a wager. If I could steal Artemis' magical silver bow, Hades would grant Selene and me protection from Apollo in the Underworld. But I had to leave my soul with Hades until I succeeded, forfeiting it if I failed."

Victoria was staring at me, riveted by the tale. "You gambled your soul for a chance at love?"

I nodded. "With no other way to approach Selene—for fear of Apollo punishing her—I wrote her notes, leaving them in our meeting place for her to later read. I wrote her poems. For forty-five days. I managed to finally steal Artemis' silver bow through trickery and deceit, but she found me before I could reach Hades' cave—cursed me so that silver burned my skin, forcing me to drop the bow.

"Artemis demanded an explanation, so I told her everything. That her brother, Apollo, had cursed me from sunlight, forcing me to make a deal with Hades to steal her bow. She took pity upon me after learning that I had done it all for love. For Selene. She made me a deal, granting me the powers of a great hunter, with the speed and strength of a god, immortality, and fangs to hunt. But Selene and I had to agree to worship only her, and none of the other gods, especially not her brother, Apollo. But Artemis was a virgin goddess, which meant Selene would have to remain a virgin, and that I could never kiss or touch her, but we could love each other from a distance. Selene agreed and we spent many years together..."

I trailed off, glancing up at the moon as it shifted into view from a momentary break in the clouds. "What happened to her?" Victoria asked, and I realized her eyes were glistening faintly.

"I was immortal," I whispered, glancing back down as the moon slunk back behind the clouds. "Selene was not. She began to age, and I knew I had sold my soul to Hades so I would never see her again. I begged for Artemis to make her immortal—honoring us for our years of worship to her. Artemis took pity on me, allowing me to touch

Selene one time. That if I bit her neck, she would see to it that we could stay together forever."

Victoria gasped. "To make her a vampire?"

I shook my head. "I didn't know anything about that yet. I was young and foolish," I said dryly. I took another breath, gathering my thoughts as I decided how best to end the story. "Selene begged me to bite her. I finally did, drinking her blood, eager to spend the rest of my days with her. But her body did not rise. Instead, a great light zipped up into the sky, making the moon glow brighter. Artemis had deceived me. Selene became Goddess of the Moonlight. Every night for my long, immortal life, Selene is always by my side, touching me with her moonbeams, but never more."

The alley was dead silent as Victoria stared up at the sky, tears leaking down her cheeks. "Thank you for sharing that with me, Sorin. I...had no idea the gods could be so cruel."

I cleared my throat, choosing not to comment in my current mood. I watched as one of the vans pulled up to the gate, preparing to leave.

"Victoria?" I asked softly.

She jolted, turning to look at me with sad, red-rimmed eyes. "I really feel like killing some vampires right now," I whispered.

The moon briefly pierced the cloud cover again, striking her moist cheeks. I felt one of those beams touch my own cheeks and I shivered at the thought of Selene bathing both of us in her embrace, wondering what it meant. *Selene...*

"Okay, Sorin," Victoria whispered, licking her lips and wiping at her cheeks. "Let's go kill some vampires."

She held her hand out and I smiled, placing mine in hers. "Thank you for listening, Victoria."

She squeezed my hand and then pulled me to my feet by way of answer. The van was already driving down the street, and the gate was closed.

Time to get to work.

31

I drew on my powers, making sure my vampire abilities were masked from detection. The sky rumbled warningly, and I saw a flash of lightning high up in the clouds. A real storm was coming to the warehouse—in more ways than one. Nature—the thunder and lightning—and nurture—the father of all vampires—was coming in to destroy everything in their wake.

Victoria did a quick check of the various weapons attached to the straps and buckles beneath her short, tight jacket. When she clasped the front closed, I couldn't see any of the implements of violence, but I knew they were only a quick reach away.

As I watched her work, a stray beam of moonlight struck her face and I almost gasped in surprise. Her pale blue eyes drank in the moonbeam, and reflected it back in a vibrant royal blue, somehow seeming to sparkle and transform their natural color as facets deep within reflected the moonlight back like precious sapphires.

"Sapphires and moonlight," I breathed aloud without meaning to, awed by the stunning transformation of her eyes, and the ripple effect it seemed to have on her pale skin, making it glow like white marble. The faint scar on her cheek flashed like freshly-polished silver—as if the substance had been used to heal her wound and still resided inside the scar tissue.

"What did you say?" she asked distractedly, glancing up at me with a curious frown.

I clamped my mouth shut and pretended to be studying the warehouse, embarrassed. "Nothing."

"Okay, that should be—wait!" she said, patting her coat anxiously. She sighed in relief as she pulled out two ornate silver sticks—the same ones she'd worn at the auction—and flipped up her hair, stabbing the jeweled sticks through to hold it in place. "Okay. Now I'm ready."

I arched an eyebrow, pointing at the sticks. "Hidden weapons?" I asked, nodding my approval.

She grinned. "I think the chop-stakes look pretty from a distance, and deadly from up close." She winked. "They look even better when I shove them into naughty vampire eyes or throats. Or ears. Once."

I winced. "Chop-stakes," I shuddered. "Remind me not to get on your bad side."

"Consider that your reminder."

I chuckled. "Okay. I'll take lead since I can sense the vampires. I'll point them out to you."

"I think I can fit through the gate, but I'll be right out in the open for all to see. The exact opposite of stealth."

I nodded. "I'll go first. Let's hope some of my old tricks are still handy."

"Maybe you need a dose of fresh blood?" she asked, blushing as she grinned at me with her teeth.

I grunted. "As lovely as that sounds, we might lose focus of what we're here to do. And I'm not sure what would happen if I tasted your blood, given our shared ties to Artemis. Perhaps your blood is poisonous to me since you're supposed to hunt down my kind. I doubt Artemis intended you to seduce me in a dark, rainy alley," I said, hoping to take the sting out of my words.

She shot me a troubled look. "You could have a point."

"We will figure that out later. Now, it's time for some good old-fashioned beheading."

"I like it when you talk dirty," she said, licking her lips as she stared at the compound. I smiled at the merry twinkle of death flashing in her eyes, feeling oddly aroused by her familiarity with murder and combat. Two hunters of Artemis—created to stand on opposite sides as some bitch of a god laughed at the cruel irony.

Later.

My eyes drifted towards the homeless man. Hopefully, he was asleep. I rose from my crouch and lifted my umbrella, extending my arm for Victoria. She accepted and tucked in close to me, dramatically nuzzling against my shoulder to get out of the rain.

Because we were pretending to be a happy couple trying to escape the rain. But my body stirred restlessly as her scent filled my nostrils. She tugged on me, urging me to cross the street in an indignant, light-hearted squawk. "Let's get out of the rain!" she laughed.

The homeless man stirred as we jogged across the street, hopping over puddles. I cast my power wide, questing for how many vampires might be lurking on the opposite side of the brick wall. There could be a dozen pressed up against it or in a shelter of some kind, manning the gate we wanted to break through.

My power sensed no immediate vampire threats beyond the wall, but it sensed one only ten feet away and I almost stumbled in surprise.

The homeless man was a vampire.

I managed to disguise my reaction as slipping in a puddle, continuing my fake laughter as I changed course to bring our theatrical jogging closer to him. I flexed my bicep, hoping to let Victoria know something was wrong. She squeezed back twice before letting go and reaching into her pocket. She pulled out a wad of cash as she neared the fake homeless man.

He was actually a scout, which was particularly clever. Hidden in plain sight.

"Oh, you poor man!" Victoria blurted as more thunder rumbled in the sky overhead, the rainfall increasing. "Go get yourself some warm soup," she urged, waving the money in front of him.

The vampire jolted, momentarily taken aback by her adamant charity, before he nodded, extending his hand. He was clean-shaven and his hair was perfectly trimmed beneath his shoddy raincoat. And his shoes didn't look cheap, confirming my vampire senses.

I lifted my umbrella high, sensing her body tense in preparation of swinging a figurative executioner's axe. She didn't disappoint. In a blur of motion, Victoria dropped her money and gripped the homeless vampire's wrist, contorting it sharply enough that I heard the distinctive *pop* of bone or cartilage snapping. Her other hand shot forward to punch him in the throat before he could cry out in alarm.

I lunged with my claws and decapitated him in an instant, using the umbrella to shield my act of murder. Victoria quickly crouched down and covered him in blankets to soak up the blood while I scanned the street and roof of the warehouse, doing my best to conceal her actions with my umbrella. I couldn't see the rooftop guards from here, so I was betting we were safe. Luckily, the dead vampire was camped beside a large drain on the sidewalk that funneled the now crimson-stained water into the sewers—the underground.

She tugged out his earbud and then shoved his head under the blankets before briskly arranging the scene so that it looked like he was merely sleeping.

The whole thing had taken maybe three seconds, and even I couldn't visually discern that the homeless vampire was now a headless, homeless vampire. Unless I leaned down to get a closer look at the water dripping into the drain—but with the cover of darkness, even that was difficult.

"We can't move him, or they might get suspicious," Victoria explained, tucking the earbud into her opposite ear. As she was making one last adjustment to his coat, she suddenly froze, staring down at his waist. A white card was affixed to his belt by some kind of clasp and extendable string. She quickly snatched it up and straightened to her feet. Then she latched onto my arm, leading me away from the gates we had planned on using. "Our friend just gave us the key to the castle," she whispered excitedly, nuzzling into my shoulder to continue our ruse of blissful romance.

Seeing her so violently and effortlessly dispatch the vampire, I wasn't sure it was much of a ruse anymore. I was pretty sure I had just tripped into a bloody puddle of love.

I grunted, eyeing the plastic card she was palming. *Blood Center of the Empire State*, the words on the front said. "Walking in through the front door will bring us face-to-face with a contingent of guards," I murmured anxiously. "Nothing subtle about that."

"Let's keep moving. I think I saw a side door, and guards often have unrestricted access. Goon privilege." She dramatically struggled to remain under the umbrella, laughing loudly again. "My hair is getting soaked!" she complained. "Where did you park?"

"Just around the corner!" I laughed, amazed at her ability to switch personas so rapidly. From swift, efficient murder to complaining about her hair. "Stop whining!"

She whispered to me under the umbrella. "I don't think anyone noticed," she whispered, obviously referring to her newly acquired earbud.

I nodded. We rounded the corner to see a paint-chipped, dented, unassuming metal door under a small awning. An electronic device was attached to the wall beside the door handle, and it showed a small red light.

Victoria shot me a look. "No camera above the door. Should we try to sneak past all the guards by the gate or use this door?" she asked, and I could tell she truly wanted my opinion rather than trying to sway me one way or another.

"Let's do it. If stealth fails, we'll resort to swift, merciless slaughter."

She flashed her teeth in a hungry grin. "The more you talk, the more I like you, Sorin. I never would have thought I'd be hunting vampires alongside the world's first vampire."

"Everything you hate about vampires happened because of Dracula and his ilk. I was long out of the picture when your dad was killed."

She nodded, a flicker of sadness entering her eyes. "I know. I didn't mean to imply—"

I pressed my finger over her lips, silencing her. "No." I felt her lips tug into a smile, but I kept my eyes locked onto hers. "My spawn, Dracula, destroyed your family. He will pay for that. I have a measure of responsibility in his actions and, for what it's worth, I'm sorry. Together, we will finally make Dracula pay for his crimes. Starting tonight," I promised, lowering my finger. "You ready?" I asked, eyeing the card in her hand.

She let out a breath, her face growing utterly calm. "Do or die."

She swiped the card and the electronic lock flashed green. She carefully turned the handle, and the door opened into a dimly lit hallway. We slipped inside like shadows, letting it close softly behind us as I kept my eyes on our new surroundings.

A sudden crack of thunder shook the building, making us both jump in surprise. The lights flickered and I crouched warily. It looked like both storms had arrived at the same time.

Victoria pointed at a wooden door off to the side. *Utility Room* was written across the top. She grinned, tugging me towards it. "I have an idea," she breathed, opening the door and ushering me inside.

The door closed to reveal a room full of pipes and machines. I frowned.

"We're going to kill the power," she whispered. "No cameras, no lights. They will blame it on the storm. As long as we get another strike of lightning," she said, opening up a metal panel on the wall. "They will have a generator to keep the refrigerators cool, but it should turn off all unnecessary electronics. If not, it will at least distract them."

I nodded. Then I kissed my crucifix, grinning at her. She rolled her eyes and gripped a switch on the panel. Thunder rumbled outside, and I wondered how much longer we had before they grew concerned for their vampire sentry posted on the sidewalk.

A sudden peal of lightning cracked loud enough to shake the walls, and Victoria slammed the switch down. The lights cut off instantly, as did all the machinery in the room. A few seconds later, a red light flared to life, blinking. "Back-up generator," she said, nodding satisfactorily. "I'm sure they'll send someone down to check on the fuse box, so we should get to work."

I nodded, casting my senses out to check for heartbeats. My eyes widened and I instantly shoved my hand over Victoria's mouth as I pressed her up against the wall behind the door.

A vampire entered the room, muttering unhappily under his breath. "Piece of shit building." He made his way over to the fuse box and I stared into Victoria's eyes from only inches away.

32

Victoria's body melded against mine in a perfect fit, the swell of her breasts momentarily distracting me. My hair hung down, casting her in shadow from the blinking red light. She blinked lazily, smirking at my obvious reaction. Her pale eyes gleamed like rubies now.

I grinned back and then glanced over my shoulder. The vampire was so distracted that he hadn't even sensed Victoria's pulse only a pace away. I turned and tapped him on the shoulder. He jumped with a hiss. I gave him enough time to see my face and bare his fangs at me before I grabbed a fistful of his hair, jerked his head back, and sliced my claws across his neck.

Blood sprayed over my face and I licked my lips hungrily, despite the faint bitterness. "Who's your father," I snarled, still holding his head by his hair as his body collapsed to the ground.

Victoria wasted no time in dragging him by the boots and shoving his body into the corner. "That makes two," she said, dusting off her hands and unsheathing a pair of wicked black blades.

I nodded, staring down at the head. "You know, I never really thought about the logistics of lugging around a dozen of these," I mused.

She grunted. "Me neither. We'll just have to pick them up later."

I studied her, distantly surprised at how calm she was in the face of such violence. Knowing how to fight and being utterly calm around excessive gore were too intensely different skillsets. Like Nosh, Victoria remained unfazed.

She noticed my scrutiny and rolled her eyes. "You won't find me sobbing in a corner anytime soon, Sorin. When I see what they've done to this city and what Dracula has done overseas, I see only a dog that needs to be put down."

I nodded my agreement. "Yet you have no problem working alongside me, another vampire."

She smirked. "Yeah, but you bring the classiness back. You always extend your arm and show unnecessary courtesies. You have charm."

I blinked at her. "So, if one of these vampires held the door open for you, you might not kill them?"

She rolled her eyes. "A woman likes to be swooned, Sorin. And don't be so absurd. Of course I would kill them. But I would say *thank you*, first. Like a fucking lady."

I laughed, lowering my head. "In my day, men looked out for their loved ones, friends, and family. Men died for them."

She nodded, understanding well since she was also an old soul. "I miss those days. When I see them, I see a predator. When I see you..." she trailed off, considering her words, "I see a *protector*. Having the capacity for violence and being cruel are not mutually exclusive."

"Much like how a beautiful woman like you can wear a ballgown one night and blades the next," I said, jerking my chin at her knives.

"Precisely." She nodded primly, tugging on a pair of gloves that smelled of oiled metal. She noticed my attention and wiggled her fingers. "Armored with reinforced titanium and Kevlar."

I grunted, having no idea what any of it meant. I cocked my head, straining my senses to press outwards through the walls. "We have six threats within a hundred paces," I said, calculating the auras that indicated vampires. I sensed a few heartbeats and sighed. "Three of them are humans. Beyond the door at the end of the hall."

Victoria nodded, opening the door. "Let's go head hunting."

I tossed the head atop the dead vampire's body and followed her, idly wondering what she intended to do to the human guards. What I wanted to do to them. Part of me wanted to eradicate everyone here, but there was a chance some of them had no idea who they truly worked for.

There was also the chance that they knew exactly who they worked for and were hoping to earn the chance to rise above their humanity and become vampires themselves.

I followed Victoria down the hall, choosing to play it by ear. She waited by the door, staring at me, obviously wondering if anyone was immediately on the other side.

"We are clear. The closest is a little more than ten paces away."

She rolled her eyes. "No one says *pace* anymore, old man," she teased. "A pace is about three feet," she said, taking three toe-to-heel steps to demonstrate. "Three foot-lengths—feet—is approximately one yard or one meter."

"Yes, little girl," I muttered dryly. "They are thirty foot-lengths away. Ten yards or maybe meters."

She grinned, turning back to the door. "I'll go left, you go right. In three, two, one!"

She opened the door and slipped inside a dim, red-lit room, hugging the wall. I followed, letting the door silently close behind me. Three guards sat at a table in the center of a large open space, playing cards. A row of glass-doored, metal boxes as tall as a man were stocked with shelves of blood bags. Victoria had told me about them—the refrigerators that kept the blood cool. White light glowed from within, illuminating the card players in a pale glow. They didn't notice our entrance.

I spotted a vampire staring down at his phone near the wall on my right. I crept up behind him, noticing another vampire just ahead of him who was writing on a pad of paper as he counted inventory of the last refrigerator in the row. I glanced back to see Victoria creeping up behind the last vampire who was reading some paperwork at a desk, unaware of her presence. He was probably numb to the sense of heartbeats nearby, subconsciously dismissing them as the human guards.

I waited for her to get right behind him and glance my way. Then I gave her a brief nod and she stabbed him through the chest with a wooden stake from over his shoulder. She simultaneously slapped a gloved hand over his mouth, preventing him from making a sound. I suddenly realized why she'd wanted the armored gloves—so the vampire couldn't bite her fingers off.

I instantly spun to my own victim and shoved my hand into his back. My claws stabbed straight through his heart and out his chest. I cradled his body, guiding it to the ground, and extracted my arm, still clutching his heart. I tipped it back like a water skin, taking a quick drink of his heart blood before dropping the organ. Knowing the other vampire would sense the sudden scent any moment, I shot towards him in a blur, covering ten paces—yards or meters—in a single second as I tapped into my powers. I snapped his neck right as his shoulders began to stiffen in recognition of the fresh blood in the room. I let my momentum carry us past the pale glow of the refrigerators and sliced his head off.

I waited, listening intently to see if the guards at the card table had noticed anything. They laughed raucously at their game, oblivious to the three murders of the most adept warriors in the room—their only hope of salvation.

I stared down at the head in my hands and peered around the corner. No matter how we approached, one of the guards would spot us. It was surprising that they hadn't noticed their overlords dropping in their peripheral vision, but the white light from the refrigerators was likely destroying their ability to clearly see the perimeter of the darkened room—much like sitting by a campfire ruined your ability to accurately observe the woods around you. Which was why sentries were always posted far away from the campfire.

And the dim red emergency lights played tricks on the eyes. Even to me it was mildly disorienting. I tapped my earbud, murmuring to Victoria, "I'm going to toss a head on their table. Get ready to move, little girl."

"*What?*" Victoria hissed back in a breathless, frantic whisper.

I gave her two seconds and then I lobbed the vampire's head up into the air, hoping my aim was true. It slammed down into the center of the table, knocking down all their drinks, plastic chips, and a pile of cards.

I was already a blur of lethal speed—an arrow of death—as the head rolled into one of their laps and all three men jumped up with cries of alarm. "What the f—"

I punched the man in the jaw, knocking him out cold before he could finish his sentence. I was already spinning to confront the other two when I saw them standing stiffly upright and shaking violently. That's when I noticed the crackling sound from behind them. The sound cut off and the men dropped like sacks of potatoes, whimpering helplessly as their bodies continued to spasm and twitch.

Victoria stood behind them with strange devices over her gloved hands, reminding me of brass knuckles—only black and not made of metal. She glanced sharply about the room, making sure my earlier assessment had been right and that there weren't more guards or vampires. She let out a breath, locking eyes with me. They gleamed like fresh blood in the red light, and I suddenly wanted nothing more than to kiss her.

Or for her to beg me to sink my fangs into her sweet, delicate neck as she writhed beneath—

I cut off the thought, blinking away the sudden visual image.

She cocked her head curiously, sensing that something significant had just crossed my mind. I waved off her concern. "What are those?" I asked, staring at the devices over her gloves. They looked to have tiny prongs on the end, not even as long as my fingernail.

She pressed down on something with her thumb and sudden arcs of lightning crackled to life between the two prongs. I jumped back a step, hissing. She laughed, releasing her thumb, and the lightning instantly cut off. "Modified stun-gun. One million volts of electricity," she said, beaming.

"You have lightning on your fists?" I asked incredulously.

She shrugged. "I guess."

I stared down at the men. They weren't unconscious, but they were whimpering in agony. Victoria calmly stunned them again and I watched as their bodies locked rigid.

I leaned down, sniffing them. "They've been bitten," I growled. "Blood donors. They know exactly what they're doing and who they're working for," I said darkly, wondering what I was going to do about it.

Victoria saved me the effort and slammed a blade down into both of their hearts simultaneously. They let out rattling groans before their bodies went limp. She calmly looked up at me. Then she glanced past to the unconscious man, arching an eyebrow.

I nodded back. "I'm feeling thirsty, what with keeping you safe this whole time. If you'll excuse me a moment, my lady." I bowed formally.

She scoffed, rolling her eyes. I made my way over to the last guard, verifying that he was equally corrupted. That wasn't necessarily a crime in my eyes, but with the vampires he worked for, guarding a blood bank and knowing full-well that it was for vampires rather than humans was good enough reason for me to end his existence.

I propped him up and sank my fangs into his neck for a quick drink. It was concerning how rapidly my powers drained after even the slightest use. I had come into the building feeling incredible—relative to my recent power fluctuations. Yet now I felt tired again. Weaker.

Closing the distance between me and the last vampire had been harder than it should have been. I could tell that my body was having to work much harder to do things I had once taken for granted. And expending a lot more energy to do so. Natalie's blood should have kept me going all night long.

The guard's blood hit my tongue and I sighed, drinking it down, relishing the sensation of it coursing through my body. I stared at Victoria as I feasted, feeling slightly self-conscious, but she was merely smiling at me encouragingly.

She began counting with her fingers before opening her mouth. "We only need seven more—"

The door behind her opened to reveal a short man in a long white coat. He gasped in surprise to see me drinking from the guard's neck. Then he noticed the other dead bodies and gagged. He dropped the pad of paper in his hand and spun, attempting to run back out the door, but he slipped or tripped, headbutting the door handle instead.

Victoria had jumped to her feet at the sound and was already running towards him. The man sobbed in terror, his nose oozing blood from headbutting the door, as he finally managed to yank the door open and stumble through. I released my fangs, snarling. He could ruin everything!

Just then, a door opened behind me and I heard a muttered curse. Two blasts of gunfire erupted, slamming into my back.

33

I rolled clear of a third and fourth blast, groaning as I fought to ignore the fire burning through my abdomen. I sprang back towards my vampire attacker, pinning him to the wall beside the door he had just used, my claw impaled through his chest.

I ripped his heart out and let his body drop as the pain from his bullets seared my abdomen like a white-hot brand. I lifted his heart over my mouth and crushed it, guzzling the steaming blood ravenously. The door beside me opened again and I blindly shoved my hand through the gap, stabbing my claws into another chest and ripping that heart out too—all while still chugging the stream of blood from the *first* heart.

It ran dry and I flung it behind me, switching to the second heart, barely pausing in my gulping. Both had been vampires. The second vampire's body dropped to the ground and I quested out with my senses to see if anyone had heard the gunshots.

There was definitely commotion, but none were an immediate threat, and I felt the wounds in my abdomen rapidly draining me of energy despite the blood I was consuming. It ran dry and I threw it to the side. "Not enough," I growled, feeling the wounds from the bullets burning hotter for some reason. I sank my fangs into the vampire's shoulder, drinking deeply. The blood instantly flowed to my wounds, but the pain hadn't ceased, letting me know something was seriously wrong. I needed more—a lot more.

I tapped my earbud, peeling my fangs away long enough to speak. "Where are you?"

Then I sank my fangs back into the guard as I waited for three infinitely long seconds.

"Okay," Victoria finally replied in a hushed whisper. "I got the scientist. Sneaky little bastard. I ran across another vampire who heard the gunshots, but I managed to stake him through the heart while he was running your way. I got his head. What happened with you?"

"I was shot twice, but I'll be fine with more blood," I lied. I glanced down and cringed to see that the two puckering wounds were smoking around the edges. It was almost as if they were burning with fever, getting hotter by the second.

"Chatter on the earbud tells me they're all coming down here. One of them called in backup after hearing the gunshots and not getting a response from their pals," Victoria said, right as she burst back through the door and into the room. She was clutching a bloody white cloth. "Figured we could bundle the others up in the scientist's coat. He won't be needing it anymore."

I clenched my fist angrily at her news as she made her way over and bent down to study my wounds. "Eight is not twelve," I told her, mentally counting the vampires we had killed. I glanced down to see the wounds in my stomach—although absorbing all the blood I'd just consumed—still looked burnt around the edges and were definitely still smoking. "Bullets hurt like hell."

She stared at it, her face paling. "They usually hurt and kill so rapidly that you never notice the *hurt* part." She grew silent, poking at it gently with a gloved finger. "Sorin," she said nervously.

"Yes?" I asked, reaching out with my senses to check for more vampires. They all seemed to be congregating a floor above us. I counted five of them, but there could have been more out of my range.

"I'm pretty sure they shot you with silver bullets—"

I dropped to my knees, hissing suddenly as my stomach muscles spasmed like she had dug her finger into the hole. I thought my wounds had burned before, but it was nothing compared to what came next. The white-hot brands were back, but this time they were scraping and prodding through my entire wound—from my abdomen to my back. I gritted my teeth, trying to climb to my feet despite the torture. "We need to get out—"

Victoria gripped my chin, waving a small chunk of silver in my face. "Sorin, *listen* to me. I've used bullets like this before. They are designed to splinter on impact. I know you say you're tough, but these are designed to drop vampires and werewolves with one shot. You were hit *twice*. If they don't immediately kill you, they poison you to death."

I looked up at her, my vision beginning to tunnel. The horror in her eyes caught me off guard. I wanted to reassure her, to tell her we would make it through this, but another flare of pain made my vision flicker with black spots. It was as if all the blood I had just consumed was fighting to keep me alive, but it wasn't enough to fight the silver fragments embedded in my flesh.

And I could feel my body drawing on my limited reserves to compensate, which was destroying my vampire strengths, leaving me as weak as a newborn kitten.

"Victoria. Get out of here—"

She slapped me. Hard.

And then she kissed me forcefully, biting down on my lip hard enough to make me grunt. She pulled away, but only a few inches. "You need blood, Sorin. Strong blood. I think your only way out of here is to get blood drunk."

I instantly shook my head, knowing what she was suggesting. "Absolutely not," I wheezed. "I'm not killing you so I can survive a couple bullet wounds."

"LISTEN!" she snapped, glaring at me with the same hostility that she'd shown against our foes earlier. "You are going to drink from me, and you are going to drink *deeply*, you stubborn bastard. Enough blood so that you are strong enough to stand up and drink the first son of a bitch who comes through that door. You are going to chug him down like a can of cheap beer. And then you are going to rinse and repeat with every single creature in this building. If that's not enough, you are going to sit your ass down at that card table and drink every single blood bag in sight," she snarled, panting.

I stared at her, struggling to keep her face in my vision through the ever-widening dark spots. "What if your blood is poisonous?" I rasped.

"Then we both die swinging."

"I don't know if I'll be able to stop myself, Victoria. I don't know if I've ever felt this kind of pain, and once the bloodlust takes over..."

She squeezed her thumb down on her stun-gun. "Oh, I'll be fine, Sorin. I've dealt with a few vampires before." She arched her neck and leaned in close, eyeing the door.

I knew I only had moments before the decision would be made for me, and I couldn't let Dracula get away with his crimes. Couldn't let my curiosity about Victoria and her shared ties to Artemis go unanswered.

And she'd kissed me...

"Promise me you'll collect the heads and get out of here the moment I'm done. Anyone left inside will be in danger. Promise me and I'll do it," I whispered, feeling dizzy.

"FINE!" she snapped. "JUST *VUCK* ME ALREADY, SORIN!" she hissed.

I blinked, my heart skipping a beat. "Vuck?" I was pretty sure I'd missed a significant segment of our conversation.

"Vuck. Vampire suck. It sounded better in my head," she snarled, blushing furiously. Then she simply grabbed the back of my head and slammed my mouth down onto her neck. "Drink, Sorin. Show me what the world's first vampire can do with a little lead in his pencil."

She gasped as my fangs sank into her neck.

And my mind exploded with blinding moonlight as liquid ice coursed through my veins, scraping my insides clean like purifying acid. But it didn't hurt in the slightest. It...was perfect bliss.

Victoria climaxed faster and louder than Natalie had—it was practically instantaneous. Her hand gripped a fistful of the hair at the back of my head like it was her lifeline in a stormy sea, and the fingers of her other hand clawed and scraped at my back, using her armored gloves for better effect. Her body rocked wildly against me as she moaned directly into my ear, clutching me tighter and tighter until I couldn't tell if she was laughing or crying. But her nails kept right on scraping my back, begging for more.

I breathed her life into mine, *inhaling* her blood rather than drinking it. My muscles twitched and spasmed, my wounds instantly growing cold enough to feel like they were frosting over. I felt my inner demon purring delightedly, throwing his head back and laughing.

YES!

My mind shattered as the demon tried to take control, wanting more of this sensation. To drink every drop of blood in the world, consequences be damned. I was a god, not a man with a curse. And I agreed, relishing in the sudden electricity of her blood coursing through my body. I'd never—ever—felt anything like Victoria Helsing's blood on my tongue. It was like my greatest memory of sunlight kissing my cheeks on a carefree day.

But then I felt my lip throb where Victoria had bitten me, and my heart skipped a beat. Before I was even aware of what I was doing, I flung myself back from her, panting desperately.

She sat on the ground, quivering as she gasped and moaned, chills sporadically ripping through her as echoes of milder climaxes struck her at the core. Her pupils were dilated and a sheen of sweat glistened on her forehead. The stun guns on both hands were crackling as she clenched her fists, unable to let go. I glanced down to see holes burned in my shirt where she had been shocking me with a million volts from each hand.

I hadn't even felt it, had I?

I flung my head back and screamed, unable to handle the power coursing through my veins. I didn't just feel as good as I had in my prime...

I felt like I'd never even come *close* to my prime until this moment.

A quick scan of the building told me that the vampires were now on the move, heading our way. Victoria groaned, climbing unsteadily back to her feet, her stun-guns still crackling. I let out a shuddering sigh to see that she was alright, but part of me wanted to tackle her to the ground, straddle her, and rip her clothes off before licking up every last drop of sweat from her body. To explore every crevice and crack of her flesh with my tongue.

And only then would I get to her unbelievably potent blood.

And I knew if I asked her right now, she'd probably agree—which instantly killed the desire of the fantasy, immediately clearing my thoughts.

I had long ago vowed to never abuse my powers that way.

"You...didn't stop," she murmured, shaking her head to get her bearings. She unclenched her thumbs and the stun-guns stopped crackling. "I'm not sure I wanted you to stop. I just knew I *needed* you to..." She twitched again, her thighs clenching at an obvious echo of her pleasure. She laughed huskily. "That was nice," she mumbled woozily.

"Are you okay?" I asked anxiously.

She chuckled throatily, licking her lips very slowly as she met my eyes. "When a girl asks you to *vuck* her, you sure don't hold back, Sorin." Her hair was a tangled mess, the chop-stakes hanging crookedly.

I smiled smugly in spite of my concern, but I was surprised by how clear-headed I felt. My inner demon was railing at the walls of my mind, begging me to finish the job, and I knew Victoria couldn't have stopped me if she had a gun loaded with a dozen of those silver bullets.

But...I was able to hold him back. Without any apparent effort.

Had I won my eternal struggle against my demon, or had Victoria's blood changed me in some way? Because I felt something entirely new living inside my soul. A trapped beam of soft, brilliantly white moon-light shining upon a pile of blue gems. And the new tenant was incredi-bly, lethally potent. Godly.

"Sapphires and moonlight," I whispered, staring at Victoria in awe.

Victoria set her hand on the table, staring at me. "You said that before, but I pretended not to notice—" Her eyes latched onto my wounds and instantly widened in disbelief. I glanced down to see my stomach coated in a bramble of thorny frost. It was already beginning to melt, since the rest of my skin felt feverish to the touch.

But I didn't have time to worry about that.

"It's time for you to go, Victoria. That was our deal. But I really think I'd like to pick up where we left off..." I said, my voice a throaty growl. "Go deliver the heads to Stevie."

She nodded obediently, scooping up the remaining heads and wrapping them up in the scientist's white coat. "You sure you're okay?" she asked, hesitating before turning around.

"Victoria," I drawled. "I'm pretty sure you *vucked* me, not the other way around." Her cheeks reddened and I caught a flash of pride in her eyes. "I can honestly say that I've never felt *anything* as pleasurable as that. Ever. And I've never felt *stronger* either." I met her eyes, making sure she understood my next words. They might be the most important thing I ever said to her. "You must *never* tell anyone about what just happened. Otherwise, Dracula would break the world to get his hands on your blood. I need to hear you promise me, out loud, while looking into my eyes. And we're about to have company, so don't dawdle."

"I promise I won't tell anyone about my blood, Sorin."

I nodded, turning my back on her. With four holes now ruining my shirt—two from bullets and two from her stun-guns—I tore the fabric off entirely, dropping the clothing to the ground as I faced the door, waiting for the vampires to arrive. "Don't forget the two heads on your way out, Miss Helsing," I murmured.

"O-okay," she stammered.

I glanced down at the torn, bloody, burned fabric on the ground and frowned. I used to wear an elegant cape. Why had I stopped wearing my cape? I closed my eyes and drew deep on my newfound power, curious what limits I had now that I wasn't constantly struggling to fight against my inner demon. I felt something soft, warm, and dependably strong settle over my shoulders and spill down my back, embracing me like a naked lover pressed against my spine as she draped her arms around my neck and rested her head upon my shoulders.

Then I imagined that it was Victoria Helsing.

I opened my eyes to see a rich cloak of the darkest shadows and hottest, purest blood rippling down behind me, constantly shifting and twitching as if I was standing before a stiff breeze.

Victoria gasped from behind me near the door. But the vampires were close, and I didn't have time for anymore goodbyes. It was time for the Devil to take his due.

To show these children that their forgotten grandfather was a force not to be reckoned with, and that I had forgotten more tricks than their father—Dracula—had ever known.

I heard the door close behind me and tracked Victoria's heartbeat as she fled the building to safety. The doors ahead of me burst open to reveal a rapidly widening storm of dazzling flashes of lightning and explosive booms of thunder.

Five figures controlled that storm, spreading out as they unloaded their guns with abandon.

But my cloak whipped and snapped, devouring the silver bullets like a swarm of bats devouring a cloud of flying insects.

Not one projectile struck me as their guns clicked empty. Five stunned vampires stared at me and then down at their guns.

"I'm clear," Victoria whispered into my ear.

And the Devil burst out with laughter, his cloak hissing and screaming with a fierce hunger.

34

I drew upon my bottomless well of power, burning away an acceptable amount of blood that allowed me to shift into a cloud of thick red mist. Rather than attacking my foes or slaughtering them in a single blast of power, I wanted to have some fun. To wield the powers I had so sorely missed since waking from Deganawida's slumber.

Knowing what I had once been capable of but being forced to get by on the bare minimum of powers for the last twenty-four-hours—and having to eat scraps like a starving dog to even do that—I'd felt increasingly inadequate. Fraudulent.

Like I wasn't the man I had once been. Like I would never be that man again.

In more ways than one, Nosh had reminded me of who I once was.

And Victoria had shown me that I could be that man again. That I could be more than that man had ever been. That it was okay to be a nightmare. A cognizant nightmare.

Selene had taught me that a single embrace of true love was worth sacrificing your soul.

Bubble had reminded me that I was a man, first, and a monster only if I chose to be one.

For those lessons, I would forever love them. They were with me even now.

But both of those lessons had left my heart torn and shattered, fearing that I was forever destined to have the desires of my heart ripped from my life and tortured before my eyes while the gods laughed at me.

Then I had met Victoria and had felt that familiar tugging on my heart once again.

Now, filled with her blood, I clearly understood the source of her power, the source of our magical ties together. The gift and curse of Artemis, the Goddess of the Hunt.

And...I was relieved to suddenly realize that it felt *nothing* like what I'd sensed upon first seeing Victoria at the auction. That the sensations that had rendered me speechless upon seeing her had nothing to do with her blood or ties to Artemis. It had been...something else. Something innocent and genuine.

Potential.

That wasn't to say that I was completely infatuated with Victoria, but there was definitely a strong connection between us. A very powerful feeling. Something worth nurturing.

To see if we could keep it safe.

And that terrified me, because I'd lost everything I'd ever loved. Everything I'd ever tried to protect. My clan of vampires, my dynasty, my legend, my first love, my wife and son...

My soul to Hades.

I had epically failed at every attempt to protect what I loved.

But...I now had one more chance to protect something that I loved.

Myself. My new outlook on life. The memory of my countless losses.

Because if Dracula won, I would die. And those losses would be forgotten forever, unavenged. I would fail to not only protect their lives, but even their memories.

And that was simply not acceptable.

It seemed that the most powerful man in the world still needed the minding of strong, independent women in order to attain his true potential. First Selene's sacrifice, then Bubble's teachings of inner peace, and now Victoria to bring it all together and remind me that I was the master of the night.

I screamed loud enough to shatter the glass in every single refrigerator. The vampires dropped their guns, clutching at their ears in agony. I screamed again and my cloud of mist exploded in every direction.

My spirit, now unencumbered, focused on the red light on the wall. In a blur, my mist shot from every corner of the room, congregating at the red light on the wall. The mist condensed, crushing it into powder and killing the red glow of electricity.

With a thought, I condensed the mist towards a spot on the ground behind the refrigerators and reformed myself into a man. A solid metal door with a security lock was set into the wall behind the refrigerators, but I assumed it was just additional storage rather than another access point for more potential attackers to flank me. I reached out with my senses just to be sure, but I felt no signs of life beyond it.

I noticed thick cords connecting the refrigerators to the wall and I smirked. I quickly ripped them from the walls, one by one. The white lights glowing from the front of the refrigerators extinguished, plunging the room into complete darkness. My cloak whipped about my shoulders, this time in utter silence. It was almost identical in design to my favorite old cloak. It even had my emblem on the back—a large drop of blood with a vertical, elegant silver bow nocked with two feathers for arrows.

I hadn't seen my back, of course, but I had willed it into existence. I simply knew it was there in the same way I knew how to flex my fist. No matter how much the cloak snapped and whipped about of its own accord, that emblem remained static, centered on my lower spine, gleaming in silver as a constant reminder...

Of the price I had paid to become the Devil.

Of Selene.

The five vampires snarled, murmuring to each other—likely through their earbuds—but I could hear them clearly. We were all vampires, after all.

"*Where is he?*"

"*Who is he?*"

"*What is he?*"

I laughed, strolling into view from behind the refrigerators. I hadn't even had to focus on my vision for it to adapt to the darkness, painting the room and my assailants in shades of gray. "The Devil has come to collect his due, my wayward children. None of you will live to see another moon because the moon belongs to *me!*"

I could have simply crushed their hearts with a single thought. I could have enthralled them into my service—mindless slaves eager to appease my every whim. I could have coughed and decapitated them. The number of new ways that I could end their existence was actually startling—thanks to Victoria's blood coursing through my veins.

I could kill them with an eternity of blinding pain, or a feather-stroke of sexual ecstasy.

Or both. Simultaneously.

My new powers beckoned to me, begging to be tested. Pleading for me to abuse these vampires, to degrade them, to set an example that Dracula would fear from halfway across the world.

But it wasn't necessarily their fault that they worked for Dracula.

And I wanted to get my claws dirty.

I dove towards them as fast as a hurled spear. No. *Faster.*

Four of the vampires leapt out of the way just in time. The fifth vampire simply exploded into pieces no larger than coins as I tore through his chest like a blade through dry cloth. I made sure to keep his head intact, knowing I would need it later for my collection. But the rest of him was simply gone. One of the other vampires gagged at the shower of gore and immediately pissed himself, but the other three tried to attack me from behind.

I spun, grabbing two of them by the throat and hoisting them up into the air. I kicked the third vampire in the chest hard enough to cave in his entire rib cage and send him flying into one of the refrigerators.

I locked eyes with the still-gagging vampire and snapped the necks of the vampires I held in either hand. I let their bodies drop to the ground and I began to walk towards the lone survivor. His eyes danced wildly, and he made as if to run towards the door Victoria had used.

My cape whipped out before him, slicing a line of fire across his outstretched arm. He tried to spin and run the other way, but my cloak shot out to impale his thigh. He began to sob in horror, stumbling backwards, away from me, as he clutched his leg, slipping in his own blood.

My cloak snapped out again, grabbing his foot and yanking it towards me, sending him crashing into the card table. His flesh burned where my cloak had touched his ankle.

He rolled to his knees and clasped his hands together before me, weeping. "Please! My name is Paul. I have a family!"

I bared my fangs, hissing at him as blood pounded in my ears.

"*SO. DID. I!!!!!!*" I roared, loud enough to make my own ears pop.

My cloak shot forward and stabbed him in the heart, incinerating it upon contact and leaving only a smoking hole in its wake. Through that hole, I saw a single playing card on the table.

The Ace of Hearts.

A single outline of a heart to replace the one I had just incinerated inside the vampire's chest.

I roared with laughter, slapping at my knees as my cloak whipped and snapped around me, seeming to purr and stretch like a sleepy cat before a fire.

My laughter soon faded, and I realized I was panting as I slowly assessed the room, inhaling the scent of fresh blood. I wasn't panting from exhaustion but from disappointment. That I had no more foes to face.

I heard a sound behind me and spun.

35

Alone vampire stood before me, blinking slowly—as if he couldn't quite believe his eyes. But he wasn't looking at the blood, the gore, or the bodies of his fellow vampires. He was looking at—

"It's *you*..." he breathed, sounding shaken to his very core. "You're alive."

I stared at him, momentarily confused and wary of trickery. He was lean but muscular, and had a short, neatly styled head of thick hair that was slicked to the side. He had a strong, chiseled, clean-shaven jaw and deep brown eyes. And he wore an elegant suit and thin black tie, unlike the other vampires I'd encountered. He looked like he was heading to an auction. Even his shoes were polished. He also had no weapons in his long, pale hands.

I'd never seen him before—of that, I was certain.

He fell to his knees with a relieved, emotional smile on his cheeks. "I can finally pay for my crime that night so long ago," he whispered.

I closed the distance in the blink of an eye and gripped him by the knot in his tie, hoisting him to his feet. "What are you talking about?" I snarled, inches away from his face.

He didn't even flinch. His arms hung at his sides; his body entirely slack, like a wet towel. "I was there the night you died."

I hissed, dropping him and leaping back a step, scanning the building for any other assailants. But it was just us. He faced me openly, clasping his hands behind his back.

I glared at him, shaking my head in confusion. "Impossible. That would make you five hundred years old. Powerful enough to hold a position of significant authority."

He grimaced. "No. This wasn't a promotion," he said, tapping his teeth with a fingernail before clasping his hands together behind his back again. His fangs weren't extended, even though I could now sense the truth to his words. He was a *very* old vampire. One I hadn't sensed when I'd first scanned the building. He hadn't been with his fellows when they planned their assault on me. "This was my punishment for failing Dracula," the man said.

I narrowed my eyes. "Get to the point," I growled, wondering what his angle was, what I wanted to do with such a potential resource, and why he was stalling with such an outlandish claim.

"Dracula bought my debts. Sent me and two-dozen others on a ship to the New World to attack a small tribe of Native Americans. I was just a human back then. Dracula threatened to murder my wife and daughter if I didn't obey. It wasn't until right before the attack that I was commanded to kidnap a child—a young boy—and bring him back for Dracula. I didn't know who you were, why we were there, or who the tribe was. But..." he took a shaking breath, struggling to continue, "as I looked into that young boy's eyes, I saw my daughter staring back at me, asking me a question. *Why would you do such a thing, Papa? How could you do this to me?*" he whispered, tears falling from his eyes.

My hands began to shake, and I realized I was panting. "My...my son?" I rasped.

He nodded regretfully, his shoulders slumping. "I grabbed him and took him into the woods, running as fast as I could. I ran until I came upon another tribe. I begged them to take the boy in and to never tell anyone the truth. That his very life depended on it."

I shook my head. "No. That's impossible," I whispered, my pulse thundering in my ears. "He died. Everyone died," I lied. Because Deganawida had told me he never found their bodies...

The man slowly shook his head. "So did you." He took a deep breath. "I knew Dracula would kill me for my failure, but I couldn't make myself do it. I didn't even have the courage to kill him instead of turning him over to Dracula, knowing that it would be a kindness. I rejoined the group and told them the boy had died in the fire, even knowing that my family would suffer for it. Dracula killed everyone who returned from our slaughter, even the werewolves and vampires. But he chose a far worse punishment for my failure. He turned me into a vampire the moment I returned without his prize, telling me that I would get to watch my family grow old and die without me. Every year on my daughter's birthday, Dracula would have me drive a carriage to my home so that he—and only he—could deliver a gift to my daughter and tell her how brave her father was."

I shook my head, still reeling from thoughts of my son surviving.

"I sat in that carriage, staring through the window from outside," the man continued. "Dracula forbid me from ever getting within thirty paces of my own flesh and blood. I watched my wife die from thirty paces. I watched my daughter get married to a man I never met from thirty paces. I watched my grandchildren grow up from thirty paces. I watched my daughter's funeral from thirty paces."

He locked eyes with me, and I saw the torn soul of a man who wanted only one thing—salvation. An end to his eternal punishment. And he would accept that salvation from only one man in the world, or he wouldn't accept it at all, preferring an immortality plagued with righteous regret over the easy death of a fraudulent forgiveness by anyone other than...

Me.

I swallowed audibly, not knowing what to do with my hands. My cloak hung entirely still.

The man cleared his throat, sounding as if he had walked a thousand miles without a sip of water. "I watched my life from thirty paces because I saved your son's life, Sorin Ambrogio," he whispered. "I might be the only vampire other than Dracula who knows your name. The only vampire who knows what your name means."

I nodded numbly. I was Dracula's dirty secret. Proof of his lies—that he was not the First.

"Dracula never permitted me to rise up through the ranks, always giving me jobs below the lowest of servants. I was a warning to all his other vampires to never betray their master. That even a five-hundred-year old vampire could be nothing more than a servant. A carriage driver."

I stared at him, gathering my resolve. "You want my forgiveness," I said in a low tone.

"No!" He shook his head adamantly. "Never. I want to die. If you don't kill me, I will attack you until you get annoyed enough to finish the job. You are the only man I will allow to kill me."

I grunted. Without Victoria's blood running through my body, a vampire as old as him would have been quite the challenge. But...he might have answers. Long-dead answers, but answers nonetheless. If he worked for Dracula, he might know my foe's vulnerabilities. Weaknesses that he couldn't elaborate on unless I broke his bond to his master.

He might know what happened to my wife and son.

"What is your name?" I asked.

"Renfield. Henry Renfield," the man said in a humble—yet somehow proud—tone.

I considered the situation in its entirety. "Renfield...which do you want more? To avenge your family or to die as a sniveling coward?" I sensed a flash of fire in his eyes—not at me, but an instinctive reaction to the term. He had fire inside him, after all.

"I am unable to raise a hand against Master Dracula," he said slowly.

"Unless a stronger, older vampire breaks that bond," I suggested, staring into his eyes.

His eyes slowly widened, not having considered the possibility. "You...would do that?" he whispered hoarsely.

"You just tried to commit suicide to confess your sins, Renfield. To confess your sins against the victim of your crime. If you simply wanted to die, all you had to do was attack me without saying a word. You wouldn't have stood a chance," I said, holding out my arms as my cloak suddenly whipped and snapped back to life. "And you had to know that. Why did you speak?"

He thought about my question in silence. For about ten long seconds. "To be honest, I was ready to attack on principle until I saw your hair. The way you stood tall. Like you owned the world. It was exactly what I saw that fateful night when both our lives were destroyed. I thought my mind was playing tricks on me, but no one even knows about you. Only Dracula and I would still know you on sight," he said, shaking his head. "The words just came out of me once I realized who you were. I didn't want to die as a nameless minion. Before you killed me, I wanted you to know that my death would give you a small taste of vengeance, so you could know that you earned at least *some* justice tonight. That maybe such a small realization would give you exactly what you needed to finish the job against Dracula, once and for all."

I stared at him, wondering if this was some sort of trap. But somehow, I knew it wasn't. Men like Renfield were few and far between. Even in my day, such honor was the thing of legend. As I pondered his story, I realized that he truly had been put into a situation where he had been given no good option to take. Slaughter a nameless tribe to save his family. To be honest, I would have done the same in his shoes. But... he'd let my son go instead. Putting my son before his own family.

I walked closer. "Kneel."

He didn't even hesitate. He sank down to his knees before me, his eyes tear-filled.

"Give me your wrist, Renfield," I commanded, closing the distance to stand over him as he lifted his wrist, staring up at me in wonder and gratitude.

I grabbed his wrist and bit into it, taking a deep drink as I stared him in the eyes.

Then I pulled away and bit into my own wrist. "Open your mouth, Renfield," I said calmly.

He closed his eyes, tilted his head back, and opened his mouth. I extended my wrist and let my blood drip onto his tongue and down his throat. He swallowed, instantly stiffening as the magic took hold without mercy—no doubt a result of Victoria's blood powering me, because it didn't typically happen as fast as this.

I continued to rain my blood down upon his mouth. "Drink, Renfield. Drink from your new Master, Sorin Ambrogio."

And he did. He drank *deeply*.

Typically, breaking a Master's bond was done gradually, over months or years, giving the vampire time to accept his decision and come to terms with it.

But Renfield had been doing that for five hundred years, and I was currently overpowered. I waited a few moments and then used my mind to reach into him, searching out my blood now coursing through his body. I found it and latched onto it, bonding it with the blood I had drunk from his wrist that was now inside of me—now a *part* of me—before my body could choose to store it for power or anything else I needed for sustenance.

"Swear your undying fealty to me, Renfield. That you will faithfully and loyally serve me, and only me, until death do us part."

Renfield did, his voice sounding even more fervent than before—as if he'd found a purpose he'd lost five-hundred-years ago. "I swear my undying fealty to you, Sorin Ambrogio. I will faithfully serve you, and only you, until death do us part."

I felt the magic take hold, a sudden flash of ice and fire that thrummed like a struck chord on a harp, vibrating in sync with the vampire kneeling before me.

"Rise, my son. Rise, Henry Renfield. Welcome to House Ambrogio."

He opened his eyes and stared up at me, a soul-deep smile in those bottomless brown eyes.

Then he climbed to his feet, letting out a nervous breath. He shot me an uncertain smile. "This is much better than death, Master. You gave me a harder path to absolution, but I think it might be the *only* road to absolution. Death is too easy."

I nodded. "There will be plenty of death in the days to come, Renfield. Rivers of blood will flow through the streets. Dracula must die, and you're going to help me do it."

"Yes, Master."

36

Renfield glanced around the room, studying the dead bodies. He pointed at the vampire who had pissed himself. Paul, I thought he had said. The one with a hole in his chest who had tried to lie about having a family. "Paul was in charge tonight. He called in reinforcements, but he didn't put any urgency in his request. Told them he would handle it but that we would need a clean-up crew for the next shift."

I grinned at the thought of the leader pissing himself upon seeing me—Paul the Pisser.

"Could you buy us some time?" I asked. "Call them back and say the situation was resolved?"

Renfield nodded. "Of course. They always believe me," he said with a bitter smile. "They know I wouldn't dare disappoint Dracula again."

I smiled. "Do it."

"Might I ask why?" I arched a stern eyebrow at him. He lowered his eyes subserviently. "In case they suggest an alternative course of action. If I know what you intend, I can be sure to guide the conversation in the direction that best suits your needs. Renfield doesn't give commands," he explained. "They would instantly be suspicious if I tried."

I nodded, seeing the sense in his suggestion. "I'm taking all of their blood. Every last bag."

His eyes widened but he nodded, pulling a phone from his pocket. I listened in as he made the call. He watched me as he spoke, making sure I didn't have any suggestions before hanging up with a proud nod. "They'll wait until morning like usual, but they want a report from Paul as soon as he disposes of the homeless man who jumped one of the guards." He glanced down at the dead Paul. "Don't forget to call, you hairy goat's dick," he muttered.

I arched an eyebrow and burst out laughing. "Well. That's one way to put it. And just so you know, he pissed himself when he saw me. I let him watch his friends die, saving him for last."

He grinned, and it was a truly dazzling look. "That makes me feel warm and fuzzy inside, Master. Thank you." I nodded, chuckling. Renfield was surprisingly handsome when he wasn't apologizing and begging for death. It was almost as if a new man had risen from the old. "They'll obviously know the truth by morning," he said carefully, "that I lied. My cover will be blown. They'll know something is up because Renfield *never* disobeys *anyone*. I was never allowed to even ask a question."

I smiled. "By morning, it will be too late."

He cocked his head curiously. "Too late for what?"

"Too late to save the Necromancer," I told him. "And for the record, I value questions, Renfield. Forget your bad habits. Immediately," I said, already walking away. "Oh, and Renfield?"

"Yes, Master?" he answered, sounding shaken by my statement.

"Could you detach those five heads and bring them with us?"

"Gladly, Master. I'll get the hairy goat's dick first," he said, sounding as if he was licking his lips. I smiled, tapping my earbud as I heard him go to work. "Victoria?"

"Sorin!" she gasped. "Oh my god. You're okay!"

I smiled. "I made a friend and picked up an extra credit point for our collection."

"Holy shit. You took on five by yourself?" she laughed. "Guess those are technically mine since I juiced you up," she teased.

Renfield stepped up beside me, hefting a black bag bulging with heads. I began walking towards the exit, smiling. "Of course, my lady. I need you to get the wolves down here, now. They have the place to themselves until dawn. I need to recover Nosh before I confront the Necromancer or they'll try to use him as leverage. By dawn, his fate will be sealed."

"Wait. He's at the police precinct. We can't just break into the police precinct—"

Renfield cleared his throat, drawing my attention. "Are you speaking of Nosh Griffin?"

I nodded. "Yes. The Shaman."

"He's here, Master," he said, pointing at the refrigerators. "He is sedated in the prison cell behind the refrigerators. Paul ordered the police to deliver him to us a few hours ago, knowing that a Shaman could easily break out of a jail cell. Paul wasn't quite sure what a Shaman could do, so he put him in the magically warded, lead-lined cell. Paul was told to deliver him to the Necromancer just before dawn when the guards changed rotations."

I blinked at him. "You're kidding me," I grunted, remembering the metal door I had seen. "Is that why I couldn't sense him? Because it's lead-lined?"

Renfield nodded. "Yes. It's also why we had so many vampires guarding the building. It's usually only a half-dozen or so."

I took the bag of heads from Renfield. "Go get him. Now. He's a scrapper, so tell him you're a friend of Sorin and that you're breaking him out, just in case he's pretending to be asleep."

"Of course, Master. Hairy goat's dick has the only access card, but I'm sure he won't mind me borrowing it," he said, smirking maliciously.

Apparently, Paul had been quite the asshole to earn such hatred from Renfield.

He turned and ran, pouring on his speed so that he was simply a blur of motion. Victoria was still squawking into my ear, taking my silence as a bad sign. "Victoria," I cut in, having to repeat her name three times before she stopped talking. "Nosh is here. Renfield is getting him for me. We'll be right out."

"Who the hell is Renfield?" she demanded.

"You'll see," I said, smirking.

"Well, I've got a surprise for you, too," she muttered, and I heard a strange slurping sound before her earbud clicked off. I chuckled, realizing she had turned off her earbud to punish me.

I turned as I heard the door open behind me. Renfield carefully came around the refrigerators, carrying Nosh in both arms. Nosh's arms, head, and legs hung limply, and his face was battered and bruised. I scowled furiously.

Renfield noticed my look and winced. "I told you that Paul was a hairy goat's dick, Master. The cruelest man I've ever met. Well, petty cruelty. Nothing like Dracula," he admitted.

I nodded, watching for Nosh's breath and reaching out to sense his pulse. It was healthy and strong but slower than it should have been. I let out a soft breath of relief. Renfield smiled down at him. "He is very tough, Master. A good friend. He laughed every time Paul set into him."

I nodded. "Remember my warning. When he wakes up, he will fight like a caged lion. Make sure you aren't standing too close to him."

Then I turned, walking towards the door to the hallway and holding it open for Renfield and Nosh. Renfield waited for me to pass before following me down the hallway. With Nosh's safety off my mind, I felt a great weight lifted from my shoulders. All that remained was the Necromancer and retrieving the journal. I still had no solid answer on why Dracula wanted the journal—just theories—but I was content with simply taking anything and everything Dracula cared about.

I opened the exterior door and took a breath of fresh, misty air. Thunder still rumbled high above, but it was distant warning sounds rather than nearby strikes of lightning.

Victoria faced me from across the street, stepping out of an alley. She was drinking a bottle of orange liquid from a straw—the source of the slurping noise I'd heard. She dropped her drink to the ground, her jaw falling open as she stared. Not at Renfield and Nosh.

At *me.*

The light rain washed over me, and I glanced down to see that I was covered in blood and gore. Completely. I brushed my hair back from my face and smiled. My cape of shifting shadow and blood snapped and cracked of its own accord, fanning out around me dramatically.

That's when I spotted Stevie sitting in a nearby van. He was staring at me in disbelief. I blinked in surprise. Victoria must have called him, informing him of my suicide attempt. That must have been the surprise she had hinted about. I scanned the street and noticed many similar vans. Benjamin and Natalie each sat behind the steering wheel of their own vehicles, as did a handful of other familiar werewolves from Stevie's warehouse. I walked up to Stevie and saw that the passenger—an older black woman—held Victoria's bundle of heads in her lap, still wrapped up in the bloody, white coat. Stevie was craning his neck to wince at Nosh's bruised, unconscious form, casting a suspicious, wary eye at Renfield. I held my hand out with a smug grin, passing him the bag through the open window.

"Five plus the eight Victoria brought you makes thirteen. Time for you to get to work."

He grunted, grabbing the bag and pulling it into the van. He unzipped it in his lap, counting under his breath. He stared down at it, shaking his head incredulously.

Renfield cleared his throat and I turned to look back at him. "We just received another shipment tonight. It hasn't been unloaded yet," he said, holding out his access card. "They were too busy playing cards—much to their ultimate misfortune. I think the keys are still inside the truck. This access card will open the gate," he said, awkwardly handing me the card he had taken from Paul.

I smiled, nodding at him as I accepted it. "Thank you, Renfield." I passed the card to Stevie.

He chuckled, snatching it away. "You crazy son of a bitch."

"You have no idea," I said, turning to walk away.

"Wait!" he shouted, leaning out the window. "Where are you going? We could use your help, caped crusader!"

I grunted, glancing back over my shoulder. "I think I've helped plenty, Stevie. I just handed you the keys to New York City. Now, it's time for me to get Nosh to my hideout below Grand Central Terminal. I can't risk the police finding him again—not if the vampires control them. Meet Renfield and Victoria there with your trucks. Make yourself at home. I'll call in a few hours if I need anything."

He grunted unhappily. "You'll call either way, because I need to make sure you're not going to blow up the world."

I smiled. "Good thing your new home is underground then. I've got a Necromancer to kill."

"That man needs a doctor!" Stevie's passenger shouted, apparently only just now noticing Nosh, judging by the sudden panicked anger in her voice.

I rolled my eyes. "He's fine. Just drugged up."

"On what drugs?" she demanded. "What if they overdosed him? What if he's allergic to the drug? And he's beat all to hell. What if there's internal bleeding? He could die right in front of you and you would just think he was asleep!"

I blinked, craning my neck to peer back into the window. "Are you a doctor?"

She nodded. "Yes, you fool! Skipping out of the building, looking like the goddamned star in a Vidal Sassoon commercial directed by Stephen King. Strutting around like a peacock with your chiseled abs, big pecs and broad shoulders, and not an ounce of intelligence beneath that gorgeous, filthy hair. Get your goddamned friend killed you goddamned idiot."

Stevie was grinning from ear-to-ear, truly enjoying the startled look on my face.

37

She didn't wait for my response, climbing out of the van and slamming the door loudly as she continued to release a steady stream of curses aimed at me and men in general. She waddled around the corner, waggling a finger up at me and Renfield like it was a riding crop and she was one second away from beating the living daylights out of us, even though she was a good two feet shorter than me. She looked incoherent in her rage, her hair slicked back against her scalp to form a perfect black bun in the back. She huffed furiously, her plump brown cheeks quivering with fury, pumping like a blacksmith's forge.

I tried to get in a word edgewise since she was still cursing in a never-ending waterfall of profanity. "In that case, would you please come—"

"I'll hear none of it, Mr. Blood-and-Brawn. I'm coming with you if I have to bend you over my knee and paddle your perfectly-shaped little rear. And don't think I won't enjoy it!"

She obviously hadn't heard my request for her to come with us.

"Thank you. My friend could use a good doctor—"

"Your friend looks like he was hit by a truck, and here you are, standing about in the rain. Your big muscles aren't going to help him. Neither is the rain. He needs a good doctor!"

I sighed, ignoring Stevie's outright laughter. I was pretty sure I heard Victoria joining in behind me, but I couldn't look away from the little force of nature before me.

I smiled politely, dipping my chin. "Let's get him into a car and out of the rain—"

Victoria interrupted me. "I have a car big enough for all of us, Doctor Stein."

Dr. Stein flung up her arms as if her prayers had been answered. "Hallelujah! Finally, someone with some sense between her ears. We need to get this poor creature out of the rain and as far away from these brooding, muscular brutes as we can. They're incredibly hopeless, I tell you," Dr. Stein clamored, shooting me a stern look. "Thank heavens you thought to bring a car, because these two only brought their chest hair."

She actually swatted us both on the ass, whipping our flanks to spur us into motion. Renfield's eyes bulged in stark surprise, but he immediately moved, staring down at the foul-mouthed doctor in stunned disbelief.

I realized I was moving, too, accepting the fact that women were insane. A hive mind of cunning viciousness more powerful than any army of vampires. And their sole purpose was to put men in their places.

And it seemed to be working.

Stevie called out as we hustled away from Dr. Stein, "Take care of them, Frankie. I'll see you all soon!"

"It's Frances, you hairy cretin!" she shrieked venomously, turning to point a furious finger at the alpha werewolf.

I grinned smugly at him, glad to be out of her immediate scrutiny.

As if she had eyes in the back of her skull, she spun and swatted my ass again. I leapt with a shout, stunned by the surprising pain of her blow. I glanced down to see she'd acquired a damned ruler at some point. "Get to moving, you hairy lummox! I don't care how pleasant you are to watch from behind! I want to see that ass *run!*" she snapped, brandishing her ruler threateningly.

I obeyed, leaping out of her range as quickly as I could. Because her feet pounded into the pavement with the power of a hammer striking a nail as she kept up a steady stream of criticisms about my lack of hygiene, my tattered cloak, and lack of respect for my betters.

Victoria was grinning widely at my rapid escape from the primordial predator behind me.

"Lovely child," Doctor Stein called out in a voice as sweet as honey, "I hate to burden you with a lost cause, but I can't very well watch all three of them when one is likely dying, one is running around like a skittish horse with my dying patient, and this buffoon has cotton for brains. Would you please tie him to your apron strings before I break out my wooden spoon?"

Victoria nodded seriously. "I will keep him in line, Dr. Stein. It's the black Lexus on the end," she said, pointing a plastic device at a sleek, expensive-looking car a few vehicles down the sidewalk. The car let out a chirp and the lights flashed.

"Sweet child," Dr. Stein cooed, pinching Victoria's cheek firmly on her way by—hard enough to leave a red blotch and make Victoria's eyes flash with pain. "Face like an angel," she smiled warmly before releasing the vampire hunter from her clutches.

I flinched as she stormed past me, waving her ruler dangerously, not immediately realizing that I was standing slightly behind Victoria for protection and that even my cloak of death had wilted behind me. Victoria burst out laughing—but softly enough for Dr. Stein not to overhear. She was too busy shouting at Renfield anyway.

"The black Lexus, you fool! Hurry!" she shouted at Renfield, who had a panicked look on his face, even though he was already opening the door to set Nosh into the backseat of the car. "Be careful and slow down, you light-blinded idiot! He's a human being, not a bale of hay!"

I stared incredulously, shaking my head at her conflicting advice. "I pray to God I'm never sick or injured," I whispered.

Victoria laughed. "She's probably one of the best surgeons in the city, even though she doesn't practice. The hospitals didn't appreciate her bedside manner. Stevie hired her on the spot, but I'm pretty sure she bullied him until he believed it had been his idea in the first place."

She licked her lips as her eyes feasted on my chest and cloak—

which had found its lost courage, hesitantly beginning to move again, but out of view of Dr. Stein. Seeing as how I rather liked the cloak's comforting embrace—and remembering that I had likened it to Victoria's hot, naked flesh pressed up against mine, I left it in place.

I kept the fantasy to myself, extending my elbow towards Victoria. "We better hurry before you get in trouble too."

She smiled warmly, slipping her arm through mine. "Who is he?"

"Henry Renfield, my batman," I said. "Apparently, he's a ghost from my past, but a man I never knew." She glanced over at me sharply but didn't comment. "Thanks to the power of your blood, I was able to turn him against Dracula. He's about to help us take over the city."

Dr. Stein was already in the passenger seat, glaring at me through the windshield. Renfield sat stiffly in the backseat, as far away from Dr. Stein as he could get without climbing out of the car, and he faced forward with a startled expression on his face. Nosh was seated in the middle seat beside him, his head lolling across Renfield's shoulder, with a long strand of drool hanging from his bloody lip.

"Batman?" Victoria asked, smirking. "Like the superhero? Shouldn't he be the Robin to your Batman? I'm impressed that you tried a pop culture reference, but you missed the mark entirely."

I blinked at her, not understanding. "A batman is a trusted associate. A personal servant who is more like a trusted bodyguard," I explained. "I don't know what a robin has to do with anything."

She squeezed my arm one time, failing to mask her amusement, before letting go and walking towards the driver's side. I made my way to the seat behind Dr. Stein, having to hug my knees to my chest since she had moved the seat all the way back, even though she was no more than four-feet-tall.

"Put your seatbelts on, boys. The hair on your chest won't protect you from a car accident," she snapped tersely. She cast a sweet smile on Victoria. "Don't forget to use your blinkers, Miss Helsing. I prefer to ride in silence, and I won't give a second warning."

Renfield sputtered. "Miss Helsing!" he gasped. "As in, related to—"
THWACK!

The ruler struck the back of Renfield's wrist so fast and hard that it snapped in two, but I wasn't entirely sure that I had actually seen Dr.

Stein move—like she had mastered the power and speed of lightning. I could barely see the top of her head through the gap between the seat and the headrest. As if she wasn't truly there.

"Foolish men," I heard her disembodied voice mutter from the front seat. "Next time it's the spoon," she promised menacingly. I saw a thick, ancient, wooden spoon rise up from the front seat as if by magic. It looked older than *me*.

I leaned my head back, wondering if the tiny tyrant could reach me with her spoon if I accidentally breathed too loudly. As Victoria pulled out into traffic, I glanced at Nosh, hoping he was healthy. I needed him to wake up soon. I had dozens of questions for all of them: him, Renfield, and Victoria, but I had to focus on priorities. Once dawn hit, I would lose the element of surprise.

But if Dr. Frances—Frankie—Stein had her way, I doubted I would be permitted to speak to Nosh anytime soon.

Maybe I would just tell Dr. Stein that the Necromancer had a stomach bug and then sit back and watch as the Warlord of Medicine marched into the vampire fortress with her wooden spoon.

38

We'd made it back to my hideout and Renfield had been ordered—by Dr. Stein, not me—to carry Nosh again as I was ordered to lead them down to my underground hideout.

After Renfield had already picked up Nosh and I'd already begun leading the way to my hideout, of course.

Dr. Stein had sniffed disdainfully at my humble shelter, but had seemed pleased at the collection of medicine Deganawida had stockpiled. After a significant argument, I'd finally convinced Victoria to stay behind with Nosh. Dr. Stein had interrupted me, suggesting the exact same thing and calling me nine kinds of idiot for offering medical advice.

Being a gentleman, I had let her have her way.

I'd been concerned that Nosh might wake up and attack the first person in sight. Now I was concerned that if he woke too early, he would find his new imprisonment worse than Paul the Pisser beating him to a pulp on a regular basis.

Not permitted to do anything else in my hideout—other than take a quick hand bath to wash off the rest of the blood and gore from my hair and body—Renfield and I had left, choosing to take the subway to pay our first and final visit to the Necromancer. We had formed a simple but effective plan, so I had put my suit from the auction back on, even though it had been bloodied up, because Nosh had been wearing a suit in his prison cell, and he'd definitely been bloodied up. It was clean enough that I could hide the bloodstains under my coat.

On the subway, Renfield had elaborated on his story but he hadn't known anything further about my son. Whether the adopting tribe had sold him into slavery or accepted him as one of their own. If he had grown up healthy and happy with a family of his own, or if he'd died in one of the later wars that had plagued the continent. Since Renfield had immediately traveled back to Europe to suffer Dracula's displeasure and his own personal hell with his family, essentially held hostage, he obviously hadn't been able to follow up on my son.

And with hundreds of years passing between then and now, I had no other leads to go on.

My only hope to fill in the gaps was Deganawida's old journal.

Stevie's werewolves hadn't offered any explanation about what had become of Lucian, other than that he had founded their pack long ago.

And I hadn't heard anything about Nero.

I finally sighed, glancing up at the screen that showed our next stop. We were close to the Museum of Natural History.

I glanced at Renfield. "What can you tell me about this Necromancer? Who is he, really, and why do they call him that?"

Renfield shrugged uncomfortably. "I have never met him. I know that he is a slave to Dracula much like myself. Much like all of us. That he's incredibly powerful and feared by every vampire I've met, and that he refuses to be seen in public, spending all his time in the museum. He spent many, many years studying death, learning spells to bring the dead to life."

I arched an eyebrow. "Why? Does Dracula have an undead army?" I asked nervously.

Renfield shook his head. "Not to my knowledge. I think Dracula chose that name to mock him—that he has a man with such knowledge under his thumb, and that he doesn't let him use it."

I nodded, pursing my lips. That sounded about right. "And you think we can just walk right in?" I asked uneasily. We'd settled on a plan after discussing and discarding at least six others as hopeless and doomed to failure. The winning plan wasn't much better, but it stood a better chance than anything else.

At even the slightest sign of violence or an attack, every vampire within miles would rush to protect their fortress.

"None of us sensed you in the blood bank," Renfield reassured me. "We only responded when we heard the gunshots. I've never seen anyone with that level of strength—to mask yourself from a five-hundred-year-old vampire. Well, only Dracula, I guess. But he's the oldest—" he grunted, realizing his mistake. "Second-oldest vampire."

I nodded, forcing my shoulders to relax. I still had Victoria's blood pouring through my veins, and I hadn't wanted to waste a single minute, fearing that it would fade away again, leaving me weakened. On the other hand, I hadn't dared to drink from her again—not so soon after the first time. It could harm her as much as me.

We climbed off the subway and I kept my head down, aimed at the ground so that my hair concealed my features from any sentries or security cameras. I followed Renfield's guiding hand with my hands tied before me, concealed from casual view by my leather coat.

I was unable to see our target building, fearing the risk of anyone recognizing me as the man from the news—the murderer of the Griffin family. Because I had seen my face on the front page of dozens of newspapers along our trip on the subway.

Renfield paused and murmured under his breath, almost inaudibly. "My apologies, Master."

I grunted. "Do it."

I felt him sigh regretfully as he tugged a black hood over my head, concealing my face and long hair. We walked for about ten more minutes, and the sense of nearby humanity soon faded away entirely. I checked my powers, making sure I was completely masked, and made sure to stumble lethargically as if I was drugged.

With Renfield's long-standing reputation as an obedient pushover with no hopes or even possibilities of higher aspirations, everyone knew he would never dare do anything to put him in a worse standing than he already was.

Because they were too ignorant to realize that a man at rock bottom had nothing left to lose.

Unfortunately, that meant I had to climb into the bottom of the well with him for our plan to work. Renfield knocked on a door and I heard a metallic *click*. He led me a few paces farther and I heard the door *click* again as it shut behind me.

"What the fuck are you doing here, stable boy? You're supposed to be at the blood bank," A low voice growled, practically dripping with aggression. I was blocking my aura even tighter than I had at the blood bank—since Victoria's blood made me so much stronger, and I didn't want to risk the Necromancer being powerful enough to sense me through my shield—so it was harder for me to sense how many vampires surrounded us. I could hear their muffled encouragement through my hood, all of them chuckling with the man who had spoken.

Renfield cleared his throat. "Paul McIntyre sent me with urgent news. You know I wouldn't be here otherwise," he murmured meekly.

The laughter cut off, all of them obviously well acquainted with Paul. Perhaps even fearful of him. It was very difficult for me not to laugh about his brave bladder.

"What orders?" the man asked warily. "You're the last person he would send here."

"Which is *why* he sent me," Renfield said submissively. "The were-wolves invaded the blood bank, trying to take the Shaman prisoner."

The man grunted. "You called and told me everything was fine," he growled furiously, and I heard the sound of fist striking flesh, jerking me to the side. I stumbled, playing along as the drugged-up prisoner I was supposed to be.

Renfield grunted, accepting the blow without offense. "That was apparently a distraction. While Paul was interrogating the homeless man I called about, someone cut the power at the building and a pack of werewolves burst in. They stole the keycard from the sentry. They beheaded him," Renfield growled disgustedly. "Paul feared one of his vampires had been compromised or spied upon, so he sent me to sneak the prisoner out while he fought back the wolves. Alex and Christopher had already fallen when I left." Several of the men gasped in outrage. "Paul said the Necromancer would experiment on anyone who tried to defy or delay his orders," Renfield added, sounding as if he was afraid of rebuke. "I'm just trying to do as I'm told, but Paul needs help. Badly. I think the wolves intended to burn the building down to destroy our blood supply."

The man grunted. "Motherfucking wolves! Why didn't you call us on your way here?" he demanded.

"Paul made me leave my phone so I couldn't be tracked."

The man grunted. "Well, get your ass up there. I'll call ahead to let them know. Looks like it's your lucky day, Renfield, getting to meet the big boss. If you even *look* at him wrong, I'll make you squeal," he warned, sounding suddenly closer.

"Y-yes, sir," Renfield stammered.

"Round up the men! Let's go skin some wolves, boys!" he snarled, and I heard growls and the stomping of many boots as they dispersed in a tidal wave.

"I've got confirmation of a fire at the blood bank!" someone shouted.

Men cursed, their footsteps growing faster and fainter as they fled to the scene.

Thank you, Stevie, I thought to myself. We'd called to tell him our plan and to make sure he got everyone out before the vampires arrived. He'd suggested lighting the building on fire.

39

R enfield let out a sigh of relief. "We're clear for the moment, but we still have plenty of vampires to worry about downstairs."

I nodded beneath my hood. "I told you that fear was a remarkable motivator, Renfield. You're doing great. I even believed you."

Renfield urged me forward. "I've had practice," he murmured. "But it was never fear of *them*. It was fear of what would happen when they tattled on me to Dracula. His capacity for pointless punishment is infinitely creative."

"Not for long," I promised. Once again, I checked on my power, knowing that I had to maintain the ruse that I wasn't a vampire or we were doomed. Because we were heading to the lower levels, and some of the inhabitants there were almost as old as Renfield.

And that they might want to get a look under my hood before permitting my delivery to the Necromancer. If that happened, we'd have to abandon my disguise and hope for the best. To shut down the threat without drawing the attention of every other nearby vampire.

I heard a musical chime, and then Renfield ushered me forward a few steps before halting. I heard him press a button. "Silence, prisoner," he snapped.

Knowing I hadn't said anything, I took it as a warning that we weren't private or that we were being observed via camera. I felt the ground drop and I stumbled in surprise, not having expected an elevator. It was only a short trip, because the doors opened a few moments after I regained my balance. I shambled forward as I heard the doors open, following Renfield's muttered directions.

It was disorienting and panic-inducing to walk blindly through hell. I lost track of how many times we turned left or right, but we didn't encounter any further vampires. At least none who stopped to talk to Renfield. Perhaps the hood over my head was a conversation killer.

But there were definitely a lot of vampires down here. I heard distant, anxious shouting, obviously a result of the attack on the blood bank. I heard ringing phones and heated arguments, but Renfield pressed on as if we were on a calm walk through the woods.

All sounds of life soon faded away, and we walked for another two minutes before Renfield slowed, squeezing my arm reassuringly.

"I have orders to deliver the Shaman, Nosh Griffin, to the Necromancer," Renfield said nervously.

I heard a man grunt. "Shaman, eh? Doesn't look like much."

"Randall Walsh said he would call ahead," Renfield answered in a respectful tone, obviously talking about the security guard from the entrance. "Paul McIntyre sent me."

"So many names dropped," the man mused dismissively. "But I suppose the stable boy must do as *everyone* commands."

"True, Lord Hugo. I've never met him," Renfield murmured. "I fear making a bad impression."

Hugo grunted. "If anyone needs to fear making a bad impression, it definitely isn't you, Renfield. You poor, despicable creature. I feel guilty even *looking* at you, as if I'm the one who beats you every night." Hugo let out an impatient sigh and I made sure to sag my shoulders, maintaining my drugged-up prisoner façade. But it was difficult, hearing about Renfield's daily torture. Whoever was behind it would pay, one way or another. "Let me have a look, first. It will be my head if I don't," Hugo said.

Renfield stammered. "Even drugged up, he is very dangerous, Lord Hugo. I was told to keep the hood on for our safety."

Hugo growled. "I will have a look or I will have *your* head, stable boy."

"Of course," Renfield said obediently.

Shit.

I knew we couldn't risk spilling a drop of blood or it would draw every vampire like a fly to manure. This close, I sensed Lord Hugo's power and grew uneasy, knowing it would be a fight that I had to end quickly, but that I couldn't call upon my power too early. Hugo lifted my hood and immediately grunted in surprise. I wasted no time, lifting my gaze to hit him with the look—the most focused, targeted, overpowered look I could manage. His knees buckled as he struggled against my enthrallment, but my power slipped over him a moment before he could properly lift his defenses. I watched his eyes glaze over just as two more vampires entered my peripheral vision.

"Hey! What's going on here?" one of them demanded.

I lowered my head drunkenly, hoping they would simply walk away. I even angled my head away from them, hoping to conceal how long my hair was in case they knew what Nosh looked like.

I breathed a command under my breath, hoping that Lord Hugo was coherent enough to obey so soon after my hasty enthrallment. "Nothing, Aristos," Hugo finally grumbled. "Just doing my damned job and making sure the Necromancer is safe. You heard about the fire at the blood bank? The werewolf attack?"

"Of course," the man named Aristos grunted.

"Then perhaps you would be better served doing something useful for once," Lord Hugo snapped. "Go find out what really happened over there. We all know Paul is a hotheaded soldier, but he's useless without orders, whereas you seem to attempt little else."

I hunched over, concealing my grin. That last bit had been all Hugo. For the first time, I was able to get a scant look at our surroundings. I stood before a tall set of double doors. Hugo manned a desk with science apparatus littered across the surface in what I took for a risky arrangement. He obviously guarded the Necromancer's chambers.

"Careful, Hugo. Every flower has a season, and I feel a frost coming on," Aristos warned.

The second man spoke up, sounding amused at their bickering.

"Put your fangs away, boys. Is this the infamous Shaman then?" he asked. "Nosh Griffin has grown his hair out."

Hugo grunted. "I never paid much attention to fashion, Valentine. By the looks of it, you haven't either."

Valentine hissed angrily. "I'm the most fashionable man here!"

Hugo gestured dismissively. "Unless you two want to explain why you're delaying me from obeying the Necromancer's orders—of which I will *definitely* inform him—it's time for the both of you to go back to braiding each other's hair and to get out of mine."

"You're bald, you insolent cow," Valentine snapped haughtily.

"Because I have to deal with imbeciles like you all too often. I keep pulling my hair out."

They sniffed pompously, turning on their heels. Hugo watched them leave—as did Renfield. Then they both scanned our surroundings and let out sighs of relief.

Hugo turned to me, looking shaken. "Who—"

I shut him down with a stern thought. "Announce our arrival—convincingly—and then get back to your duties. Keep everyone away and I might let you live."

Hugo nodded woodenly, motioning us to the giant doors. Renfield tugged the hood back over my head and I readied myself for war as Hugo knocked on the doors with a resounding *thud-thud-thud*. He paused, and then thumped the door one last time—some kind of prearranged code, perhaps? I could only hope that it wasn't a prearranged alarm and that Hugo had found a way to worm out of my control.

The fact that the Necromancer hadn't sensed the brief pulse of power I'd used was surprising, but maybe he simply mistook it as his minions bickering back and forth.

"Come in, Hugo," a smooth, commanding voice called out.

Hugo opened the doors and spoke in a clear tone, ushering us inside. "Henry Renfield and Nosh Griffin, the Shaman prisoner, my lord," he said by way of introduction. "Paul McIntyre sent him over early due to a werewolf attack at the blood bank."

Then he wisely abandoned us so as not to accept any responsibility for the news update. I heard the doors close behind me as Renfield guided me deeper into the room.

Deeper into the belly of the beast.

Ahead of me, somewhere, was the infamous, secretive Necromancer.

40

I stood in silence, wanting nothing more than to lunge forward and destroy everything before me, but I didn't know where the Necromancer stood, and I didn't know how powerful he was. I was clamping down on my power so tightly that I couldn't sense anything—almost like I was mortal.

"So, this is the man causing me so much trouble. Well, causing Dracula so much trouble," the Necromancer said, striding closer. I frowned beneath my hood, a strange sensation tickling the back of my neck. I suddenly wanted nothing more than to yank the hood from my head. "Rise to your feet, Renfield. I hate a man who grovels too much."

"Yes, Necromancer," Renfield stammered.

Every muscle in my body was suddenly fighting against me, and I gritted my teeth, fighting it down. The power deep within me sloshed and sprayed like waves against a cliff, fighting to wear it away and press forward.

"Mina Harker mentioned the Shaman had an ally. I think she said she was framing him for a murder, but I lost interest in her prattling on, flashing her breasts all over the room. I told her to get back with me when she had more results than tits, but I haven't heard from her since her goons delivered the journal."

Renfield was utterly silent.

"Well? Has she caught him yet?" the Necromancer demanded impatiently.

I heard Renfield licking his lips anxiously. "I haven't heard from Miss Harker, but the suspect's picture was put on all the media outlets," he said nervously.

The Necromancer grunted. "Well, I don't have time for the media outlets. I have you. Who is this man and why do we care about him?"

Renfield stammered awkwardly and I wanted to burst out laughing. The Necromancer hadn't seen my face, even though it had been blasted all over the news. "I think he's still at large, Lord Necromancer."

He grumbled unhappily. "That blood strumpet is more trouble than she's worth," he cursed. "Only useful because Dracula likes to hump her almost as much as he loves fresh blood."

I blinked, feeling deliriously pleased with myself at learning I had killed Dracula's bedmate.

I heard the Necromancer advance closer, pausing thoughtfully. "I've always wondered why Dracula hates you so much, Renfield. The fact that no one knows the truth is what emboldens their cruelty. I'm sure you're unable to speak of it, knowing Dracula's penchant for privacy," the Necromancer murmured, sounding bored. "Since you don't seem to have a brain cell in your head, we may as well get this over with. Let's have a look at the dangerous Shaman. I'm required to check the inventory before putting it on the plane for our trip back home."

I steadied my nerves, hanging my head low as I debated a dozen courses of action I might take. His boots stopped no more than a pace away from me.

"That would mean *now*, Renfield."

"Of course, my lord," Renfield stammered, likely having no idea what I expected him to do. "Just nervous, my lord."

The Necromancer sighed impatiently. "I'll just do it myself!"

His hand grabbed the hood and yanked it off. Thankfully, the room was dimly lit so I didn't wince on instinct. I slowly lifted my gaze, panting anxiously as I waited to confirm my suspicion—the suspicion I'd had the moment I first heard the Necromancer speak.

The Necromancer stared at me, his smug grin rapidly fading into a visage of horror.

I stared at him, narrowing my eyes, recalling that night so long ago when my tribe had been attacked. When I had felt magic blanket the area, blocking me from sensing the attack soon enough to prevent it.

"It's so good to see you again, *old friend*," I snarled, twisting my wrists so that the fake, knotted rope binding my wrists fell to the ground.

Nero—the world's first warlock—stared back in utter shock, dropping the hood.

"Sorin..." he breathed, his voice shaking. "You're alive."

"Just in time to watch you die, traitor."

And I lunged for his throat, wanting to rip him in half with my bare hands.

My old warlock friend, Nero, was Dracula's Necromancer.

My old warlock friend, Nero, had betrayed me and destroyed my family.

I was truly going to enjoy this...

41

I slammed into a wall of solid air and snarled viciously. A lamp came flying from behind me and struck Nero in the jaw, causing him to stumble and release his shield of air. I lunged through his magic and gripped him by the throat, snapping my fangs at his face. My hand didn't rest on flesh, but a wide band of metal around his throat.

Nero stared at me—not in fear, but in shock. "How?" he rasped.

I slammed him down to the ground so fast and hard that the back of his head struck the wooden floor first, his boots thumping to the ground two full seconds later. His eyes rolled, dazed by the blow, but he didn't cast any magic at me. I punched him in the side with my free hand, breaking one of his ribs to jar him back to his senses with pain.

Renfield picked up the discarded lamp and slammed it down into Nero's knee with a sharp crack that broke bone and shattered the lamp, causing the Necromancer to squeal in agony.

"Why?" I demanded, baring my fangs as I stared into his eyes. The eyes of a man I had once called a friend. One of my two best friends.

"It wasn't me, Sorin," he wheezed, clutching at his broken rib and knee, whimpering. "But I know how this looks—"

I picked him up and flung him into the marble fireplace. He grunted as his back struck the mantle, knocking the breath from him before his body crumpled to the floor. Still, he didn't cast any magic at me. The only magic he'd thrown had been a wall of air to keep me *back*, but he'd simply stopped trying after that.

He stared at me, holding his palms up in an innocent gesture, gasping through his numerous injuries. "Lucian and I came back to find the camp destroyed. Deganawida told us you *died*, Sorin. What the fuck?"

"Yet here you are," I snarled, holding out my hands to indicate his richly furnished chambers.

He nodded guiltily. "Lucian stayed behind to defend the Americas and build a new pack. I went to Europe to hunt Dracula down. I..." he trailed off, looking sick to his stomach. "I failed, Sorin. He caught me." And Nero very carefully tapped the collar around his throat, hissing suddenly—as if merely touching the collar with his finger had caused excruciating pain. It took him a moment to regain his breath. "He sent me back to betray Lucian," he finally whispered. "I had no choice. This collar prevents me from disobeying Dracula. I'm just a puppet—" His eyes suddenly widened with panic. "Oh, no! You have to get away from me before he senses—"

Nero's body abruptly stiffened in an entirely unnatural way. His head flung back and he rasped in pain. Then his body stilled and grew relaxed as if he'd fallen asleep—or died.

I shared a quick glance at Renfield who shook his head. "No idea..." he murmured uneasily, shooting his attention back to Nero.

My old warlock friend slowly rose, sitting up. His face was utterly calm and relaxed, and his eyes were suddenly solid red, his pupils *gone*. They narrowed upon seeing Renfield. "What is the meaning of this, stable boy?" he snarled suspiciously.

But his voice no longer sounded like Nero. It was cold, sinister, and dripping with the arrogance of a self-righteous emperor. A voice I would recognize anywhere for its unique baritone.

Dracula.

He turned to me and visibly flinched, blinking rapidly. Then he leapt to his feet, pointing a finger at me. "You!" he snarled in that same voice, hobbling on Nero's broken knee.

"Dracula," I growled, my claws flashing out. The collar apparently allowed Dracula to possess Nero's body. Which was an incredibly efficient way to rule two hemispheres.

"Sorin, my old friend," he mused, his lips curling up into a macabre grin. "You just won't die, will you? Perhaps you would like to join your friend? I have another collar especially for you."

I seethed, panting as Victoria Helsing's blood seemed to scream within me, begging to avenge her father. My inner demon railed against my control, wanting nothing more than to skin Dracula alive. Neither cared that Nero was stuck in the middle.

"Let Nero go and face me yourself, coward," I hissed.

"This answers *so* many questions, Sorin. You have no idea what you've done."

"Come to me, Dracula. Face me in person. I will wait for you."

Dracula grinned. "Oh, I will. Now I have a *reason* to come to New York. But not yet. First, I think I'll watch you kill your old friend, Nero."

And he laughed a terrible laugh as he lifted up a hand, preparing to hurl devastating magic at me. Faster than I could blink, Renfield darted in front of me, slicing off Nero's hand at the wrist. Dracula laughed, even as Nero's face contorted in agony—giving me a horrifying juxtaposition. Nero's body and soul were being tortured, and Dracula was not letting him address it, using his body like a puppet.

Before I could think about what I was doing, I tackled Nero to the ground, gripping the collar with both hands. Dracula's voice spilled out of Nero's mouth. "No! Stop!"

Dracula beat at me with Nero's bleeding stump, causing Nero blinding pain but not caring about his host's injuries. Dracula was perversely *enjoying* it. We struggled, rolling over across the floor as I tried to tear off the collar. Renfield dove in, pinning my foe's shoulders down as I loomed over him, flexing every muscle as my claws squealed against the cold, seemingly impenetrable metal. But with Dracula's constant squirming, I couldn't get a proper grip.

Then the crucifix necklace fell from beneath my shirt, the chain having snapped in our struggle. The crucifix fell onto Nero's forehead...

And Dracula—not Nero—squealed like a stuck pig.

Renfield redoubled his efforts, trying to keep Nero still as he thrashed and bucked in a desperate attempt to get the crucifix off his forehead. I gripped him by the throat and slapped my palm over the tiny, simple cross.

It began to smoke, searing Nero's flesh as it grew hot to the touch. And then it grew *hotter*. The scent of scorched flesh didn't solely belong to Nero. My own palm blazed with fire, and I sensed Victoria's blood fighting to freeze it and save me the pain.

I stared down at Nero, watching his eyes, waiting for the red to disappear.

Dracula panted hoarsely, cursing my name, my wife and son, my friend Lucian, but most of all, Nero.

I leaned close. "I'm coming for you, boy," I promised him.

"You'll never get near me! I *own* the travel industry! I will crash every plane and sink every ship leaving your shores!" he snarled, spittle flying from his lips as the red began to fade and slip away. "I own *everything*! I will throw the *world* at you, Sorin Ambrogio!"

I stared into his eyes, smiling sadly. "I actually pity you, Dracula. Because you bought your own façade. You, who stood on the shoulders of a giant and convinced yourself that you were actually flying. Well, the giant is waiting for you. In New York City—which is now *mine!*"

Dracula's eyes danced madly, wildly, furiously. "I will kill every vampire in New York City! On the spot—"

And Nero's body suddenly slumped, falling unconscious the moment Dracula was finally banished. I flung the crucifix across the room with a snarl. I stared down at Nero and the cross branded into his forehead. I glanced down at my palm to see an identical scar, shaking my head angrily as I thought on Dracula's parting threat. Then I gasped in understanding.

Seeing Nero's wrist still freely bleeding, I quickly grabbed it, spitting my venom onto his wound to halt the bleeding. I shot Renfield a panicked look. "You have less than sixty seconds to collect as many vampires as you can find and bring them to Hugo's desk. After that, they are all dead." Renfield nodded, racing out from the room in a blur. I closed my eyes, pulled deep on my augmented blood, and cast a protective net as far and wide as I could—covering maybe a hundred paces. I hoped it was enough to save some of the vampires from the curse Dracula was no doubt already performing. These vampires had the answers I needed, which was why Dracula was willing to kill them all—to keep them from me.

I quickly searched Nero's collar until I found the original clasp. It had been fused over with melted metal, judging by the burn scars on Nero's neck, but I knew there was still a weak point beneath or Dracula never would have gotten it onto him in the first place. My muscles bulged as I strained, fueling my strength with Victoria's blood. I screamed, the metal growing hot in my hands before it finally snapped in a resounding *crack* like a felling tree.

I couldn't be sure that Nero hadn't been lying to me. That he hadn't called Dracula himself. But I knew his injuries would keep him unconscious for a good long while.

I felt a lead blanket of death abruptly press down upon the entire building and I cursed.

Dracula had begun.

42

I hissed at the sensation even though I knew it wasn't lethal to me or Renfield since we weren't bonded to Dracula. The curse would only be able to kill his own bonded vampires. The reason I'd never been able to do such a thing to save my own empire was because Dracula had been influencing them with his blood long before I knew about the coup. That was the only explanation.

Because I'd secretly tried to kill them all—much as he was trying to do now—and I'd failed.

I dashed out of the room to find Hugo wincing against the unseen force.

I sliced my wrist and held it over his mouth. "Dracula is trying to sever all bonds to his American vampires. You have less than thirty seconds before I can no longer hold him back." Then I bit into his forearm without permission, sucking down a quick gulp of his blood. There was no time for anything else—do or die. I tore my fangs away and released him as he frantically began to gulp my blood. I withdrew my hand. "My name is Sorin Ambrogio," I said hurriedly, realizing I hadn't officially told him yet. "Swear your undying fealty to me. That you will faithfully and loyally serve me, and only me, until death do us part." He repeated the oath faster than I had, panting at the effort. I latched onto our shared blood and forced it into submission with a snarl—not having the time to do it gently like I had with Renfield. But it worked, the sensation of fire and ice actually making me hiss in pain.

If I hadn't had Victoria's blood in my veins, it would have been impossible.

Hugo's shoulders slumped as Dracula's pressure instantly backed off, no longer a threat.

Renfield rounded the corner, dragging two overly pretty men by their overly pretty hair.

Hugo muttered an annoyed curse to see the chosen survivors as Renfield kicked the back of their knees, sending them to the ground with a thud. Then he yanked their hair back violently. "Aristos and Valentine were all I could find, Master."

"My name is Sorin Ambrogio," I snapped hurriedly, feeling Dracula's dread power swamping over the building with greater malevolence. I fought back as best I could, redoubling my efforts to shield us for one more minute. "Dracula is trying to kill everyone. Swear fealty to me, and you get to live."

They nodded without hesitation, lifting their arms. I bit into each of their wrists, took quick gulps, and then tore my other wrist open. I held my arms over each of their mouths so they could drink my blood. Then I repeated the oath with them.

Once they swore fealty and I bound our magic together—doing them both simultaneously—they collapsed in relief. I, on the other hand, stumbled at the stabbing pain of fire and ice, gasping hoarsely. Renfield caught me by the shoulders, steadying me for a few moments.

"Thank you," I whispered, shaking my head as the pain faded.

My three new vampires stared at each other, looking bewildered. A palpable hush suddenly pressed down over us, like heavy cloud cover drifting across the full moon.

Death quietly fell over New York City, and I knew every vampire with ties to Dracula had just died. It was stunning in scope, but not surprising as a tactic.

"Why would he do such a thing?" Aristos whispered.

I grunted. "He knew I could steal your fealty. He wasn't punishing you, he was trying to prevent me from gaining an army."

They suddenly seemed to recognize me. "You...are the man from the news."

I narrowed my eyes. "Yes. The man Mina Harker tried to frame for murders he didn't commit. She died under mysterious circumstances upon meeting me at an auction."

Renfield chuckled and they shot him an instinctive, reprimanding frown.

"I am the world's first vampire. The man who turned Dracula."

Their eyes widened incredulously, but they didn't dare voice their doubts. Not less than a minute after I'd just saved them.

I smiled as I watched the machinations and politics begin to start, their eyes narrowing as they sized each other up, vying for power. Unbelievable. They were about to realize that I ran things quite a bit differently than Dracula.

That I refused to make the same mistake twice.

As the three newly saved vampires were still sizing each other up, internally preparing their pitches to inform me how they could serve me better than their colleagues, I shot Renfield a macabre smile, holding out an inviting hand for him to handle it as he saw fit. The three noticed this, frowning warily.

Instead of answering their curious looks, I turned my back on them and began walking back to Nero's office. "Renfield is my number one. Before you comment on my decision—even respectfully—you should think extremely hard on how you've treated Renfield over the past centuries. And you should know that I trust him implicitly. Enough to close this door right now and leave you three in his most capable hands." I glanced over my shoulder. "Come see me when you've finished getting them in line. I want to know what they've been doing for Dracula and the Necromancer. Immediately."

"Yes, Master Ambrogio," Renfield said, dipping his chin. For the briefest of moments, his eyes met mine, and no amount of words could have relayed how grateful he was for my trust.

For the second chance I had given him.

I nodded back, acknowledging the silent thoughts. "That will be all, Master Renfield."

I let the door click shut behind me.

I stared down at Nero's unconscious form for a few moments, thinking. Then I stepped over his beaten, bloody, and burned body, and sat down in his chair, kicking my feet up on top of his desk. Deganawida's journal sat on the corner, and I let out a sigh of relief.

But I didn't touch it.

A strange device with a pad of numbers and a retractable attachment that looked eerily similar to the *call* icon from Nosh's expensive phone sat atop the desk. I frowned at it for a few moments. Then I pressed the order of numbers to call Stevie's phone, curious how the device worked. Nothing happened. I scooped up the attachment and heard a rapid series of beeps from within. I held it to my ear, grinning as it began to ring in a familiar fashion. I grunted victoriously, waiting for Stevie to answer.

Victoria answered instead, sounding frantic. I smiled. "Sapphires and moonlight," I murmured. "It is done..."

I heard her responding purr through the phone, and it made the hair on the back of my neck stand on end. We spoke for about two minutes before she cut me off and told me she was coming to see me in person. I smiled eagerly. "That sounds delightful."

She hung up before I could ask about Nosh.

Renfield opened the door, peering inside. "I have them gathering pertinent information that I thought you might want to see, but it will take them some time."

I nodded. "Miss Helsing is on her way. Have one of them ready to receive her and show her every courtesy."

Renfield nodded. "Valentine will suffice."

I nodded, glancing down at the unconscious Nero. "Do we have any sedatives here?"

Renfield nodded. "Certainly. We also have fully furnished rooms available for guests who are here on an extended stay." I cocked my head, frowning. "Warded prisons, Master Ambrogio," he explained, smirking.

I nodded. "Even better. Let's do both, just to be safe. I want to take a shower without worrying about him."

Renfield bowed and walked up to Nero. He grabbed him by a boot and simply began dragging him across the floor. "I'm afraid the elevator doesn't descend to the dungeon," he said, not sounding the least bit disappointed.

I chuckled. "Stairs it is, then." I was entirely certain that Renfield had no intention of carrying the warlock over his shoulder. He would either drag Nero down the stairs or get one of the other vampires to do the dirty work.

Case in point, Renfield forgot to hold the door open so it banged shut on Nero's head, eliciting a pained groan from the sleeping warlock.

The door finally closed and I sighed contentedly, lacing my hands behind my neck. I spotted fresh wood beside the fireplace and two doors leading off from the main room. I walked over to find that one was an elaborate bathroom with a luxurious shower similar to the one I had used in Nosh's parents' penthouse. The other room was a large master suite, complete with dressers of fresh clothes and a large closet.

I nodded satisfactorily. "This will do nicely," I murmured, making my way back to the bathroom to turn on the shower. As the water warmed up, I walked back out to the main room and started a fire.

"Much better than the subway," I mused. "Probably smells like wet dog down there now anyway."

43

I sat on a couch beside Victoria, listening to the crackling fire in Nero's old office. She had teased me several times about my robe —something I had found in Nero's closet that had looked ridiculously soft and fluffy—but the look in her eyes told me her teasing was closely tied to envy.

Renfield had returned, confirming that our guest was enjoying his new accommodations that we had provided, and that he was currently resting. Translation—Nero was buttoned up tightly in his warded prison cell, sleeping off his sedatives.

Stevie had accompanied Victoria, and Renfield had discovered an exquisite bottle of wine from my new collection, filling everyone's glass to the brim. Her blood coursing through my veins was still present, but it had significantly faded after my struggle against Dracula.

On the other hand, bonding four vampires—old, powerful vampires—had given me a boost of power all my own. I knew it would be some time before I was back to my full strength without the assistance of Victoria's potent blood, but no one else knew about that. I wondered why I couldn't sense that power in her veins from a distance. She smelled enticing, but no more than other immortals I had met in my life. Nero, for example.

Stevie had given me an update on Nosh, stating that he was perfectly fine but that Dr. Stein was refusing to let him get out of bed—which was a cold pallet on the floor, with dozens of werewolves stepping over him every five minutes.

"The only vampires left in New York City are mine, Stevie. You don't have to live underground if you don't want to. The choice is yours, of course. But there is a new rule. If a wolf kills a vampire—or vice versa—they die. Unless a crime was committed."

He nodded. "We'll have to figure out a way to judge that. A way we can all agree on."

I nodded. "In time. For now, you will give me the responsibility in exchange for freeing you of your vampire problem. I imagine there is now a large power vacuum for your werewolves to fill. I have no problem sharing."

Renfield cleared his throat politely. "Hugo is gathering financial reports for you so we can review the various business operations that were in play."

I nodded, eyeing Stevie. "Operations that suddenly need new management."

He finally nodded, reading between the lines. "That sounds nice. I can make that work."

I smiled. "I have no desire to become a king again, Stevie. This is a large city. Plenty for us to share."

Victoria cleared her throat. "We aren't the only players in town. The witches are silent but powerful. They usually stay out of town, but that was a result of the infighting between werewolf and vampire."

"And now werewolf and vampire are allies—an even greater force."

She shot me a grim look. "Technically, it's a much weaker force. Hundreds of vampires dropped dead, and that's impossible to hide. People are already talking."

I nodded. "We have a lot of work to do, and Dracula is still out there."

"Should we meet again tomorrow?" Stevie asked me. "I'm sure you have a lot to catch up on," he said, gesturing at the door and the vampires diligently working outside. I nodded. "The police are still looking for you, and you don't have them in your pocket. Whatever evidence they had on you is still out there. The DNA thing will be hard to beat," he said, setting his drink down and climbing to his feet.

I kept my face composed as Victoria shot me a stern look, shaking her head. Stevie hadn't noticed since he'd been climbing to his feet. "I'm looking into it," I said carefully, not sure what Victoria had been trying to tell me.

"We should probably head out," Stevie said, glancing at Victoria.

"I think I will stick around for a bit longer. I want to talk to Sorin about something."

He smirked, holding up his hands. "I don't want to know," he said, chuckling. He turned, accidentally bumping into a side table with an ornate chest on it. "Whoops." The table stood firm and he let out a relieved breath, shaking his head. "This mysterious Necromancer had nice taste," he mused, tapping the ornate chest with a fingernail. Renfield stood, guiding him from the room.

I stared at the chest, not having noticed it before Stevie bumped into it. My hand began to shake as Victoria said something to me. Rather than respond, I abruptly climbed to my feet and hesitantly made my way over to it.

"Sorin? Did you hear me?" Victoria asked.

I opened the chest, holding my breath. Inside was a familiar silk pouch, and I let out a gasp of surprise. Victoria was suddenly standing beside me, gripping me by the shoulder.

"Sorin! What's wrong?"

I pointed down at the silk pouch. "Dirt. The son of a bitch found it."

"Found what?" Victoria asked, sounding frustrated and nervous. "How will a box of dirt help you?"

I smiled down at the box, my mind suddenly racing with possibilities. I thought this chest had been long lost. My safety net.

"Dirt," Victoria repeated, sounding concerned.

I nodded, turning to face her. "I need a large open place without a lot of people."

"Why?" she asked, looking baffled.

"I want to get into real estate."

She arched an eyebrow, looking suddenly concerned for my sanity.

"Well, the only vacant land in New York City without people is probably Central Park. But that's not for sale. Period."

I shrugged. "I'm not looking to buy it. I want to build something there."

She didn't look relieved by my answer. "With dirt? Are you sure you're feeling okay?"

I nodded excitedly. "This is my *coffin dirt*. The coffin dirt of the oldest vampire in the world. It's tied directly to my castle. No matter what Dracula claims, that castle is *mine*. If I can't travel to him..."

She gasped incredulously. "That story is true? About your coffin dirt establishing a portal to Castle Dracula?"

I narrowed my eyes. "With this coffin dirt, I can bring Castle Ambrogio to *us*."

She made the sign of the cross. "Shit. If you want to do anything in Central Park, you better start praying."

"Why?"

"Because it's consecrated ground. The Nephilim own Central Park. Not even the vampires risked setting foot there."

I stared at her, stunned. "The Nephilim are in New York? The offspring of Angels?" I'd never met one, but I was well aware of the dangers rumored about them.

"And the witches...

I nodded. "It seems we have a lot to think about," I said, feeling suddenly optimistic.

She paused, pursing her lips. "You weren't listening to me earlier, were you?"

I frowned. "I'm sorry. The dirt distracted me. I'd buried it long ago and hadn't known Nero recovered it. I thought it was lost."

She nodded stiffly, guiding me back to the seat. I complied, wondering what she had said that had her so rattled. "You look as if you've seen a ghost," I said carefully.

"It's about Nosh," she said. She took a deep breath and then spoke haltingly. "The police found DNA at the scene of the crime. They dismissed his parents' DNA, but they found two other sets."

I shrugged. "What is DNA?"

She let out a breath, looking frustrated. "Right. That wasn't a thing in your day. DNA is evidence tied to a specific person. Everyone's DNA is different. They use it to confirm someone was at the scene of a crime. Fingerprints, hair, blood, saliva," she explained.

I blinked at her. "I showered at their penthouse," I said, suddenly understanding her concern. "It puts me at the scene of the crime."

She nodded. "They found Nosh's DNA too, of course."

I waited. "Well, he spent a great deal of time there, so that's not surprising."

She shook her head, looking sick to her stomach. "Sorin...your DNA matched Nosh's DNA," she whispered. "You two are related somehow..."

All thoughts of exploring the bedroom with Victoria suddenly evaporated from my mind.

All I could think about was a tiny little boy learning how to walk near a campfire before his world turned to fire and blood...

Did this mean that Nosh...

Was my *son*?

The Devil of New York City returns on 11.25.2019 in DEVIL'S CRY.
PREORDER HERE!

Turn the page to read samples from Shayne's other worldwide bestselling novels in **The TempleVerse**—*The Nate Temple Series, the Feathers and Fire Series, and the Phantom Queen Dairies.*

TRY: OBSIDIAN SON (NATE TEMPLE #1)

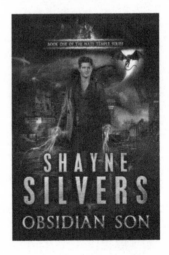

T here was no room for emotion in a hate crime. I had to be
cold. Heartless. This was just another victim. Nothing more.
No face, no name.

Frosted blades of grass crunched under my feet, sounding to my
ears alone like the symbolic glass that one shattered under a napkin at
a Jewish wedding. The noise would have threatened to give away my
stealthy advance as I stalked through the moonlit field, but I was no

novice and had planned accordingly. Being a wizard, I was able to muffle all sensory evidence with a fine cloud of magic—no sounds, and no smells. Nifty. But if I made the spell much stronger, the anomaly would be too obvious to my prey.

I knew the consequences for my dark deed tonight. If caught, jail time or possibly even a gruesome, painful death. But if I succeeded, the look of fear and surprise in my victim's eyes before his world collapsed around him, was well worth the risk. I simply couldn't help myself; I had to take him down.

I knew the cops had been keeping tabs on my car, but I was confident that they hadn't followed me. I hadn't seen a tail on my way here, but seeing as how they frowned on this kind of thing I had taken a circuitous route just in case. I was safe. I hoped.

Then my phone chirped at me as I received a text.

My body's fight-or-flight syndrome instantly kicked in, my heart threatening to explode in one final act of pulmonary paroxysm. "Motherf—" I hissed instinctively, practically jumping out of my skin. I had forgotten to silence it. *Stupid, stupid, stupid!* My body remained tense as I swept my gaze over the field, sure that I had been made. My breathing finally began to slow, my pulse returning to normal, as I noticed no changes in my surroundings. Hopefully, my magic had silenced the sound and my resulting outburst. I glanced down at the phone to scan the text and then typed back a quick and angry response before I switched the cursed phone to vibrate.

Now, where were we...

I continued on, the lining of my coat constricting my breathing. Or maybe it was because I was leaning forward in anticipation. *Breathe*, I chided myself. *He doesn't know you're here.* All this risk for a book. It had better be worth it.

I'm taller than most, and not abnormally handsome, but I knew how to play the genetic cards I had been dealt. I had shaggy, dirty blonde hair, and my frame was thick with well-earned muscle, yet still lean. I had once been told that my eyes were like twin emeralds pitted against the golden-brown tufts of my hair—a face like a jewelry box. Of course, that was two bottles of wine into a date, so I could have been a little foggy on her quote. Still, I liked to imagine that was how everyone saw me.

But tonight, all that was masked by magic.

I grinned broadly as the outline of the hairy hulk finally came into view. He was blessedly alone—no nearby sentries to give me away. That was always a risk when performing this ancient right-of-passage. I tried to keep the grin on my face from dissolving into a maniacal cackle.

My skin danced with energy, both natural and unnatural, as I manipulated the threads of magic floating all around me. My victim stood just ahead, oblivious of the world of hurt that I was about to unleash. Even with his millennia of experience, he didn't stand a chance. I had done this so many times that the routine of it was my only enemy. I lost count of how many times I had been told not to do it again; those who knew declared it *cruel, evil, and sadistic.* But what fun wasn't? Regardless, that wasn't enough to stop me from doing it again. And again. Call it an addiction if you will, but it was too much of a rush to ignore.

The pungent smell of manure filled the air, latching onto my nostril hairs. I took another step, trying to calm my racing pulse. A glint of gold reflected in the silver moonlight, but the victim remained motionless, hopefully unaware or all was lost. I wouldn't make it out alive if he knew I was here. Timing was everything.

I carefully took the last two steps, a lifetime between each, watching the legendary monster's ears, anxious and terrified that I would catch even so much as a twitch in my direction. Seeing nothing, a fierce grin split my unshaven cheeks. My spell had worked! I raised my palms an inch away from their target, firmly planted my feet, and squared my shoulders. I took one silent, calming breath, and then heaved forward with every ounce of physical strength I could muster. As well as a teensy-weensy boost of magic. Enough to goose him good.

"*MOOO!!!*" The sound tore through the cool October night like an unstoppable freight train. *Thud-splat!* The beast collapsed sideways into the frosty grass; straight into a steaming patty of cow shit, cow dung, or, if you really want to church it up, a Meadow Muffin. But to me, shit is, and always will be, shit.

Cow tipping. It doesn't get any better than that in Missouri.

Especially when you're tipping the *Minotaur*. Capital M.

Razor-blade hooves tore at the frozen earth as the beast struggled to stand, grunts of rage vibrating the air. I raised my arms triumphantly. "Boo-yah! Temple 1, Minotaur 0!" I crowed. Then I very bravely prepared to protect myself. Some people just couldn't take a joke. *Cruel, evil,* and *sadistic* cow tipping may be, but by hell, it was a *rush*. The legendary beast turned his gaze on me after gaining his feet, eyes ablaze as he unfolded to his full height on two tree-trunk-thick legs, hooves magically transforming into heavily-booted feet. The thick, gold ring dangling from his snotty snout quivered as the Minotaur panted, and his dense, corded muscle contracted over his human-like chest. As I stared up into those brown eyes, I actually felt sorry... for, well, myself.

"I have killed greater men than you for less offense," he growled.

I swear to God his voice sounded like an angry James Earl Jones. Like Mufasa talking to Scar.

"You have shit on your shoulder, Asterion." I ignited a roiling ball of fire in my palm in order to see his eyes more clearly. By no means was it a defensive gesture on my part. It was just dark. But under the weight of his glare, even I couldn't buy my reassuring lie. I hoped using a form of his ancient name would give me brownie points. Or maybe just not-worthy-of-killing points.

The beast grunted, eyes tightening, and I sensed the barest hesitation. "Nate Temple...your name would look splendid on my already long list of slain idiots." Asterion took a threatening step forward, and I thrust out my palm in warning, my roiling flame blue now.

"You lost fair and square, Asterion. Yield or perish." The beast's shoulders sagged slightly. Then he finally nodded to himself in resignation, appraising me with the scrutiny of a worthy adversary. "Your time comes, Temple, but I will grant you this. You've got a pair of stones on you to rival Hercules."

I pointedly risked a glance down towards the myth's own crown jewels. "Well, I sure won't need a wheelbarrow any time soon, but I'm sure I'll manage."

The Minotaur blinked once, and then bellowed out a deep, contagious, snorting laughter. Realizing I wasn't about to become a murder statistic, I couldn't help but join in. It felt good. It had been a while since I had allowed myself to experience genuine laughter.

In the harsh moonlight, his bulk was even more intimidating as he towered head and shoulders above me. This was the beast that had fed upon human sacrifices for countless years while imprisoned in Daedalus' Labyrinth in Greece. And all of that protein had not gone to waste, forming a heavily woven musculature over the beast's body that made even Mr. Olympia look puny.

From the neck up he was entirely bull, but the rest of his body more resembled a thickly-furred man. But, as shown moments ago, he could adapt his form to his environment, never appearing fully human, but able to make his entire form appear as a bull when necessary. For instance, how he had looked just before I tipped him. Maybe he had been scouting the field for heifers before I had so efficiently killed the mood.

His bull face was also covered in thick, coarse hair—even sporting a long, wavy beard of sorts, and his eyes were the deepest brown I had ever seen. Cow shit brown. His snout jutted out, emphasizing the gold ring dangling from his glistening nostrils, catching a glint in the luminous glow of the moon. The metal was at least an inch thick, and etched with runes of a language long forgotten. Thick, aged ivory horns sprouted from each temple, long enough to skewer a wizard with little effort. He was nude except for a beaded necklace and a pair of distressed leather boots that were big enough to stomp a size twenty-five imprint in my face if he felt so inclined.

I hoped our blossoming friendship wouldn't end that way. I really did.

Get your copy of OBSIDIAN SON online today!

*Turn the page to read a sample of **UNCHAINED** - Feathers and Fire Series Book 1, or **BUY ONLINE**. Callie Penrose is a wizard in Kansas City, MO who*

hunts monsters for the Vatican. She meets Nate Temple, and things devolve from there...

(Note: Callie appears in the Temple-verse after Nate's book 6, TINY GODS... Full chronology of all books in the Temple Verse shown on the 'BOOKS IN THE TEMPLE VERSE' page.)

TRY: UNCHAINED (FEATHERS AND FIRE #1)

The rain pelted my hair, plastering loose strands of it to my forehead as I panted, eyes darting from tree to tree, terrified of each shifting branch, splash of water, and whistle of wind slipping through the nightscape around us. But... I was somewhat *excited*, too.

Somewhat.

"Easy, girl. All will be well," the big man creeping just ahead of me, murmured.

"You said we were going to get ice cream!" I hissed at him, failing to compose myself, but careful to keep my voice low and my eyes alert. "I'm not ready for this!" I had been trained to fight, with my hands, with weapons, and with my magic. But I had never taken an active role in a hunt before. I'd always been the getaway driver for my mentor.

The man grunted, grey eyes scanning the trees as he slipped through the tall grass. "And did we not get ice cream before coming here? Because I think I see some in your hair."

"You know what I mean, Roland. You tricked me." I checked the tips of my loose hair, saw nothing, and scowled at his back.

"The Lord does not give us a greater burden than we can shoulder."

I muttered dark things under my breath, wiping the water from my eyes. Again. My new shirt was going to be ruined. Silk never fared well in the rain. My choice of shoes wasn't much better. Boots, yes, but distressed, *fashionable* boots. Not work boots designed for the rain and mud. Definitely not monster hunting boots for our evening excursion through one of Kansas City's wooded parks. I realized I was forcibly distracting myself, keeping my mind busy with mundane thoughts to avoid my very real anxiety. Because whenever I grew nervous, an imagined nightmare always—

A church looming before me. Rain pouring down. Night sky and a glowing moon overhead. I was all alone. Crying on the cold, stone steps, and infant in a cardboard box—

I forced the nightmare away, breathing heavily. "You know I hate it when you talk like that," I whispered to him, trying to regain my composure. I wasn't angry with him, but was growing increasingly uncomfortable with our situation after my brief flashback of fear.

"Doesn't mean it shouldn't be said," he said kindly. "I think we're close. Be alert. Remember your training. Banish your fears. I am here. And the Lord is here. He always is."

So, he had noticed my sudden anxiety. "Maybe I should just go back to the car. I know I've trained, but I really don't think—"

A shape of fur, fangs, and claws launched from the shadows towards me, cutting off my words as it snarled, thirsty for my blood.

And my nightmare slipped back into my thoughts like a veiled assassin, a wraith hoping to hold me still for the monster to eat. I froze, unable to move. Twin sticks of power abruptly erupted into being in my clenched fists, but my fear swamped me with that stupid nightmare, the sticks held at my side, useless to save me.

Right before the beast's claws reached me, it grunted as something batted it from the air, sending it flying sideways. It struck a tree with another grunt and an angry whine of pain.

I fell to my knees right into a puddle, arms shaking, breathing fast.

My sticks crackled in the rain like live cattle prods, except their entire length was the electrical section — at least to anyone other than me. I could hold them without pain.

Magic was a part of me, coursing through my veins whether I wanted it or not, and Roland had spent many years teaching me how to master it. But I had never been able to fully master the nightmare inside me, and in moments of fear, it always won, overriding my training.

The fact that I had resorted to weapons — like the ones he had trained me with — rather than a burst of flame, was startling. It was good in the fact that my body's reflexes knew enough to call up a defense even without my direct command, but bad in the fact that it was the worst form of defense for the situation presented. I could have very easily done as Roland did, and hurt it from a distance. But I hadn't. Because of my stupid block.

Roland placed a calloused palm on my shoulder, and I flinched. "Easy, see? I am here." But he did frown at my choice of weapons, the reprimand silent but loud in my mind. I let out a shaky breath, forcing my fear back down. It was all in my head, but still, it wasn't easy. Fear could be like that.

I focused on Roland's implied lesson. Close combat weapons — even magically-powered ones — were for last resorts. I averted my eyes in very real shame. I knew these things. He didn't even need to tell me them. But when that damned nightmare caught hold of me, all my training went out the window. It haunted me like a shadow, waiting for moments just like this, as if trying to kill me. A form of psychological suicide? But it was why I constantly refused to join Roland on his hunts. He knew about it. And although he was trying to help me overcome that fear, he never pressed too hard.

Rain continued to sizzle as it struck my batons. I didn't let them go, using them as a totem to build my confidence back up. I slowly lifted my eyes to nod at him as I climbed back to my feet.

That's when I saw the second set of eyes in the shadows, right before they flew out of the darkness towards Roland's back. I threw one of my batons and missed, but that pretty much let Roland know that an unfriendly was behind him. Either that or I had just failed to murder my mentor at point-blank range. He whirled to confront the monster, expecting another aerial assault as he unleashed a ball of fire that splashed over the tree at chest height, washing the trunk in blue flames. But this monster was tricky. It hadn't planned on tackling Roland, but had merely jumped out of the darkness to get closer, no doubt learning from its fallen comrade, who still lay unmoving against the tree behind me.

His coat shone like midnight clouds with hints of lightning flashing in the depths of thick, wiry fur. The coat of dew dotting his fur reflected the moonlight, giving him a faint sheen as if covered in fresh oil. He was tall, easily hip height at the shoulder, and barrel chested, his rump much leaner than the rest of his body. He — I assumed male from the long, thick mane around his neck — had a very long snout, much longer and wider than any werewolf I had ever seen. Amazingly, and beyond my control, I realized he was beautiful.

But most of the natural world's lethal hunters were beautiful.

He landed in a wet puddle a pace in front of Roland, juked to the right, and then to the left, racing past the big man, biting into his hamstrings on his way by.

A wash of anger rolled over me at seeing my mentor injured, dousing my fear, and I swung my baton down as hard as I could. It struck the beast in the rump as it tried to dart back to cover — a typical wolf tactic. My blow singed his hair and shattered bone. The creature collapsed into a puddle of mud with a yelp, instinctively snapping his jaws over his shoulder to bite whatever had hit him.

I let him. But mostly out of dumb luck as I heard Roland hiss in pain, falling to the ground.

The monster's jaws clamped around my baton, and there was an immediate explosion of teeth and blood that sent him flying several feet away into the tall brush, yipping, screaming, and staggering. Before he slipped out of sight, I noticed that his lower jaw was simply *gone*, from the contact of his saliva on my electrified magical batons. Then he managed to limp into the woods with more pitiful yowls, but I had no mind to chase him. Roland — that titan of a man, my mentor — was hurt. I could smell copper in the air, and knew we had to get out of here. Fast. Because we had anticipated only one of the monsters. But there had been two of them, and they hadn't been the run-of-the-mill werewolves we had been warned about. If there were two, perhaps there were more. And they were evidently the prehistoric cousin of any werewolf I had ever seen or read about.

Roland hissed again as he stared down at his leg, growling with both pain and anger. My eyes darted back to the first monster, wary of another attack. It *almost* looked like a werewolf, but bigger. Much bigger. He didn't move, but I saw he was breathing. He had a notch in his right ear and a jagged scar on his long snout. Part of me wanted to go over to him and torture him. Slowly. Use his pain to finally drown my nightmare, my fear. The fear that had caused Roland's injury. My lack of inner-strength had not only put me in danger, but had hurt my mentor, my friend.

I shivered, forcing the thought away. That was *cold*. Not me. Sure, I was no stranger to fighting, but that had always been in a ring. Practicing. Sparring. Never life or death.

But I suddenly realized something very dark about myself in the chill, rainy night. Although I was terrified, I felt a deep ocean of anger manifest inside me, wanting only to dispense justice as I saw fit. To use that rage to battle my own demons. As if feeding one would starve the other, reminding me of the Cherokee Indian Legend Roland had once told me.

An old Cherokee man was teaching his grandson about life. "A fight is going on inside me," he told the boy. "It is a terrible fight between two wolves. One is evil — he is anger, envy, sorrow, regret, greed, arrogance, self-pity, guilt, resentment, inferiority, lies, false pride, superiority, and ego." After a few moments to make sure he had the boy's undivided attention, he continued.

"*The other wolf is good — he is joy, peace, love, hope, serenity, humility, kindness, benevolence, empathy, generosity, truth, compassion, and faith. The same fight is going on inside of you, boy, and inside of every other person, too.*"

The grandson thought about this for a few minutes before replying. "*Which wolf will win?*"

The old Cherokee man simply said, "*The one you feed, boy. The one you feed...*"

And I felt like feeding one of my wolves today, by killing this one...

Get the full book ONLINE!

Turn the page to read a sample of **WHISKEY GINGER** *- Phantom Queen Diaries Book 1, or* **BUY ONLINE**. *Quinn MacKenna is a black magic arms dealer from Boston, and her bark is almost as bad as her bite.*

(Note: Full chronology of all books in the Temple Verse shown on the 'Books in the Temple Verse' page.)

TRY: WHISKEY GINGER (PHANTOM QUEEN DIARIES # 1)

The pasty guitarist hunched forward, thrust a rolled-up wad of paper deep into one nostril, and snorted a line of blood crystals—frozen hemoglobin that I'd smuggled over in a refrigerated canister—with the uncanny grace of a drug addict. He sat back, fangs gleaming, and pawed at his nose. "That's some bodacious shit. Hey, bros," he said, glancing at his fellow band members, "come hit this shit before it melts."

He fetched one of the backstage passes hanging nearby, pried the plastic badge from its lanyard, and used it to split up the crystals, murmuring something in an accent that reminded me of California. Not *the* California, but you know, Cali-foh-nia—the land of beaches, babes, and bros. I retrieved a toothpick from my pocket and punched it through its thin wrapper. "So," I asked no one in particular, "now that ye have the product, who's payin'?"

Another band member stepped out of the shadows to my left, and I don't mean that figuratively, either—the fucker literally stepped out of the shadows. I scowled at him, but hid my surprise, nonchalantly rolling the toothpick from one side of my mouth to the other.

The rest of the band gathered around the dressing room table, following the guitarist's lead by preparing their own snorting utensils—tattered magazine covers, mostly. Typically, you'd do this sort of thing with a dollar-bill, maybe even a Benjamin if you were flush. But fangers like this lot couldn't touch cash directly—in God We Trust and all that. Of course, I didn't really understand why sucking blood the old-fashioned way had suddenly gone out of style. More of a rush, maybe?

"It lasts longer," the vampire next to me explained, catching my mildly curious expression. "It's especially good for shows and stuff. Makes us look, like, less—"

"Creepy?" I offered, my Irish brogue lilting just enough to make it a question.

"Pale," he finished, frowning.

I shrugged. "Listen, I've got places to be," I said, holding out my hand.

"I'm sure you do," he replied, smiling. "Tell you what, why don't you, like, hang around for a bit? Once that wears off," he dipped his head toward the bloody powder smeared across the table's surface, "we may need a pick-me-up." He rested his hand on my arm and our gazes locked.

I blinked, realized what he was trying to pull, and rolled my eyes. His widened in surprise, then shock as I yanked out my toothpick and shoved it through his hand.

"Motherfuck—"

"I want what we agreed on," I declared. "Now. No tricks."

The rest of the band saw what happened and rose faster than I could blink. They circled me, their grins feral...they might have even seemed intimidating if it weren't for the fact that they each had a case of the sniffles—I had to work extra hard not to think about what it felt like to have someone else's blood dripping down my nasal cavity.

I held up a hand.

"Can I ask ye gentlemen a question before we get started?" I asked. "Do ye even *have* what I asked for?"

Two of the band members exchanged looks and shrugged. The guitarist, however, glanced back towards the dressing room, where a brown paper bag sat next to a case full of makeup. He caught me looking and bared his teeth, his fangs stretching until it looked like it would be uncomfortable for him to close his mouth without piercing his own lip.

"Follow-up question," I said, eyeing the vampire I'd stabbed as he gingerly withdrew the toothpick from his hand and flung it across the room with a snarl. "Do ye do each other's make-up? Since, ye know, ye can't use mirrors?"

I was genuinely curious.

The guitarist grunted. "Mike, we have to go on soon."

"Wait a minute. Mike?" I turned to the snarling vampire with a frown. "What happened to *The Vampire Prospero*?" I glanced at the numerous fliers in the dressing room, most of which depicted the band members wading through blood, with Mike in the lead, each one titled *The Vampire Prospero* in *Rocky Horror Picture Show* font. Come to think of it...Mike did look a little like Tim Curry in all that leather and lace.

I was about to comment on the resemblance when Mike spoke up, "Alright, change of plans, bros. We're gonna drain this bitch before the show. We'll look totally—"

"Creepy?" I offered, again.

"Kill her."

Get the full book ONLINE!

MAKE A DIFFERENCE

Reviews are the most powerful tools in my arsenal when it comes to getting attention for my books. Much as I'd like to, I don't have the financial muscle of a New York publisher.

But I do have something much more powerful and effective than that, and it's something that those publishers would kill to get their hands on.

A committed and loyal bunch of readers.

Honest reviews of my books help bring them to the attention of other readers.

If you've enjoyed this book, I would be very grateful if you could spend just five minutes leaving a review (it can be as short as you like) on my book's Amazon page.

Thank you very much in advance.

ACKNOWLEDGMENTS

I couldn't do this without my readers—those wayward souls who crave adventure, encouragement, tears, laughter, danger, and confidence. You are all enablers to my madness.

And I love you for it. I'll keep wording, you keep reading. I'll do my goodest.

Also, take a gander at that kick ass cover! I know a wizard, obviously. Check her out here:

Cover Design By Jennifer Munswami - J.M Rising Horse Creations

ABOUT SHAYNE SILVERS

Shayne is a man of mystery and power, whose power is exceeded only by his mystery...

He currently writes the Amazon Bestselling **Nate Temple** Series, which features a foul-mouthed wizard from St. Louis. He rides a blood-thirsty unicorn, drinks with Achilles, and is pals with the Four Horsemen.

He also writes the Amazon Bestselling **Feathers and Fire** Series—a second series in the Temple Verse. The story follows a rookie spell-slinger named Callie Penrose who works for the Vatican in Kansas City. Her problem? Hell seems to know more about her past than she does.

He coauthors **The Phantom Queen Diaries**—a third series set in The Temple Verse—with Cameron O'Connell. The story follows Quinn MacKenna, a mouthy black magic arms dealer in Boston. All she wants? A round-trip ticket to the Fae realm...and maybe a drink on the house.

Shayne holds two high-ranking black belts, and can be found writing in a coffee shop, cackling madly into his computer screen while pounding shots of espresso. He's hard at work on the newest books in the Temple Verse—You can find updates on new releases or chronological reading order on the next page, his website or any of his social media accounts. **Follow him online for all sorts of groovy goodies, giveaways, and new release updates:**

Get Down with Shayne Online
www.shaynesilvers.com
info@shaynesilvers.com

facebook.com/shaynesilversfanpage

amazon.com/author/shaynesilvers

bookbub.com/profile/shayne-silvers

instagram.com/shaynesilversofficial

twitter.com/shaynesilvers

goodreads.com/ShayneSilvers

BOOKS IN THE TEMPLE VERSE

CHRONOLOGY: All stories in the TempleVerse are shown in chronological order on the following page

NATE TEMPLE SERIES

FAIRY TALE - FREE prequel novella #0 for my subscribers

OBSIDIAN SON

BLOOD DEBTS

GRIMM

SILVER TONGUE

BEAST MASTER

BEERLYMPIAN (Novella #5.5 in the 'LAST CALL' anthology)

TINY GODS

DADDY DUTY (Novella #6.5)

WILD SIDE

WAR HAMMER

NINE SOULS

HORSEMAN

LEGEND

KNIGHTMARE (TEMPLE #12) — COMING SOON...

FEATHERS AND FIRE SERIES

(Also set in the TempleVerse)

UNCHAINED

RAGE

WHISPERS

ANGEL'S ROAR

MOTHERLUCKER (Novella #4.5 in the 'LAST CALL' anthology)

SINNER

BLACK SHEEP

GODLESS (FEATHERS #7) — COMING SOON...

PHANTOM QUEEN DIARIES

(Also set in the Temple Universe)

COLLINS (Prequel novella #0 in the 'LAST CALL' anthology)

WHISKEY GINGER

COSMOPOLITAN

OLD FASHIONED

MOTHERLUCKER (Novella #3.5 in the 'LAST CALL' anthology)

DARK AND STORMY

MOSCOW MULE

WITCHES BREW

SALTY DOG

CHRONOLOGICAL ORDER: TEMPLE VERSE

FAIRY TALE (TEMPLE PREQUEL)

OBSIDIAN SON (TEMPLE 1)

BLOOD DEBTS (TEMPLE 2)

GRIMM (TEMPLE 3)

SILVER TONGUE (TEMPLE 4)

BEAST MASTER (TEMPLE 5)

BEERLYMPIAN (TEMPLE 5.5)

TINY GODS (TEMPLE 6)

DADDY DUTY (TEMPLE NOVELLA 6.5)

Made in the USA
Coppell, TX
11 July 2020

30686964R00173